THICKER THAN SOUP

THICKER THAN SOUP

KATHRYN JOYCE

Matador
9 Priory Business Park,
Wistow Road
Kibworth Beauchamp
Leicester LE8 0RX, UK
Tel: (+44) 116 279 2299
Fax: (+44) 116 279 2277
Email: books@troubador.co.uk
Web: www.troubador.co.uk/matador

ISBN 978 1784622 640

British Library Cataloguing in Publication Data.
A catalogue record for this book is available from the British Library.

Printed and bound in the UK by TJ International, Padstow, Cornwall
Typeset by Troubador Publishing Ltd, Leicester, UK

Matador is an imprint of Troubador Publishing Ltd

To David
Another journey shared.

Part 1

CHAPTER 1

Chocolate Sin Cake

Sally slammed John's car door. *The Restaurant*, he'd said. *Seagrams, Seagrams.* It was all about his beloved restaurant these days. The weekend at her mother's had been agreed months before, when she'd decided to go to the Bakers' Guild AGM. But now, at the last minute, he'd decided he had an auction he really *had* to go to. Damn him!

Seeing a vacant ticket window she moved quickly. "Return to Paddington," she snapped, "back on Sunday."

The teller raised an eyebrow and snapped back. "Running late. An hour."

"Sorry, er…please," she apologised and then realised he'd told her something. "Pardon?"

"Weather. Train's late. Sixteen-fifty, platform two."

Turning at the blast of a car horn she watched John narrowly avoid a taxi and curling her toes in her boots she recalled her father's words from childhood; *Kick a rock when you're angry and your own foot will hurt.* She sighed. Of course Seagrams took John's time, and the auction was important. And yes, she'd kicked another stone.

Huddled into a corner of the nicotine browned café she stirred sugar into coffee and waited for her train. It hurt to be left out of John's plans and, it had to be said, his lack of interest in her recent work hurt too. He knew little of the Board meeting in November and the fight she'd fought and lost – on her birthday, of all days – to avoid redundancies, or the distress of ensuring

3

the retail bakeries targeted for closure were staffed throughout Christmas whilst informing staff they'd start 1981 without their jobs. Just over a year ago, when she'd been invited to join the Board as Personnel Director she'd seen an opportunity to influence, to participate in the future of Black and Emery. At only thirty-one, and the only woman, she'd welcomed the challenge. What a fool she'd been to consider herself a co-member of the timeworn grey-beards. She'd been no more than salve on growing rumblings of inequality. In trying to persuade the male bastion that closing thirty retail outlets and the Research and Development Lab, known fondly as The Kitchen, was ill-considered, they'd combined their strength. They hadn't listened or even, she was sure, read her report. Fools them, she'd decided, to believe her a mere makeweight in their baker's dozen. *'We must invest our way out of this recession'* and *'outsourced services will be beyond our control'* she'd protested. But they'd dismissed her. *'Give a woman a…'* someone had started to say, and she'd snapped back *'Cocks may crow, but it's hens that deliver eggs!'* Then James Black, heir to the Chair, had spoken, "*My father's decision is based on many years of experience, and he knows…* Sally cringed as she recalled his final words, *'Oh yes, and I believe birthday congratulations are in order'*. The tactless and inappropriate words had brought muttered greetings from around the table that had in effect, dismissed her. And so, despite growing evidence that Maggie Thatcher's free markets and new entrepreneurs would soon be leading the county to prosperity, Lawrence Black's decision to 'prune' Black and Emery had been made.

Back on the platform Sally tugged her scarf tighter and shrank inside her coat. She longed for a chat with Diane who, as head of The Kitchen, had been her good friend since they'd both joined Black and Emery seven years ago. But Diane had received her redundancy news by clearing her desk and declaring their friendship equally redundant.

In the icy wind and darkness the January afternoon enveloped and filled her and it took the lights of a train emerging from the gloom to chase away tears that threatened to spill.

Inhaling the heated air gratefully, she placed her bag on the adjoining seat, lit a cigarette and blew smoke at the non-smoking sign. What did a cigarette matter, she thought, when so many people, many of them women who'd traded poor pay for stale Friday cakes and misplaced loyalty, were losing their jobs.

Unfolding her newspaper she read of Rupert Murdoch's attempts to buy The Times and then read with more interest an editorial about Tory Wets being left out of the Cabinet. Maggie, it seemed, was surrounding herself with men willing to do things her way, a tactic she admired ruefully.

When, still grinning from an encounter with an enormously obese cat that lived in the Paddington Ladies, Sally heard her name being called she turned towards the tall slim figure striding towards her with a fixed smile belying a sinking heart.

"James. What a nice surprise." She'd expected to see him or his father at the AGM but had hoped to avoid their presence before then. "We must have travelled on the same train. I didn't see you. Where were you sitting? I thought you were driving up." She was talking too much and too quickly and wishing very much that he hadn't spotted her.

"No. I decided the train was more comfortable. I'm taking a taxi to the hotel – I assume you're going to the Charing Cross. Join me?"

"Lovely," she lied.

By the time she'd reached her room Sally had reluctantly agreed to meet James for dinner. But an early meal, she'd insisted, as she had a call to make. She wanted very much to not sleep on the argument.

From the middle of the huge bed in the cavernous room Sally sought refuge in Anita Desai's world of bougainvillea and cane-chaired verandas until overwhelmed by the heat, she tossed the book aside and opened the window. The room cooled quickly, but preferring freshness to stuffy heat she snuggled under a blanket thinking wistfully of the blankets at home, now neglected in storage bags along with the patchwork Kantha quilt her father's family had sent from Pakistan many years before. She disliked the new continental quilt – or duvet as it was apparently now called – with its giant pillowcases. But, like the built-in wardrobes and John's paintings, they were what Diane would say were, 'so today'. As was living together, or living in sin as her mother called it, often adding that her father would spin in his grave if he knew. She escaped into her book.

An hour later, with pale colour applied to her lips and the marquisate butterfly pendant John had given her for her birthday fluttering at her throat, Sally found James in the bar with his fluorescent green cocktail almost finished. Ordering a wine-cooler for herself she suggested taking their drinks straight to the dining room.

"Ah. Actually, I've reserved a table in a little place in Covent Garden. I'm sure you'll like it."

The conceit! "Oh, really! I was planning a simple meal and early night."

"Yes, I'd like that too and I think you'll find L'Hirondelle fits the bill."

"Really." She sipped her drink silently, awaiting acknowledgment of her disapproval which when it came, sounded surprisingly gentle.

"I have the feeling I've upset you though I've no idea how or when. I apologise. Unreservedly. I'd hoped we might have a pleasant evening together. After all, we do have quite a lot in common."

"We do?"

"Well, yes. We're both challenged by working for my father for a start."

The comment was so startling she couldn't help laughing. "I'm sorry; I don't mean to be rude. Yes, working for your father can be challenging, and er, no, you haven't said or done anything wrong." Other than, she told herself, replicated your father!

"Well that's good news." James drained his glass. "So drink up and let's go and eat."

Seated at a red leather studded booth with matching menus, Sally forced James to shorten his own deliberations by choosing quickly and ordering for them both, he requested a bottle of Orvietto.

"My favourite." Her acerbic tone was either not perceived or ignored as James handed his menu to the waiter.

"That was all very decisive. Are you always so quick to choose?"

"Well, no, not always. John's a chef and knows about food and wine. We often spend ages choosing because he's so interested. But I usually know what I want as soon as I see the menu."

This new James was unsettling but maintaining her cool demeanour would have been churlish. He looked different too. Quite handsome, in the diffused glow of the Victorian wall light. Had she given him a fair chance, she wondered?

"It must be nice having a chef in the house. I suppose he does all the cooking and you eat wonderful food all the time."

"Well no, as it happens; he works awful hours. I do the everyday stuff, and, though I say it myself, my curries are better

7

than his because my father taught me how to mix the spices."

James grinned. "We eat Vesta curries! Your father's a chef too?"

"No. He did work in a restaurant, but as a waiter. Sadly, he's … no longer alive." Even after ten years Sally still struggled to say the word dead in relation to her father. "He was Anglo Indian, and came to England in 1948 after Partition."

"Ah. I'm sorry." James lifted his wine glass. "That's after India and Pakistan separated?"

"Yes."

"Your father was caught up in it?"

James, it appeared, was adept at polite conversation and Sally found herself telling her father's story. "When the British – Mountbatten it was – rushed through the Partition boundaries based on out-of-date maps, ten million people suddenly found themselves to be in the wrong place." She paused, judged if he wanted this history lesson and encouraged by his apparent interest, told him how the people of the The Punjab didn't know until the last minute if they were to be Pakistani or Indian. "With the new borders slicing through the middle, families and communities; Muslims, Hindus, Sikhs, Christians, Buddhists, were forced to move. People were confused, and angry. By the time it was all over more than a million people had died."

"Your father's family ended up on the Pakistan side?"

Sally nodded.

"They're Muslims?"

"No, Christians. There're a lot of Christians living in Pakistan." Her father's stories had been shocking. "I'd cover my ears when he told us what happened." She sipped wine, remembering. "My grandfather didn't get home one night. They found his body in Heera Mandi, the red light district in the old city, where he would never have gone. There were so many deaths and his was just another. So suddenly, as the eldest son, my father was the breadwinner and decision maker for the family. It's hard to believe that people who'd lived together for generations suddenly hated each other in the name of religion, isn't it?"

"It is." The waiter refilled their glasses. "And your father came to Britain to start a new life?"

"Yes. And lost his college education. That's why he was strict about ours. He made sure we – my brother and I – didn't take our free British school for granted. Before he left for work in the evening he'd check our homework. If it wasn't good enough we'd suffer the indignity of him crossing it through and making us repeat it. We hated it, but he wanted us to have what he hadn't. He was very proud when we both went to university."

"Yes, I can imagine. So your grandfather was Indian?"

She shook her head. "He was in the English army and met my grandmother in India." Sally thought of her wedding photograph of the stunningly beautiful bride and her upright soldier. "She was the daughter of an officer in the Indian army and traditionally would have had an arranged marriage, but my grandfather convinced her parents that he was a suitable boy. Most of the family still live in Lahore. I have my grandmother, uncles and an aunt, and cousins I've never met."

James raised his glass. "So that's where you get your beauty," he toasted, "I wondered about your heritage."

The compliment was unexpected and she looked away, flustered.

"I'm sorry, I spoke without thinking." James touched her hand lightly. "Please. Tell me more. Is your mother Pakistani too?"

Encouraged, she continued. "No, she's English. She lives in the East End, in Bethnal Green. It's where she came from and where my parents lived all their married life, and where I grew up too. I'm going there tomorrow after the meeting."

The wine was loosening her tongue, and she found herself relating her favourite childhood story. "My parents met here in London. My father was young, only twenty, when he arrived here, and he missed his family very much. The cold wet streets in London were full of closed doors and curtained windows and he didn't like the strange food. One day he was travelling home from work on a bus when he saw, through a window, people dancing. The next day he looked for the window again and saw a sign above a door, but the bus passed before he was able to read it. When he passed the next day he read *Thames School of Dancing*. The next day, he saw the next line, *Instruction in All Forms of Dance*. This was a way to make friends, he thought. He'd learn to dance. The following day, he got off the bus, crossed the road, went up the stairs, and enrolled. And that's where he met my mother who, every Tuesday and Friday, went with her friend Lillian to dance. According to my father, his light-footed and elegant movements impressed my mother and she was overwhelmed by his handsome face, jet black hair, blue eyes, and creamy complexion. They married within eight months, and I was born just six months later. Not that I knew that until I got my birth certificate when I was twenty-one. Mum was reluctant to hand it over. It came as something of a shock to realise that my birthday was actually in December, not March! When I was a child my birthday parties had always been in March. Even now I still have a little extra celebration on 7th March, and occasionally give the wrong date when filling in forms! And if that's not enough, the name on my birth certificate is Sarah, not Sally. I insisted on being called Sally when I was about five and it stuck."

The waiter set and adjusted plates and tilted an eyebrow in silent question towards the empty wine bottle. Laughing, James nodded and asked for water too. "Perrier please." He turned back to Sally. "Your father sounds like he was a character. He must have been quite young when he died."

James, so distant at work, had managed to make her feel he was a friend. Nevertheless she wasn't ready to tell him how much her heart still ached for her father. "It was a traffic accident, ten years ago," she told him. "Sadly, such things happen. But what about you. What do you do in your spare time?"

James lifted his glass and looked through it at her. "I was happy talking about you. But, well, what do I like to do?" He chewed food. "I walk, often in the hills. Last year I went to South America, to Peru. Have you been there?" Sally shook her head and he told her about the Andes and somewhere she hadn't heard of called Machu Pichu. He told of people living on floating islands, and mountain people who ate mildly hallucinogenic coca leaves to combat altitude sickness. "Apparently, Himalayans have adapted to altitude, but the Andean hasn't." He drained his glass. "I'd like to go to Pakistan. Did your father know the mountain areas?"

Sally knew little of the mountains. "He talked of a village, Thandiani, in the north where they escaped the heat of summer. But he talked mostly about Lahore." Plates had been cleared and Sally scanned the dessert menu for chocolate. "Are you having dessert?"

James nodded his head. "Yes, I love puddings, and these tiny portions are all very pretty but they don't fill you up much, do they?"

"Well, I'm full but I can't resist chocolate. Have you had this Chocolate Sin Cake? It sounds like heaven."

"Hmmm. They say that researchers have discovered chocolate produces the same reactions in the brain as marijuana. They also discovered other similarities but they can't remember what they are."

Sally laughed at the joke. "Didn't chocolate come from

South America originally? Maybe the Andean people made it from those cocoa beans you were telling me about."

"That was coca leaves," James corrected, "which are used to produce cocaine, not chocolate. I think chocolate originated in Central America. Didn't the Aztecs use it as an aphrodisiac?"

"Really? Well, wherever it came from and whatever it does, I'm glad it's here!"

James ordered. "Two Chocolate Sin Cakes, and coffee please." He looked at Sally. "I take it you'd like coffee? And a brandy or something? I thought I'd better order coffee straight away or that early night you wanted won't happen."

Looking at her watch Sally was surprised to see it was ten o'clock. "Good idea, but no brandy thanks; I've a call to make." The restaurant had almost emptied and as their desserts and coffees arrived James asked for the bill.

"Not so fast." She looked at the warm, dark cake on her plate. "I refuse to rush this." Picking up her spoon she separated a small slice from the cake and inhaled the chocolate aroma. "Sensational!" she breathed, and putting it into her mouth let it slowly melt.

James watched in amazement. "I've never seen anyone eat so wickedly!"

Sally smiled but spoke no more until she'd scraped up the last crumb with her finger. "You know, I could give up chocolate but I'm not a quitter."

They walked towards the hotel in companionable silence until James said he thought they had a number of things – beyond work – in common. "For example," he said, "we both had strong fathers who insisted on their own idea of what made a good education. Your father sounded strict but fair. I'm afraid mine was just strict."

Sally sensed resentment. "You were away at school?"

"I was happy to board; it was less regimented than home. I suppose I shouldn't be saying this but you already know my father sets high standards and likes to be in control. He, and Black and Emery are hard acts to live up to." His breath seemed to dissolve in mist.

They reached the hotel and curiosity about James and his father encouraged her to agree to a nightcap. "So after Rugby you went to Oxford."

"I did. I was fortunate to have all that but what I really wanted was music. I played the viola moderately well and wanted to play professionally. My music tutor wanted me to try for the Royal College but for my father, music was merely a hobby."

"Do you still play?"

He shook his head. "There isn't time now. But Felicity, my youngest is musical. Her future will be different." James raised his glass. "To our new found friendship."

"Cheers." Sally drank the toast and noted intentions for a daughter's future that echoed a father's control. "Well it sounds as if Felicity is talented and I wish her good luck. It's been an enjoyable evening but I must go." She rose unsteadily and giggled. "Woops. Perhaps I shouldn't have had the Tia Maria after all."

James walked beside her up the stairs and along the first floor corridor. When he rounded another corner she was about to assure him she could find her own way as he unlocked the door before hers, which, as the rooms would have been booked at the same time, wasn't as surprising as it seemed.

It was eleven-fifteen. She dialled home and waited eight, nine, ten rings then cut the line. Someone, a maid, had turned down the bed and closed the window and it was hot again; too hot. Kicking off her boots, she removed her thick warm tights and pulled her sweater over her head, struggling to undo buttons she'd forgotten to unfasten. A bed-side lamp careered to the floor and bending to retrieve it, she felt the room sway. "Water." Freeing herself of the reluctant sweater she drank deeply from the bottle provided as the phone started to ring.

"John?"

A disinterested voice told her she had a call then the line clicked and she heard John's voice. "Hello?"

"John! I thought I'd missed you." The bottle slipped from the edge of the table and a small wet pool spread across her discarded jumper.

"I've just got in. I guessed it'd be you."

He sounded abrupt. "Oh. Erm. How are things?"

"You sound happy."

"I'm all right." Conversation faltered.

"How's your hotel?"

"It's alright."

"And you're alright."

"Yes. Thank you. How are you?"

"I'm alright."

"John, please. I don't want to argue any…."

"Everything's alright then."

"John, please…"

"You're having a nice time in a nice hotel care of Black and Emery who've kicked your friends out of their jobs."

She caught her breath. "What? You mean Diane? John, I'm staying here because I need to be here and as for Diane, it seems to me that you are benefiting from her availability all too well!"

"At least she's interested in what I'm doing which is more than I can say about you, cosying up there with your Board cronies!"

She couldn't help herself; she kicked the stone. "For your information I've had a very nice evening with James. It's nice to find someone who's actually interested in me for a change!" She kicked again, harder. "So do what you want and GO TO HELL!"

There was no satisfaction to be had in slamming the receiver. Retrieving the spilled water bottle she hugged her knees and felt a desperate need for John's arms when a knock on the door startled her. Rising unsteadily she called softly. "Who is it?"

"Are you all right? I heard shouting. Is everything all right?"

It was James. Pulling on her wrap she opened the door. "I'm sorry," she apologised, "I, er, I..." James's concern broke her last defence and she turned back into her room to hide unstoppable tears.

"What's happened?"

"It's nothing." Her voice wavered. "Oh God, I'm sorry. I'll be all right in a minute."

"Are you sure?" The door closed. "You look pretty upset to me. Can I do anything?"

An immaculate handkerchief appeared. "Here. I haven't used it, I promise." He wiped her cheek and placed the handkerchief in her hand. "If I can help, you will say, won't you? After all we're friends now, you and I, aren't we?"

His arm moved and she registered how tall he was as he pulled her the few inches towards him. As his other arm wrapped around her waist she felt her face lift into a kiss that fired every nerve of her body. His hand moved inside the silk wrap, grazed her breast and slipped the strap from her shoulder before unsnapping her bra in a smooth, shockingly exquisite movement. She gasped. The hand returned to her breast. Hands – hers – released his shirt from the belted trousers and moved inside the crisp cotton, up, across the coolness of his back and as the loosened shirt rose over his head they fell together, backwards on to the bed, skin on skin, belly on belly.

Her teeth bit his ear as he took her nipple into his mouth and her back arched as his tongue, sharp and pointed, flicked then licked whilst a hand tugged her skirt up over her hips and found its way between her thighs. He was unfastening his trousers when a moment of insight released a half whispered "No" that meant nothing as she felt him push, deep, and the brief awareness disappeared as her body responded in the ancient primal rhythm that took her quickly into urgent, gasping, arching orgasm.

She woke with a feeling of great thirst. A little surprised to find the bedside light on and more surprised to find herself still partly dressed, she remembered. Humiliation burned a wave of shame. Thankfully she was alone in the bed. The clock told her she'd slept for around three hours and groaning, she turned on her side, curling below the covers and smelling what they'd done. Tossing aside the covers and peeling off clothes she went to the bathroom, dropped her pants in the bin and let a scalding shower sting as she scrubbed mercilessly, seeking pain until, wrapped in a large, hotel robe, she took her undried body back to the bed and lay rigidly above the soiled sheets. "Stupid, stupid, stupid."

With aching head and parched mouth she went in search of aspirins in her toilet bag, washed them down with several refills of the tumbler, and returned to the blankets.

The toilet bag! Her birth-control pills? Snapping on the light she ran to the bathroom and searched the bag. The contents cascaded into the sink; face cream, perfume, lipstick, nail file. The pills weren't there. It was Thursday and she was away from home until Sunday. Her head pounded. "Idiot!" Item by item she replaced her toiletries and returned to the bed where the clock glowed the hours and minutes for the rest of the night until at six she got up. Another shower freshened, and with make-up applied carefully she left the room in search of an unaccompanied breakfast.

James was already there, reading the paper. Swallowing a wave of embarrassment she lifted her chin. "Good morning." A shadow of uncertainty that crossed his face gave her some satisfaction. "May I join you?"

"Er, well. Actually, I've almost finished. But, yes, do sit down."

Ordering coffee from a hovering waitress she took the seat opposite. "About last night." She smoothed a napkin across her lap. "I think that we should assume it didn't happen."

"Of course. If that's what you want." James put aside his paper. "But of course, it did."

The skin on her neck and face burned and she spoke quietly. "I don't think it would have happened if I hadn't drunk so much and even accepting that, it's not something I go around doing. It won't happen again."

"It could, you know." James smiled a thin smile. "There's no harm done."

"No harm…?" She kept her voice low. "What if John, or your wife, or someone at work found out?"

"Why would anyone find out? I'm hardly likely to tell my wife – I'm a happily married man! Likewise, you're hardly likely to tell your boyfriend."

"Happily married? You…," she failed to find a word she was prepared to use.

"Oh Sally. Grow up!" James leant forward. "It was sex! I don't love you, but I enjoyed last night. What's wrong with that?"

Where was the charming man she'd dined with? She leaned forward too. "No James. It wasn't just… It was a mistake. A big mistake. And it won't happen again. I sincerely hope that neither of us will ever mention it again."

"Well, that's one thing my father is right about; it's the sort of thing that happens when women get men's jobs. They can't handle it. But if that's what you want," he condescended, "consider last night undone!" He prepared to leave. "But I'm not sorry it happened. I enjoyed it."

Did he seriously think she'd sleep with him again? And... the sort of thing that happens when... As he walked away humiliation won over indignation. The Black family machine was truly indomitable.

By the time Sally arrived at her mother's house it was all she could do to sit and drink tea before escaping to the innocence of her childhood bed for a few hours. When later, she found her mother still – or again – in the kitchen, she apologised. "Sorry, Mum. It's been a busy time."

"Feeling better? You looked done in. John's not coming then? I'd made the bed." Her mother, still finding it impossible to tolerate them sleeping together, had prepared her brother's room. "I hardly ever see you together." A peeled potato plopped into a pan. "I suppose you'd do things together more if you were married but..."

"No, Mum. We wouldn't." The conversation had taken place many times. "It's the same. A piece of paper won't make any difference."

"Well, your father and I never gallivanted around like you do, I know that. We lived together too you know."

It wasn't worth an argument. "Shall I check the oven?"

"Thanks, love. It should be nearly done. It's lamb casserole. You still look a bit tired. Tell you what, make some tea and see what's on the TV for later."

Sally didn't need to be told she looked tired. She was tired of remembering. Each memory washed over her, refreshing shame with a stomach crunching guilt that craved forgiveness that John would never give. She poured boiling water over tea leaves and picked up the Radio Times. The next day she'd go home, apologise for their scrap, and be sorry for so much more.

CHAPTER 2

Poulet au Vin de Xérès

When Sally slammed the car door without a kiss, a wave, or thanks for driving her to the station, John didn't feel like telling her he'd miss her either. Her short fuse was, at times, a tad too short. After all, it had been *her* mother she was visiting and a weekend shared with Jane Lancing wasn't *his* idea of togetherness. And Sally hadn't been much fun recently either; she'd shown little interest or enthusiasm for something that was going to change their lives! Given the circumstances, it wasn't unreasonable to expect her to see the significance of an auction where catering equipment was being liquidated. He admitted he'd waited until they were on the way to the station before breaking the news but given her fiery temper, he'd been deliberately circumspect.

With his head echoing accusations of *selfish* and *obsessive* he pushed the gearstick into drive and pulled out – only to stop urgently at the blast of a horn. Mouthing *sorry* at the other driver he focused on his driving. "Mirror, signal, and ..." He manoeuvred cautiously into the traffic.

Sally's anger, he mused, hadn't masked her pique when he'd told her it was Diane who'd told him of the auction and, declaring it to be a 'fun day out', had offered to go along. He knew Sally missed her friend and it had been his intention to broker a peace during the day out. It was to be a day of resolution; a repaired friendship, equipment and furnishings secured, and, if he could persuade Diane to work for him too, his front of house vacancy would be filled. A perfect day.

Better than creeping around Sally's brother's single bed at her mother's!

His thoughts turned to why Alain had asked him to come to work early that evening. For a chat, he'd said, and John's heart had missed a beat. Had he found a replacement already, two months ahead of his departure? It had been seven years since Alain had made him Chef de Cuisine at Le Goût du Goût in Bath, and returning to his home town after the comfort of London's anonymity had been daunting. But with Sally at his side he'd faced his skeletons and grown to know that now, with his inspiration, his dishes, and his cooking, diners came back to Alain's restaurant again and again. Alain didn't cook, but he understood food and how to run a restaurant. '*Non madam, we 'ave no tables, et oui, we arrre foolly booked ce soir.*' Adding a Gallic shrug for authenticity, John chuckled. Alain was his mentor and friend, and Le Goût du Goût had sown seeds of a dream. Leaving would sadden them both.

As he parked behind the restaurant he saw Alain emerge from the wine store and felt a flutter of irrational jealousy at the thought of someone else doing his job.

"Hey, Alain."

"Ah, Jean. You are here. Oui, we will go to my office." Alain gave no indication as to the forthcoming chat. "We have a nice special for tonight, oui?" John nodded. "My mother used to cook the poulet like this, but with not so much sherry. She used vinaigre more. I have memories of our family lunches in the garden, eating this. Your dish, it has a richer flavour; it is better for here. I hope I can find someone who can cook like this before you go."

John relaxed; a replacement hadn't been found so easily. Perching on his desk Alain indicated that John should sit in the chair. "Jean, I have been wondering how you are getting on with your new restaurant?"

Tilting his chair on its back legs, John wondered where the conversation was going. "I've signed the contracts and should exchange next week. It's full steam ahead." Perhaps, he thought, Alain was about to ask him to work on Saturday. "But there's a lot to do. That's why I've booked Saturday off – I know it's difficult, so very sorry, but I'll do as much as I can tomorrow. Hill's are auctioning bankrupt stock on Saturday and I have to see that stuff."

"Yes, I am sure." Alain nodded. "In fact, that's what I wanted to talk to you about."

He couldn't work on Saturday. "If I…"

"I have a proposal. I will be very brief because you are busy and I want you to go away and think about what I have to say and then come back with your thoughts. D'accord? I have been to Bathampton and seen your place." The front legs of John's chair returned to the floor. "I like it. And also, I know you. I think you will have success. But I also know how hard it is to start a new business. So I offer my interest. For a share in your restaurant I would be happy if you allow me to invest in your project. I have thirty thousand pounds."

John's mouth dropped open. "You're joking!"

"Non. I never joke about investing my money. I'm interested in what you are doing and think you are a good investment. My offer is provisional; I need to see your accounts and working plans, but I hope you will like this idea?"

"Wow! What can I say? "John rubbed a hand over his mouth "I like it. I like it a lot." Investment. What did that mean? "We'll have to agree terms and things; I mean, what do I do if you suddenly need your money back or something?"

Alain nodded. "Jean, for both of us, we need to agree terms, so I have drafted some here." He passed a brown folder to John. "But I don't want your answer tonight. I want you to read this and to think about it. We will talk again, in more detail I hope?" Alain tapped the folder. "Of course, this is only a draft. By

22

coincidence, I have an arrangement with my accountant next week; perhaps you can give me your preliminary ideas after the weekend? We can talk in detail in the next few weeks if we decide to move forward in this."

"Yes, of course I can." John shook the outstretched hand. "Thanks, Alain, thanks a lot." Leaving the office he almost punched the air. Thirty grand! It would make a huge difference to the start-up. He couldn't wait to see Sally's face. Then his euphoria dipped. Would she be interested? She'd be pleased, but would she really care? Nevertheless, he wanted to share his news with her and he tried to recall where she'd said she'd be staying. It was one of the big hotels, somewhere expensive. He'd thought it insensitive at a time when people were being made redundant and though Sally had said something about corporate rates and budgeted money he'd still thought it extravagant.

Work levels in the kitchen increased. Vegetables were scrubbed, washed, chopped and made ready to pre-cook. He set to work on a tray of chickens, quartering and removing skin, fat and bones quickly. Shallots, garlic and tarragon were ready and bottles of Amontillado and sherry vinegar were placed alongside the array of seasonings he kept to hand. Soured cream was missing. A call for *Soured Cream?* brought an immediate response of *Fridge, John.* It looked chaotic, but it worked.

As the first order came in, activity in the kitchen, already vigorous to the casual eye, cranked up a notch. Two Rillette de Tours, one Avocado Mousse with Smoked Salmon, and one Chicken Liver Paté followed by two Normandy Pork à la Crème and two Poulet au Vin de Xérès. Two skillets hit the flaming hobs and John reached for the garlic. He was cooking.

The next morning John woke with a dull head. He pushed his tongue round his mouth and recalled the disastrous conversation with Sally. Afterwards, he'd re-dialled, but the receptionist's monotonic voice had got in the way. "Wrong number," he'd said, and replaced the receiver with the absurd exchange still between them. It wasn't what he'd wanted but she'd sounded as though she was having a good time, and perhaps even a little drunk when he'd been expecting an apology. If she'd been drowning her sorrows, she'd done a good job!

A whisky to drown his own sorrows had turned to several – large ones. And now he regretted both; the whisky and the row. Looking at the clock he saw she'd be at her meetings. And it was Friday; he'd be at work until midnight.

Distracted with strong, sweet coffee and marmalade smothered toast, the first page of Alain's proposed investment demanded his full attention. The restaurant, he read, should be guided by the Partnership Act. Alarm bells sounded; he didn't want a partner! Picking up a pen he marked '1' and on a clean sheet of paper wrote *Business Agreement*; *1 – query Partner. Associate?* He read about access to accounts, how the investment would be maintained, and reporting schedules. Alain wanted involvement in decision making and a return on profits. He scribbled '2'; *what happens if there isn't any profit?* After writing the word *profit* he paused, then added; *need to agree what 'profit' is.* If Alain was to become involved, his parents' money would need to be formalised. It made sense to clarify their position as much as his own.

The document seemed to address all eventualities but by the time he'd finished there were two sheets of notes on everything from management to what would happen if one of them died. He retrieved his business plan from the small bedroom that was increasingly an office and added it to the file alongside the Estate Agent's details he no longer needed to read. *Casa Romana*, it said, *Italian Restaurant .... Prime location .... 80 covers plus function room*

… Scope for development … Two-bedroom apartment above restaurant … Open to offers. What it didn't describe was the scratched paintwork, the faded wallpaper, the out-of-date style. But redecoration was easy and the shabbiness justified change. He'd sketched and made notes and taken pictures, and ideas had tumbled over ideas. A new bar at the back of the main dining room, with droplights from crossbeams, would soften the cavernous pitched roof, and the smaller room, now battered by stored tables and boxes, would be transformed with moody lights, picture covered walls and intimate seating.

If the dining rooms were the personality of the restaurant; the kitchen was its soul. Here, the black ranges and stainless steel worktables he was to inherit were sound and he already saw himself there, slicing and seasoning, sautéing and flambéing. Two tall glass fronted chillers by the serving door would move to make way for a servery where Sally's foodie friend, Diane (if he could persuade her) would manage the transition between kitchen and eager diners.

Adding his sketches and photos to the growing file, he saw again the final picture he'd snapped – a faux wishing well – and sang to himself; '*No well, No well, No well, No well, I'll be the King of…*' What? He still needed a name.

Lighting a cigarette he inhaled deeply. A voice of reason warned of recession and interest rates and failed businesses. He'd saved some money, and his parents promised to help if – when – he started a business, but it wouldn't be enough. The bank manager had explained about business plans and loans and interest, but until John had something concrete he'd been unwilling to be specific. "Well," John addressed his snaps, "you can't get more concrete than bricks and mortar." Alain's money was attractive. But it was *his* dream and he wasn't prepared to give it away.

If Alain was impressed when he returned with the draft the next day he passed no comment but responded by sitting down immediately. "So you plan to display work of local artists and sell pictures for a commission? I didn't know about this idea."

A muscle in John's neck solidified and he circled his head to release it. "That'll be independent, otherwise the figures will be skewed." John could cook. And he could draw too, but he needed an income and it was cooking that paid. Artistic talent and a couple of scraped 'A' levels had got him through interviews to art college in his late teens, and once there he'd discovered hippies and psychedelic music and friends like Barrie Bates who'd introduced him to free love and easy drugs. It had been wild until Janine said she was pregnant. He couldn't even be sure it was his child, but she'd said she would prove it. After that he hadn't known if it was the black dog depression that fatigued him or the medication they gave him to relieve it. Days had been spent drifting in and out of the sleep that evaded nights until he hadn't been able to live without medication. They'd locked him up then, in a place where the hell got worse. For a time. More than two years had passed before he'd recovered and during that time he'd heard little about Janine or the baby, other than to be assured it was his.

He hadn't done drugs after that, not even the antidepressants prescribed by the doctors, but babies had become synonymous with depression and he intended never to face either again. His adoptive parents, ever loving Frances and Michael, had supported the child and mother financially until he was well and then he'd taken over. But he kept his distance. The child had her mother. He knew from bitter experience that she didn't need a parent who didn't want her.

He'd found work that paid as a kitchen assistant, discovered a passion for cooking and taken himself to cookery school. Then Sally had come along, and Alain. But art had still been in his soul.

When he'd needed to reflect, to think, to work things through, he'd gone to the galleries to connect with the Masters, particularly Rothko, where he'd meditate into the floating planes of the Seagrams murals until nothing else existed. He'd permitted himself a humble empathy with the great man, a bond born from the depths of despair that went beyond life. Rothko had taken his life and John admired him for finding the strength to do so. He hadn't compare his own battles with Rothko's – who could tell what drove such a man – but he knew of the black spaces a mind could reach and had some understanding of the journey that had taken Rothko's mind from creative inspiration to destruction.

Few had the talent of Rothko. John hadn't, and nor had any of the aspiring artists he'd met at College. Some were good and some were special – like Barrie, or Billy Apple as he'd launched himself in New York. David Hockney had been there too and he'd been extra special. But most were just good artists who needed a break, and his restaurant, he'd decided, would do something for the ordinary, good artists.

Suddenly, in a clear minded moment of random thought John discovered the name for his restaurant. *Seagrams*. It seemed so obvious he'd wondered why he hadn't thought of it before. Inspirational!

Alain too, had an interest in art and was praising him. "This is good thinking. I think you can sell the art from the restaurant."

"Yes, it'll make the restaurant different from others; an edge that'll attract custom." The bank manager had complimented him on this proposition, and John displayed his endorsed business acumen proudly.

"Oui, I can see that," nodded Alain. "It is a good idea." He asked for copies of the forecasts and suggested his own accountant should manage the accounts.

The muscle in John's neck pulsed. "I can't do that," he said, "my mother is doing them and as you see my parents are providing some of the finance. Mum's an experienced bookkeeper and she'd be insulted if I tell her I don't want her." Alain opened his mouth but John pressed on. "And actually, though I like your offer very much, I see you as an associate more than a partner. The advantages of your financial involvement are clear but I have the greater share as well as being active and therefore a greater involvement." There. He'd said it. He'd been going to do it without Alain and could still do so.

Alain pursed his lips. "So. You want my money, but not me. Well, I appreciate that control is important to you. But I expect you can also see that if I am to invest thirty thousand pounds, I need to have some say in how it is used."

"Yes," John agreed, "that is why we are discussing this so carefully." He paused. "My mother will do the books, but your accountant should audit them."

"D'accord. I understand you want less of me in your business than I feel I should have. I think I can help you more than you realise; I have been doing this for a long time. It is important for me to know how my money is used but I can agree to being what you call 'associate' or perhaps what I would call a sleeping partner. I am less happy about having little say in how the money is spent. However, I admire your determination and I think you are a good risk. So with agreement of quarterly reports, accounts, and forecasts, I will let you use my money. We will meet formerly, quarterly. But, I say again, if you need help, you must not hesitate to talk to me, huh?"

John held out his hand. "I will be happy to take thirty thousand of your pounds and turn it into gold."

"I would be happy if you do that, but I don't mind if it takes a few weeks!" Alain shook his hand. "You know there are no formal rules for these sorts of business relationships, but I hope you agree that it is a good idea for us to have a written agreement to guide us in our future discussions?" John nodded his assent.

"So, I will instruct my solicitor to draw up an agreement around what we have discussed, oui?"

"Oui!" Some clouds, he told himself, had gold linings. "Now I must go and do some work here or you'll be stopping my pay, and as you can see, I need that too."

It was still dark when he stopped the hire-van outside Diane's house but her face was already at the window.

"Phew! Does that heater go any lower?" Diane unfastened her scarf as she clambered into the cab.

"It was cold when I started." With his eyes glued to the road he twisted the knob a half turn. Frosty grass verges sparkled in the headlights and he'd already felt the tyres slip on the glistening, untreated side road. "You had breakfast?"

"No. You?"

"No. Let's grab a bacon bap at the trucker's place near Keynsham."

The roads were almost empty and it wasn't long before they were on the Bristol Road. "We're rollin'." John grinned. "Y'know, I'm looking forward to this, especially now that I can afford pretty much anything I need."

Diane turned her head. "Go on."

"Guess what's happened." His grin widened.

"You've won the football pools?"

"Nope."

"Your premium bond's come up!"

"Nope."

"You've inherited a fortune from a long lost uncle?"

"Nope." He'd been too late to ring Sally the previous evening, and he was bursting with his news. "Ok. I'll tell you. You'll never guess anyway." He paused for effect. "Alain is putting up thirty grand." He glanced over quickly, savouring the surprise on Diane's face.

"What?" Her eyes were wide. "Why?"

"Well he thinks I'm going places and wants a piece of the action." He looked sideways again. "Now all I need is for you to say you'll work with me and I'm on my way."

Diane shook her head. "Sorry, no can do." She paused. "Actually, I've got my own piece of luck to tell you about. You'll never guess… no, not that again. I'll just tell you. We're both burgeoning entrepreneurs. I've signed a lease; I'm taking on The Kitchen." Even in the dark John could see her beaming smile. "I'll be doing a lot of the same stuff as at Black and Emery but for other firms, and even some stuff with Black and Emery too!"

It was hard to feel pleased at Diane's news; he'd been confident she'd join him. "That's great!" He hoped he sounded genuine and wondered if Sally knew. He also wondered who he would now entrust the crucial role to.

Energised by bacon rolls and coffee, they registered details at the reception desk and entered a maze of multi-tiered rows of fryers and griddles, coffee machines, utensils, and saucepans and skillets of every shape and size. Bar equipment led to glassware, cutlery overflowed into crockery, and baking trays mille-feuilled alongside cloths and clothes. Keeping an eye on potential competitors, John noted lot numbers until just before nine-thirty when they made their way to the auction hall and leaned nonchalantly against a heavy oak dresser behind rows of already seated punters. A clock struck the half hour and platform lights came on, illuminating winter gloom dulled further by dirt smeared windows. Buzzing chatter subsided. The auction was about to begin.

The first lot, a fryer, went quickly, too quickly for John to spot who was bidding against the auctioneer's rat-a-tat patter. More lots went quickly too and before long lot fifteen, his first item, was called.

"Lot number fifteen. A countertop boiler in stainless steel. As seen. What are we bid?" The auctioneer's eyes scanned the room. "Forty? Who'll start us off? Forty pounds. Thank you sir, we have forty pounds. Forty pounds, we have forty. Forty five? Thank you. Fifty? Fifty. We have fifty five? All done then at fifty?"

He'd marked eighty pounds in his catalogue and discreetly nodded his head in the direction of the auctioneer but to his dismay the auctioneer raised the gavel and was calling, Going... going... John's hand shot up before the gavel descended. "Yes!" he waved frantically.

The auctioneer acknowledged him. "We have Fifty-five. Sixty?"

The previous bidder shook his head and John congratulated himself; he was off to a good start.

By mid-afternoon he had many of the items he'd wanted. "Good day, eh?"

"You did well, once you got the hang of it." Diane chuckled.

"I did ok!" he protested. "I only went over my limit on the sideboard – which is fabulous – and the outdoor stuff, but I got everything else for less. On balance I'm up. I stopped bidding when the drop lights went over my head."

Diane groaned at the pun. "Like I said, you did well. But what about those lights? They'd have been perfect. You need something like that or the place will be dingy."

"I'll find something." He should have bid more, he knew it.

Along the road, silhouetted trees and stratum of blue-grey clouds backlit slashes of golden winter sun and as they neared Bath, Diane invited him to eat with her and Malik. "It's only spaghetti bolognaise, but if you're on your own....?"

It was tempting, but he had much to tell Sally and was eager to call her. "Thanks, but better not. I need to offload this lot into my parents' garage and get the van back by seven. And go home, have a shower. All that stuff." John gave his attention to the roundabout he was negotiating before he spoke again. "Y'know, Sally will be really chuffed to hear that you're taking on The Kitchen. You don't mind if I tell her about it, do you?"

Diane turned away and looked out of the side window. "If you want."

"Right. I'll tell her then." They stopped at traffic lights and watched whilst a girl crossed in front of the van, her breath misting like speech bubbles on the evening air. "I just wondered if you wanted to tell her yourself."

"John, it's none of your business."

"Well, actually Diane, I disagree with you. Sally is more upset about losing you as a friend than you know, and friendship is important. And it is my business because not only do I care about Sally but I value you as a friend too. So in my book that gives me the right to say I think it's gone on for too long. You two were great friends, how can you ignore that?"

"Yes, we were good friends. And as good friends I'd have thought Sally would have let me know I was about to be kicked out of my job. She must have known about it for months. But no, not a word!"

"Well, I hope that I never upset you." The lights glowed green. "So you're going to stay angry forever are you? Have you any idea how much Sally fought that closure? She agonised over it. Do you think it was easy for her? And, then, after making what was, in her eyes, a difficult but ethically correct decision, she lost her best friend!"

"As a so called 'best' friend I'd have...."

He cut in. "Diane, I don't want to fall out with you over it. I can see your side too. In fact I think you both had valid points. So the choices are to either accept the differences and move on or end a great friendship."

"John, you've made your point." They drove on for a few minutes. "Are you sure about the spaghetti?"

"Y'know what? I'm going to London." It was a spur of the moment idea, and crazy, but sometimes it was right to be crazy.

"Tonight? You old romantic, you." They'd arrived at Diane's house. "Malik's here. Are you sure you don't need a hand to offload the stuff?"

Assuring her that he and his father could manage he rejoined the jam of vehicles vying for end of the day space. In urging Diane to make up he'd suddenly yearned to be with Sally. He loved her and wanted to be with her – even at her mother's. He pictured her thick, almost black curly hair that she plaited at night and her prominent cheekbones with the three pinprick scars that twitched when she laughed – the curse of chickenpox in childhood – and her exotic blue eyes inherited from her Pathan grandmother, fringed as they were with rich, dark lashes that didn't need mascara to frame them. He thought too, of her determination, her optimism, even the quick temper that was soon tamed. They were her and he saw and understood them. They were specific, unlike the preciousness, the shared desire that excluded all else when they made love, and the shared intimacy that was so mysterious and fragile. Over the years he'd dared to trust love and worry less that beautiful Sally, one day, might find him wanting.

His father must have been waiting; he was out of the house and opening the van before the engine had been turned off. "Good day was it?"

John pursed his lips as he unlocked the back of the van. "So so."

"By the way, your mother wants you to sign something for the bank. She told me to tell you." Michael hovered at John's shoulder as the rear doors opened. "My goodness! You've enough here to start a restaurant."

The icy air chilled and once unloaded John was glad of the warmth of the house and a hot drink. Keen to be on his way, he told his parents quickly of Alain's proposal. "So I think we should formalise the money you've lent me." Frances started to protest but John shook his head. "It's important Mum. Alain will have a share of the profits so I need to make sure that they're clear of all expenses – including your time and your money. It all needs to be recorded. Properly."

Frances sliced banana cake. She'd done the books for Neil Jackson, supplier of fruit and vegetables to supermarkets and green grocers, for more than twenty years and was friends with him and his wife, Linda, who had gifted the cake. "We'll sort it out." She passed cake to John and then Michael. "I wish Neil didn't buy so many bananas!"

The winter freeze had emptied the roads and by ten-thirty he'd driven through Bethnal Green and into the supermarket car park. Leaving his car next to night staff cars he walked briskly past the children's playground, empty of even the older kids who usually hung out there until late. The icy wind burned at his ears and covering them with his gloved hands he almost ran along the indistinguishable rows of identical houses. Yes, he was on Coventry Street; he saw the corner shop with Rasheed behind the counter, ready to serve anyone at any hour. Seven doors more and then two brass '3's above the letterbox. He knocked gently and waited. His ears stung with cold and he knocked again, harder this time. There was movement and a voice inside.

"Sally. It's me. Let me in." Bolts grated and a security chain rattled. Pushing through the gap as soon as he could he closed the door quickly, grateful for the warmth in the house.

"Sal. I'm sorry," he dropped his bag. "I've missed you." She felt like home and he knew it was alright again.

"I can't believe you're here." From upstairs Jane's voice called out and Sally told her all was well.

"Can I stay then?"

"Can you sleep in a single bed?"

"With you?"

She nodded.

"No problem!"

CHAPTER 3

Pasta alla Puttanesca

A bucket of daffodils, daringly sunny in the April breeze, caught Sally's attention as she passed the flower shop, their cheerful disposition giving hope that Spring was around the corner. Picking out two bunches, then a third, she took them into the shop.

"Haven't seen you for a while." The florist ripped a sheet of paper from a roll. "You're looking well."

"Oh! Thanks." Handing over a pound note, she waited for her change. "It must be the spring air!"

As she left the shop she reflected that she did, indeed, feel particularly well. Her own work had slowed to a manageable pace and John's restaurant would be opening in one more week. It had taken almost four months but from the carnage of renovation, elegance had been forged. And in the process John's excitement had become hers too.

Humming under her breath she snipped the bunched daffodil stems, released them into a vase on the windowsill and added water from a milk-bottle. Thinking how John's mother would have snipped the flowers individually and arranged them with foliage she pushed them around a bit then decided they brightened the day just as they were, defiantly unadorned. She made tea, tuned the radio and settled down to listen to her secret passion, The Archers.

As Peggy's voice faded into the evergreen tune she retuned to Radio Two. John teased her about the 'everyday story for odd folk' she'd listened to alongside her mother as a child. And, no doubt, her mother would have been listening to this episode too. She dialled the London number.

"Hello, Mum." Sally listened to news of the big new supermarket and how Mrs Bhatti had to wait for eight months for a hip replacement and the local council were laying new paving slabs. With toes curled against the front door draught she wiped dust from the spider plant fronds between her fingers and flicked pages of her diary. Noticing the red dot on the previous Sunday – the day to expect her period – she frowned. Had she marked the wrong week? Counting back four weeks and then forward again, she shook her head. Her periods came on time; she was on the pill. A thought formed. "Sorry Mum, I've got to go; er…there's someone at the door." Replacing the receiver she counted the weeks again. Her last period had lasted for only three days and like the one before, she'd put it down to the pressure at work. But she'd not missed a period. From the depths of doubt came worms of fear; the pill, she'd heard, could trigger periods when a woman was pregnant. And some women said they didn't know they were pregnant until they gave birth. Her legs felt weak. "No, please no." She counted the weeks between the dots again and shivered.

Dr. West was running almost an hour late when Sally arrived at the surgery and sitting between a middle-aged woman with swollen legs and an acne-pitted youth she looked at faces resigned to waiting and wondered what brought them to seek advice. A tired young woman, not much more than a child herself, shuffled a baby on her lap and yawned as her neighbour asked the age of the child.

"Two months."

"Your first?"

"Yes." The baby started to whimper.

"Boy?"

The mum nodded.

Sally picked up a *Woman's Own* and opened it from the back, looking for the problems page. What advice, she wondered, would Marje have for her circumstances?

Finally her number was called and feeling the bulge in her handbag that was a small sample bottle she went to Dr. West's surgery.

"Good afternoon Miss Lancing, and how are we today?"

Usually the doctor's greeting made her want to giggle. But not today. Today, a dip of paper into her bottle and there was the evidence.

"Congratulations Mrs...er Miss Lancing." Her doctor glanced at his buff record folder then peered over his glasses. His smile had disappeared. "Er, yes. Miss Lancing."

"Thank you." Her inner woman mutinied. Thank you? How dare he look down his nose at her! But the inner girl felt the last slither of hope melt into trepidation that far outweighed indignation and clutching the leaflet he gave her, she left him to his rightousness.

She was pregnant, she didn't know who the father was; why, she wondered, did she feel nothing. Pulling John's baggy sweater round her shoulders she wondered why she wasn't angry, or frightened, or weeping? Then she realised what she was. She was numb. She'd left the surgery crushed by Dr. West's confirmation as well as by his judgement and now, with arms folded on the kitchen table she cursed her lying periods that hadn't warned her and lowered her head to her folded arms. A draught from the future chilled and she pulled the sweater tighter; what was she going to tell John? How would he take it? And if he knew.... what happened. She thought of the child he'd already fathered... and rejected. Sitting at the table like a child a primary school refrain echoed; *forgive us our trespasses as we forgive them who trespass against us, and lead us not into temptation…* And then *…if I die before I wake…*

The clunk of the front door roused her and John appeared, his cheerful voice discordant in her ears.

"Hi Sal. Oh good, you haven't eaten yet. I'm starving. What do you fancy?"

Grateful for once at his single-mindedness she saw how happy he was; happier than she'd ever known him. And she made an instant decision to postpone telling him about the baby until Seagrams had opened and was under way. Forcing a smile she didn't feel she put her arms round him and kissed him on the cheek. "Things gone well?"

"Yep!" He looked at her. "You ok? You look bushed."

"Mmm, I'm fine. Just a bit tired. I'd dozed off to sleep. How's today gone?"

"Great. The decorator's almost finished, the blinds are up, and I've rearranged some of the tables. It looks fab. And almost all the people I invited to the opening night have replied." Cupboards were being opened and closed as he searched through them. "Jack from Radio Bath is coming and Alex Manning from Homewood Park Hotel is bringing his boss." A long, blue wrapped pack of spaghetti appeared in his hand and he thrust it towards Sally. "Pasta alla Putanesca? Fast and easy or hot and spicy?"

Sally turned away then remembered she had to be her happy, worry-free self. "Oh, fast and spicy." Did John give her a questioning look? "I'll er, set the table." His enthusiasm was all-embracing and as he regaled her with plans for wine and food and people she began to believe she'd get through the week without him knowing something was amiss.

Standing by his side outside Seagrams Sally both felt and shared John's elation. She, too, had cleaned and scrubbed and polished and set tables but it was his achievement and the pulse in his temple, his clenched hand in hers, and the brightness in his eyes gave evidence to the palpable excitement that almost overcame her one little cloud of apprehension; Diane would be coming. She'd sent a card, a white flag of peace, when she'd heard Diane had taken on The Kitchen, but it seemed there was to be no reconciliation.

Facing them immediately as they entered the restaurant was the painting John had commissioned. She liked the colours well enough but preferred almost any of the other pictures that now created a gallery of the walls. These, and the candlelit glasses and cutlery and flowers arranged by his mother were, thought Sally, what brought the room alive.

"It's wonderful, John!"

Misinterpreting her meaning, John pulled a chair toward his painting. "Yeah." Climbing up, he draped a muslin cloth from the frame, replaced the chair in its perfectly aligned position and headed for the kitchen. But not before she'd seen apprehension behind the shine of his eyes and she knew that withholding her news had been the right thing to do.

Leaving him to his kitchen she went to the bar, flicked the switch on the new hi-fi system and found Billy Bang's *Sweet Space;* lazy Jazz was perfect. Leaning against the bar she let the music wash over her until, hearing the door open, she turned with a warm smile.

Diane spoke first. "Sally."

"Diane." She turned the music down. "It's been a while."

"Hasn't it."

Separated by more than the room Sally longed for the old friendship. "I, er, you…"

"Oh God. This is so stupid!" It was Diane who came forward. "I've missed you Sally, and life's too short for this rubbish."

"Oh Diane! It is!" The women hugged and laughed. "I've missed you. And wonderful things are happening – you've started a business too?"

"Yes! And Black and Emery are paying more than they used to too!"

"Ha! I told them they would. Serves them right."

Diane spluttered something about absurd insanity and held her friend at arm's length. "You look amazing. You should wear red more often, that dress is gorgeous." Grinning, she pushed forward her chest, "And it fits you perfectly…."

Sally saw John approaching, carrying champagne. "A drink! There're things to celebrate."

His arm slid round her waist. "Hey, you two! It's been too long!" He winked at Diane. "If that dress is a bit on the tight side, it's my fault; too much of a good thing!"

"No!" Diane clapped her hands. "We're celebrating more than one new beginning! Wonderful! Congratulations. I thought you looked well Sally; you must be one of those lucky women that pregnancy ….." Sally's and then John's expressions cut her words. "Oh no! I'm sorry. I think I've just put both my big feet in it."

Sally recovered first and asking Diane to start filling champagne glasses she pulled John into the small dining room. Her legs trembled. "John, I…."

"Sally?" His words were low and precise. "Tell me it isn't true."

But her face told the truth and she saw disbelief become anger then rage, rising and filling him so that she stepped back against the wall, fearful of something she'd never seen in him before.

"No!" The single word, mouthed rather than spoken, hung before her as he turned, moved, almost ran.

Pain jolted as the door rammed her shoulder and she slumped, her legs folding, so that she crouched against the wall, trembling.

Moments later Diane was there. "Sal?" she whispered. "Are

you ok? Can I do anything?" She, too, crouched. "He didn't know, did he? I'm sorry. I thought you didn't want children but you looked so happy when you said you had things to celebrate and when John said you'd put on weight and it was his fault I thought… I'm so sorry."

Her shoulder burned and she cupped it gently. "I didn't think he'd noticed my…" Holding out a hand she smiled weakly. "Help me up? It's not your fault, Diane. I was saying that as well as celebrating the restaurant, you and I had made up." She stood shakily, flexing her shoulder. "Don't worry; I'll talk to him," and added with more strength than she felt, "Look, I've got to get out there and give a hand. Can you come to my place tomorrow, around three? I could use a friend."

Diane nodded. "Yes, I'll come. And you do look terrific – especially when you smile."

Grateful for the encouragement she returned to the dining room and with a glass of orange juice in her hand smiled at a wiry, bearded man who she recognised as Alex Manning.

Through the evening she excused John's absences, explaining his food demanded him and that he would join them as soon as he could. When, eventually, she went to find him in the kitchen and he turned from her as if she'd ceased to exist she didn't wait to see the unveiling of the picture or hear the speech he'd been practising all week. Quietly, she left the restaurant.

The sofa wasn't a comfortable bed and Sally was irritated when she woke at around four o'clock. John would have seen her when he arrived home – why didn't he wake her? Then memory caught up. The empty bedroom confirmed his absence and the rest of the night filled with images of car crashes and accidents until daylight brought rationality and she guessed he was probably still at the restaurant, alone. At eight o'clock she called

Seagrams but when the continuous ringing merely drummed the pounding ache in her head she replaced the receiver as nausea swept over her. Was this morning sickness, she wondered. If so, it had chosen a fine time to start. A slice of toast contracted her throat so she took tea to bed and prayed for sleep to blanket suffering, at least for a time.

It was early afternoon when she woke to cold tea and a still silent house. She rang the restaurant again and was greeted warmly by someone she didn't know. Echoes of conversation sounded in the earpiece as she waited.

"He's er ... busy just now. He said he'll talk to you when he can."

Nursing the silent receiver until she became aware that her feet ached with cold she moved to the sofa. Talk when he can. When? What does he mean? With her feet curled under a coat she tried to unravel her mind. There'd been a baby once before. And it had been John's baby. With a girlfriend, at art college. He'd left her – walked away from his own child. Had he been ill or had it made him ill? The knots became tighter. If, in January, she hadn't… Diane was due to arrive in little more than an hour. It would be the first time since… Where did Diane's loyalties lie? Her friend had worked with John during their rift and despite the pretence of indifference Sally admitted she'd been jealous. First and foremost, Diane had been *her* friend. The three of them – then four with Malik – had spent holidays and happy times together, and the friendship had deepened, but was Diane now the friend she'd once been? Sally's thoughts returned to the previous evening and she assured herself that Diane had been genuine. Her heart warmed; the quarrel was over. It had to be, she decided, she needed her friend more than she had ever done.

"He'll come home, Sally. He has to."

Sally wasn't comforted; Diane couldn't know how

wholeheartedly against fatherhood John was. Or how decisive he could be. "Hmmm, maybe to collect his things."

"When's the baby due?"

"I'm not ... sure." Sally's hand moved across her stomach. "It's not exactly planned; I was on the pill until a few weeks ago but I forgot some in January so I think it's probably due in October." She looked down, ashamed of the truth and wondering what she could tell Diane. "There're a couple of problems." She hated that she couldn't have a cigarette. "Firstly, we don't want a baby. Not now. Not ever. John's even more against it than I am. And you know what happened to him at college."

"But he was only a kid himself then and he's older now. And he loves you. Surely, that makes a difference?"

"I hope so, Diane, I really hope so." Sally felt nauseous and it wasn't morning sickness.

"What about you?"

"I'm pregnant. I don't have a choice. I guess it'll grow on me." She laughed mirthlessly at the pun.

"But you're worried about John."

"Ah, there's the rub." How, she feared, would Diane judge her? "It's not as simple as that." But it was too much to bear alone. "I don't know... if John is the father."

"You what?" Sally didn't think she'd ever seen a jaw drop before. "Sal? What happened?"

What happened? It was an appropriate question and Sally told her friend about 'what happened', finishing with, "so you see, it could be James's baby." She dropped her eyes, waiting for condemnation.

"You idiot." Diane's voice didn't sound damning. "It could have been anyone, you know. James is a bastard. Does anyone else know – apart from James?" She touched Sally's arm. "Sally. Look at me."

It felt unreal. Rousing herself she looked at Diane. "No, I don't think so. Or at least, I doubt it."

"You poor thing." They stared at each other until Diane spoke again. "Do you want to know what I think you should do?"

She nodded.

"Much as is grieves me that 'Daddy's boy' will get away with it, the baby probably is John's and he must never believe otherwise. You're not James's first conquest…"

"You…?"

"No, not me, but there were others. You don't need to know. He's a predator. But you and John, well, you'll be terrific parents. John's older now, and he loves you. He'll be back once he's got his head round it. He might even grow to like it! The baby's his; it will grow up with John as its father which will make him so. Think about it Sally, life's tough enough without letting bloody James Black ruin it for you both – in fact, for all three of you."

Words were easy. Sally shook her head then stood wearily. "I'm going to make some tea." Once in the kitchen she sat and it was Diane who made the tea.

"Here. Tea – panacea for all that ails."

"Thanks. You may be right but I don't think John deserves to have a baby dumped on him."

"No, Sally, he doesn't. But he isn't going to have a baby dumped on him. You need to start getting used to the idea that the two of you are going to be parents. Together. Otherwise… well, you're going to ruin the lives of three people over one mistake. You're going to suffer, whatever you do – that's punishment enough. Don't ruin John's and the baby's futures too. Don't you think that James has some blame for what happened? I'll bet he's not thrashing himself to death over it!"

"He…"

"I know he doesn't know. But he'll know soon enough, and he's bound to wonder."

"You don't think...?"

"No fear! He won't let you get in the way of what he wants. But if I were you I'd watch your back where he's concerned. Sally, think of it this way. If it had been me who'd been seduced by James, would you, as my friend, forgive me?"

She answered without hesitation. "Of course I would, and I wasn't seduced. I'm sorry to say I participated."

"We're talking in circles. Think about it, Sally, forgive yourself, and get on with it."

When Diane had left Sally felt more alone than she'd ever felt. "Fool," she mumbled, "stupid fool." Scrambled eggs and toast went un-eaten and calls to Seagrams were unanswered. Midnight came and went and at one o'clock she went to bed whispering, "Awful, awful." Saturday became Easter Sunday and the days seemed pointless.

She'd taken tea and work papers back to bed when a key rattled the lock at the front door. Papers scattered and from the bottom of the stairs John's sunken, pink rimmed eyes looked at her.

"Hi." She descended the stairs slowly, hesitantly. He was here. "Tea?" she asked. He seemed to struggle for words. "It's what people do when they don't know what to do, isn't it?"

His silence was unsettling. She passed a mug and jumped as he caught her wrist and held it despite spilling hot tea that hurt.

"Sal..." At last he spoke. He swallowed, and spoke again. "Sally. I'd been looking forward to this Easter more than I can tell you. The restaurant; my dream. But... I've been to hell and back."

He wiped tea from her hand and tears prickled at the gentleness of his hand brushing hers.

"My mind's been taken over. By what was said. And not said. On Friday."

His voice crackled and she could hardly bear his suffering. She had to tell him the truth, to release him. "John, please. I…"

"Sally, let me finish," he urged, "or I don't think I can say what I have to."

She held her breath; her heart was breaking. He didn't deserve to suffer like this; he had cause to go, to leave without guilt. She listened as he said he didn't want a child; the idea horrified him. But because he loved her – which he did, he said – he would learn to accept their child. Their child; his words pierced like arrows. It wasn't right to deceive him. She hadn't simply bought a pair of shoes without telling him, this was fundamental to their lives. But the truth might destroy him and all he was working for. She couldn't tell him! Diane had been right; she would suffer either way, but in keeping her secret John and the baby needn't.

"You'll have to help me, Sally, to be a father. You will, won't you? With you, I can do it."

She'd longed for him to come home but now she felt all the happiness she'd ever known drain away and leaning forward her forehead rested against his. "Oh my love. I…. I… I don't know what to say to you. I wish I wasn't pregnant more than I can tell you." She wanted to tell him she was scared, and that she wished desperately that it was his baby, that she could have an abortion and not live the rest of her life with the decision, and that she didn't have to live the rest of her life knowing she'd deceived him. But she couldn't.

Throughout the day and into the night they talked. Of their families, their feelings, their futures. About childhoods, parenthood, and changes to be made. They talked of their parents; when they should tell them; how surprised they'd be. And John talked of marriage. He said he wanted to give his family a foundation, and she sidestepped. "Marry in haste," she stalled. Having hurtled down a path of duplicity, marriage was a deceit too far. Before exhaustion eventually overcame her later that night, and with her back spooned into John's warmth, she felt the strength of her love and knew it to also be the weakness in their bond.

When the phone woke them it was John who went to answer it. Minutes later he was back, saying he'd turned down a bank holiday ramble with his mother to spend the day with her.

The news pleased her. "What time do you need to be at work?"

Saying he had until six o'clock he lay down again, close so that he touched her side, and for a while she watched his face and tried to read his thoughts. "How long do you think we can keep this er... to ourselves?" The word 'baby' didn't come easily.

He didn't answer and she was about to repeat the question when he turned to face her then saw the blue-purple tennis ball bruise on her shoulder.

"How did you do that?"

"Oh, I slipped. In the bath." She lied as she recalled the moment he'd unwittingly slammed the door into her. "It doesn't hurt much."

John touched the bruise gently. "You must take care."

She rolled towards him, moved by his tenderness.

"If Diane guessed so easily, your mother and mine will too. We'd better tell them. What do you think?"

Life was galloping ahead and she was no longer holding the reins. "Not yet; soon."

To her relief he nodded then asked if she'd like to have breakfast in bed.

Though they barely mentioned the pregnancy in the coming weeks, Sally's mind dwelled on little else. Her guilt, now shared, weighed less and though practical and financial matters added layers, she more comfortably set them aside. Income from the restaurant couldn't yet be relied on. Her salary was already paying the bills. She'd work for as long as possible and return as soon as she could afterwards. Her immediate predicament was her colleagues. They, she feared, would see her pregnancy as evidence that she didn't belong in the boardroom and assurances that six weeks leave of absence was all she needed would be easy compared to convincing them she could be a mother and still be professional.

A month passed without her condition being disclosed, but as she discarded a fitted skirt one morning in favour of a looser dress, she knew it was only a matter of time before her body gave away its secret. As the weekly exec meeting ended she invited the one Board member she felt treated her as an equal to the King's Head.

Andrew was a perceptive man. "It's nice to have lunch with you Sally, but I get the impression there's more to this than pleasure?"

"Hmm." Sally took out a packet of cigarettes. She wanted one badly. "I'm going to have a baby."

His surprised smile quickly dissolved. "I'd like to say congratulations, but your expression tells me otherwise."

"You're right; I'm not pleased. And neither is John, though he's being amazingly positive about it. We didn't plan for this; in fact, we planned for it to never happen. But now it has, and it couldn't be at a worse time with Seagrams just up and running." She sipped her orange juice. "I suppose you're shocked that I'm not being all mumsy, aren't you?"

Unintelligible chatter filled the gap as Andrew considered his reply. "Well, how you feel about having a child is none of my business. Everyone's different." He lifted his glass. "But I suppose what you're telling me is that you'll be leaving us. I'm sorry…."

"No, Andrew, that's what I don't want!" Without a cigarette she bit the skin at the side of her thumb. "I need my job – for money and for sanity. I'm scared stiff of being at home with nothing but nappies all day." Her cigarettes lay on the table and she offered one to Andrew.

"I gave up."

"I'll have to." Sally lit a cigarette. "My worry is Lawrence and the others. I need your support, Andrew. And your advice on how to win them over."

"I'd like to support you Sally, but seriously, how are you going to be able to do your job when you have a baby? Jenny didn't work for nearly six years after we had ours and even now she only does part-time."

So she was up against Andrew too. "Andrew, believe me, I can do it." She held his eyes. "I'll sort out childcare; John's Mum will help, and I promise you it won't affect my job. Please Andrew, help me with the others."

Andrew flicked a beer mat at the edge of the table and fluffing the catch, bent to retrieve it. "You've got guts, I'll say that. If anyone can do it you can. And you've never let me down on a promise, so yes, I'll do what I can. But if you have any difficulties you must talk to me before they become problems."

It was what she wanted to hear. "Thanks Andrew."

"I mean it Sally. Times are tough and I watch my own back these days too."

At the next management meeting Sally's formal announcement that she intended to take six weeks maternity leave during October and November was greeted with silence from the old stalwarts but as it wasn't contested. All she had to do, thought Sally determinedly, was to show them! Everything was falling into place even if, she thought, it felt like a conspiracy.

On a hot day in early August Sally sat at her desk feeling grotesque and wiped moisture from her face. Beyond the open window drone bees made drowsy by heat encouraged somnolence as bruise coloured clouds pondered the storm they threatened. When the phone rang she welcomed the distraction. It was Lawrence's secretary informing her that he would like to see her in his office at four o'clock. With less than ten minutes warning she resented the arrogant assumption that she had nothing more important to do and knowing it was unlikely to be important increased her resentment. Sighing, she finished signing the weekly payroll cash requisitions, touched up her lipstick and locked her office.

"Ah, Sally." Lawrence indicated an armchair next to a coffee table. "Do come in and take a seat." James was sitting in another of the chairs and as she sat he asked his father if he should stay.

"Oh, stay, by all means. I think it's good practice to have a third person to oversee the discussion, you know, that sort of thing. " He turned to Sally. "That's correct isn't it?"

She looked from Lawrence to James then back to Lawrence. "We need a third party?"

James answered. "Oh, I think it's the thing in these situations isn't it? You would know of course, being the expert."

Alarm bells sounded. She'd expected to advise on a contractual issue or similar, but what she was hearing implied something personal. "If it's necessary for a third party to be here – for my benefit – I have the right to say who the third party should be."

James rose with a conceit that confirmed her fears. "I'll say goodbye then." He was a man used to getting his own way.

At her request Andrew was summoned and over a cup of untouched coffee Lawrence informed her that the Board had reached an unfortunate but unavoidable decision; due to reduced staff numbers a Director of Personnel at Board level was superfluous and as they had a Personnel Manager already in post the function was to be restructured. Her role was redundant and sadly they were going to have to let her go. Generous compensation and augmentation of her pension on top of her statutory allowance were hers, plus of course, she'd receive three months pay in lieu of notice, tax free under the circumstances. She should leave immediately and consider herself on garden leave until the end of the notice period. And they would, of course, be happy to provide a reference to a future employer if asked, and they wished her well for the future.

She heard the words with mounting disbelief. There'd been no discussions about restructuring her department. This was due to her pregnancy. And James. She was being paid off!

"Did you know about this?" Andrew's face disclosed that he had indeed, known, and she gained some satisfaction from his discomfort. "So you've cooked it up between you."

Lawrence began to speak. "My…"

But Sally was coldly furious. "You condescended to put a woman on your board, but a pregnant woman, well that's too much of a challenge isn't it! This isn't redundancy, this is dismissal. And it's unfair dismissal." Standing up she smoothed her top over the seven month bump and walked proudly to the door. "You haven't heard the last of this. I am, after all, the Employment Law expert here."

She went to the Executive Ladies – its very existence an anathema to the Board – where she knew no one would follow her and addressed the dark, flush-stained face in the mirror. "They've used what you've taught them and they've won. You're finished." The emptiness of her farewell comment hit and she gripped the sink in furious and helpless frustration. "Damn, damn, damn." Swallowing disgust, she splashed cool water over her face.

Her office contained little of personal value. A pen, a glass paperweight – a present from Andrew one Christmas – and a packet of tissues. Taking the paperweight she re-locked the door, dropped the payroll requisition on Paula's desk (it wasn't her fault) and walked out of the building, tossing her keys and paperweight in the car-park bin. It was a small victory.

Slamming the door, she kicked her shoes fiercely so that they ricocheted across the corner of the hall.

"Sal? You ok? "

Finding John still at home was a surprise. "Apart from being fired from my job, I'm fine!" She marched into the sitting room and stared at the window. She didn't want John to be home; she wanted to think, to work things out. Before she had to tell him that their future had just skidded round another hairpin bend.

"Fired from your job?" John appeared in the doorway, hair tousled, feet wet, and clutching a towel round his middle. "Why?"

"They've dressed it up. Redundancy! But we all know it's because of this!" She pointed at her stomach. "Everyone knew; including Andrew! You know who your friends are when the chips are down."

John came towards her. "Calm down, Sally. You'll hurt Hughie."

"It's not called Hughie!" She hated that he'd given the unborn child a name, especially that ridiculous name. "It's not any bloody thing! I don't want this bloody baby. You don't want it either. You know what? The only people who are pleased are your parents and my mother. Well, they can have it. With pleasure." She stabbed a finger at the bump. "All those years of hard work ended with this! There're three million people unemployed out there, who's going to give me a job when I'm tied to a baby? It'll be years, decades, before anyone takes me seriously again." She knew she was ranting but at least it drowned John's useless comforting words. She didn't want his platitudes; she wanted the clock to go back. "Y'know what I think? I think we should get it adopted." She saw her comment hurt – as intended – and shrugged his arm from her shoulders. "How are we going to pay for all the things the baby will need without my salary? Where's the money going to come from?" As her father had when her parents had argued about money, John started to offer solutions; things would work out, he said. It hadn't been her father's fault they'd been poor but she'd hated it. And now she hated John. She didn't want his solutions. "Go to work, John. You're going to be late." She backed away as he moved towards her. "I'm fine. Go to work. We'll talk tomorrow. I'll call Diane and see if she'll come over."

It was enough. John looked relieved and made to leave. "But if you need me you'll ring me? Ok?"

Nodding resignedly she sighed with relief as he left. She felt dull, tired, and fat. And she'd been fired. John didn't understand; he'd got Seagrams, and he was a man. She didn't want his attempts to placate, she wanted understanding. And sympathy. And not to have to face two more months of inactivity before this baby would take over her life.

Inactivity was something Sally wasn't very good at, as gleaming windows, dust-free skirting boards, and orderly kitchen cupboards testified to. Even the spider plant glowed with health.

The cycle of time-filling activity, rather than dulling her thoughts, became meditatively rhythmic and set her mind on the road to the future. As soon as the baby was old enough new, increasingly impressive CVs would be ready to be sent to a growing list of prospective employers.

In this way, though tiring, housework had been unexpectedly rewarding. But with only days before her baby was due to be born, it was just tiring. Everything was. Resting on one side and then the other it was impossible to find a comfortable position. She'd woken early that morning feeling energetic and had cleaned out the airing cupboard. Sheets and towels had been shaken, re-folded and re-stacked, and after John had gone to work, she'd re-organised it again so that the soft towelling nappies had a home. Now, with the baby unusually active it was impossible to rest. Heaving herself to her feet she moved towards the bathroom feeling like a Spanish galleon gathering sail when suddenly water gushed down her legs. Grateful that John wasn't there to see the embarrassment of her having wet herself she tossed a towel to the floor and padded it with her foot when a shockingly painful tightness gripped her belly. There'd been feelings of tightness over the past few weeks but not like this – this hurt! Then she realised. This was what they'd said could happen when labour started. Her waters had broken and that was a contraction.

A call to the maternity unit confirmed the baby was probably on its way and, advised to not rush but come in directly, she called Seagrams. John's voice was less calm, but he assured her he would drive carefully.

They'd hardly set off for the hospital when another, stronger, contraction brought a gasp of pain causing John to brake sharply and pull over to the side of the road. "Don't stop!" She bit her lip and counted her breath; 1-2-3 in, and 1-2-3 out until the worst of it passed. "It's not too bad – I just feel…very constipated!" Half laughing she urged him on. "Get me there, but safely please."

At the hospital her protests that she could walk went unheeded and directed by a nurse, John pushed the wheelchair along disinfected corridors echoing with infections and infirmities and into a small room where another contraction distracted dark thoughts. "It's only minutes since the last one," she gasped. "John, stay with me. Promise me you won't leave?"

The nurse patted her hand. "You're fine, lovey. We'll look after you. Put this on and get yourself into bed. I'll be back in a 'mo'." She turned to John. "Come with me, Dad."

"No, er, I'm staying with her."

She raised an eyebrow at his stained chef tunic. "Sure you are, but not like that."

Sally watched him leave with dismay then looked anxiously at her surroundings. A high, plastic sheeted bed surrounded by hostile looking screens, trolleys and a crane-like hoist countered all that she'd naively expected to be natural about childbirth, and as she began to nervously remove her clothes, tears threatened.

"Not in bed yet? Here, you need to get into this." An oversized, back-to-front shirt-like robe was shaken and held for her to slot over her arms. Tapes secured a minimal degree of dignity and clinching it behind her she got on the bed and pulling the cold cotton cover over herself, turned her face gratefully into the pillows.

The nurse busied herself straightening the sheets. "There. Midwife'll be here soon. You'll be fine." She folded away Sally's clothes. "And look, here's your husband."

Encased from head to toe in various green garments, John looked uncomfortable and self-conscious, and to Sally's relief didn't correct the nurse's assumption that she was his wife. And she was extremely grateful to have him back. "Ha! You look like a clown!"

"Wait till you see my tricks," he said, "you'll split your sides."

An hour passed slowly. She gripped John's hand and as each contraction stalled conversation, they became silent. Despite advice she'd heard and read, nothing could have prepared her for this. It was awful. And the birth would be the truth. She glanced at John and prayed the baby would resemble him. Or her. Or anybody but James. She'd hated the pregnancy, and feared her attitude might have affected the foetus. Tormented by fears of deformity she closed her eyes. She'd once told Diane of her worries and been told she was being ridiculous, but now the demons gathered in readiness. Another contraction took hold and she swore to herself. No matter what it was like, no matter who it looked like, she didn't care so long as this would end. She tried to breathe; 1-2-3 in, 1-2-3 out, but agony took the breath away and sent John rushing for the nurse.

"Lovely," the nurse told them. "Five centimetres. We're well on the way."

"How much longer before the baby will be born?" gasped Sally.

"Oh, a while yet." The nurse dabbed her forehead and told her not to worry. "Don't be afraid to use this." She handed Sally a mask with a tube running from it. "Gas and air. It'll help you to relax." She turned to John. "If I'm not back when she wants to start pushing, press this." Indicating a button on the end of a lead, she left them alone.

"Push?" John asked. "What does she mean?"

"I don't know." She thought about the things she'd read and slipped the mask over her face. "I've read about it. I think I'll know when it happens." Even to herself her voice sounded distant.

When 'pushing' gained meaning, gas and air merged with pain and time until, before long, the midwife held a blood and mucus streaked baby for her to see. Its tiny first cry of life brought a gasp of amazement, and when the squirming baby was

CHAPTER 4

New World Mussel Salad

With a mind not yet clouded by the approaching storms of paternity, John opened an eye and squinted at the radio clock. Nine twenty-eight. One day, he promised himself, he'd not set the clock and would trust his mental alarm, honed as it was to remarkable precision and which, on workdays, invariably woke him minutes before the alarm clock.

It was the first working day of the week when his restaurant would open, and the first full working day for his new team. The enormity of the reality still awed him; it really was quite astonishing that he, John 'nobody', was about to be somebody! It had to succeed. The need started at his solar plexus, extended through his chest and knotted his neck. He breathed deeply and reminded himself that though starting a business during the worst recession for fifty years was risky the silver lining was that builders, plumbers, electricians and decorators had been available so that the refit had been completed below budget and on time. Suppliers had been keen to curry business too, encouraging him with discounts, whilst out-of-work kitchen and waiting staff were eager to find jobs. These were good omens. He tossed aside the quilt and leapt from the bed, eager to start the day.

John Lennon's voice floated *Imagine* from the bedroom radio and John sang along as he admired his more slender profile in the mirror-glazed wall. "Food," he sometimes quipped, "is not only my bread and butter, it's my jam too." The reality was that his work as a chef made food easy and sport difficult. Unsocial hours meant unsocial activities and though gyms were open during the day he didn't like the idea of them at all. All those Kevin Keegans and Henry Coopers tossing towels and flexing muscles as they splashed their perfumes! Sucking in his breath he commended himself that, in the hard work of Seagrams, he'd reduced his belly to no more than a slight paunch, unlike Sally, he'd noticed, who seemed to have gained a few extra pounds testing so many of his delicious new dishes.

Wrapping the lead around the drill and tucking the plug into the cable, he placed it with the stack of paintings next to the front door and returned to the spare bedroom for the last picture; the large panel that leaned against the wall. All the paintings were intended for Seagrams 'gallery' but this one was different. It had been commissioned after he'd discovered art student, Roly, whose work spoke of Rothko. When Roly had told him he liked the relationships between primary and secondary colours John had felt a shiver of destiny and the immediate bond led to this painting that for John, represented the Seagrams dream. The semi opaque dark red rectangle floated like a heat haze over yellow and dark blue so that greens, purples and oranges hovered between the planes. It would be the last thing he hung. The other paintings would cover the walls but this would be unveiled at the celebration evening and, unlike all the others, it was not for sale.

Driving time was thinking time and John planned the day in his head. Firstly he needed Neil, his new sous chef, to understand the recipe for the mussel salad. Sally had suggested a switch; croutons for olives, and having tested it on his parents a few days previously he'd found the contrast of crunch and sharp saltiness worked well. Neil, like several others had started early and turned their hands to things that had never been discussed during interviews. The previous day Neil had cleaned windows and fixed window blinds, and today John intended to pass him the job of organising an engineer for the recalcitrant freezer and chasing up the clothing order. And later in the day the first team meeting would take place, with some staff meeting for the first time. Julia, for example, had been interviewed only last week. In his quest to persuade Diane to take the front of house role John had left it late and then despaired at finding the right person until Alain had come to the rescue with the wife of a wine merchant friend. She was, he'd said, passionate about food and wine though having a six-year old might pose a problem. Not pretty in the conventional sense, Julia's boyish physique and unfashionable short straight hair gave her a gamin look that, along with a presence that emanated confidence, John found to be inexplicably engaging. She'd impressed him with enthusiastic suggestions for New World wines and an au-pair and he'd offered her the job on the spot. That she'd accepted immediately had pleased him greatly; a woman in the role was symbolic of his New World style – phrasing, he felt, that had a ring of modernity. It was 'after' Seagrams, as they said in the art world.

Arriving at the same time as Neil, John commandeered his services to offload the paintings from his car. "What do you reckon?" He held up a monochrome still life depicting a simple, almost transparent wine glass behind opaque black grapes set against a pale grey background.

Neil took the painting from him. "It's good. The reflection on that glass and the drop of water on that grape look real." He placed it next to an unframed canvas with dark, spider-like paint bursting from one corner. "That one though, what's that supposed to be? Anyone could do that. My kids could do it."

John smiled. He'd enjoyed painting abstracts at college and engaging with abstract art. "If you don't like that, wait to see what I'm putting opposite the entrance. You'll hate it," he said.

"It's your place." Neil shrugged and followed him into the kitchen. "What time's the staff meeting?"

Telling him two-thirty, John headed for the cupboard-size

room he used as an office. The final self-addressed envelopes he'd sent out with invitations to the celebration dinner sat on the desk, alongside another envelope with the embossed name Keith Floyd on it. He opened it quickly. It had been a bold move to invite Floyd, but seeing the expected refusal brought a pang of regret. The audacious Floyd at his opening night would have been a catch but consoling himself that he had at least replied, he opened the other envelopes. Most were acceptances and he grinned happily, ticking names against his master list until a polite cough made him turn. It was Julia, holding a bottle of wine.

"Hello! Didn't expect to see you 'til this afternoon."

Julia moved into the room. "Hope you don't mind me dropping in but I wanted to get this chilled. I think you should taste it." She held out the green glass bottle. "New Zealand, Sauvignon Blanc. Perfect for your mussel dish and wonderful with salmon too. It has a taste of gooseberries and lemons and I have to say, it's quite delicious."

John's eyes widened. "Wow, you don't waste time, do you?" He pointed towards the wine store. "You know where to find the chiller." He watched her walk away. "Er, you going now?" he asked.

She turned. "I don't have to be anywhere this morning."

"It'll save time if you want to check the wine delivery against the order and log it into the wine store."

"Sure! That's a great idea."

When later John found the bar ready for business he congratulated himself; he'd been right to employ her.

By afternoon the restaurant was almost functional and as two-thirty approached his team gathered in the small dining room. John looked into expectant eyes. These were his staff and it was terrific. The dream was happening.

A few days later he stood next to Sally, and even though he'd been there in the afternoon, he was unprepared for the effect of this first real entrance. His first night was about to happen and he see-sawed between elation and terror. Alain had insisted on a formal dress code but at the last minute he'd exchanged his hired tuxedo for the same uniform the waiting staff would be wearing; black Levi 501's and dark blue open neck shirt with the Seagrams Rothko-style logo forming the breast pocket. It was, he decided, the appropriate attire for the evening.

"John, it's wonderful."

Sally looked stunning in her low-cut crimson cocktail dress and strappy stilettos but the Rothkoesque panel directly opposite demanded his attention. The colours looked less translucent in artificial light but still levitated, hovering slightly from the surface of the wall. He scanned the room, approving each table with its blue iris that replicated reflections of the long droplights in the glasses and cutlery. High seats against the bar invited drinkers and along the walls spotlights lifted paintings from shadows. Turning back to his painting, he walked forwards until he stood inches from the surface and let his fingers brush the surface. A label, similar to those below other pictures, explained nothing ; 'Untitled. Not for Sale.' Picking up a white gauzy cloth and pulling a chair to the front of the picture he climbed up and draped the face of the painting. Then taking a deep breath, he stepped down and replaced the chair to its table. Suddenly he was nervous that everything would go terribly wrong and he glanced quickly at Sally. She and this painting were his luck; he inhaled the spirit of both and went to the kitchen.

"Everything ok?" he asked no-one in particular. Looking around he saw trays of cooked mussels taken recently from the fridge. Shirley rinsed salt from aubergines and Neil trimmed Portabella mushrooms. Behind Neil were the portioned chickens and pears to be roasted. Red wine waited to be combined with cooking juices and Bob, the young but keen kitchen hand, was immersed to the elbows in cold water and spinach. The glass door of the dessert fridge screened New York cheesecakes chilling above handmade chocolates and mini jugs each with raspberry coulli and dark chocolate sauce waiting to be placed on dessert plates. The menu for this night had been chosen to surprise and delight, a meal that would be memorable beyond the evening, enthuse and impress guests so that they would remember him, tell others about his food, and return again and again. Predictable dishes would not to be found in this establishment.

Julia was filling trays with champagne flutes. "Thought you were coming dressed as a penguin?" she laughed.

"Couldn't do it," he responded. "Here, let me help." Picking up some bottles he backed through the swing door into the dining room where, to his happy surprise, Sally was hugging Diane. There'd never been quite the right moment to discuss Diane's presence that evening and hearing Sally demand champagne because they had things to celebrate was a great relief. "Hey, you two. It's been too long!" He twisted the wire on a cork and winked at Diane. "If that dress is a bit on the tight side, it's my fault; too much of a good thing!"

Whether it was Diane's words or Sally's expression that triggered his horror he wasn't sure, but too shocked to speak he let Sally guide him, stunned, into the small dining room.

"Sally?" At last words came. "Tell me it isn't true."

She didn't reply; she didn't need to. A cage closed, trapping every 'No!' in his world in his head. Light dimmed as the red of her dress filled his vision and his clenched knuckles cracked as he fought with them to not hit. Crunch! He thumped the door. And ran. To the safe haven where the searing heat of the flames, the slicing blade of the knife, and the furious frenzy of effort captured the violence of his rage and absorbed it into the energy of cooking.

The next morning Sally's face was the last thing he remembered distinctly. The rest of the evening was a haze of half-memories that, when he tried to recall them in sequence, were disordered and disjointed. There'd been quizzical looks from Neil and Julia – probably when he downed whisky in the kitchen – and he'd dropped a pan of roasted pears. People and happenings and emotions tripped over each other; his bruised knuckles must have been before the desserts but it seemed later and the speech must have been after Alain had insisted he greet his guests. When had Sally come into the kitchen? He recalled applause after his speech and the unveiling of his canvas to reveal flat, lifeless patches of muddy colour. The evening had lasted forever and been over in an instant.

When everyone had left he'd locked himself in with a bottle of whisky, and in darkness spared by a thumbnail of moonlight he'd assessed the day that had started with him as King and ended with him… 'no better than he ought to be'. The phrase was Sally's mother's. Sally, in her red dress, glowing radiantly. Unless some wonderfully fortunate misfortune struck, Sally would have a child who, like him, shouldn't be. In the dark recesses of his mind fat rats of self-doubt scurried and lines from a poem of Larkin's that they'd read at school and loved because it gave them permission to use 'that word', mocked. But behind schoolboy sniggers the truth of the poem had resonated and though he couldn't recall the lines he recalled the conviction. Kids were not for him.

Through the night he'd drunk whisky to drown the fug-grey days and slow motion nights that had followed Janine's pregnancy, and quaked at the prospect of well intentioned white coats when death would have been preferable.

By the time dawn broke and the whisky had failed to do its job he replaced the stopper. He knew he couldn't walk away this time; Sally wasn't Janine and he wasn't that John. But a child would change things. Forever. The bright future of yesterday had shattered and dawn brought only the fear of the dreaded black dog that would wipe out his dreams before they'd started. A business, full of risk and uncertainty, had get-out clauses. And if it all went wrong, you could start again. But there were no get-out clauses with a child. You couldn't sell off tears, tantrums, teenage rebellions. You couldn't buy extra love, extra support when it ran low. You couldn't change your mind after a few years, as his own mother had. He'd been almost two when she'd given him away. Swallowing to push down the lump that had curled into his chest he thought of the life he'd dared to hope he would share with Sally, unshackled by the ties of children and poverty. His beliefs were as strong and compelling as they'd ever been. He hadn't changed. The fear was that he would have to.

His eyes were gritty, his tongue furred and dry. Stretching stiff legs and aching back he eased himself from the floor. He'd not felt cold in the night but now he shivered and his limbs, heavy as if drugged, dragged to the bathroom. The remaining whisky flowed down the sink and filling a glass with clean cold water he drank the sweet freshness.

His second day of business began. Anger threatened to boil at a smudged glass, the unsharpened knife, coffee not brewed strong enough, but each time he regulated it, refusing to let it control him. Did he imagine Neil about to speak, and glances that darted away? When Julia asked if he was pleased with the opening night he laughed brilliantly and said it had been a wonderful success. The day passed. Food finished and diners left, until alone again at last, he sat in his office chair – the most comfortable in the restaurant – and turned the tormented fears that had raged blindly the night before into nurtured thoughts and finally intentions that, with the new morning became the decision that was the only one he could live with. Unshaven and unchanged for two days and nights and carrying the stale odours of body and work he returned home.

Standing in the hall and looking up he saw Sally's face, always an open book, looking drawn and apprehensive, and the words he'd practised in the car failed to materialise. She descended the stairs and he read her pain too, and vulnerability, and yes, resentment, and he searched for concern and hoped to find understanding as she said something strangely normal about making tea.

Searching his silence for words he followed her to the kitchen and watched as she gathered cups, teabags, milk, and made tea. He caught her hand. "Sal…" His voice faltered and he started again. "Sally. I'd been looking forward to this Easter more than I can tell you. The restaurant. My dream! But instead, I've been to hell and back. My mind's been taken over. By what was said. And not said. On Friday." He sat down, mistrusting the strength, or lack of it, in his legs and interrupted her as she began to say something. "No. Sally, let me finish. Please. Otherwise I don't think I can say what I have to." His eyes were sore and he massaged them with the heel of his thumb. A sentence escaped, "You know that I never wanted to be a father, you know how I feel about…." She was looking at the table and he couldn't read her face. Unless he spoke quickly words would fail him, "but I can't walk away from you. I love you. More than anything. I can't let you do this alone. I need to… to face up to this. It's our baby. Please, Sal, please help me to…to…have this child, to be a father, to be a family. Please…" Tears intruded and he rubbed them away crossly.

Sally was leaning towards him, her forehead resting against his and she was whispering that she loved him and didn't want a baby either and needed, really needed his help to get through what was happening too. Her words shocked him; in his own wretchedness he'd assumed nature delivered delight and joy as preparation for motherhood – or at least he'd not considered otherwise. They were in the same boat! The realisation that

Sally needed him gave him strength and with a new tenderness he began for the first time to believe that together, they would manage. It would be nothing like Janine, whose child existed only in thought and namelessly. Amanda. That was her name. He'd held on to the anonymity that her namelessness sustained, allowing his financial support to suppress responsibility. The child would be fifteen or sixteen now and he wondered what she looked like. Janine had been slim, leggy, and though not particularly beautiful her arty, mildly bohemian manner and willingness to sleep with him had made him feel a part of the college scene. She'd been nineteen, he twenty, and consequences were light years away. If he felt anything now it was regret sprinkled lightly with guilt for a life created irresponsibly. But she'd been Janine's child, always, and for the first time he wondered if she – Amanda – ever asked about her father and hoped if she'd been told anything, that Janine had been kind.

The bedroom was light and bright with day when a dream that included the incessant ringing of a phone became reality. John opened an eye and saw Sally sleeping beside him and heard the phone continue to ring. It was later than he'd thought, almost ten. With joints stiffened by two nights spent in the restaurant he slid from the bed.

"Goodness me," his mother's voice said, "You weren't still in bed were you? It's a lovely day!" Unaware of their drama, she was suggesting a walk in the spring sunshine. "We can have lunch out and you can tell us your weekend news." Momentarily taken aback he realised Frances was referring to the first days of Seagrams, and promising to ring back he returned to Sally's warmth with a still dazed head and a desire to do no more than spend the day with Sally. Edging towards her warmth he stirred a degree of wakefulness and whispered that he didn't want to walk with his parents. She whispered sleepily she was of the same mind. With his body spooned into hers he considered the conundrum of love which, when shared, doubled instead of halved. It was impossible to balance the fury of two nights ago against the bursting love of now when in reality little had changed. He was still going to be a father and though it didn't please him, he'd reshuffled the cards and the joker had lost. Sally needed him. For the first time he would have to care for and support her. That, in itself, was potent.

Sally's voice sounded in his ear. "How long do you think we can we keep this to ourselves?"

He didn't answer for a moment. Who would they tell first? Turning towards her he noticed a vivid yellowish bruise on her shoulder. "Oh my God! How did that happen?" There was only so much he could look after.

After the bank holiday it was quiet in the restaurant and John found time to explore the possibility of converting the upstairs flat, which he'd hoped to let, into office space so that the spare bedroom at home could be cleared for the baby. The task, it seemed, was relatively simple. By moving a door so that the smaller bedroom opened from the hallway a slightly smaller, one-bedroom flat could still be let. The perfect tenant, he mused, would be someone who might work in the restaurant. It wouldn't be a bad arrangement and he concluded that such a change would lose little in the way of income.

"My, you timed that well." His mother was sitting at the kitchen table, coffee cup in hand when he arrived. "I thought I'd get five minutes peace. Ah well. Make yourself a cuppa; the kettle's hot."

He kissed her on the cheek and dropped a carrier bag on to the table. "Invoices from last week." He busied himself making a drink.

"Well we knew they were coming so if they're as expected it'll be fine." Pushing the bag aside she looked at her son meaningfully. "And how are you?"

"What do you mean?"

"Oh, I think you know what I mean. But to remind you, you were not your usual self on Friday. Something was wrong. So, how are you?"

He held up his hands in submission. "Ok, I give in. I never could hide things from you could I? Do you think anyone else noticed?"

Frances gave a wry smile. "I think anyone would have had to be blind to not know something was amiss but many might have put it down to nerves. And you look better today. So?"

"Well…." John paused. They hadn't yet agreed to divulge the pregnancy but in the circumstances there was nothing to be done but tell his mother. "It seems that… I'm going to be a father."

Frances's cup slipped so that tea slopped over the table. "Goodness! I didn't expect that." She mopped up then looked John in the eye. "And how does it feel?"

She didn't mention Janine or Amanda but he wondered if, or how often, she thought about them as it occurred to him that Amanda would be a grandchild as much as the baby Sally was expecting. "Not as bad as I thought when I first heard, by accident, just before the opening on Friday. The news did shock me. But we've talked and it's ok. Mostly. I'm fine."

Frances exhaled. "Then that's all right, isn't it?" she kissed the top of his head. "In fact, it's wonderful. John, I'm so happy. And you know that we'll do anything to help don't you."

But beyond her joyful words he saw foggy ghosts. "Do you ever wonder about Amanda, Mum?"

The answer didn't come and he was about to say it didn't matter when she spoke. "I'd be lying if I said never. But it was a long time ago, and I don't think about her often. We never knew her, did we?" Her hand covered his. "It's different this time though. Sally and you, you're different. Older. And… together."

"Oh, Mum. We didn't plan it. And with the restaurant and everything, well, it's not easy. But it'll be ok. Believe me."

"I hope it will, John, I really do. Dare I ask… if you'll marry?"

"Aha, that old nut." The question irritated; why should it be assumed that a having a child would change their beliefs? But strangely it had and though he wasn't ready to admit it, it *was* what he now wanted. "Too soon to say." He changed the subject. "Dad playing golf?" Frances nodded and so John described his idea to turn part of the flat above Seagrams into an office and realised that things were coming together as though having babies happened all the time; a thought he found somewhat unnerving.

As the months passed, work left little time to think about pregnancies and babies. A culinary clash with Neil led to his departure and without him it was noticeable that staff meetings became more widely creative. It seemed everyone had aspirations; even young Bob's chocolate fudge cake found its way on to the menu. By June, John had a replacement sous chef and by August the restaurant was paying its way. With the smaller dining room established as a wine bar, not-so-hungry diners relaxed amongst art hung as in the Royal Academy summer exhibition and dreaming of bagging an early work, bought a painting or two. Though the commissions didn't greatly increase his bank balance the sales brought joy to starving artists and did what he'd hoped for – built his reputation.

It had been a hot, humid day when, standing in a cool shower before work and dreaming of early evening diners he heard the front door slam. Sally? It was too early. "Is that you, Sal? You ok?"

The shower drowned her words but anger and one word, 'fired' came through. Pulling a towel round his middle he ran, dripping, down the stairs. "Fired?" It was astonishing news; unbelievable! "Why?"

She was shaking with anger and telling him she'd been made redundant. "Everyone knew except me," she yelled, "even Andrew!"

Though sick at the prospect of losing her income, her frenzy was his immediate concern. "Calm down, Sally. You'll hurt Hughie." That absurd name – an amusing fillip during bouts of morning sickness! The name inflamed her; the baby, she spat, didn't have a name, it didn't have anything. She'd paused and said, with added venom, that it should be adopted! The cruellest threat, loaded with need and pain and recrimination was intended to hurt but sympathy and fear for the unborn baby strengthened him. She'd lost her job and it wasn't her fault. "They're morons," he told her, "they've wanted an excuse for ages. It isn't about the baby." The words were half true and he'd clung to the true half. She hadn't deserved it; she'd worked hard. She was entitled to be upset. He tried to pull her into his arms. "It's not the end of the world," he soothed, "we'll manage, we'll sort things out, together."

"How are we going to pay for all the things the baby will need without my salary? Where's the money going to come from?"

His eye was on the clock. They needed to talk rationally but with time pressing all he could offer was promises. "We'll manage," he placated. "It's time I started to take a bit more money each month. It's been a good summer." It was an empty promise but with early diners arriving in less than an hour he was fretting about food and preparations. He tilted her face but she turned away and he watched helplessly as she bit the skin on her thumb in the way she did when she was disturbed.

"Go to work." She told him she'd ring Diane, and worrying, he left.

Driving quickly to recover lost time he tried to think ahead to the evening in front of him but Sally's news resounded. Managing without her income was inconceivable and he wondered how much her payoff was to be. The wheels clipped a kerb and he swore. If Sally could get another job quickly things wouldn't be too bad. Her record was impressive and she was ambitious, but who would employ a woman with a baby? And she'd change; they'd change. He pictured her slumped with tedium but seeing traffic lights on green he told himself if he got through it would be a sign that all would turn out well. He made it, but cheer changed to fear as he steered wide out of the corner and registered the driver's shocked expression as he clipped the side of a Mini.

Cursing a ragged tear in the fibreglass of his wheel arch he crossed the road. "Sorry, mate. My fault completely."

"You can say that again!" The driver made up for in voice what he lacked in stature. "What the bloody hell were you thinking of?"

"Yeah, I know. Actually I've just had a bit of really bad news, and I'm afraid I was in a hurry. But I was going too fast. Look, I'm very sorry, and yes, it's clearly my fault."

The man was without an argument. "Well you're bloody crazy to drive like that. You shouldn't be on the road. I hope you've got insurance and stuff."

With details exchanged, John returned to his car and discovered a flat tyre. By the time he arrived at Seagrams he was fraught and in no mood for humour.

"Morning!" Julia was at the bar. "Overslept?"

Ignoring her witticism he headed for the office, found his car documents and rang the insurance company. A schoolgirl voice wasted his time with a million irritating questions before agreeing to send a form in the post and then he spoke to the garage who, more efficiently, booked the car in for the next morning. Early diners had already arrived in the restaurant and he rushed into searing steak, blackening butter, and pan frying sole as Sally's news continued to tighten its grip on his guts. He knew it was unlikely that she'd find another job, and losing her job meant she'd change. They'd be a family. He didn't know how to be a family. He worked unconsciously until the last diners paid their bills then, oblivious of the clearing up and cleaning going on around him, he slumped into a seat.

Julia rested against her elbows on the bar and watched him. "If I told you the till is very full would it make you feel better?"

John looked up. "Sorry?"

"You're in a world of your own tonight! I was saying that we've had a good night. For a Thursday."

"Oh." John blinked. "Oh. Yes, thanks. Great."

"There you are; all ready for the safe." She dropped the money bag and till roll on the table in front of him. "You look like you've got the world and his dad on your shoulders this evening."

"Thanks." He took the cash bag. "Yeah," he sighed, "I think I have."

"You seem distracted."

The easy warmth that melted customers worked its magic on him. "Coffee before you go?"

"Sure. And I tell you what, I'll make it too."

By the time she returned John was nursing a large scotch. "Something to chase the coffee down?" he offered, indicating his own glass.

She shook her head. "No thanks. Erm… driving?"

Her disapproval was gently damning. "Yeah. I suppose I am."
John pushed the glass away. "One accident a day's enough.
Better go good, huh?"

"Ah" said Julia. "That's what this is about. You've had an
accident?"

John sighed. "I guess you could say that. Yeah. Indeed. An
accident. That's what I've had." He laughed without humour
and they chatted for a while. About wine.

As the months progressed the restaurant flourished.
Reservations were made days and even weeks in advance and
customers were being turned away at weekends. A novice
teacher moved into the flat and supplemented the waiting staff
when they were busy and a trainee chef covered weekend nights
too. And Sally's unexpected availability lessened the paperwork
burden until, one October afternoon as he wiped a sleeve across
his forehead and tried to marry orders with invoices, the phone
rang. "Seagrams. John speaking."

Sally's voice sounded calm and in control, and though he'd
thought himself ready the shock was astonishing. Standing
quickly, his chair shot backwards and papers fluttered to the
floor. "I'm on my way. Now." He made to replace the receiver
then raised it again. "You ok?"

"Yes, I'm fine. Don't panic; there's plenty of time. Please
drive carefully."

Plan Birth Day went into action. He called Alain to instigate
the promised replacement chef, pushed a note under the door
of the teacher tenant-cum-waiter, cleared the stairs in three leaps
and told the staff, "It's on its way!" A cheer sent him on his way;
they were on their own and knew what to do.

On reflection, the lead up to and the birth rolled like frames in
a film. Sally in monotone, grasping her huge belly dramatically

and groaning as she struggled out of the car at the hospital. He, walking behind a wheelchair whilst she protested it was ridiculous. Someone – a nurse – had escorted him from her room and believing himself about to be excluded from the birth he'd protested weakly. But they'd given him paper robes, paper shoes and a silly hat and there was no escape. He'd looked ludicrous and Sally had laughed, briefly before a spasm of pain gripped her and fear gripped him. He'd held her hand, praying she knew what to do and then walked round the bed. Her medical chart said she had the same 'A' blood group as he had; it had – irrationally – pleased him. They'd been alone a lot and once he'd had to find the nurse who'd told them calmly that everything was going well then left again, and he'd wished she'd stayed as in her absence he didn't feel any better for her assurances.

Later the same nurse returned and instructed Sally to inhale through a mask. It seemed to calm her and he'd wondered if he could inhale the gas too but she returned before he'd had the courage and brought a midwife who'd instructed Sally to breathe or pant. He'd found himself breathing and panting too and was pleased to be at the head end where he'd tried to look useful mopping Sally's forehead with a damp cloth and holding her hand. Eventually the midwife had commanded Sally to push and to his amazement a screwed up face appeared, then a tiny red, mucus-smeared baby slid into the midwife's waiting hands. It didn't move and for a moment he'd feared it was dead then the mouth opened and a mewling sound sent him staggering against the wall. He'd felt faint and looked at Sally whose face, so recently haggard, suddenly radiated with joy. She'd said they had a son without looking at him and an ominous wave had washed over him; this helpless baby, his own child, felt like a threat.

CHAPTER 5

Beef Stroganoff

Sally switched the Christmas tree lights on and off and on again, chuckling as her son's tiny mouth and eyes popped open in amazement. She didn't much like having lights on the rubber tree plant but their brightness cheered the late afternoon dusk on what was the shortest – and possibly coldest – day of the year. She sat by the window and tucked a blanket round them both, sharing warmth in Sammy's rhythmic suckling until the central heating clock would click into action. Outside, street lamps shone haloes into icy air and an elderly couple walked slowly by. What errand or pleasure sent them out in this bitterest of afternoons, she wondered, when anyone who could stay indoors would justifiably do so? She watched them pass, cheered by their arm-in-arm affection and dismissing the possibility that the icy pavements may have compelled their togetherness.

The street appeared poised, as if waiting for something to happen. All the world's a stage, she thought, and the men and women, players. She wanted to be a player. This bit-part she'd landed was dispiritingly dreary. Her beautiful son asked so little and John had a starring role at his restaurant. Diane had her Kitchen. But she missed her spotlight.

"A few more days and we'll go to Grandma and Grandpa's for Christmas," she told Sammy, "and then Daddy will have his holiday and we'll have a happy time." The week after New Year, when John was closing the restaurant, glowed like a beacon in the darkness. "Yes Mr Sammy Sommers," she kissed his sweet-smelling cheek, "and after that, we'll go to see Granny in

London too. We'll go to Whitechapel Gallery; nobody minds babies there. We'll have to go to church with Granny but we don't mind that do we? Will you be quiet?" Sammy kicked his legs. "You will? What a good boy. Yes, we'll have a nice time." He'd finished feeding and wrapping him warmly in his carrycot she curled the blanket round herself, picked up the newspaper folded at the cryptic crossword and examined the blank squares. "Hmmm…Suitcase ricocheted round the station. Seven letters, third letter a 'g'. Ah, Bagshot!"

Sally's eyes drooped as she struggled to understand why the entire book of short stories seemed to be a passage of Rose's and her stepmother Flo's lives. She flicked back a few pages then put aside the book and switched on the TV. Sammy lifted a hand in protest then settled again as she turned down the volume. Moira Stuart reported a disease that had claimed the lives of seventy five men in America was being blamed for the death of a London man. Distracted by the newscaster's arching eyebrows she yawned, and noticing the book she'd bought John for Christmas lying on the table for all to see, jumped up. It was a valuable facsimile of an old American book of cookery that had cost more than she'd intended to spend, and she was sure he'd love it. Then she remembered a whimsical piece she'd read in her magazine, describing the essential elements of a date as entertainment, food and affection. Over time, it said, the latter replaced the former, but on no account could food ever be omitted. She'd intended to show it to John, but now she snipped it out and slipped it inside the book before wrapping it in carefully smoothed paper she'd saved from the previous year.

Returning to Alice Munroe she warned Rose not to marry Patrick. "Don't, Rose," she whispered, "You've got your scholarship; you can do what you want." John teased her about talking to herself, but she'd always done it. It slowed thinking and helped her work things through. But recent self conversations had been tedious. "I'll get my coat so we can go and keep warm in the library," was all well and good but it lacked direction, and though talking to Sammy might appear more acceptable, telling him that another job rejection letter had arrived didn't make her feel any better. "I've got to *do* something," she said, aloud.

Diane's New Year's Eve party was the highlight of her Christmas, and though it meant Sammy had to go too, she wasn't going to miss it. "Shall I take him upstairs?" she asked, unwrapping her sleepy bundle.

Diane pulled the hood from Sammy's face. "Aah. Who's a warm little bunny?"

"Bunny? You should see his elephant legs; he's a greedy boy!" Sally shrugged her coat from her shoulders.

"He takes after his Daddy then, don't you?" Diane cooed into his face. "Who's a bootiful boy." She stroked his soft dark hair and caught the hand that lifted upwards. "You want to come to me do you?" She took him from Sally and started up the stairs. "I'll put pillows round him in the middle of our bed. You go on in."

African music played to an almost empty room as most of the guests congregated in the kitchen. Catching Malik's eye she nodded at the bottle of wine he held aloft and eased round chattering drinkers. "Miriam Makeba?"

Malik grinned. "Sure is. Recorded live in Conakry. I was there."

"Yeah? Wow. Did you ever meet her?" They chatted about Makeba and Guinea Conakry and then Senegal until Malik told her Diane had instructed him to look after people's glasses so he better had. Joining a small group who were debating the army's involvement in Northern Ireland she listened to their increasingly voluble views until she saw a group of Diane's old colleagues and joined them, laughing with the others as Carol explained the calendar they'd made as a parting gift for Angie. They'd mounted photos of various men Angie had admired over the years, and rolling her eyes, Carol added, "We could have put several on every page!"

"Dish of the day, it was!" Angie chortled. "A hunk on every page."

It was good to be in the middle of it all again; Sally felt alive. One of the drivers she recognised as Gerry tapped her on the shoulder and asked her to dance, then she joined a group of women she vaguely knew who danced together. She talked to friends of Malik's, to people she knew and people she didn't and when John arrived at almost two the party was swinging.

"A drink to toast the New Year?" When he shook his head she held out her glass. "Just a sip. A welcome to 1982." But his exhaustion flattened her wine cheered warmth and she pulled on her coat, tucked the blanket round Sammy and said her thanks and farewells to her friends.

"What a great party." Still full of energy she recounted the evening as John drove. "Everyone was singing at midnight, bursting balloons and poppers – I'm amazed Sammy slept through the noise." Seeing his last dregs of concentration were focusing on the short drive home she became silent. "I'll try not to disturb you if Sammy wakes; you look just about done in." She squeezed his arm. "But you had a good night?"

John smiled weakly. "Thanks. Yeah, fantastic night, in turnover. But it's been hard work. I need a week of nothing and I'm looking forward to it."

Her heart sank. The vision that had sustained her throughout the last month threatened to evaporate and she recalled how that very morning she'd shaken a clean sheet over their bed and felt her life mirrored in its downward glide.

Inactivity was suffocating and now the forthcoming week was threatened too. She bit the skin at the side of her thumbnail and sighed.

"That's a big sigh. Everything ok?"

"Yes. Yes, I'm fine."

"Sammy ok?"

"Yes. He's fine too. Everything's fine. No, I was yawning, not sighing."

"Good." His hand patted her leg. "Talk to me, eh? I need something to keep me awake 'til I get us home."

She chattered again about the evening, telling him she'd wished he could have been there too, and how Sammy had woken around eleven and wowed them all with smiles. "He looked at Malik and just smiled" she chuckled, "even though Malik didn't do anything. I'm glad you're home next week – he'll be smiling at his Daddy too."

"Well, I'll try and co-ordinate sleep patterns so that I can catch a few. It should be easy; we both want the same things; sleep and food. Oh, and of course, a few cuddles. That's my resolution for 1982; get more sleep."

She put her hand over John's and as if cued, a resolution came to mind; she could compile John's recipes into a book. She had a typewriter and time in abundance and Diane could do food photography. Here was sanity! She'd think about it, plan it, then delight John with a draft that he would find irresistible. "Happy New Year my love." She squeezed his hand.

"Yeah." He yawned. "You too."

A few hours later Sally woke with a start; she'd overslept and hadn't heard Sammy's cry for his five o'clock feed. She ran, and found him pink-faced in his cot, sleeping soundly after his previous evening's first solid food – a piece of rusk. She placed a finger in his hand and relished the feel of the soft, tiny fingers that curled around hers. "Hello little one. Welcome to 1982," she whispered.

It was three more days before John came down to breakfast at a normal time, looking relaxed and, thought Sally, like the John she used to know. Picking up the newspaper he asked, "Coffee?"

"Aha, back to normal," she teased and gave Sammy to him. "Post?"

"For you." He passed her a blue airmail envelope. "It's from Pakistan; there's an address on the back." Jiggling Sammy on his knee he sang, "Sammy's a little Paki boy."

"Don't call him that!" She'd been called 'Paki' at school and it hadn't been nice.

"Well, he is. It's ok."

"He's not Paki. He's part Pakistani. Like me. Don't say Paki. It's horrid." Indignation dissolved as she watched the two darkly tousled heads bobbing together as John sang 'Sammy's my little Pakistani boy' and Sammy blinked in confusion.

John sat Sammy on his lap. "Any chance of toast?"

"Lost your legs?" She'd been about to open her letter. "No, don't move – I can feed two babies."

"No wonder I love you." John helped himself to Sally's slice of toast, catching Sammy's attention. "You'll be asking for toast before long, won't you? Well you can't have it. Not yet. You're already too fat for your carrycot. You're a very big little boy."

"He's all right for a while." John was right; Sammy *was* getting too big for the carrycot. "He can sleep in it when I go to Mum's next week then I'll look around for a second-hand travel cot." She'd picked up the airmail letter and turned it over. "Oh! It's from my grandmother in Lahore. She doesn't write often; I wonder why she's written." She ran the point of a vegetable knife carefully along the flap releasing a number of ten dollar notes that fell to the floor. "Oh my goodness! She's sent some money!"

John picked up the dollars and examined them. "Did you tell her about Sammy?"

"Well, yes, I sent a card. Wait, let me read her letter. Her writing isn't very clear." She read for a moment or two and confirmed that the money was indeed, for Sammy. "She says she's happy to hear about the baby and pleased we've named him Samuel after my father and grandfather. She'd like to see him but she's over seventy and couldn't come to England. However, if I'd like to travel to Pakistan I'll be welcomed." She paused. "I guess she means you too, though I think she'd find it hard to understand why we're not married. She's very Christian. And probably old fashioned too."

John handed the dollars to Sally. "Well maybe you should use the dollars for one of those travel cot things. There might even be some spare."

"Sure." She was still studying the letter. "My cousin Jai got married last year and also has a baby, a daughter called Ipsita." She looked up. "It's strange to think that Sammy and Ipsita are related; their lives will be so different." She folded the letter. "I wish I'd known my cousins. I used to hear about Jai and his sister Aamina when Dad was alive. There were more letters then." She pushed the letter into her pocket, wondering if they'd have been friends.

Suddenly John slapped the table, hard, causing Sally to jump and Sammy's bottom lip to tremble. "Whoops, sorry little fellah." He continued excitedly. "Let's go to Pakistan! We could save some money, get married, and honeymoon in Pakistan." He sank to one knee. "Not quite what I'd have planned, me holding the baby and all but would you do me the honour etc, etc?"

Despite his humour Sally knew the proposal wasn't a joke. Marriage had been raised several times and so far, she'd managed to side-step it. To start with, pregnancy had been a good reason, and then it had been too soon after Sammy's birth. Then their finances were too insecure. On each occasion he'd accepted the reasoning but each time her doubts about Sammy's paternity deepened the pit. She searched for the man in the boy and the boy in the man and told herself that the dark hair and solid, stocky body were John's, and that when Sammy's blue eyes changed colour they'd be green. But marrying John cemented permanence of a deceit that was a deceit too far.

Her mind raced for a convincing rejection as she played to his theatre. "Why sirrr, this be unexpected." With her head on one side she appeared to consider her answer. "Can a girl be bowled over by a man 'olding a baby?" She twisted a long curl round her finger. "An 'oneymoon, y'say? Well, it be an attractive offer; I'll 'ave to give it some thought. D'you have anything else to offer? Maybe a gold ingot or two?"

"O'll be werking on it m'dear." Country John responded and then sat back on the chair. "But seriously Sal, we could do it y'know, if we work it out."

Relieved to have again bought time Sally hid behind laughter. "Well let's see how things go shall we?"

A postcard on her mother's sideboard gave Sally another idea; printed postcards could be offered for sale at the restaurant, not only to market the art, but also for sale in their own right. It was a good idea, she decided, cheaper to produce and possibly even better than the cookery book. She turned the card over and saw it was more than a year old, testimony to the fact that her mother threw nothing away. Replacing the card she sat in the rocking chair that had been as much her favourite as her father's, now without the cotton antimacassars that had protected it from her father's oiled hair. It was the chair she and her brother had fought over until their father's voice had chastised them and made them sit on the settee silently for what seemed like an eternal five minutes. She remembered the day her parents had brought the furniture home, proud of their purchase, saying it was a cottage suite and a bargain. In adolescent superiority she'd announced grandly that she'd have preferred something contemporary and her father had laughed and said to her mother, "Did you hear that? 'Contemporary' no less. What would we do with 'contemporary'?" He was right of course, the pink fringed lampshades were old fashioned even then but had complemented the wallpaper roses. Over time the faded fringing on the shades drooped and the faded wallpaper roses disappeared behind magnolia emulsion. But an eclectic mix of cheaply framed Indian art, English landscapes and Christian imagery had tolerated time alongside crocheted doilies and embroidered cloths that were as comforting as the gentle rhythm of the rocking chair. A modern television now stood on top of an old radiogram and next to it, protected from dust with one of the embroidered cloths, was a video recorder. Her mother loved to watch films. That very morning they'd been persuaded by a picture of Mel Gibson to take home 'Gallipoli' from the rental shop in the High Street and later, once Sammy was settled, they'd watch it together.

Water splashed in the kitchen and she could see and hear her mother 'oooing' as she bathed Sammy in the kitchen sink. She called through, "Do you want any help?"

"No. We're managing very well thank you." Sammy was held, dripping, above the water. "Just look at those legs; he wants to stand already. Before you know it he'll be playing football." There was a shift in tone. "I don't suppose you've thought of making him legal? He could get bullied when he goes to school, y'know, without a proper Dad."

"Mum!" She'd been given a number of reasons why she

should marry, but Sammy being bullied was a new one. "First of all, he's not 'illegal'. He's registered, has a birth certificate, and his parents' names both appear on it. He has a proper Dad, as you call it. John and I are proper parents, and we'll be bringing Sammy up together. And why would anyone bully him? No-one will know his Mum and Dad aren't married and even if they did, they wouldn't care. It's 1982 you know, not 1952!"

Her mother cuddled Sammy in a towel and muttered, "Come the day, come the deed."

Sally changed the subject. "How did you cope, Mum, when Matt and I were little? Weren't you lonely with Dad at work every night?"

"Well, sometimes. 'Course I was. But you two kept me busy. And anyway, we couldn't afford much that wasn't needed. Mostly I'd watch telly. Or listen to some music. His night off was always a bit special though; you remember – either he'd do one of his curries or I'd make something a bit special. We went out sometimes but we were never ones for gadding about. I did my embroidery and your Dad always had a book on the go. He loved his books." She dried Sammy as proficiently as if she'd been drying babies only the day before.

"But you went to work too."

"Well, I had too, didn't I? We needed money. But only when you two went to school, and only part-time."

Sally took Sammy and laid him on a sheet on the floor. "Look at him kicking his legs! He loves to be free of his nappy." Draping the damp towel over a radiator she returned to the conversation. "But you liked working in the pharmacy."

"No, not really. My feet and my back used to ache from standing for hours on end behind that counter. And I used to have to get up early to get my chores done before I went to work. I remember feeling tired a lot. But I did enjoy chatting with Bob and Brenda. I wonder what happened to them after they sold up."

Sally remembered her mother often fell asleep in front of the TV; she and Matt had teased her about it. "We should have helped you more; why didn't you tell us to do things instead of trying to do it all yourself?"

"I did. And you didn't do it properly."

She wondered what was true and if time and perception had changed things much. "What about when we were little, Mum. Did you enjoy being at home then?"

Jane narrowed her eyes. "What's this about, eh? Is it about me, or might it be about you?"

"Well, you of course." Sally shifted in her chair.

"You're sure, are you?" Sammy gurgled and kicked his legs and blew bubbles at his grandmother. "Hello beautiful boy," Jane encouraged him, and then spoke to her daughter. "It's not like the films, is it?"

Suddenly she saw a woman who was more than her mother. Behind the old fashioned ways was a perceptive and caring person who had always put the needs of her family before her own until one by one, they'd all gone. She'd have expected her children to follow independent lives but nothing could have prepared her for the early loss of her husband, and immersion in a personal grief that was, at times, still fragile. Sally realised she'd never sought to know much about her mother's loss. Her mother had accepted and adjusted, but silently and privately, she still grieved for her husband.

"Are you lonely, Mum?"

Jane was putting a nappy on Sammy, cooing and gurgling with him so that she almost repeated the question just as her mother began to reply. "Lonely? What's lonely? No, I'm not lonely. I'm happy with what I do and what I have. I have you, and Matt, and now your families to think about. And I have church. And friends. I've lived here a long time and I have lots of friends. There's always somebody to talk to and there's things going on. Being lonely and being alone are different things, you know. Being alone is a gift. It gives me chance to see clearly, to see what's right. There's no distraction. I'm happy with it. But lonely, that's different. Being lonely is being unloved. And I'm not unloved. So I'm not lonely."

There was the truth. Sally couldn't say she was lonely either; Sammy was a joy and after all that had happened, she and John still loved each other. She had her mother and her friends too. When she'd been working she'd longed for a day at home and now she had plenty of them she was soaking in self-pity! Her mother's words echoed. Lonely? No. Alone? A gift. With an indefinite but not infinite time span. With renewed vigour she vowed to use her time so that when it ended she'd look back and be proud of what she'd done. Taking Sammy from her mother she prepared herself to feed him. "Do you... Do you miss Dad?"

"More than I can tell you." Jane's gaze turned inwards. "I carry him with me. Every day." Then she was back in the present. "But thinking about being without him is a way to be miserable, so I don't let the past change the future." She spoke complicitly, "Y'know, when nobody's listening, I talk to him. He even answers me sometimes."

"That's where I get it from! I talk to myself too; John laughs at me. But I don't often get answers. What does Dad say to you?"

Encouraged, her mother divulged the proof of her husband's spirit. "At the supermarket last week, I picked up two packs of bacon, and wondered whether to get the large or the small one – I couldn't remember if I had any in the fridge, you see. And so I asked your Dad. He knocked the larger packet clean out of my hand and it fell on the floor. I picked it up and put it back on the shelf, and when I got home, he was right – I had some there already."

"Oh Mum. You are funny and I do love you."

Travelling home, Sally meandered thoughtfully through the

week's memories. The visit had been unexpectedly uplifting and feeling a new equality in the relationship with her mother she resolved to spend more time with her during this time that she had on her hands.

The train pulled into the station almost ten minutes late so it was a surprise to not find John there to meet them. Finding change she dialled home, then the restaurant, then home again. Sammy started to whimper; he was hungry. "Shhh. Where's your Daddy?" He sucked on Sally's finger for a few seconds before finding it unsatisfying and began to cry determinedly. "Shhh, shhh. We'll be home soon. We'll find Daddy. I expect he's fallen asleep. Silly Daddy. Don't worry, I'll feed you soon. Shhhh."

A light shone through the glass of the front door. "There you see, Sammy. Daddy's home." She paid the taxi driver and struggled to the front door with relief turning to irritation. No doubt she'd find him asleep on the sofa. "Hello!" Was it too much to expect him to get to the station on time? "We're home." The smell of fresh cigarette smoke told her that his resolution to give them up hadn't lasted long, and pushing open the sitting room door she saw him – awake and sitting in a chair!

"Where...."

She stopped. His face was tense, his eyes cold as granite. "John?" Something terrible had happened. She laid Sammy in the carrycot. Something in John's expression frightened her. "John? What's happened? What is it?"

Sammy's whimper faded beyond awareness as John stood and a terrible premonition made her raise a hand protectively over the carrycot as he moved towards them both. "What..."

He pushed her roughly to one side. "Looks like me, does he? What do you think?"

Sally's heart gave a huge thud, seemed to judder, and then

resumed a drum roll beat. "What... what do you mean?" She was in the middle of one of her nightmares; soon she'd wake and everything would be normal.

"I asked you if you could say he looks like me. It's not a difficult question is it?" The words were spoken precisely, slowly, as if to a recalcitrant child.

"Well, I don't know. He's got your build, but..."

"But whose blood has he got? Answer me that, whose blood has he got?"

Sammy's screams scythed the nightmare. "I have to feed Sammy. He's hungry; he's missed......."

"No!" John's roar silenced Sammy for a moment then a fearful whimper replaced hungry screams. Sally moved but John grabbed her arm, jerking her violently so that her face was in front of his. She'd never known him like this. Violence wavered and she tried to pull away but the grip tightened, pinching her arm. "You'll not feed him. You'll answer me. Whose blood does the bastard have?"

Breath left her body in a single, rapid 'hummph' as her legs folded. He knew. He knew. This was her worst dream; the nightmare was real. "Oh my God." She gasped for air and shuddered as oxygen forced her lungs to work again. Pain in her arm increased then subsided as he dashed it aside.

John's body deflated and his face crumpled. "It's true, isn't it? You're not even going to deny it. You're not even going to lie. It's true. He's not my child." He whispered and his voice cracked. "How could you? How could you!"

She hadn't any words. She couldn't lie. She never had. John had believed he was Sammy's father because he'd had no reason to think otherwise and because she'd been unable to wound him with the possibility that he wasn't. But she'd dreaded such a moment as this since the pretence had claimed its passage as truth. It had nagged maliciously and needled her conscience and she'd tried to tell him but he'd silenced her. His adjustment to fatherhood had been alarmingly complete and his happiness had restrained her as effectively as a gag. Now her secret had exploded and her worst fears had materialised. Had Diane told him? Sally couldn't believe she'd have told him, at least not deliberately. Had she told him by accident? At her side, Samuel gnawed miserably at a fist. "How did you know?" She trembled uncontrollably.

Taking a piece of blue card from his pocket John thrust it in front of her face. "This told me," he said, "It's on the record card if you know what you're looking for. And I wasn't even looking."

Sally looked at the card. "I don't know what you mean," she said. "This doesn't...."

"Look at his blood group. It's 'O'."

"I don't understand."

"Clearly."

Sally's brain wouldn't function. Blood group 'O'? There wasn't anything unusual about that.

"Mine's 'A'."

Confusion still clouded Sally's mind. "What are you saying? I don't understand"

"Yours is 'A'.

A sliver of light broke through the fog and she tried desperately to remember biology lessons from school. If they were both 'A' group, then Sammy should also be 'A', shouldn't he? Was that right? She couldn't remember. But wasn't 'O' the group that anyone could be? Or was 'O' just compatible with other types? But it didn't matter whether she knew or not, whether he was right or wrong. John knew, without doubt, that Sammy's parenthood was not as he'd believed. "I...I'm sorry, I..."

Sammy was whimpering and John looked at him. "You'd better feed him. Poor little bastard. I'll get my things and come back for the rest."

She watched the ghost of his departing back long after the front door slammed. "What have I done?" she whispered, "oh, what have I done." One crazy evening; a few stupid drinks and she'd destroyed the thing she valued most in her life. The mistake of her life. Irreversible. Her chest hurt. It really hurt. She wanted John to come back and hold her. She wanted him to understand it had been a mistake. But everything was spoiled now. Sullied. Impossible. He'd tell his parents she was a slut and a liar and it was true. And they'd hate her too. They'd hate her for what she'd done, for what she'd done to John, and for destroying their own dreams. And her own family? Shame almost drowned her. For the first time in her life she was glad that her father wasn't alive. He'd never know; never be so completely disappointed in her.

Sammy's cries broke her catatonic state and shrugging off her coat she tugged at the buttons of her cardigan and lifted his tear wet face to her breast. "I'm sorry," she whispered, "I'm so sorry." Sammy's legs jerked and he shouted his frustration. Pinching her nipple she edged him upwards, encouraging him with soft words. "I know, you're hungry. Come on little one, here you are." But his knuckles tensed, his back arched, and his scream pierced the air. The angry voices, her trembling body, his need for food that had passed, and hungry though he was, he couldn't feed. Hugging him to her she rocked them both, backwards and forwards and wiped away her tears from the face of her innocent son.

Days weighed heavily as self recrimination and regret were interrupted only by Sammy's feeds and needs. "I'm sorry," she told him repeatedly, "it's my fault." She searched for fugitive hints of paternity as she struggled to remember her schoolgirl biology, convinced that John was mistaken yet knowing there was no going back. She'd as good as admitted her guilt and it was evidence enough. She embraced wretchedness, pain, welcoming it as if taking it all could lessen John's share. Sleep came intermittently, sometimes on the sofa, sometimes in a chair. The bed was too full of memories and reminders and though she sometimes lay on it during the day, night-time had too many ghosts. The only thing that grounded her, that had any definable meaning, was her innocent son.

By the end of the following week Sammy's hunger seemed insatiable. He was taking all she had and crying for more and it didn't take long to realise that her milk was drying up. She had to do something, if not for herself, then for him. She explored the kitchen and finding not much more than milk in the fridge made herself drink sweet milky coffee. She made a breakfast of a half packet of ginger-nut biscuits, dunking each one into the coffee and eating them one after the other until the packet was empty. Realising her hunger she searched again. A slice of curled ham, a half wrapped pack of butter and three overripe tomatoes littered the fridge, and the freezer offered packs of solid meat, the inevitable packet of frozen peas, plastic pots of John's frozen herbs, lamb chops she could chip off, and a small carton of soured cream that John must have bought, for stroganoff possibly. But no ice-cream. Eating required shopping, and shopping required more energy than she had. But Sammy's grizzle urged her on. She transferred the cream to the fridge. "Shopping list." She was talking to herself again. "Two pints of milk, a pound of minced beef, rice." She amended the list to half a pound of minced beef, and disheartened anew, drifted again into the groove of despair that filled her days, until the phone startled her.

"It's too early," she mumbled, "Go away." It continued to ring. She closed the kitchen door but on it rang; on and on. "Damn it." she muttered and went into the hall, lifted the receiver and dropped it decisively into its cradle.

Within seconds it started again and in sudden hope thought it might be John. She grabbed the receiver. "Hello."

"Sally? Are you all right?"

She sat on the stairs, raw with disappointment at hearing Diane's voice.

"Sally. I can hear you. Talk to me. Please."

No-one else had known about James. "What do you want?"

"Sally, are you all right?" Getting no reply, Diane continued. "I've called loads of times, and I've knocked on your door. Sally, talk to me."

"What do you want?"

"You sound angry, Sally. Are you angry with me? I saw John yesterday; he looked awful. He told me he isn't Sammy's father. Why did you tell him? What happened? Sally? I'm worried about you."

So Diane hadn't told him. "You'd better come round. This evening, later, after eight?"

"Here, I brought red." Diane put a bottle down. "You sounded like you could do with a drink. What on earth's happened?"

"Sorry Diane, not for me. I'm struggling to feed Sammy. But you have some." She finished chopping an onion and picked up the mushrooms.

"Then keep it for another time; I'd just as soon have a cup of tea. Shall I make some?"

"Mm, please."

Diane filled the kettle and set out the cups. "So. Are you going to tell me what's happening?"

Her tears, mostly onion tears, felt real. "Diane, did you talk to John whilst I was at my Mother's?"

"Yes, of course. Why?" Diane looked puzzled.

"Did the question of Sammy's paternity come up in any way?"

94

"What? No. I only saw him for a minute. He picked Malik up and they went for a game of squash. I thought at the time he looked as though something might be bothering him but he often looks a bit stressed these days." Diane put a hand on Sally's arm. "You're not thinking I told....? Sal! No way! I haven't told anyone. Not even Malik."

A weight lifted. "I didn't think you'd told him. Not exactly. I wondered if something might have been said by accident, or maybe you'd told Malik and he'd let something slip. Maybe."

"No way. Malik doesn't know." Diane put tea in front of Sally. "You don't think.... James..."

Sally shook her head. "He had too much to lose. And anyway, apart from timing, he's had no reason to believe that Sammy might be his child and he'd definitely prefer it that way. But something must have made John wonder. For some reason he'd checked Sammy's clinic card and saw that he's blood group 'O'. He's A, and so am I. So he decided that Sammy can't be his."

Diane knew straight away. "But that's not right! Almost any combination can be 'O'. 'O' is universal. Sally, we've got to tell him. He's wrong!"

Turning the down the heat below the sizzling frying pan, Sally shook her head. "He's not, though, is he? He's not wrong. I couldn't lie to him, Diane. I've never lied to him. I deceived him – I cheated on him, and I went along with things I knew weren't true, but I never deliberately lied to him. And so when he asked me, directly, if he was Sammy's father, I couldn't deny it." Mushrooms went into the frying pan. "So now he knows."

"Oh God. And he's left you? Oh, Sal. I'm sorry." Frying mushrooms seemed absurdly mundane given the conversation. "But he must be Sammy's father. Sammy looks like him! Sally, you've got to talk to him. Tell him it was a dreadful mistake. Once! Only once. And you must tell him that 'A' and 'A' can make 'O'."

"It wouldn't do any good." She crushed ice crystals from the cream with the spatula. "He won't accept what I've done. He'll never forgive me for sleeping with another man; his pride won't let him."

"It's crazy. Did he never sleep with anyone else?" A look of disbelief on Sally's face hurried Diane on. "I don't mean whilst he was with you, but I bet he's had a few one night stands along the way. Talk about double standards! Women are expected to be pure and virginal on our wedding day whilst men are wimps if they don't sow their wild oats. There's a lot of healed virginities out there!"

"John's old fashioned like that; he's never talked about previous relationships, not even Janine. But you're right. All's fair in love and war, but only for men."

"But he knows you're not that kind of woman. He knows you wouldn't sleep around. I can't believe he's left you and Sammy." Diane spooned stroganoff over rice and they started to eat. "Mmm. Nice." She swallowed. "Can't you get a test done to prove who the father is?"

"Can you imagine John agreeing to that? And anyway, it's not just about Sammy. It's about what I did." The wine bottle was still on the table and she looked at it then moved it, and temptation, out of the way. "I'm glad you've come round. For one thing, at least I'm eating." She forked some meat. "You're right. There are double standards but people are different too. Some women do and some don't. And some men respect women and some don't. John has strong views about women and he respected me. Now he doesn't."

"But what about Sammy? He'll have a right to know who is father is one day. What'll you say to him?"

"I don't know, Diane, I really don't know." Her fork dropped to the plate. "I can't eat any more. I don't know what's going to happen, but John and I are finished and I have to make a life for

Sammy and me. I'll not pursue John. He's free to do what he wants. One day, I suppose when Sammy is old enough, I'll tell him what happened."

"Oh Sally. What a mess. What are you going to do?"

What indeed. So many questions and so few answers. She'd never felt so helpless.

CHAPTER 6

Eve's Pudding

John dipped his finger into the brandy butter and considered what was needed to balance the flavour. Vanilla, or a pinch of cinnamon? Certainly some lemon to cut the butter. He mixed three small portions. "Hey, Graham." The chef he'd hired for the Christmas period looked up. "Come and try these; tell me what you think."

Graham savoured the first, the second, and finally the third. "That's bland," he said, indicating the second. He tried the first again, then the third. "That's the one." He pointed to the first. "Cinnamon. That's good."

"Yeah, I agree." He tasted the three again and made a note to amend the recipe. It had been Alain's idea to serve complimentary mince pies and brandy butter during Christmas but producing them was a tiresome burden with a full quota of lunches and evening parties spanning almost three weeks.

Picking up the staff rota he noticed the date; December 21st. The shortest day. Or, more relevantly, the longest night. He yawned and rotated his head, easing the muscles in his neck. Free time came in minutes these days and it wasn't going to be much of a family Christmas. Sammy wouldn't know and Sally, he was sure, would understand, particularly this first year. He'd make it up to her after the New Year parties were over, when the restaurant would be closed for a whole week. They'd have their Christmas then.

The staff rota showed the temporary waiters, all students from Bath College, were spread evenly across lunches and evenings. He changed them so that one covered lunches and three did evenings for the next three days and deciding that Julia could work out the logistics, helped himself to a mince-pie and escaped to his office. There, if only for a few minutes, he could eat his pie in peaceful solitude. Closing the door softly he sank gratefully into his chair, raised his feet to his desk, and with eyes closed let the world disappear – except for the caramel waft of fresh-from-the-oven sugary pastry. Opening one eye he saw, neatly framed in the 'V' of his feet, his mince pie sitting squarely in front of a photo of Sally holding newly born Sammy. Already, at two months old, he was hardly recognisable. This newcomer, this stranger who'd appointed him father. Labels were discomforting; 'businessman' or 'restaurateur' didn't sit well but they were at least pleasing. 'Father' was unsettling, an illusion that had become reality. Or a delusion. Guilt sat heavy below his heart, wedged against a rib and twisted the knife he'd pointed at his own parents since he'd known he'd been adopted; it's unnatural to not love one's own child. He wrapped his arms across his chest. "Like mother; like son," he muttered. Love, affection, tenderness, an innate drive to nurture and protect, where were they? A branch tapped the window as a robin landed. Sally, like a bird, fed and cosseted Sammy to the exclusion, it seemed, of all else. Including him. She'd been besotted from the start and seemed to know exactly what to do, whereas he was clumsy and inadequate and covered his confusion with a mask of pride and humour as everyone fussed and cooed and uttered ridiculous comments about resemblances. And after Sally fed, bathed, changed and dressed him she'd hand him over like a wrapped gift and he'd feign infatuation with his tiny son. He said the right things, kept his fears hidden, and prayed that affection would grow as Sammy did.

The mince pie disintegrated as he bit through the perfect

pastry into the warm, toffeed fruit and dripped its juice onto the bookings diary. Dabbing it clean with his fingers he saw every line of every day was full to New Year's Day. And that evening, more than half of the tables were scheduled for two sittings, including two office parties. With walk-ins too, Julia would need energy, foresight and a deal of conjuring to manage food flow, drinks, and the performance of the student waiters.

With pre-orders already in for the parties, tables were being set up as John passed through the restaurant. His practised eye paused on Rick, one of the students, setting up one of the party tables. Young and keen, Rick's enthusiasm was blunted by clumsiness, and though it had been easy to laugh when he caught his apron on a door and halted abruptly so that the door had swung back and hit him from behind sending a tray of cutlery to the floor, it hadn't been so funny when a mishandled attempt to catch a dropped butter knife had toppled a dirty plate into a customer's lap. It had cost John a cleaning bill, a complimentary meal, and possibly lost customers too. Accidents were too frequent to be ignored and he admitted sadly that Rick hadn't been the best choice.

Rick saw him watching. "Looks good, eh?"

"Not sure." Crackers between glasses made it difficult to see where each place and glass belonged. "Looks a bit crowded to me." He stacked crackers in woodpiles in the centre of the table. "Try that, eh?"

"Good thinking." Rick set about collecting the crackers only to knock over a glass and, in saving it, dropped the crackers and sent a fork cascading across the floor.

"Guess that proves the point." John moved away. "Good save though, and keep smiling." All hands would be needed over Christmas and Rick was Julia's problem. He hoped she'd give him safe work or find a way to tone down his eagerness.

"Ok, where are we all?" It was five-thirty. "Let's talk." The daily meetings had been Julia's idea to combine the needs of the restaurant and kitchen and had soon proved their worth. "Now, if you thought last Saturday was busy let me tell you, it was an appetiser." He watched faces. "You all know what you need to do tonight so I'm not going over any of that. Any questions on the menu or timings, talk to Graham or Julia. That's their job. Ok?" Heads nodded. "Graham, I need the market orders before we finish tomorrow. Any minor changes you need to make, I'll trust your judgement. Any doubts let me know." Graham nodded and scribbled in a notebook. "Julia, you did a great job on Saturday. Keep your waiters on the ball like that and it'll be fine. But I saw a dirty knife go back to the kitchen. Not good enough. Make sure your waiters see things like that before a customer does, and Bob, you make sure it doesn't happen! Right? Questions?"

"Yes, I've a question." Shirley half raised a hand. "Can someone help plate up tonight? Beth's busy with early prepping but should be done by then. Otherwise I don't know how we'll serve the parties together."

John looked at Graham then at Beth. Both nodded. "Good idea, Shirley. But keep an eye on presentation; it's new to Beth."

Within ten minutes the meeting ended and he tried to think of something uplifting to finish with. "Great stuff." He remembered the daily motto on his calendar that morning. "Remember, it's not the ingredients in the dishes that lead to excellence, it's the ingredients in the restaurant. Knowledge, discipline and expertise. Aristotle said that excellence isn't an act, it's a habit. We're not acting here, so let's have an excellent evening." Despite a wry eyebrow raise from Graham, John was pleased with his off-the-cuff motivator which would, he was sure, inspire the students.

The evening rolled by, as did the next day, and the next week. John had worked through Christmases before and many a New

Year's Eve had been spent in a kitchen. But he'd never worked twelve double shifts in a row and by the end of New Year's Eve he found himself struggling with a batch of invoices, unable to sort them into alphabetical order. As the door closed behind the last customer he lowered his aching body into a chair and lit a last cigarette. Sally had given up and he'd promised her that his New Year resolution would be to quit. So, tomorrow. Sucking smoke into his lungs he looked at his Rothkoesque painting. If someone had suggested he was superstitious he'd have decried such nonsense but every day he'd touched the painting and as he did now, drawn strength from it. Taking a last pull on his cigarette he stubbed it out. "That's the last one," he told the painting. In response blue and green lured his turgid brain into a sense of serenity so that had Graham not shaken him he might have succumbed to its hypnotic powers. Finding strength from somewhere he checked the alarms, double checked his cigarette was out, and wishing his painting a prosperous New Year locked the doors on nineteen eighty one.

John felt Sally slip from the bed. He looked at the clock; five-twenty something. He clung to the comfort of sleep and luxuriated in the warmth of the bed until noises from the kitchen indicated the day had begun. Looking at the clock again he struggled to comprehend it was it now ten-fifteen. Saturday had already disappeared in a haze of coffee and sleep and Sunday was in danger of doing the same. Stretching his limbs he visualised coffee and a cigarette, then remembered he'd stopped smoking and immediately longed for a cigarette. Food, he thought, would distract him. Bacon! He hoped there'd be bacon in the fridge.

Ski Sunday flickered silently on the TV and filled the late afternoon with blue light. Across the room John saw that Sally had fallen asleep with Sammy still at her breast and his artist's eye framed the picture; her face, Madonna-like in the blue cathode light with a single tendril of dark hair falling across the whiteness of her breast directed his eye towards Sammy's glowing contentment. It was an evocative mother and child. He rose from the sofa and resisting Sally's drowsy constraint took Sammy from his mother's lap. Turning the sound down on the TV he settled back with Sammy and watched skiers swishing through slalom poles at seemingly impossible speeds. He'd never skied and imagining the thrill of speed on snow thought he'd like to. Tensing as a skier almost lost balance he watched another skier accelerate faster and faster through the poles until suddenly a barrier was hit and skier, skis and sticks flew. Oblivious of Sammy he jumped – then remembering the small body on his knees clutched at him quickly. To his amazement a smile appeared on Sammy's face which, on catching John's eye turned to a chuckle. John gasped; for a second he doubted what he'd seen and heard but there was no mistake. His son had smiled and laughed with him. He'd communicated with him. The icy stone lodged in his chest melted and skiers forgotten he folded Sammy to his chest and breathlessly suppressed his unmanly tears.

The next morning John woke before eight feeling refreshed and ready to get on with life again. Putting his head round the nursery door and seeing the cot empty he felt an unexpected disappointment that Sammy's day had started without him and went to find him in the kitchen with Sally. Exchanging him for an airmail letter he'd picked up on the way, he stole Sally's toast whilst she made him some coffee and tried to raise another smile by singing to his son. "Sammy the little Paki boy."

"Don't call him that!"

He didn't understand. "Well, he is. It's ok."

Sally objected indignantly. "He's not a Paki! He's part Pakistani. Like me. Don't say Paki, it's horrid."

Relenting, he sang again. "Sammy the little Pakistani boy." As Sally neither approved nor disapproved – she was too busy opening her letter – he danced his slice of toast in front of Sammy. "You'll be asking for toast too before long, won't you? Well you can't have it yet; you're already too fat for your carrycot. You're a very big little boy."

Some notes slid from Sally's envelope. Green dollars. When he'd toyed with going to The States around ten years previously, a pound had bought about two dollars, which, if it hadn't moved much, made this around forty pounds; enough for the travel cot Sally talked of and with some left over. He knew little about this grandmother who Sally said had sent the money other than she was said to have been a great beauty. Suspended as he was in a generational vacuum it was as well to accept the futility of wondering if his own grandmother, or indeed his mother, had been beautiful, though it was conceivable his father, whoever he had been, might have once thought so. Sally talked about a family she knew little of but she did, at least, know who and where they were. Suddenly an idea struck him. They'd go together to Pakistan! What a wonderful idea! He shared his excitement with Sally. "We could go to Pakistan! The restaurant's done well over Christmas, and you'll probably get a job again soon. We could save some money, get married and blow the rest on a honeymoon in Pakistan." Buoyed by the boldness of his idea, he secured Sammy under an arm and kneeling in front of Sally proposed to her – for some reason in a jovial West Country voice. "Not quite what I'd planned, me holding the baby and all, but would you do me the honour, etc, etc?"

He saw her face cloud but it was a passing moment and then she was his Sally again, beautiful and playful and answering him in an even worse accent than his own with… well, not quite yes but definitely not no. Feeling blessed, he stood and rubbing his knee – the floor was hard – dared to believe that at last, happiness was his. The restaurant was going well. He'd discovered fatherhood. He'd given up smoking for three days. And Sally had agreed to marry him – almost. Life was good.

The icy air was oddly calm when he went back to work and after kicking aside mail and turning off the burglar alarm he turned the thermostat up. It was early to be at work, none of the other staff would be in for hours, but having taken Sally and Sammy to catch the London train his day had already started. He re-acquainted himself with his painting, then listened to the answer-phone, recorded a message of greeting for the New Year and putting his gloves back on went to his office, pleased to have come in early enough to get the place warm after the break. He turned on the radio and continued to sing along with Blondie as Jimmy Young closed his programme on the pip of eleven as a weather warning was announced. Heavy snows, it cautioned, would hit the south and west. Police advised people to stay at home. Looking out of the window he groaned; flakes were already falling. In terms of business, the last thing he wanted in January was a weather warning.

An hour later snow blinded the windows and by two, the few reservations had cancelled. As staff arrived John sent them home and resigned to losing an evening's takings, retrieved files and paperwork from the office, set the heating to stay on, and locked up. Snow squalled in his face and hair as he crossed the car park and sweeping the white blanket from the windscreen he wondered how the roads would be. With snow melting into his socks the possibility of a long walk home was distinctly unattractive so, when the engine of his beloved Scimitar car fired he gave the dashboard a tap of appreciation and crept across the eerily silent gravel on to the tarmac. He'd bought the car just a year ago, when the last New Year's witching messenger parted him from his final Alain bonus. 'Carpe Diem', it had urged, 'It's the 80's, a new decade'. Sally, he remembered, had been less enamoured. She'd wanted new carpets. But carpets were just carpets and the sleek, fibre-glass Scimitar GTE was, he was sure, set to become a classic. Below him the tyres crunched snow-hushed roads as they crept slowly home.

Throughout the night and into the next morning the snow continued to fall and John rang his staff to tell them the good news; they had another day's holiday. It was less good news for him; twenty four hours earlier he'd been positive, energised, and eager to start the New Year and now he was frustrated and inanimate. To some extent disappointment was mitigated by the knowledge that closure was at the quietest possible period but the two-for-one promotion would flop and he'd still have to pay his staff. Layering bacon rashers across the grill pan he buttered slices of bread and spread lashings of ketchup. A weekday bacon sandwich was little consolation but it made the day feel better and dulled the ache of tobacco addiction in a way that strong coffee didn't. Forcing his attention towards paperwork he sorted invoices, read letters, and after half-an-hour rang Sally instead. Finding her out and no doubt enjoying herself felt unfair and after the briefest of polite conversations with her mother he returned to his papers. Sally's glossy magazine, bought for her journey to London lay forgotten on the sofa, and he flicked aimlessly through the pages, pausing at a photo spread around the old year's headlines. No-one would be allowed to forget the royal wedding; the same old pictures featured everywhere with Diana looking coy, Diana looking radiant, and so on. And it seemed that being a world leader demanded nerves of steel; where assassination attempts on President Reagan and Pope John Paul had failed, President Sadat of Egypt had been less fortunate. Dangerous work indeed. There were pictures of

Bobby Sands and Bob Marley, also dead; who'd remember any of them in years to come, he wondered. But Mark Thatcher's failure to navigate out of the desert had been amusing. A leaflet slipped from the magazine and seeing Cranach's 'The Fall of Man' on it aroused his curiosity. All evil, it stated, had been brought about by Adam and Eve. Tossing it aside he sighed and forced himself back to his quarterly reports only to realise that the December accounts were still with his mother. How easy procrastination became when time had few demands. And watching snow fall was an unexpectedly calming pleasure.

During the night the snow stopped but arctic air crusted the surfaces and even salted paths and roads froze over. Newscasters spoke gloomily of the infamous winters of '63 and '47. It was unlikely that anyone would turn up at the restaurant despite it being Saturday and John stayed at home. By mid afternoon he decided to brave the conditions and walking slowly along the icy pavements he reached the corner shop to find newspapers hadn't arrived and were no longer expected. Taking what appeared to be the last bottle of milk from the fridge and a bag of porridge oats, he added bread, bacon and half a dozen eggs to his basket and went to the till, where he saw the cigarettes. "Ten JPS, please." Ten, he told himself, weren't as bad as twenty.

Monday morning came and John wandered from the hall to the kitchen and stared out of the window where the small garden, colour-washed with white, inspired a few sketches of hoar crystallised twigs and lace patterned puddles. It had been a while since he'd sketched and with his mind roaming freely Sammy's smiling face appeared. Turning to a fresh page he let his pencil tell the story.

Satisfied at last with the drawings he went back to the hall and stared at the phone. Sally had told him yesterday that they'd been to Camden and the Whitechapel Gallery, and today she planned to go to Portobello Market with Sammy. The house was too quiet without him – them! She was having a good time and all he had to tell her was that he'd walked to the supermarket and got the quarterly report figures he needed over the 'phone. And watched the snow fall. The next day's meeting, he determined, would go ahead even if he had to walk all the way to Le Goût du Goût.

Noticing a matt film on the picture frames he stretched his cuff over his finger and ran it along the tops, removing dust and nudging them awry. He straightened them and thought of the gallery walls at the restaurant where pleasingly good sales over Christmas had left gaps. Sally had grumbled for months about pictures being stored in Sammy's nursery and with a sense of purpose that banished inertia he bounded up the stairs.

Sammy's cot blankets had been pushed aside and touching the softness of the sheet John was irrationally surprised to find it cold. Straightening the covers he placed a teddy-bear where Sammy might see it and pulled open the curtain to reveal a photo of the three of them. Happy family, he thought, and meant it. A basket, where Sammy's creams and lotions were usually kept looked sadly unused without its usual clutter and picking up the blue clinic card that lay in the bottom, he read the printed label: *Samuel John Lancing Sommers. 14/10/81. Boy.* Inside was his weight table, half filled, and showing that Sammy had grown on each recording. He was thriving. John flipped the card over and saw the immunisation record, dated and initialled up to December, and with empty lines waiting for more. "Poor fellah," he muttered and dropped it back into basket. He was about to turn away when he noticed; *Blood group: O.* He blinked, and looked again. It stated clearly Sammy's blood group as 'O'. His own was 'A' and so was Sally's. The clinic must have made a mistake – but if they had it was a serious one. A letter had arrived a few weeks after Sammy's birth, explaining a heal prick blood test that had screened for genetic diseases; John recalled how he'd wondered if the test could be done for him. The folder labelled 'Baby' was in the bottom drawer with their files and as yet, it contained few papers. The letter was near the back. Scanning the page he saw it. 'O'. Sammy was 'O'. There could be no doubt. The clinic hadn't made a mistake. Something cold, clammy and indescribable clenched his guts. Sammy should be 'A'. If Sammy was 'O' then he, John, couldn't be Sammy's father.

Nausea swept over him. Not Sammy's father? His heart thumped. Blood drained from his limbs. Sally? He couldn't believe it. But.... He loved Sally more than anything in the world but was he blind? His legs weakened so that he folded into the chair – where Sally had so recently nursed their (her?) son. Sally? An affair? When? They'd been through a tough time about a year ago, but ... Who? Was it still going on? Did he know about Sammy? He read the letter again, searching for rationality; there had to be an innocent explanation. The wrong baby? It happened. They'd given Sally the wrong child! But Sammy eyes were his mother's eyes, and the mouth – that beautiful mouth. He had no doubt that Sammy was Sally's child. But if the same blood sample had been used for the letter and the card.... Yes, that must be it. One had been copied from the other. He checked the dates on the documents. The heal prick had been done at the hospital but the card, two weeks later at the clinic. His fingers tangled his hair and pulled, searching for sense. If Sally had a lover – a thought that offended and tormented him – he couldn't bear it. He'd fought his demons for her. He'd taken on fatherhood. For her he'd feigned delight and suppressed anxiety. He'd done it because he loved her. Then an amazing thing had happened; Sammy had laughed with him and changed him forever. The psychotherapist had once told him that babies were hardwired to be attractive; their survival depended on it. It was knowledge had formed some of his guilt, but when Sammy had laughed at him it was as if he, John, had

Alain feigned affront. "We can and we do. For us it is also Eve's Pudding you know. You think Adam and Eve were English?"

"I hadn't thought of it but I suppose no, not necessarily. But it's an English pudding! You can't put an English pudding in a French menu!"

Alain threw his hands open in mock derision. "Non? How do you say Tarte Tatin in English, eh, or Crème Caramel? And how about soup? You think this is your word eh? And whilst we are on the subject, how about the word 'restaurant'? Ha! I think I have you, lock, stock and barrel as you say, in English, I believe?"

Alain was light-hearted but John was irritated. "Even so, Eve's Pudding is English through and through, and this is a French restaurant. All your menus are in French. It looks absurd. Eve's Pudding. I wouldn't have done it."

"Non?" Alain looked at John. "You have some anger. Why?"

John's eyes fled to the menu. "Don't be ridiculous." He forced lightness into his voice. "I'll have the Lapin and then Eve's Pudding. I'd better try it."

Alain appeared to be preoccupied with his menu until he said, "Well, if you want to know, we were influenced by your menus. We decided to try something not French, although I have to admit, it's not what you might call your 'New World' either. But you haven't answered me. You have anger. What has happened?"

John breathed a long sigh. "Ok. Yes, I'm upset. But it's nothing to do with the restaurant and therefore nothing to do with why I'm here. I prefer to talk business." He picked up his briefcase and extracting a brown file, handed it over the table. "Here you are. It's looking good." He briefed Alain on the figures, skewed by Christmas, and agreed with him that the early part of the next quarter would buck what looked like a trend.

"What about promotions? Do you have plans?" asked Alain.

"I was thinking of a wine evening, with a speaker and a special menu. Or a diner's club? What do you think?"

Alain nodded. "They are ideas. But I'm not sure you should diversify too much. You are getting a name for good food, and also for your gallery. Perhaps there is something in a wine evening."

"That was Julia's idea; she knows a lot about wine and her husband is a buyer." John mused. "What do you think about having an artist in the bar area, or the small room? A sort of artist in residence. Perhaps sketching some of the diners – with their permission, of course. We could have an artist day each week; say on a Tuesday or Wednesday, when it's quiet."

"Non, I think the aroma of paint is not good with the food." They ate their food and continued to discuss possibilities until Alain made a suggestion. "What about a book of your recipes?"

"No." John spoke sharply. "Definitely not."

"You are so sure, Jean? Why do you say 'Non' like this?"

"It's, well, it's…. No. I don't want to. That's all."

Alain frowned. "John, what is the matter today? You are not yourself."

John looked away then back again. "Sal…" He coughed, finding it hard to continue. "Sally said she'd do a recipe book. But, well, she won't be doing it now." His next words appeared. "I think… we're splitting up."

Alain's eyes opened in amazement. "Splitting up? Non! I can't believe it! What has happened?"

John stared at his square of golden sponge sitting on top of glistening apple. It was the first time he'd voiced leaving Sally and the words echoed in his ears, mocking him. "I guess our Garden of Eden got so boring that she wanted a new apple." Despite a sick feeling in the pit of his stomach he poured crème Anglaise and picked up his spoon. "So, here's your English Eve's

Pudding with your French copy of English custard."

"Of course." responded Alain. But the banter had disappeared.

John lit a cigarette, inhaled, and looked from the hospital letter to Sammy's record card. *Blood Group 'O'*. Sally's return was imminent and he searched for some rational explanation that would put his world back to normal. She'd be at the station now, and wondering where he was. But he couldn't meet her there. He couldn't deal with this publicly and he couldn't hide it once he saw her so he waited in the home they'd made together. The phone had rung twice and he'd ignored it, sure that it would be her. Screwing his cigarette into the ashtray he folded the letter and put it and the clinic card into his pocket, asking again how it could possibly be wrong and praying that it was.

Then he heard her voice, outside. He could hear her talking to Sammy, hear the key in the lock, the door opening. She was in the room. He couldn't look; couldn't bear to see either the truth in her face, or more lies. She was asking what was wrong, and at last he forced his face towards the woman he'd thought he'd known. She put Sammy, crying and kicking and waving into the carrycot and stood, looking not at Sammy, but at him. Rising from his chair he moved until he could see Sammy. "Looks like me, does he? What do you think?"

Any hope of an explanation vanished as Sally's shocked face revealed the truth and in that moment his last hopes vanished. He opened his mouth but there were no words. Then he found a voice, one that cracked and broke as it spoke. "I asked you if you would say that he looks like me. It's not a difficult question is it?"

"Well, I don't know. He's got your build, but…"

He couldn't bear it. "But whose blood has he got? Answer me that, whose blood has he got?" It was a surreal bubble where

Sammy screamed in a peripheral blur. Sally moved, towards the baby. "No!" he yelled. How dare she turn away when their whole life was shattering around them? He seized her arm, twisting her to face him. "You'll not feed him," he said through gritted teeth, "you'll answer me. Whose blood does the bastard have?"

Her body seemed to concertina as she collapsed downwards, endorsing his nightmare. He thrust her away, rubbing clean the hand that had touched the woman who'd birthed a bastard and passed it off as his son. "You're not even going to deny it. You're not even going to lie any more. It's true. He's not my child."

Her words were no more than breath. "How did you know?"

Anger coursed through his body. She asked how he'd seen through her lying façade! She thought she'd been so clever. He took the record card from his pocket and flicked it towards her. "This told me." He said. "It's on here and you didn't know how to hide it."

Sally picked the card up and turned it over then opened it and looked again. "I don't know what you mean," she said. "This doesn't...."

"Look at his blood group. It's 'O'."

"I don't understand."

"Clearly." He watched her confusion. "Mine's 'A'."

"What are you saying? I don't understand."

"Yours is 'A'."

There was glimmer, a dawning. "I...I'm sorry, I..."

Sorry! The word smacked the walls and came back at him, hard. She wanted to apologise! His life was ruined, and she was saying 'sorry' as though she'd merely forgotten to buy the milk. How little he knew her, he thought. He wanted to go, to be away from there right then. He didn't want to talk to her, to be with her. "I'll take what I need." He looked down at Sammy who whimpered for comfort and couldn't know that not being his son was breaking his heart. "You'd better feed him. I'll be back for the rest of my things."

It was Valentine's day when he moved from his parents' house to the flat above the restaurant, and hearing from Diane that Sally had gone to live with her mother he returned to claim what he wanted from what had been their home. She'd taken very little; had he been able to afford the mortgage he could have continued to live there – except for the echoes. Within minutes he'd filled a box with books and music and dragged it to the hall. In the kitchen the drab winter morning light reflected the table in the patio door, a reminder of meals like the one on her birthday when he'd first told her about the restaurant, little more than a year ago. A cupboard revealed one – only one – of the two small coffee cups they'd bought in Italy, and his painting of Bath Abbey – an abstraction he'd been pleased with – had disappeared from the wall. In the bedroom their bed, neatly made, chilled him yet the empty dressing table echoed her absence. From the empty wardrobe top he saw she'd taken the old-fashioned blankets and folding the pillows and duvet together, he dropped them next to the door and went to Sammy's room. It was almost empty. The cot, the chair, his few clothes. All gone, except for a small teddy-bear that lay with a discarded teething ring on the carpet. Pressing his head against the cold door frame John breathed in, out, in, and out, until a wave of dizziness passed and then picked up the teddy-bear, adding it to the pile he was taking with him.

Back in the flat he tossed bedding on his bed and flopped on top of it, emotionally drained. What, he wondered, was to be done with the house and remainder of their possessions? He would write – a businesslike letter stating his intention to instruct an agent to clear and sell their house. Sally could communicate through a solicitor. There'd be no need to make contact again.

A knock disturbed his thoughts. "John? Are you there?" It was Julia's voice.

He sighed and grumbled. "Oh, for goodness sake!" Living in the flat was convenient but proximity to work was a nuisance. A definitive line between his privacy and the restaurant was needed, and deciding to instigate it by ignoring the knock he lay quietly until he heard the footsteps recede. "Ha!" It had been easy; he'd won. Removing his shoes he rose from the bed and walked quietly across the floor until he saw, to his frustration, that an envelope had been pushed under the door. He snatched it up and tossed it aside until, within moments, curiosity forced him to open it. Julia wanted a meeting. He read again, disturbed by the formality of the request; they talked regularly and in structured meetings there were always opportunities to speak out. With a cold dread he concluded she intended to give notice. He ran down the stairs.

"You want to talk?" Julia looked apprehensive. "My office, now."

Closing the door behind her he moved to his desk, and waited, silently watching her discomfort and waiting to hear how she would dress and present the news that one of his competitors – no doubt – had enticed her to go to work for them.

"You've read my note." It wasn't a question.

"It says you want to talk to me. So talk." John folded his arms across his chest and leaned his chair backwards so that it touched the wall.

"Well, it's all of us." John waited, surprised. Surely, he thought, all of them couldn't be leaving! "Not just me I mean. I've been asked to talk to you on behalf of everyone."

She was twisting a ring, nervously, on her finger, waiting for a response, but John was confounded. "What do you mean, 'on

116

behalf of everyone'?" They'd sent an emissary? Irritation simmered. "Julia, will you please do me the courtesy of telling me what the hell's going on." She was looking down at the ring, twisting it round and round. "And damn well look at me!"

She jumped. "That's why!" She snapped back. "That's why John. You intimidate people! You .... I. We. We don't want to work like this." She tugged the neck of her sweater as if to release the red flush that was spreading up and into her face. "I'm sorry, I didn't mean to say it like that, I wanted to discuss ....."

Intimidate people? What on earth, he wondered, was she talking about? "I don't intimidate people!"

She'd pulled a tissue from her pocket and dabbed at her hands. "You've no idea, have you? You're in some dreadful world of your own and you don't see any of us anymore."

Dreadful world of his own? Intimidate people!

Seemingly encouraged by his open-mouthed silence, she continued. "It used to be fun working here. Even Christmas, despite the hard work, was fun. We worked together, all of us. We're a good team, including you, and we want to keep it that way. You made us a good team; you're our leader. But since Christmas you.... well, you've become intolerant and unfriendly, and we're all walking on eggs. It's not very nice." Her voice faltered but then recovered. "We know you've had a tough time and we're all very sorry about you and Sally but we're ....."

His hand slapped the desk as, unwilling to listen any more such... babble, he interrupted. "Julia, you've no idea what you're talking about. And it's none of your – or their – damned business."

"You're wrong!" Julia snapped back. "You've made it our business. We've all made allowances for you but all you do these days is shout or complain." Taking a deep breath, she started again. "Look John, I just know that if I hadn't seen my little boy for ages I..."

His fingers gripped the edge of the desk and words shot

from his mouth. "Well you would wouldn't you. He's *your* child, isn't he!"

As the impact of his words made sense, Julia's confusion gave way to shock and turning away he wished there was some way he could unsay them.

"Sammy's not your child? No! I… I can't believe it. John?"

"Julia, I didn't mean to say that. Please, it's private." Crumpling into the chair, his hands covered his face and rubbed his eyes as if all that existed could be erased.

"That's why you and Sally…"

"It's private. I don't want to discuss it." The words 'intolerant' and 'unfriendly' reverberated in black hollowness as images of gossiping staff rolled behind his hands. "And it's not general knowledge." Dropping his hands he snapped, "And if they find out you'll know what 'intolerant' and 'unfriendly' really mean. Right?"

Julia's face hardened. "You don't need to threaten me and you've no call to speak to me like that. You may have problems but I'm not a part of them, so if you speak to me like that you must expect me to respond likewise." Pushing away her chair, she made to leave.

"Sorry Julia." He grimaced. "Looks like you might have a point, eh? Sit down." He couldn't afford to alienate her – and he didn't want to. "Please." But… intolerant! Unfriendly! Unable to face her he turned and looked out of the window. "You're probably right, I haven't been myself recently but in my defence there's been significant provocation." Outside the resident robin landed on a twig and he envied its liberty. "They say birds are monogamous, don't they." He didn't want an answer. "If I've been difficult recently," he began, "I, well I… Look, I need to give this some thought. You can tell everyone that I'll talk to them. Soon. But I need to think."

Julia's chair scraped the floor and he felt her reassuring hand on his shoulder before she left the office. Beyond the window the bird flew away and he envied it anew.

What, he asked himself, could he say to the staff? Julia was right; they were a good team. He'd worked hard to make it so, encouraging ideas and placing himself in the middle of things despite carrying the world of responsibility that gave them their jobs! Unfriendly and Intolerant? Absurd! Absentmindedly he opened a packing box and saw his art books. 'The Early Impressionists', 'History of Modern Art', 'The Romantics'. Stacking them on the floor he picked up '20th Century Art'. Kandinsky, Matisse, Braque. It had been a long time since he'd looked at these books; years in fact. They'd been away, out of sight. He placed them in piles around the room; some on a small table, some by the fireplace, others on the top book shelf, and reached again into the box. This time he found his green, hardback sketch-pad. Laying the spine across his hand he let it fall open at his last drawing and found, from just seven or eight weeks previously, Sally and Sammy, his 'Mother and child'. A scribble that had whiled away long snowy days when they'd been in London. He made to rip the page from the pad but stopped. It was a good sketch; simple and not overdone. Telling himself that given the long absence from drawing it was worth keeping, he turned to the previous page and found Sammy's laughing eyes looking directly into his as they had on the magical Ski Sunday. This time, alone, tears flowed. Sobs racked his body and his heart felt dislocated. How could this baby, not even his child, and whom he'd never see again, cause such heartache?

It didn't take long to unpack the boxes, particularly if he didn't find homes for the contents. Surrounded by clothes, books, linen and even more boxes he realised that he'd have to put some of the things away before he unpacked any more.

Removing towels, sheets and a pillow from a chair he sat and assembled his thoughts. His limbs and head ached but the conversation with Julia had to be dealt with. Her words still hurt, and affronted, he saw unfairness and ingratitude in their complaint. Being loved by staff was not a priority but he'd nurtured them; encouraging, supporting and being flexible. He hadn't sought thanks, but neither had he expected a unanimous revolt when he wasn't feeling quite so magnanimous. Intolerant! Perhaps some had seen Rick's sacking as intolerant but the damaged picture had been priced at more than a hundred pounds. Sacking him quietly might have been less 'intimidating' but it had been the final straw in a string of catastrophes and he'd had to go. Perhaps, he admitted to himself, there were times his behaviour might have been perceived as less than friendly but being cheerful when your world had turned upside down was asking a lot. And, he decided, if intolerance was to be ascribed, it could more easily be attributed to them! But resentment, he knew, wouldn't keep the doors open and something had to be done. Groaning at the prospect he found a sheet of paper, sat at the table, and stared at its blankness. He lit a cigarette and thought. Three words appeared on the paper; 'apology', 'reasons' 'unacceptable'. It galled him to have to say he'd behaved unacceptably but he'd do it to pour oil on the troubled waters. Adding 'thanks for hard work', 'individuals offended?', 'tolerance / two way', 'way forward' he lit a second cigarette.

Troubled by dreams that left a crash of memories he got up and began to find homes for clothes and books and pots and pans. By the time dawn broke there was a new, calm orderliness and he wished he could realign the past so easily. Taking the kitchen dishcloth he wiped dust and dirt from the table, the bath, the door, the phone, until, in the smeary glass of the mirror, he saw beyond the heavy grey eyes, unkempt hair and dirty t-shirt to the child he used to be; naïve and vulnerable. Taking up his sketch pad and pencils he sat on the edge of his bed and let his pencil work.

It was done quickly. More than a caricature but less than a portrait, it interpreted the relentless cloak of sadness he wore, and that had, he realised, disrobed itself whilst he'd been drawing. Freed – at least for the time being – from the unforgiving weight of heartache, he inserted a new blade into his Stanley knife and with a lightness of spirit slashed the carpet around the bay window and set up his easel. He found brushes, pigments, white spirit, pencils, and putty rubbers dried into soft grey pebbles. He had an urgency to paint. With masking tape he attached a sheet of textured paper to his easel and unable to find his palette squeezed yellow ochre and dark umber and cadmium on to a plate. His brush loaded, a trail forged across the pristine paper.

CHAPTER 7

Mango Fool

Victoria Park Gardens were, as most gardens are in late January, bare and dank, though bunches of snowdrops and aconites were starting to hint at colour. It had always been a favourite spot where, at this time of year, an empty bench could be relied on. Sally pulled Sammy's buggy round to face the watery sun so that it warmed him as he slept and pushed her hands into the pockets of her coat. It had been a year in which John was a daily thought and everyday activities induced his image. That morning marmalade had dropped on the morning paper and a few days ago, when her mother had touched up the woodwork round the front door, the smell of white spirit invoked his presence – and absence. As a matter-of-fact girl, one who lived in the present and looked to the future, backward tugging anchors were troubling, but after the flat and most of their furniture had been sold and she'd received a cheque without even a note from him, the solicitor's impersonal communication had closed their lives together. Since then, she'd become adept at forcing her mind elsewhere – at least for most of the time.

Sammy woke. "Hello little one." He was walking, and talking a bit, and babyhood was disappearing. "You've had a nice sleep, and we're going home now." Sally replaced a mitten he'd removed as smiles became grumbles and he demanded freedom.

"Anma, Anma!"

"Yes, yes. We're going to see Grandma, but keep your mittens on." Life with her mother had its conveniences and Sammy loved his grandma, but it wasn't what she wanted. She needed a home for herself and Sammy and had half-heartedly looked at several flats. But the next move had to be significant; it had to be a home. A duck waddled across the grass, at home in its park and unruffled by the cold wind that rumpled its feathers. It quacked its song into the pale day. "Duck, Sammy. Quack, quack," she pointed, tucking his mitten encased hand below the blanket. Perhaps a holiday, some sunshine, she thought, knowing as the idea formed that it wasn't the answer. She wanted more than a diversion. She was seeking a life.

Her perfect son, almost hidden beneath his warm covers, glowed pinkly in the winter air. Drawing crisp cold air into her lungs she strolled with him through the park, pondering the more urgent challenge of what she should do about a letter that lay in her bag. Diane had written that she and Malik were marrying and hoped it would be possible for Sally as well as John to come to the wedding. Torn between the desire to see her friend marry and an aversion that clashed with an undeniable desire to at least see John again, she was at a loss to know how to reply. In the year of remorse, regret, anger and finally bearable sorrow, she'd reached a plateau; but could she manage the wedding? Perhaps, she thought, if she didn't take Sammy – the evidence of her downfall. The idea of herself as a fallen woman brought a grin to her face and she looked at her son wondering how such a term could have ever been associated with this beautiful, precious perfection!

At home another letter was waiting, and to her excitement she saw it was from Pakistan. Slicing carefully into the flimsy folds she looked quickly at the signature; it was from her cousin, Aamina, who she'd heard about long ago in some of her father's stories, and then sometimes in the decreasing – since her father had died – exchange of letters. She read it quickly then again, more slowly. Few women in Pakistan, she believed, went to school or work, and it surprised her to find Aamina had finished a Bachelor's degree in Business Studies and was planning to move on to her Master's. The course, Aamina wrote, was conducted in English (another surprise), and she asked if Sally would like to exchange letters to help improve her language. The letter reawakened forgotten fantasies that had formed when she'd exchanged letters with an Indian girl, a penfriend arranged by a Geography teacher at school. When the girl hadn't replied to her second letter Sally had concluded that life in London must have been too ordinary for her exotic friend, but Aamina's letter recreated visions of magical markets and delicious spiced foods, and, excited at the prospect of hearing about her father's family, she began to form a reply in her head.

Along Roman Road, aromas of cumin and cardamom-infused frying lamb and displays of mangoes, papayas and yams tempted Sally. Later, she decided, she would write descriptions of the shop selling sari silks, another selling yams and lentils, and try to create images of life in London for her cousin Aamina. She smiled to herself at the irony that she would be writing about a life that Aamina might find unexpectedly familiar. A display of golden mangoes caught her attention and she bought two, wondering how much they would cost in Lahore. She'd ask Aamina. She'd like to know about life in Pakistan. Her father had captivated her and Matt with stories of his life but he'd left in 1947. Much would have changed in thirty-six years. Recalling her lost Indian penfriend Sally vowed to make her letters interesting.

At home her mother was trying to encourage Sammy to give her his spoon rather hold it in one hand and use the other to feed himself. Shrugging off her coat, Sally took the dish of food. "Here Mum, let me take over."

Seeing his mother transformed Sammy's disgruntled

complaints into a lip-smacking smile. "Mam mam mam…"

Taking advantage of the distraction Sally took the spoon from his hand, loaded it with mashed potato, and filled the smiling mouth in front of her. "Good boy!"

Watching, his grandma tutted. "Little tinker." She rinsed a milk bottle and dropped it in the Tupperware milk bottle carrier. "I'll put the kettle on." The silver foil top, also rinsed, joined others in a box on the windowsill.

As Sammy accepted spoonful after spoonful without further displays of independence Sally chatted about the activities of the days. "Oh, by the way, I bought those." She indicated a paper bag on the table.

"Mangoes. Ooh, lovely. Your father loved mangoes. He's always nudging me to buy some; they remind him of home."

Sally looked at her mother. "What did you say?"

An abashed smile lifted the corners of Jane's mouth. "Well, I mean they reminded him of home. I see them in the street and I think to myself, I'll get some of those. I feel like I have to, remembering how your father always wanted me to buy them."

Sally remembered the mangoes, or more precisely, the mango fool her mother had made and the rest of the family had made predictable jokes about. But it wasn't mango fool that fired her excitement. "No, I don't mean that. You said they reminded Dad of home. Mum! You're fabulous! You've just given me an answer! I know what I'm going to do." Sally experienced a rush of exhilaration and could hardly bring herself to say it out loud. But she knew she was going to do it. "I'm going to Lahore!" She turned to Sammy and clapped her hand. "We're going to go on holiday, Sammy. We're going to Lahore."

Part 2

CHAPTER 8

Chicken Boti

The air-cooler blocked most of the window, though propped against pillows, Sally could just see a triangle of washing lines where her heat stiffened laundry, washed by a maid with detergent coarsened hands, waved solidly. She'd quietly tried to launder their things herself but both the maid and her aunt had protested and she'd backed down.

Tucked into the edge of the cooler were the three photographs she'd brought with her, their edges curling in the heat. The larger one showed her parents smiling happily, eating ice-cream on Brighton promenade one sunny afternoon a few months before the accident had killed her father. It was the latest one she had of him and she'd wanted his family to see him happy in his English life. Below it was the photo of Jai's wedding, creased and shabby edged from handling as she'd tried to absorb the faces of these people; her uncles, aunts and cousins, who she would meet in Lahore. In the bottom picture her sepia grandparents stared out fixedly. Her grandmother must have been about fifty but looked younger than the serious moustached man standing stiffly behind her. It was this woman that Sally had longed to meet, the one who her father had repeatedly and proudly told her she resembled.

On the mattress next to her Sammy twitched his baby dreams and she eased to one side to let cooled air from the enormous box contraption blow between them. The three weeks since their arrival in Pakistan had fused sights, sounds, and senses and she was grateful for the parting gift Diane had given her, a journal, that had prompted her to record the kaleidoscope of clamour and bustle that had filled her eyes and invaded her heart. Brought up with the notion that daytime activity was right and proper and anything else was undeservedly self-indulgent, Sally found the enforced afternoon rest each day trying and afternoon siestas had become writing time. As the household rested she immersed herself in the buzz and bedlam of Lahore life, writing anew and re-reading days that had passed. Opening the book at the beginning she started to read.

Tuesday 12th May, 1983.

…wide streets full of life with grandly painted lorries, laden with onions or melons, heave and bellow impatiently at horse-drawn carts whose drivers, standing like Ben-Hur or sitting on top of overstuffed sacks, ignore the clamour. Young men swing from the backs of buses, hollering their destination, miraculously collecting passengers without stopping. Cars head the wrong way down the carriageway to shortcut right turn junctions. Motorcycles and bicycles, cars and vans, motorised rickshaws and taxis are an undisciplined chaos I've never seen the like of.

Sammy, excited by the elaborately decorated vehicles, keeps pulling my face round and shouting "Lowwy!" I feared for the lives of pedestrians who crossed roads, oblivious of the dangers. Aamina pointed out the shopping areas; Mall Road, Anarkali Street, Gulberg, and Jai detoured through the old city to show us the Badshahi Mosque, such a contrast to the Museum and Lahore Railway Station; the Mosque, Mughal, and the others, Colonial.

All excitingly different three weeks ago, now already familiar. But reading again evoked the excitement of that first journey from the airport in Islamabad to her aunt's home in Lahore.

… arrived at an area called Model Town, where spacious, tree-lined streets and some very grand houses hide behind gated walls. After the city, it seemed impossibly sedate. We stopped at one of the smaller houses; Jai and his parents, my uncle and aunt, Daniel and Yalda, along with Jai's wife Saima, their daughter, Ipsita, and my cousin, Aamina all greeting

me warmly and I caught my first glimpse of a life that my father might have had if he'd spent his life in Lahore. And I and Sammy would never have existed.

Fanning her still sleeping son she skipped to the meeting with her grandmother. *…long grey plait coiled tightly round her head, framing her nut brown face and eyes that glistened like river washed gemstones. Words failed and we embraced. All I could think of to say was "I'm so happy to meet you." My grandmother didn't let go of my hand for ages and all my nerves disappeared!*

Sally recalled the clamour of hugs, kisses and gifts. Even little Ipsita had dutifully kissed Sammy which he'd enjoyed enough to kiss her right back! Of all the greetings, only Aunt Zarah's had felt merely dutiful and her un-kept promise that they'd be spending a lot of time together was, as she neared the end of her stay, not something she was sad about.

She turned a page. *…Yalda showed us to our room. It's quite dark and small, and Sammy and I sleep together on a mattress on the floor, which is no different than any of the others. It was already after six so I bathed and dressed Sammy for bed and everyone was very amused to see the pyjamas, as bedtime, even for Sammy, doesn't happen until around midnight.*

Sammy had adjusted easily to the afternoon siestas, and Sally wished she could escape the heat so easily. She read on. *…Later in the evening I was encouraged to leave Sammy playing with Ipsita and in Saima's care whilst Daniel drove Yalda, Aamina and me to Liberty Market where, although it seemed unnecessarily extravagant, Yalda insisted her tailor would transform the gifts of fabric into new shalwar kameezes. The market made me feel quite dizzy. Instead of rows of stalls, it turned out to be a noisy, brightly lit shopping complex full of restaurants, malls, shops and street vendors. Apparently shopping areas are called markets here. The whole place thronged with mostly women, even though it was after nine o'clock. I thought there must be a holiday or a festival but Yalda said not, and that this was normal. It's cooler to shop in the evenings and everywhere stays open until people go home!*

On our way into the covered area we passed rows and rows of garish sandals and glitzy handbags and near the entrances were piles and piles of wraps, shawls and stoles which we had to squeeze by to get into a warren of fabric stalls. Thankfully Aamina took my hand and guided me past dozens of alcoves where owners sat or stood, watched TV, or shouted their wares and prospective buyers haggled over damasks, silks and chiffons. I hung on to Aamina as we squeezed through the crowds. Even so, elbows dug into me and my toes were trodden on many times. Yalda was quite majestic, dismissing stallholders' invitations to view their glittering or sequined fabrics, many draped across headless mannequins. "Ugh! Made in China," I heard her say several times. Loudly.

We went down some stairs, passing soft drinks sellers who looked at me in a way that made me feel uncomfortable; I was relieved that I'd borrowed Saima's shawl and that my long shirt covered my bottom. Below stairs was an Aladdin's cave of riches! I saw one artist (for that's what he must be!) painting iridescent peacocks, copying from a piece of fabric on to soft silk to create a matching dupatta. Another man stitched seed-like beads on to stretched silks – I worried about his eyesight. Shop windows displayed scarlet wedding dresses woven with gold thread and jewels, which Aamina said cost more than a lakh rupees, which is quite a few thousand pounds. I thought people were poor in Pakistan!

We caught up with Yalda in a small workshop, where she'd already opened up my new fabric pieces. She told me to choose from styles on a sample rail at the back of the shop, but when I turned I saw a false half-ceiling, just above my head height, with four men sitting cross-legged as they whizzed fabric through sewing machines. I was horrified! I told Aamina, very quietly, how dreadful I thought it was but she was more interested in pulling samples from the rail. She laughed and said that I shouldn't worry as the men were all part of the family and that they earned plenty of money because they did good work. I didn't like it and didn't want to have them make my clothes but Aamina assured me they'd be much worse off if everybody was like me because they'd have no work.

Though Sally had visited the market a number of times

since, nothing would replace the impact of the first time. In a few days, when she and Sammy went home, she knew she would read and re-read these journals to keep these memories alive.

Wednesday 13th May, 1983

One day only and my clothes are ready! They're beautiful but a bit loose round my middle. I suggested a few darts but Yalda insisted loose garments are more comfortable in the heat. I hope she's right; I'm finding the heat exhausting and they tell me it's not hot yet! The clothes are certainly more comfortable and infinitely more beautiful than my jeans and shirts. I can't wait to wear them – they feel thrillingly exotic.

She'd take some of the clothes home, at least one for herself and one of Diane. Her mother, she knew, wouldn't wear such a thing. The others she'd leave behind – the maid would be glad of them.

And one day, she promised herself, she'd return. She knew already that she'd miss them all very much, particularly Rachel, Daoud's wife, who she'd met after collecting the clothes from the Market. They'd returned home to find an extraordinarily beautiful woman remonstrating with two noisy, excited boys who on seeing Sally, had switched smoothly from Urdu to perfect English, "Look, here's a new auntie for you," she'd told the boys. "Do you want her to think that boys do not know how to behave in Pakistan, eh? Now say hello nicely to auntie." Dutifully the boys greeted her in unison before running away giggling. "I'm sorry," Rachel had said, "We've been travelling for many hours and they're letting off steam. You must be Sally. I see the family eyes." She introduced herself and her 'naughty' twins, Sohail and Tariq. The room became crowded as Daoud, her uncle from Abbottabad appeared with three more, older boys who he'd introduced as his older sons, and a minute later, Sammy had hurtled into the room and thrown himself at her legs. Conversation had been impossible and Yalda's instruction to prepare to go out to dinner was welcomed. But Sally had realised they must have forgotten how young Sammy was. "What about Sammy?" she'd asked, "he's too young. I can't go!"

Her protest had been brushed aside. "Of course you can," Yalda had assured her, "there'll be lots of families. Saima's bringing Ipsita and Rachel's bringing the twins." Rachel had nodded and she'd guessed this beautiful new aunt of hers was not much older than herself.

Aamina had helped her to wash and dress Sammy and she tried to glean more. "Rachel's very beautiful."

"Isn't she!" Aamina had chatted readily. "Rachel is Daoud's second wife." She'd rubbed a flannel over Sammy's face. "Daoud's first wife died in childbirth. It was very sad." There'd been a respectful pause. "But then he met Rachel and married her. Do you know she's twenty years younger than him! Unbelievable! He's ancient; I think fifty seven or maybe eight and she's only thirty seven!" She'd shuddered dramatically. "Can you imagine sleeping with someone who's almost sixty?"

Amused at her cousin's chatter Sally had protested that Daoud was still attractive, even at fifty-seven, and soon, dressed in her new clothes and feeling exotic, Aamina had announced them dramatically. "Ladaa! Here we have the handsome Master Sammy and his beautiful Ammi, wearing this season's exciting creations by Malik Malik, tailor of repute!" Sally had fussed self-consciously with the strangeness of her dupatta until Daniel had moved forward and placing an arm round her shoulders had said, "You look stunning. I am proud to call you my Pakistani daughter." In that moment Sally had both missed her father and loved her new uncle.

Finding the account of the evening in her journal, Sally read' *...The restaurant was full of noisy families. I wanted to know Rachel better so when I saw her take the twins to a low table I took Sammy over to join them. We chatted about little boys and about Abbottabad, which* *is much smaller than Lahore. It's cooler too and snows in winter, which sounds like heaven. It's hard to imagine snow from the heat of Lahore.*

The big surprise had been the discovery that Rachel had been born in Middlesex, which explained her perfect English. But the story she told Sally was very different from her own. Coming to Pakistan as a twenty-year old bride in an arranged marriage, she'd met her husband only once before. She'd lived with his family near Peshawar where, without friends and not allowed to leave the house alone, she'd been homesick. Joy at the birth of her baby son a year later had turned to sadness as her mother-in-law took over the child, and when, another two years later, her husband became sick with TB and died, his parents accused Rachel of being a bad wife and mother and demanded she return to England, alone. But she'd stayed in Pakistan, hoping to see her son again. Sally had asked why she didn't just take him, and Rachel had replied, "I'm a woman and this isn't England."

When sounds of movement came from her grandmother's room Sally was eager to restart the day and finding the light switch in the half light of the tiny, windowless kitchen at the back of the house, she turned it on. Then off and on again, and found load-shedding – which Sally had soon discovered were all too frequent power cuts – had begun. In the dim light, she felt around for the candles.

"Sallyji. Chai. Very nice."

"Saima!" Sally jumped. "I didn't hear you! Haan, yes. I'll make a large pot – I heard Daadi stirring too." It amused Sally how English blended with Urdu, and with so many English words a component of the language, her self-appointed task of learning was less difficult.

The kettle whistled its alarm call and soon the household settled into familiar camaraderie, sipping sweet milky tea and chatting. Their grandmother's bent fingers slowly but skilfully plaited Aamina's oil-shined hair and Sally recounted how she'd once squawked as her mother had pulled out knots caused by her father's attempt to dress her hair for school. Saima ran fingers through Ipsita's dark, baby hair, already curling round her tiny neck, and Sally hugged Sammy and kissed his mop of uncontrollable spikes.

As the heat dissipated they moved to the veranda, shifting rattan chairs into soft breezes that might drift their way. Saima had changed into a new, electric blue and silver shalwar kameez in readiness for Jai's return from work and Sally fondled the silky dupatta. "You have many beautiful clothes, Saima."

"They are wedding presents; I had many pieces." She smiled at Yalda, the bestower, and Sally wondered how many pieces there'd been when, after three years of marriage, some were still being made up.

At her feet Sammy dressed one of Ipsita's dolls with strips of fabric he'd taken from curtaining that Yalda and Saima's were considering for rooms that had been built above the family home in preparation for the second child Saima expected in a few month's time. She was eager to be mistress of her own domain even though it was still part of the family house and wrinkled her nose at Yalda's choice of neutral stripes. Retrieving her own choice, a contrasting purple and green floral pattern, Sally observed their positions in the family; the classical older woman and the younger one with brave new ideas. The cohesive family scene reflected Sally's own dreams; she too, had a need to call somewhere her own, though a home of her own wouldn't include the family support that Saima enjoyed. It was an idealistic scene and Sally wondered about her own goals and pondered how expectations had predestined her journey through school, university, and career until motherhood swept her off course. Was it a pathway she'd merely 'careered' along?

The sound of voices heralded the men's homecoming and signalled the end of the working day. With Sally's visit declared reason enough to abandon the kitchen in favour of another evening outing, Aamina's suggestion of the upmarket M M Allam Road was overruled by Daniel who wanted traditional Gawal Mandi street food.

Inching the car alongside other vehicles in the heavy traffic they, too, ignored the red traffic light of Kalma Chowk as Daniel entertained them with stories of childhood. "Your father, Sally, was very kind and very serious. We, that is Daoud and I, were often troublesome, but your father would take the consequences. He was the eldest and therefore responsible, you see." He recounted how, as young boys, they'd delighted in throwing stones on to the tin roof of a building. "I threw the first," he said, "and the noise was wonderful. It rattled and clonked then fell to the ground with a thud. I did it again, and then Samuel threw one, and Daoud did too. Soon we were throwing many and the noise was even better! Then, goodness me, I noticed a man with a very angry face coming round the side of the building. Daoud and I ran as fast as our legs would go but not Samuel. He stayed. The man was very angry but Samuel stayed and apologised. Afterwards he said that he couldn't run because his legs had been too heavy with fear! But really, he was much braver than us!"

Sally chuckled. "That sounds like my father. He teased us a lot, but he was strict too. I remember him being upset once because Matt and I had lied to him. He'd instructed us that we must not go to the fairground without him and said that he'd take us on his free evening. But we couldn't wait and went anyway, then were late home. When he asked why we were late we said that we'd helped to clear rubbish from the school field, and he congratulated us for taking part. A few days later Matt's friend came to do homework with him, and Dad joked about his friend's scruffy school bag. 'Did you pick that up from the school field?' he asked. Of course, his friend didn't know what he was talking about and we were caught out. He was angry that we'd been to the fairground, but he was upset that we'd lied. He wouldn't let us go anywhere for two weeks, but losing his trust felt a bigger punishment than anything."

"Your father was a good man, Sally." Daniel steered the car round a corner and they travelled by the murky canal. "You see that water?" he asked. "As boys we used to escape the heat by jumping into it."

"That explains a lot," Jai said, "that water's toxic. It can do a lot to damage a boy's brain."

"Ah, so you swam there too, eh?" Saima cut in.

The banter continued until Daniel parked the car behind others on a central reservation in the busy road and promised ten rupees to a barefooted boy to look after it. Holding a hand against oncoming traffic Jai led them over the second carriageway with Sally carrying Sammy and hoping she appeared equally unperturbed as vehicles swished around them.

Gwal Mandi was already busy with people walking and looking, many already seated at tables that covered the pavement and much of the roadway. Shop and restaurant fronts were strung with bright light bulbs and glowing braziers illuminated shiny faced chefs who juggled dishes of steaming food into the hands of dancing waiters. Plates of curries, breads, pickles, salads, and runny golden dhal were slipped amongst battered metal water jugs and tumblers. Coca-Cola, Fanta and 7-up bottles rattled and plates clattered as waiters called 'kahari', 'roti', or 'saag'.

Mouths watered with expectation as they moved up the street comparing menus and inspecting arrays of meat or fish on braziers or tandoories until, decision made and table selected, Sally edged round a barefooted, sad-eyed woman selling cigarettes. A ragged child, presumably the cigarette seller's, offered chewing gum whilst keeping a wary eye on a policeman across the street. Buying a packet of tissues from another grubby child Sally reaped the reward of a gap toothed smile when she refused change of as much as the cost of the tissues. It was hard to imagine this chaotic street drama of paan and falooda makers, street entertainers, jewellery hawkers, balloon wallahs, and jalebi fryers dispersing as, later, sweepers transformed it back into its daytime persona; another traffic choked Lahorian street.

A menu appeared in Sally's hand and looking at the romanised script she realised how little Urdu she knew. She understood gosht was meat and aloo was potato, but what was rutabaga?

Yalda's voice came across the table. "What would you like to eat Sally?"

"Please, you choose for me," she laughed, "I don't understand the menu. But I love chicken tikka – if it's not too spicy."

"They do the best boti in Lahore over there," she said, pointing across the street. "It's like tikka but the pieces are small. Maybe Sammy could try some."

"Yes please, and maybe some rice and dhal for Sammy too; he likes that. Oh, and some plain lassi – we can share that. But no salt."

From the next seat her Uncle warned her to save some space. "We're going for ice-cream afterwards." His smile replicated that of his brother, Sally's father, and a momentary sadness clouded her face. "Do you not like ice-cream?" Daniel misinterpreted her look. "I thought everyone like ice-cream!"

"No, I mean yes. Sorry. Yes, of course I like ice-cream. It's just that, well, you look so much like my father sometimes; I miss him even more now I'm here. I've been so happy with you all and I wish I could tell him about it. It would have pleased him greatly to know that we'd met."

Daniel placed his hand over Sally's. "He knows, Sally. God is good."

Daniel's Christian confidence didn't persuade Sally but she appreciated his well intentioned words which sounded much like something her mother might have said. "I wish you'd met my mother too," she told Daniel. "Or more to the point, I wish we'd been together more over the years."

Lifting her hand Daniel clasped it in both of his. "Sally, it has been a great pleasure to meet the daughter and the grandson of my much loved brother. Our family have missed Samuel ever since he left for England nearly forty years ago. We thought then that we would all be together again within a short time, but it wasn't to be. Our mother mourned her son when she lost him to England and then again, when she lost him to God. You coming here has filled some of that gap and reduced the pain of our loss. You are our daughter."

The sincerity of his words moved Sally to respond from her heart. "Thank you, Daniel. I wish we'd met before and I wish we had family memories to share. When we go home next week I don't know how long it will be before we'll meet again and I'm going to miss you all very much. The holiday's gone so quickly; you'll be a gap in my life. I'm not sure I understand it myself but it's as if coming here has made me more complete."

Plates of food smacked the table. "Chicken boti," the waiter called as he dropped the first dish into a gap at the side of naan bread. "Fried fish." The second dish slid by the water jug and shunted a plate of salad dangerously close to Sammy's hands.

"Ha. Food." Daniel released her hand and handed a slice of cucumber to Sammy before moving the plate out of his reach. "I have a great hunger. Let's eat. We will talk again before you leave us."

A stack of roti landed alongside paper napkins and tasty morsels appeared on her plate as everyone insisted she try this or that. Tempted by the deliciously aromatic chicken boti she helped herself, and taking some naan proffered by Aamina, dipped it in something she recognised as dhal and placed it in Sammy's grabbing hand. Her mouth watered as the mild earthy aroma drifted upwards and dipping a second piece for herself, she let it slide over her tongue before folding more naan round a glistening morsel of boti. Lost in its juicy pungency she didn't see Sammy's empty hand until he shouted and pulled at her hand. "Greedy boy!" she laughed and caught hold of his outstretched hand, "you've eaten that too quickly!" Tearing a tiny piece of tender chicken she popped it into his mouth.

"I think you'll have to leave him behind when you go back to England, Sally," Aamina said, "He likes his Pakistani food too much."

"He likes all food too much." She'd adopted the common 'too' in place of 'very' and chuckled. "You'd be surprised how easy it is to get Pakistani food at home, and anyway," she promised, "we'll be back for more!"

During the night Sammy's screams and dirty nappies told their own stories. Dawn light smeared the eastern sky as Sally tried to muffle his cries with her wrap and quietly unfastening the door to the garden, she slipped, bare footed onto the cool, dew-damp grass. Fresh air cooled her face and she fanned Sammy's clammy skin, singing softly, *Lavender's blue, dilly dilly. Lavender's green. When you are King, dilly dilly, I shall be Queen.* Beyond the high walls the crank of a squeaking bicycle marked the start of a new day, and nearby she could hear a yard already being swept. A cockerel crowed and someone coughed, then the electronic crackle heralded the Azan. Lights appeared as neighbours rose to perform their morning prayers and water ran as they performed their ablutions. Sally sat on a garden seat and listened to the rise and ebb of the Mullah's chant. His fine voice, despite the electronic vibration on the high notes, was calm and reassuring in the early morning. Sally felt compelled to cover her head respectfully, but with her dupatta wrapped around a now sleeping Sammy, she rose and carried him gently indoors.

To her surprise she encountered her grandmother. "Oh Daadi! I hope we didn't disturb you? I'm afraid Sammy's tummy's a bit upset."

Her grandmother shook her head. "Nahin. I am old. I do not sleep. Sorry for my English. I forget." She beckoned Sally. "Come. Sit with me."

Laying Sammy gently on the divan she took the chair next to her grandmother. "I think your English is very good," she complimented, "I wish I could speak Urdu as well as you do English."

Chuckling, her grandmother held out a hand. "I was better when your Dada was alive; I had to speak English because his Urdu was too bad. I made the children speak English too; it important to have good English so they have good life now." She looked at Sammy. "Your baby a fine boy," she nodded, "khoobsoorat."

The eyes, so blue in the early light, belied her grandmother's seventy six years. "I think he's got your eyes," smiled Sally. "They're very beautiful too."

"Ah, yes. Beautiful. I forget. Yes. Your baby is beautiful child." A short, silence preceded her grandmother's next question. "Sarah, what happened....Ah, sorry, I mean Sally. It is difficult; you have been Sarah for me since your father wrote me of your birth. Sally. Yes. Sally. What happened? Where is your husband?"

Fearing attitudes in Pakistan might judge her, an unmarried mother, as shameful, she'd resisted talking of Sammy's father, and as everyone had so far been too polite to ask outright, she'd admitted the truth that John had left her and hidden behind an implied assumption that it was all too painful to talk about. But now her grandmother voiced the question that most of the rest of the family were probably asking each other, and it shook the sack of guilt she carried as a memento of behaviour she believed immoral in any culture. What happened, her grandmother now asked. Faced with a need to explain herself, she hardly knew where to begin. "His name, Sammy's father that is, his name is John. He's a good man." She stalled, unable to admit that John wasn't in fact, her husband, and worse, might not be Sammy's father. Deciding on a simpler truth she told her, "It went wrong. Horribly wrong. Now I have my son."

Her grandmother nodded. "Does this John not want his son?"

She swallowed. "No, Daadi, he doesn't. But he has reasons. It's complicated."

"I'm sure there are reasons. My life has taught me it is usually the people who are complicated." Her grandmother paused. "But you still love your John?"

The questioning, already difficult, was getting harder. "I see him in Sammy," she admitted. "It's hard not to think of him. But I've learned to live without him." Sally couldn't say she still loved John, but she couldn't say she didn't either. "It's in the past Daddi. We have to get on with life."

"A good man who leaves his family will have strong reasons. And I do not think you would have been wife to a bad man. So I am sorry for you all." Her tolerance was moving and Sally understood why her father had talked so lovingly of her. "Your father didn't have to leave a wife and child but he too made a painful decision to leave his family. He was a good man too. Sometimes there are reasons."

"Yes, he was a good man." She'd heard stories from his siblings but she wanted to know more. "Tell me about him, Daadi," she asked gently. "What was he like when he was young?"

The old eyes brightened and a smile touched the corners of her mouth. "Samuel bahut bahut chaalak. More chaalak than his brothers, and they bahut chaalak." She nodded to herself, then seeing Sally's lack of comprehension, she thought for a moment. "Mafi, I mean clever, too clever – at school. But sometimes he too much clever. Sometimes he clever naughty. I tell you a story. One day he rip his school shirt. New one, and expensive when we had small money. His father tell him 'Money – it not grow on trees. You too careless. You not care. I stop you pocket money.' So Samuel, he thinks, nahin mushkil – no problem – he take money from friends to do mathematic homework! He have more than pocket money very quick!"

Sally laughed. "He helped me with maths too; he was good at it."

"Sarah," her grandmother said, again using the name given by her father, "he should have been doctor like Daoud or a businessman like Daniel. He…" Her grandmother's voice faltered as she raised a hand, pale and almost translucent, to her mouth. "He was the eldest; he did what he had to." Something from the past haunted her eyes. "It was too terrible." Grief, unrelieved by time, resonated in the silence between them.

Holding her grandmother's papery hand, Sally encouraged her to speak some more. "He told us stories when we were young, about terrible things that happened. I see people here now, ordinary people, living ordinary lives, and it's hard to understand what happened."

Her grandmother seemed to shrink in her chair and a full minute passed before she spoke, so softly that Sally had to lean forward to catch the words. "Nineteen forty seven. What started it all?" She shook her head. "It started before. Years before. British make India join their war with Germany. Ghandi, he say this not India's war. He start the Quit India Movement for Independence. But some Hindus and some Muslims don't like it. Hindus do not honour Islam. Muslim League and Indian National Congress want different Independence. Jinnah, he start the Pakistan Movement. 'One country, one culture, one language,' he said. So Britain, their war finished, they give Independence to both by cutting in half." Her eyes opened wide as she looked at Sally. "Suddenly, everybody is living in the wrong place! Bah! What did Mountbatten know of Punjab? He just chop it! Hindus and Sikhs, Muslims and Christians. We live together. Hindu temples, Sikh temples, Mosques, Churches. What is the difference? Eid, Christmas, Diwali, Usavas. We shared them all as friends." She paused and sighed and, in Sally's eyes, looked frail. "Then came the fighting. One day friend, next day enemy!" Her eyes looked inwards. "Terrible. Terrible. My friends, Deepta and Leeora, they were Hindus. We grew up together. Like sisters. We went to school, we got married. We had babies. We were together, always. I loved my friends like sisters. Deepta went to live in Gujranwala, but she visited Lahore many times." Her voice faded until she repeated, "many times" and she closed her eyes, drawing curtains over the painful memories and Sally wondered if she had fallen asleep. But she continued. "There was a massacre in the market place. They say mothers killed their babies by jumping with them into wells. I don't know. I never saw Deepta again." Another silence extended. Sally waited; her grandmother's silence was far from peaceful. "Everyone blame each other, but all sides kill." Again, silence. "Leeora's brother's head…. delivered to his mother, in a box." A tear ran from behind the closed eyes and the sting of tears burned Sally's eyes. Tugging white tissues from the box she put one into her grandmother's hand and dabbed her own face, wanting to hear no more but needing to listen. "Leeora's family, they leave Lahore on the refugee train. Just one hour, they have, to pack and settle their affairs. They leave with nothing. Many people go; they have no time for packing or goodbyes and some people here get very rich very quick from what they left. I don't know if Leeora's family arrive in India or…." Shadows on her face didn't need words but what was said next was horrifying. "Trains of corpses arrive here, and there too. Blood run from carriages. One side kill. The other kill back. Maybe Leeora die quickly; she get shot or stabbed. Maybe raped. I don't know. But maybe. People disappear." She tutted. "People. They thieve and lie and torture friends. How can it happen? I don't understand; not before, not now. How can I understand? It was people. Now? I don't trust anymore." Her eyes opened and looked towards a framed photograph; a portrait of her husband and Sally wondered what evil had befallen her grandfather. He was neither Hindu nor Muslim, nor was he Pakistani. But he'd been a victim just the same. Her father had told her that his mother hadn't spoken for weeks after his body had been discovered and that the shock had turned her hair grey. She wanted to know more about him and waited quietly for her grandmother to continue but rising stiffly and without voicing the outrage, the final, unspeakable evil, she went to her room leaving Sally to see that time hadn't salved her grandmother's losses; she'd merely learned to live with them.

Looking at Sammy, sleeping soundly on the divan, the horror of murdering one's child made her shiver. Her father's accounts of India's history and Partition had been shocking but less explicit, and, in the safety of their London home, less vivid too. Here, in Lahore, in the stillness of an early morning, the immediacy of her grandmother's stories stunned her. Grief, which still hovered below the surface of the family, had been shared, and the sharing had made it hers too. She was family. With the first rays of sunshine touching the window, she gently lifted her sleeping son, carried him to their room and lay with him on their mattress, her hand gently but protectively rubbing his sore tummy.

By the time Sally woke the sun was high and Sammy played happily with her necklaces which, she saw, would take an age to disentangle. Remembering that Zarah would soon be arriving to escort her on a gift-buying shopping trip she jumped from the mattress, disengaged her beads and chains from Sammy's hands and after bathing him, handed him over to Maria, the maid, to be fed roti and egg. Taking a roti for herself she washed and prepared herself quickly, reluctant to keep her aunt waiting. Gift hunting amongst the gaudy extravagances of Ichara Market had offered nothing she wanted and when Zarah – who loved shopping – had offered to take her to a shop in the smart Gulberg area where she said stylish textiles and jewellery were popular amongst Westerners, Sally had accepted gratefully.

Like many of her friends, Zarah was an experienced shopper; knowledgeable about the wares, ways and wiles of shopkeepers and skilled at bargaining. In air-conditioned comfort Sally selected scarves, bags and pieces of unusual but distinctly Asian jewellery for her mother and her friends. She found woven table mats for Matt, and a linen kameez for Diane. Impressed with the quality and persuaded by the prices – expensive in Pakistan but much cheaper than London – she sorted through sumptuous bedcovers, table mats, cushions and rugs, trying to decide which would reflect her Pakistani roots in the home she intended to make for herself and Sammy before long. An array of purchases spread out next to the cash desk; enough for Zarah to negotiate and be granted an attractive discount so that, once paid, Sally insisted on providing lunch with her savings.

Regaled with stories of parties, weddings, picnics and shopping expeditions, Sally ate a chicken and mango salad until, as they finished with ice-cream topped iced coffees, she commented, "Being here has been a revelation to me; I thought Pakistan was a poor country!"

"Life is what we make it, Sally. It hasn't always been so good, but we have peace and prosperity like we've never had before. Businesses are booming and Pakistan is growing." She cast her kohl-lined eyes casually around her and lowered her voice. "We have to be careful what we say in public and not attract attention because we're…" She lowered her voice even further, "Christians." Sally almost laughed but it was clear that Zarah was serious. "We'll talk at home, but not here." She whispered then laughed loudly as though they'd shared a private joke. Catching the eye of the waiter she signalled for the bill and when it arrived, passed it dutifully to Sally.

Adjusting her dupatta around her hair, Sally sat beneath the shabby cantilevered canopy of a motorbike rickshaw enjoyed the ten miles-an-hour breeze that provided respite from the afternoon heat. A motorcycle carrying a family of four weaved alongside them, the mother riding pillion and anchoring her flapping dupatta around a sleeping baby whilst a strappy sandal dangled casually from one foot. Wedged between herself and the driver a second child wore bright yellow sunglasses to protect his eyes from the dust and Sally realised how familiar Lahore had become when such sights no longer surprised her. Now, she sat calmly as they avoided buses, cars, bikes and pedestrians and listened to Zarah talk of the farewell party that Daniel and Yalda were organising for her, pleased to know that Daoud and Rachel would be coming. As they reached their local market Zarah spoke rapidly to the driver, instructing him to pause whilst she selected oranges and lychees from a roadside cart then ordered him forward to buy cauliflowers from a second cart. Accepting package after package the driver waited patiently as they visited a bakery and the pharmacy, and when finally they arrived at home and the driver had offloaded their purchases into the hands of Maria, Zarah dropped a few coins into his hand. Adding a few more as a tip, Sally wondered wryly if London taxi drivers would be so accommodating.

"Hello baby." Holding out her hands to greet Sammy she

kissed him on the cheek. "Have you been a good boy for auntie?"

Already putting a kettle to boil for tea, Maria turned and nodded. "Lovely boy. He too happy so I happy."

"Thank you Maria, Sammy looks happy too."

As Sally returned to the sitting room, Zarah told her, "You don't need to thank her you know, she's paid to do these things."

The family's lack of interest in Maria's welfare irritated Sally and glancing towards the kitchen she spoke quietly. "That may be, but thanks cost nothing. Looking after Sammy isn't part of her job so it's kind of her to do it. And I'm grateful." Defiantly, she decided to give one of the silk scarves she'd bought that morning to Maria as a farewell gift; they were certainly better than anything she had seen Maria wear, and why shouldn't she have something nice?

Zarah patted the space on the divan next to her "Come and sit here. You're just not used to having servants. Here, even maids have maids. No-one wants to do their own chores, but who you work for makes you important." Pulling a mosaic-mirror lipstick case from her bag, she glossed her lips. "I'm sure that I would find many surprises in England. It's not so rigid here in the city but if you were to stay in our provinces you'd find things very strict. Lahore is more sophisticated; you're lucky we live here and not in some parts of this country." She put away her lipstick and stroked Sammy's cheek with a heavily ringed finger. "But even here there are problems. I said I'd tell you about being a Christian here didn't I. You see, we're a minority group and our country is run according to Islamic laws." Zarah's mascara-heavy lashes fluttered dramatically. "We're discriminated against and marginalised."

Although she didn't think her aunt was lying Sally found it hard to trust what she was being told. "But Christians fill the church. St Andrew's was full when we went."

"Oh, there are thousands of us! But we're still a minority. It didn't matter once. During British rule we were respected. We had good education – many of the schools here were set up by Christians – and we had good jobs. Hospitals too. But after Partition we became…, well, we became Dhimmis." Zarah spat the word in disgust. She explained for Sally. "Dhimmis were people who, when invaded by Islamic forces, were granted limited rights. That's how it is for us. Even though Pakistan is our country our freedoms are barely tolerated. For example, as Christians we're allowed to eat pork and drink alcohol. But only by licence. And under conditions they regulate. How kind! When the British left and Pakistan became independent we Christians were reduced." She paused for a second, thinking. "I mean separated, made less important. Now it is normal to be discriminated against. Zia Ul-Haq makes Islamic law Pakistani law, and Muslims say our religion is a Western religion being spread through schools and colleges. Ten years ago they nationalised the schools and colleges. And the hospitals. Many Christian teachers, doctors and nurses have lost jobs they had for many years. Daoud has been fortunate; he keeps his job because obstetricians are needed. But it's becoming more difficult for him. Some men won't allow him to treat their wives; he wonders how long he will be able to keep his job."

"You mean he might lose his job because he's Christian?"

"Of course. It's even worse in the North-Western province where he lives. He drives an old car and lives in a small house so that he doesn't draw jealous attention. He's worried."

Was Zarah exaggerating? Sally had overheard Daniel talking to Yalda about an allowance he gave Zarah to pay their boys' college fees and Sally wondered if she was jealous of her brother's successes. She knew that in Daniel's knitwear business Muslim and Christians worked together, and Aamina's good friend at college, Xainab was Muslim. What she'd seen didn't suggest Christians were unfairly treated. "Aamina's at a mixed school, isn't she?"

"Yes, it's a girls' college. It used to be run by Christians and it takes Christians and Muslims, but there are many more Muslims."

"But wouldn't you expect that? There're more Muslims than Christians in Pakistan."

"That is true. People want their children to go to the old Christian schools because they're good, but preference is given to Muslim families. It's difficult for our children to get accepted. And when it comes to work, they don't even get to interview."

"But how do they know they're Christians?"

Zara looked surprised. "Our names, of course. We have Christian names."

"Zarah Masih is Christian?"

"That's not my name. I'm Zarah Wakil. Zarah, wife of Wakil. But many people now choose your western way, like my mother, your grandmother. She took my father's family name, Lancing, probably because he was English. Some people keep their own names too. I do. My full name, when I need to be official, is Zarah Lancing Wakil. But our children are Masih, which is a Christian family name, from Messiah."

"It must be complicated to know who belongs to which family, or to trace families."

Zarah looked surprised. "Trace families? We know who they are!"

So many differences were hard to absorb. "But surely not all names identify religion, do they? When you apply for a job, or register your child at a school, how do they know what your religion is if your name doesn't make it clear?"

"They ask. It's on all the forms too. Don't you do that in England?"

"Not always. Lots of forms, such as hospital forms, ask. But it doesn't matter; it's just for records, or so that they know if you need anything special."

"Well here it does matter. If you're not Muslim you're not important, no matter how educated or qualified you are. More and more, Christians are becoming less educated and poorer, and soon, Christians will only get the jobs no-one wants to do. And there's nothing we can do about it. Daniel and Daoud were lucky; our mother was the daughter of an officer in the Indian Army and our father, of course, was English, and then, they were both respected. But it's changed. For our children it's harder. They're only at good schools because we pay the fees and I wonder how much longer that will be enough. You know the university where my father, your grandfather worked?"

Sally nodded. "Foreman's Christian College?"

"Yes. A very good college; one of the best. Daniel and Daoud both went there. After our father was killed the staff – many of them Christian too – gave them places. But that wouldn't happen now. Nazih – our eldest – wasn't accepted, even with very good results. He's a very clever boy. He would have been accepted before nationalisation." Zarah's voice was bitter. "Being discriminated against is bad, but persecution is worse. There are many stories of attacks against Christians. In the past few years some of our churches have been burned and we hear of Christians being turned from their homes. What can we do? The laws of our country do not protect us, and the army enforces them." Behind her make-up Zarah's face was flushed with resentment. "Wakil used to be Muslim – did you know? He converted to Christianity."

It was an afternoon of surprises. "I had no idea!"

"That's why his name is Masih. He took the name when he converted. He was at an Army school but he had to leave. He finished his HSC – Higher Secondary Certificate – at an ordinary state school then trained to be a nurse."

"Why did he convert?" She was more than curious.

"Wakil objected to fighting. A few years before Partition, violence here was escalating as Ghandi and Jinnah formed their different movements. Wakil found Christianity... more approachable. Little did he know how things would turn out."

The complaining voice had a whining, petulant quality that Sally found hard to sympathise with even though she deplored such inequality. "I'm sorry, Zarah." She patted her arm and made to stand, bringing the conversation to an end.

Zarah restrained her. "I sound dreadful, don't I? Mostly it isn't so bad. Most people are decent and nice." She smiled. "We have friends who are Muslim; they don't like the discrimination any more than we do and they're horrified at the persecutions that are happening. But if they don't support the changes they appear to criticise Islam, which is dangerous for them too."

As the one family member Sally hadn't warmed to it was easy to believe Zarah exaggerated the discrimination and problems she talked of and though Sally was interested, the conversation was unsettling. "Why do you stay? Why don't you go and live somewhere else?" It seemed an obvious thing to do.

"Sally, why did you come to Pakistan?"

"What do you mean?"

"You came to be with your family?" Sally nodded. "Maybe you came to discover who you are?" Again, she nodded. "That's why we stay, Sally. We are Pakistani. This is our home."

When Zarah had left, Sally continued to ponder the truth of her words. No-one else had talked of religious discrimination. Had they, she wondered, wanted to shield her from such uncomfortable aspects of life so that she took home an image of a comfort and stability despite the horrors of recent history? It was hard to believe. They'd taken her into the family honestly and openly and she'd felt truly comfortable in their home. And for the first time in many years, she felt comfortable with the 'home' she called herself. Her only shadow was the imminent departure.

"Let's go for an ice-cream." She told Sammy as she fastened the straps on his buggy.

"I-keem. Sammy I-keem." Sammy's hands clapped with delight.

Yalda laughed. "I like ice-cream too. Can I come?"

Sally manoeuvred the buggy through the gates and into the street. "It's so hot." The scorching heat was one thing she knew she wouldn't miss.

The shady walkways of Model Town Park were always a few degrees cooler than the sun-blasted streets and it was a lively place in the late afternoon. People were already striding, jogging, or strolling and chatting their way round the shaded perimeter path, navigating between those who'd entered at different gates or who travelled in the opposite direction. Sally identified a few regulars, returning nods and smiles of recognition. At the rose garden she stopped; the peach coloured Peace rose had been her father's favourite. Cupping a full bloom in her hand she lifted it to her nose, darkening the petals with the trace of her fingers as she inhaled its perfume. A memory of her father pruning old thorn strewn stems in their small garden came to mind, his voice telling her again that God had made roses perfect whereas man, in trying to emulate him, lost the essence. She sent him a thought; 'not from this one, Dad, this is one of yours'.

Back at the main entrance, Yalda sent Sally to find a seat whilst she bought the ice-creams. "Vanilla?" she asked, "and Chai?" In the shade of some trees they squeezed a Lipton's tea bag against the sides of cups and added sugar – something Sally never used in England. The metallic Pakistani tea was impossible to drink unsweetened and, to her surprise, she'd grown to enjoy the sweet milky drink almost more than its English counterpart.

"I'll miss tea like this when I get home," she admitted as she crushed tea-soaked sugar lumps.

Yalda popped the last of her ice-cream into Sammy's mouth, sipped her tea, and then said, "You don't have to go home yet if you don't want to."

Sally blinked, and wondered if she'd misheard. "Pardon?" Yalda merely tilted her head to one side, and Sally realised she'd heard Yalda's words perfectly well. "Of course I do. Our flight goes in three days."

"And I'm saying you don't have to go home yet if you don't want to. We'd like you to stay longer and your grandmother will be too sad to see you go. You have brought her son back to her. And to Daniel too; he and your father were close as boys." She offered Sally the complimentary biscuit from her saucer.

"No thank you." Sally shook her head then laughed. "I mean to the biscuit."

Sammy pulled at his mother's kameez. "Cookie. Sammy." He'd learned the word 'cookie' from Aamina who, in Sally's opinion, watched too many American films.

Giving the biscuit to Sammy she admitted to Yalda that she'd love to be able to stay. "But how can I?" she asked, "I have to go and find a job and a home. And my mother will be missing us. And, well, I have my friends. And…" She paused. "But I'd love to stay" she said quietly.

"You could get a job here if you felt you needed to, a good job. You have an English degree. That's of great value, and plenty of women work, especially if they're educated."

"But I don't speak enough Urdu, and I'd have to find somewhere to live, and how would I look after Sammy if I went to work?"

"What do you mean?" Yalda looked surprised. "Many people speak English. And you'd live with us. You're our family. And we'd look after Sammy. This is not a problem. Is it normal for you to not live with your family and help each other in England?"

"I, well no. Of course we support each other when we need to…"

"When you need to?"

They'd debated questions of culture and values on several occasions and always agreed that they were different. Could she live with Daniel and Yalda and have help with Sammy if she found some work? The idea seemed equally sensible and preposterous.

"Oh Yalda, it's different. People are more independent; we're encouraged to be individual. Family is very important to us too, but …. well it's different."

"Well it seems very strange to not want to live together and help each other. But it's for you to decide. It's easy for us – Saima and Jai will be moving into their new rooms in a few weeks and we have enough room. Think about it. If you want to stay with us you'll make us all very happy. If you cannot stay, then we hope you will come back again. Very soon. Now, what do you think of the curtains Saima has chosen?"

Once the seed was planted it was impossible for it not to germinate. The following morning Sally waited in one of the rows of seats at the Pakistan International Airlines office, clutching tickets and passport and waiting for her turn at the counter. A couple went to a vacant position; he attentive, she pregnant. They looked so young. With a pang of sadness she realised that she'd miss Diane's wedding and for a moment faltered. But though missing her friend's wedding would sadden her, the desire to stay was strong.

Half an hour later, and with tickets extended for five months, elation assured her she'd made a good decision. It would take most of the money she'd put aside for her and Sammy's future, but, she rationalised, it would focus her mind when she did eventually return home.

CHAPTER 9

Fallen Angel Food Cake

As the TV faded John felt himself drawn, Alice-like, into a celestial vortex of perpetual white. He blinked and focused on a pile of books until the retinal impression faded and then, turning off the now silent TV, felt the crush of emptiness it had dispelled. He both longed for and yet recoiled from the clamour of the earlier celebrations that seemed to have happened in a distant, if parallel time; an evening in his honour that had celebrated the restaurant's first anniversary and lent itself to a degree of retrospection.

The evening had been Alain's idea; success, he'd said, breeds success. There'd been spontaneous speeches praising John's talent, his ingenuity, his flair, and vows of friendships and enduring promises had been sealed with quaffs of wine. Julia's husband had honoured him with a case of vintage Napa Valley, and Alex Manning's request that he appear as Guest Chef at Woodhome Park was proof of prowess. He'd planned a speech, but after the tributes, praise inspired and wine loosened words had come from his heart. But now, alone, the stillness of the flat echoed with emptiness and silence. On a normal day it refreshed, but tonight he buzzed with celebrity, and solitude thumbed its nose at him.

Unable to resist, he'd brought a plate of dessert upstairs with him. A pool of sweet cherry compote surrounded two crescents of the lightest of cakes, one richly dark, the other snow white; Angel and Devil Food cakes in an amusing synergy, with cherry 'sauce' adding to the joke. Dipping a finger first into the devil frosting then the angel sugar glaze, he licked the sweetness, recalling how the naughty double-entendre dessert had enticed some of the more imbibed guests to high spirits. The duo of cakes had been an inspiration; they'd been the 'icing' on the meal. The idea for the confection had come from the old American recipe book that Sally had given him the previous Christmas, and which despite the association, he couldn't resist using. A book, he told himself, was just a book. But his cake, he thought, looking at the plate, wasn't just cake. Sally would have liked the cake, particularly the devil, and a crazy stray thought that he would save her some made him question his sobriety. She'd gone, but she wouldn't leave him alone. He hadn't seen her since the day she'd betrayed herself in the cruel irony that mocked his misunderstanding over blood groups and dried up his love for her as though it had never existed. No, worse. It had existed; he'd loved her almost since he'd first met her though he hadn't known it to start with. Now, he knew love was nothing more than an intangible, fleeting mood, a device conjured by poets and storytellers to weave dreams. He'd almost believed it could last. Almost. But Sally had confirmed what his birth mother had taught him. She, who had given birth to him had taught him that love didn't endure and he'd believed it before Sally. But it had been hard to give up on and he'd dared to trust her. She'd been everything; his lover, his best friend, his soul mate. Her happiness had been his. He'd begun to understand and then trust when she'd told him that in loving him her own freedom to love grew. And he'd dared to share it with her.

Love was a deceit, that he was sure, but what he couldn't explain and didn't understand was the child. He massaged his temples. He missed him so much it – love? – ached. A line from somewhere came to mind; *Tis better to have loved and lost, than never to have loved at all*, and muttering "Tosh!" he licked the final sauce from the plate.

The celebrated chef slept and woke as sober John. Both had been there the night before. The chef and ordinary John. Jekyll and Hyde. John had hidden behind Chef and watched the evening; an observer who couldn't take part. Now he re-lived the evening, hearing again Alain's accentuated Frenchness sprinkled liberally with absurd mispronunciations and pronounced Gallic shrugs. As Chef basked, John wilted. "We 'ave ze man oo iz giving us ze nouveau umpire, out in zis field of iz own." He'd gone on to play on his 'empire' corruption by adding "zis strong competition from zis new player iz, as you say in Inglis, just not cricket." He pronounced it 'crickette' as though the word belonged to the French, and though Chef had laughed along with the others John had resented the Francophile distraction from his New World style as much as his own lack of repartee that might have bowled Alain's 'crickette' out. He envied Alain's assurance and acknowledged the debt was greater than mere investment, but in the cold light of a new day, it was he who'd made Seagrams successful. His hard work, not Alain's banter.

Leaning against the cold red bricks outside the back door John raised his face to the morning sun and let it ease the grittiness of another long Saturday night as he chewed his bacon sandwich. A cigarette, the first and best smoke of the day followed, and in the quietness of the spring morning he savoured the calm before the storm. This second Easter Sunday would be twice as busy as last year's. Lunches would start shortly after midday. From ten onwards they would be flat out, and John enjoyed the last of the peace with the last of his cigarette. In his mind, he scheduled shoulders of spring lamb with rosemary, chicken ballotine, and salmon en croute until the sound of a car on the gravel in front of the restaurant distracted him. It was early for any of the staff, and certainly too early for a customer. Grinding the butt of the cigarette under his heel he walked round the side of the building.

"Morning."

"Morning. Can I help you?"

He recognised the woman walking towards the front door as having been at the anniversary dinner with Alex Manning and his wife.

"Sorry. I know it's early. I lost an earring on Thursday, probably at your party." She put out her hand. "I'm Sandy. Alex Manning's sister-in-law." A gap between her front teeth was attractive. "I couldn't come before; I've been in London. I suppose I could have rung."

It wasn't surprising that he remembered Sandy. Everyone at the party had probably remembered her spiky copper coloured hair and green day-glo dress. Now, her hair gleamed like polished metal in the sunshine, and her short, sleeveless dress displayed a tan that went beyond the deep 'V' of her neckline. "Yes, I remember. You asked for a second dessert."

Sandy's laugh was as loud as her hair. "Sorry – too much wine. But who could resist a Fallen Angel?"

She'd almost purred 'fallen angel' and his Sally chilled libido spiked into life. "My fault entirely." Her eyes were green and accentuated with black khol. "Well, let's see if we can find your earring. Hold on, I'll get the key and let you in."

Dodging dustbins, kitchen tables, servery, and finally, restaurant tables, he unbolted the front door. "Hi. Come on in. What colour's the earring; you've brought the other one?" He pulled a box from under the bar. "We keep lost property here."

"Ah. That would have been a good idea, wouldn't it? But no I haven't brought it. It's silver, with three jade stones. It's not precious, but I like it and it's part of a set."

They searched the box without finding it and then Sandy

almost disappeared under what had been her table. John looked on, enjoying the spectacle. "I don't think it will be on the floor. It's been cleaned a few times since Thursday. Are you sure you lost it here?"

Sandy was almost under another table. "No, not really. But I don't know where else it might be. I hope you don't mind me coming over." She stood up, revealing the extent of her tan.

Averting his eyes reluctantly he assured her he didn't mind. "Look, I was just going to have some coffee. Would you like some?"

Wishing he had more time to spare he brewed fresh coffee and found Sandy in front of his iconic Rothko-like panel. He waited, curiously, whilst she stepped back then forward again, and peered closely. People either loved or hated it and he wondered which camp she would stand in.

"This is unusual. It looks a bit like Rothko but his are more opaque than this." She pointed to the sides. "You can see the different colours this artist has used here, and here, quite easily." She looked at the label. "No title. And no price either. How much is this?"

The mention of Rothko and obvious regard stirred his interest but this picture was not for sale. "It's mine."

"You painted it? You're an artist as well as a chef?"

He shook his head thinking how deep – and captivating – Sandy's green eyes were. "No. I mean no, I didn't paint it, but yes, I'm also an artist, or used to be." He explained how the artist, like himself, had been influenced by Rothko, and that he'd commissioned the painting. Intrigued by her interest, he asked if she painted.

"I wish I did. I studied art history but I've no talent. It's my mother who's talented." She told him her family had moved to France when she was seven years old. Her father, a wine merchant, had bought a vineyard south of Béziers, which was where they still lived. "I'm going home on Tuesday," she told him, "I've been here on a short holiday, visiting my sister."

Enjoying the conversation as he was, John was aware of the work to be done. "Look Sandy, I've around eighty people for lunch today and need to get on. I'm sorry about your earring. Why don't you give me your telephone number then if it turns up I can ring you?"

Over the first new potatoes of the season, John let Sandy merge with Toyah Willcox, so that it was Sandy, rather than Toyah who strutted her rebel punk on Top of the Pops. He'd loved the irreverence and distinctive, magnetic voice and Sandy looked very much like her. A brief dalliance was tempting; her imminent departure suggested fun without commitment, and leaving the potatoes to cook he dialled the number she'd given him.

"Bonjour."

"Sandy?"

"Oh! Sorry. I was expecting Alain."

Alain? Alain was calling Sandy? Why? Righteous anger clashed with fluster. "Er, no. No, I'm sorry. It's me, John, from Seagrams. I....... I wondered if your earring turned up."

"Oh, forgive me. I expected my brother."

Indignation turned to relief and feeling slightly foolish he asked again if she'd found her earring.

"No. And it sounds like you haven't found it either."

"No. Sorry, but no." He soldiered on, telling himself she could only say no. "I was wondering, perhaps you might like to have ..." he almost said 'another look' but realised how ridiculously transparent that would sound and searched for an alternative option. "...coffee. Or a drink. Not here....... I close this evening." He warmed to the idea. "There's a wine bar behind the Abbey in Bath: The Three Tuns. Would you like to go there? With me?"

For the first time in more than ten years he had a date! Checking his wallet for funds he danced an excited jig and sang, *Do you want me baby, Do you want me, Oh…,* as he went to explore his wardrobe. The black button-collared shirt? Or a t-shirt and leather jacket? Jeans? Her father was a wine merchant, so the wine would have to be good. Should they eat? The Italian near the bridge? He stopped short; where would he get condoms on a Sunday evening? In case…

Light from a three or four day wedge moon turned Sandy's hair from copper to gold as he propped himself on an elbow and ran a hand over the surprisingly soft spikes of her hair. "You could stay."

"I have to go home. I have to go to work on Wednesday."

"I meant tonight. Stay tonight. The restaurant is closed tomorrow. I have a free day."

Sandy chuckled. "Mmmm, I could." Head tilted to one side she made a drama of considering the options. "I'd better call my sister or she'll send out search parties."

His eyes caressed her nakedness as she made the call. There was an audacity about her that daunted yet had permitted her to come easily to his bed, and in that, it pleased him. It had been quite an evening; they'd enjoyed an acceptable bottle of Rioja at The Three Tuns, eaten a Coq au Vin they'd both agreed to be chicken stew at The George, and moved on rapidly after his appalling line, 'Would you like to come and see my etchings?' Conversation about music and art had started interestingly but with outrageous flirtation needing little encouragement his flat became more attractive than dessert or coffee. Now, Sandy was telling her brother-in-law she'd be back some time tomorrow. She both attracted and intimidated him.

Flipping the tape over in the cassette player, the sound of

Queen's *The Game* album filled the room and she sashayed in time to the music. An absurd vision of his mother's likely reaction to the scene brought a grin that Sandy interpreted as an invitation, and she re-joined him on the bed, narrowing her feline eyes and purring as they sang *Crazy little thing called love* together with Freddie Mercury. He rolled her over on the bed, enjoying being shocked by her enough to overcome any sense of respectability. She'd be returning to France shortly and in the meantime, she was here, she was agreeable, and he was having more fun than he'd had in months.

Later he slotted another cassette in to the player. "Do you know the words to this?" he asked. Toyah Willcox's voice sang *I wanna be free.*

When Sandy left with no promises other than a breezy "Next time," John was happy. She wasn't his kind of girl he told himself, and then thought again. She was exactly the kind of girl he wanted. Free, fun, no promises, and the antithesis of Sally.

CHAPTER 10

Chicken Biryani

Sally replaced the receiver and mopped her face with her dupatta. She wished it had been possible to make an international call at Daniel's home instead of in this crude and cramped booth, where her news had been broadcast to anyone who chose to listen. Shouting "I'm staying in Pakistan" and "No, we're not coming home" had cruelly quashed her mother's excitement at the call and imminent return. She'd felt heartless and self-indulgent as she'd tried to explain, at volume, "the wonderful opportunity to understand my heritage." Above her head a small fan stirred the hot air, clicking at each revolution; tck-t, tck-t. "Oh shut up!" she muttered, and gathering her things, backed out of the tiny cubicle.

"You've called your mother? Her health is good?" Taking a nod as sufficient response Yalda pulled her into the living room. "We're going to Abbottabad," she enthused, "we're going to visit Daoud and Rachel instead of having your farewell party." In the corner her grandmother beamed too. "Daadi hasn't been to Abbottabad for many years, and she likes it there too much. You know she was married there?" Again, a nod was enough. "We will leave early tomorrow morning, at eight. You must pack something warmer, a pashmina for you and something for Sammy. And some shoes for the hills." Yalda hugged Sally. "Oh, I like Abbottabad too much, it is too beautiful!"

By the time they'd been in the car for four hours and passed through Islamabad, all – apart from Daniel and her – had succumbed to the steady motion of the car. Sammy snuffled, Yalda ground her teeth and her grandmother snored, but fighting eyes heavy with torpor Sally took in all about her. They passed Saeed's book shop, where she'd been told she could get any book in the world, and another Yummy's Ice-Cream Parlour, as in Lahore. Modern, expensive restaurants and cafes hinted at high cuisine from behind trimmed hedges and smoky street grills emitted aromas that made the mouth water. The busy streets, straight, wide and dusty with criss-cross junctions and finger-post signs to F Block and D Block brought Milton Keynes to mind until purple-hazed hills in the distance hinted at something more exotic. Daniel identified the hills as being the Marghalla Hills, foothills of the Himalayas and where, she thought, lay Abbottabad. But hopes for the journey's end were dashed as they left Islamabad and Daniel pulled into a filling station. Waking Jai to take over the driving he said they still had at least two more hours to travel. Such distances were unheard of to her; Bath to London was almost too far and visits to Matt in Glasgow rarely happened. But here they were, driving a distance that took more than six hours, for little longer than a weekend! Her grandmother had prepared well, bringing along cushions and wedged between Yalda and Saima they all slept comfortably. But as the road twisted and turned through villages and followed rivers that meandered through ever more hills she fought sleep's persistence until finally, hypnotised by the seemingly endless journey, it won.

Then Daniel announced they were coming into Abbottabad and everyone stirred. Sally blinked and looked eagerly at her new surroundings. She'd expected something akin to Lahore's old city and was surprised to see traffic moving in an orderly fashion along a street lined with crumbling colonial buildings that still displayed remnants of elegance. They passed a park, complete with bandstand, and then a double storied Victorian building. She laughed in astonishment, "That's a school! It's got separate entrances for boys and girls! Just like at home!"

Her grandmother's beautiful eyes gleamed. "There are many British buildings here; Abbottabad was British garrison town. Your grandfather, he stationed here. We meet at Abbottabad." She pointed at a gothic church. "Look," she said, "St. Luke's. We marry here. And near is hospital where your father is born." She pointed out other memories as they turned first one corner and then another, happily reminiscing. "Oh, it is too many years since I come here."

Slowing in front of tall, black painted gates, Jai hooted the horn. "We're here!" he announced, and the gates swung open to reveal Daoud, Rachel and all five boys spilling from a small, block of a house. Daoud was helping his mother out almost before the car had stopped, whilst Sammy, alarmed at the sudden excitement, burrowed into his mother's neck and attached himself like a limpet. Noisy greetings continued through a doorway and into a room where a small table containing condensation crazed glasses of fresh lemonade waited for them. The house had seemed small from outside, possibly just two rooms wide and two high, but inside she could see the long 'L' to the left that she'd thought to be another house was also part of her uncle's home. Around the room, heavy wooden furniture might have appeared dark and inhospitable were it not for colourful kilim rugs and cushions that padded the chairs, sofas and stools, and small hexagonal tables, inlaid with shiny mosaics that reflected light from windows draped with silk fabrics. Curiosity overcame Sammy's shyness and he dared to inspect the silently flickering screen of the largest television set he'd ever seen, leaving Sally to sink into one of the chairs, grateful that the journey was over.

In the evening, conversation turned to possible activities. "You are here at the hottest time of our year." Daoud held up a hand as Sally tried to speak. "Yes, I know. Lahore is much hotter. But we're coming to our wet season so the humidity here is high. We are fortunate; we have hills around us where it is cooler. You cannot come to Abbottabad and not climb Shimla Pahari. Do you like to walk?" From the corner of her eye she saw Daoud's eldest son pull a face. Daoud saw it too. "Aah Farouq, you don't want to walk eh? Nahin mushkil. No problem. Daadi will go on the bus; you can accompany her and carry the picnic for us all." Even Farouq saw the humour through his teenage angst.

Rachel tapped Daoud's hand. "And Sally and I will go to Gurdwara Bazaar in the morning to buy chapatti and salad. The chicken biriyani is ready but Sally must see our bazaar whilst she's here."

Recalling a biriyani of grey glutinous rice, sinewy chicken and viscous vegetable curry she'd once faced in a Bristol Bengali restaurant, with some effort Sally managed to hold back her disgust.

"Oh no, not the baz…" Daoud's voice trailed as Rachel raised her eyebrows. He tried another tack. "Why don't you send…." until realising the futility of arguing he finished with, "Please, at least be back to walk up the hill in time for a picnic, no?" Rachel smiled sweetly at her husband and he turned back to Sally. "Shimla is too beautiful. We will walk up through the woods and from the top we will see the whole town. I think you will like to go there. It will take maybe one hour to walk, maybe a little more with the children." He looked down at the sandal she dangled from her toes. "You have shoes?" She assured him she had. She'd seen women in the park wearing sneakers with their elegant shalwar kameezes and soon learned that there were times when looks didn't count. Her own sneakers were in her bag.

It wasn't yet seven when, with the boys left in Yalda's care, Rachel led her to the bazaar through streets already jammed with rickshaws and carts, trucks and bicycles, buses and trucks, so that, along with other pedestrians, they squeezed through gaps in the congestion and inhaled air tinged with diesel fumes, cooking oil and hot bread. Yet it felt fresher than Lahore and she felt more energetic than she had for weeks. Sidestepping a flat, tyre imprinted bunch of bananas Rachel stopped by a huge urn strapped to the back of a bicycle. "Aha! Tea." She handed over a white china cup brimming with pale pink steaming liquid. "I don't think you will have had this before. It is Kashmiri chai, made with cardamom and milk and sometimes with almonds too."

Sally sniffed, then sipped. "It's, er, it's different." She drank more deeply and gasped as the sickly drink brought tears to her eyes as she sought to swallow the scalding liquid as quickly as possible.

"Oh Sallyji, please don't drink it. I can see you don't like it. Here, give it to me." Handing a coin and the cup back to the vendor, Rachel said something in rapid Urdu that stretched his walnut wrinkled mouth into a gap-toothed smile.

They moved on, past stalls laden with everything from chickens in cages to plastic buckets to woven hats. Goods were more functional than in the glitz and glamour of the Lahore markets, and more randomly distributed. A tailor, resting against his sewing machine, smoked a cigarette and brushed water from his sandal as the greengrocer next to him watered bunches of coriander and piles of shiny peppers. Another man stirred an enormous metal bowl of white liquid over a brazier and Sally tugged Rachel's hand. "What's that?"

"It's yogurt. Or at least it will be, when it's ready." A rack of metal shelving contained more of the large bowls. "Look, that's it. Would you like some?"

She looked dubiously at the dirt crusted layer and frowned. "Sammy likes yogurt; is it safe?"

"We'll get it from below the surface. The flies sit only on the top."

Clutching a small, tightly knotted plastic bag of clean white yogurt, they moved on. "I'm amazed they sell this stuff in bags. How on earth do people get it home safely?"

Rachel shrugged. "People bring bowls. It's normal."

Along the street a small crowd watched two men seated cross-legged on a raised platform flip and flatten balls of dough into round discs against a paddle, then slap them inside the smoking holes of tandoori ovens. Rachel pushed Sally to the front so she could watch as the dough expanded, balloon-like as it cooked. Toasted flour singed her nostrils as within minutes, the baker hooked and flicked the discs to a youth, who bagged the steaming bread and passed it to waiting hands. A few minutes later they too had acquired a steam filled bag and edging their way through the constantly renewing crowd they shared a hot chapati.

"Mmm, delicious."

"Irresistible!" Rachel agreed. "Come," she said, "we'll go home now, but a different way so you can see some more."

Sally stopped next to an old stone archway. "Look at that! What is it?"

"It's municipal offices." Rachel rubbed flour from her fingers against the stones. "It used be the Gurdwara. The Sikh temple. It was finished only a few years before Partition, and has been deserted since the Sikhs left. Beautiful, no? It is why the bazaar is called the Gurdwara bazaar." She pointed to the stones above the arch. "Can you see that writing?" Faded script decorated the stone. "That's Punjabi. It says 'God lives in this place'." Eating the last piece of her bread she urged Sally on. "Come, we must go. There are many abandoned temples. You've seen the old Hindu temple in Model Town, near to Daniel's home? Next to the market?"

She'd wondered at the origin of the red brick ruin that gave home to a number of families and considered the stories it and this Gurdwara might tell when, created in faith they'd been abandoned in faith too.

Humidity slowed the Shimla Hill walk to a lumbering trudge, and sipping water Sally understood why Daoud had warned her. Meanwhile the twins, oblivious to the heat and energetic as ever, raced backwards and forwards whilst Sammy protested at being held captive in his buggy. Sally was grateful when Daoud instructed the older boys to take turns pushing Sammy up the hill until, as they cleared the trees and arrived on an open, grassy slope, the gentlest of breezes stirred pine scented air, and the majestic vista Daoud had talked of opened itself before them. All was worthwhile. Daoud and the older boys went to meet Farouq and their grandmother from the bus, Rachel spread a picnic rug and, captivated by the views, Sally took out her camera. Tiny yellow flowers poked through the pine-needle carpet and Sally focused her camera on them, then keeping her back to the ugly low hotel behind sought out tiny squares of green roofed bungalows squatting untidily amongst apple and pomegranate orchards below, and further below, the sprawl of Abbottabad that packed itself into the valley floor. She clicked and clicked, capturing the images and trying to imprint it all into her mind to be written into her journal later. In front of her, conifers framed a clear blue sky, and opposite, haze-blurred hilltops fringed the saucer-shaped valley. Delighted to be released, Sammy ran crazily after the twins as she knelt to capture the natural composition of them running into the magnificent scenery that was too beautiful not to record. Absorbed in the moment she was unaware of Rachel's voice. "Sally! Sallyji," Rachel touched her shoulder. "Meet Arif. He's a good friend of ours. He's enjoying Shimla today, too."

Looking up towards the sun she saw little more than the silhouette of a tall slender man dressed elegantly in well-cut jeans and checked shirt, but when he moved to cast shade on her face she saw dark – almost black – eyes that smiled into greying temples.

"Assalamu Alykum." Even his voice was beautiful.

She didn't move. Caught unawares, she hesitated, confused, and felt her eyes widen as his narrowed before reality asserted itself. Rising quickly to her feet and forgetting it was offensive for a man to shake the hand of a woman, she held out her hand. He glanced towards Rachel then placed his hand on his chest, inclining his head slightly as he did so. A blush coloured her cheeks and she dropped her proffered hand to merely straighten her shalwar kameez. "Assal...erm, Wa'alaka salam." The exchange lasted seconds but each slow motion detail imprinted itself into her mind.

Rachel looked at her curiously and then turned to Arif. "Er…. would you join us for lunch? It's only a simple picnic, but we have plenty."

He spoke English well, if slightly accented. "That's too kind of you. Shukria, thank you. But we're having lunch at the restaurant. Faiza and the children are waiting for me. I came out to enjoy the view but it's too difficult for the wheelchair out here." Turning, he excused himself to Sally and made to leave, then paused. "But please bring your guests for tea whilst they're in Abbottabad. Perhaps tomorrow? I'll telephone."

Bidding each other 'Khuda Hafiz', Rachel waited until Arif had moved out of earshot. "Sally?" It wasn't a question and Sally knew what she meant.

"What?"

"Are you all right? Why didn't you greet Arif?"

"I did! Well, no. I.., well, no, I don't know. I forgot what to say in Urdu." She busied herself, adjusting her camera and cursing for behaving like a Victorian heroine, swooning at the first eligible bachelor – which he was unlikely to be – and giving him reason to believe she was both rude and silly. And why, she wondered, was her heart racing like it was?

As she'd done every night, she lay in bed and invited the day's events to lull her to sleep. But tonight's recollections started with and stalled at Arif, elaborating so that he accepted the invitation to join the picnic, sat next to her and talked about Abbottabad, his work, her trip, books they'd both read. He peeled an orange, and passed segments to her until she insisted he ate some too. It was an agreeable meander until common sense brought reality back into focus. Nevertheless, she hoped the invitation to tea would materialise, so that she could replace her false impression with that of a mature, interesting and intelligent woman. Forcing her mind elsewhere, she re-lived the bazaar; the tea, the chapattis, the yogurt. They'd used the chapattis as spoons, scooping the salty sour yogurt and unexpectedly delicious biryani into their mouths. When Rachel had first opened the flasks of biryani even the tantalizing aromas of cinnamon, cardamom and roasted chicken hadn't tempted her and she'd denied hunger, insisting on a small portion which she'd then lathered with yogurt and tested gingerly for Sammy. To her surprise the flavour seduced her to a second taste, and with her mouth watering she'd bashfully confessed and gratefully accepted a full helping before demanding the recipe from Rachel.

"The secret is in the spices, and of course, the way it's cooked." Yalda had told her. "Everyone has secret ingredients and no-one will tell you how to make it."

Sally was supervising Sammy's afternoon milk when Daoud announced an invitation to tea with Arif.

Her pulse quickened. "I expect we'll meet his family?" she asked tentatively.

"You didn't meet them yesterday?" Daoud sounded surprised. "Ah, well, Faiza is Arif's wife, Pazir is their daughter, and there is a son, Karim, a nice boy. The twins like him too much."

Faiza. His wife. She chastised herself for the disappointment. Of course he was married! "Arif mentioned a wheelchair – has someone had an accident?"

"No, not an accident, Faiza's been sick for a long time. She's had many troubles but now she has Encephalitis." Sally's raised eyebrow brought forth an explanation. "It's a brain virus that is usually not too serious. But Faiza is not responding well to treatment. She's not very strong." He nudged his glasses up his nose. "She may not join us this afternoon. She gets very tired. But if she does, don't worry; it isn't contagious. We think she contracted it from a bite, possibly a mosquito." He lowered his voice. "The poor lady has suffered too much in the past few years. There was a third child; a little girl, but she died from measles when she was two years old! It was a terrible shock. Faiza became too depressed after she lost her daughter; it was a bad time. I don't think she has come to terms with it, even though it must be three years now."

Sally shivered; no mother could hear of the death of a child and not feel the shoes on her own feet. "Oh, Daoud! That's awful! But Faiza will recover from the En…sorry, what's it called?"

"Encephalitis. Yes, I think so. She has some new drugs now." He sighed. "It has been difficult for them all. I hope Faiza is able to join us; I think you'll like her. And she'll be interested to meet you. She has a brother in England, studying, so she'll probably want to ask about your home."

Sally wiped milk from Sammy's mouth then took his cup

to the kitchen where Rachel was washing vegetables. "Did you hear? We're going to see your friend for tea, er... he's called Arif, I think?"

"Arif. Yes. He's a colleague of Daoud's. I met him when my first husband was in the hospital; Arif was his doctor." She elaborated. "When I left Jabil's home I got a job at the same hospital. Nursing is good work for women – like teaching – and I had to earn some money. I'd been there for only a few days when I saw Arif again; he was with Daoud. And, well, the rest you know. Later I met Faiza too. We sometimes have picnics, or go out together."

"You didn't tell me you're a nurse."

Rachel laughed. "I'm not! I didn't even start the training; I met Daoud and married him and didn't need to work anymore."

"But you could have still become a nurse, couldn't you?"

Rachel wiped around the sink mechanically. "I suppose I could, but it wasn't appropriate. I got married." She dried her hands and hung the towel on a hook. "Right. We'd better get changed and make sure the boys are clean. They like to play with Arif's son, Karim. He's six years older but always finds something for them."

In front of the mirror Sally pulled a brush through her hair and pondered the parallels and differences in her and Rachel's upbringing. Having grown up in England, each with a Pakistani father though of course, Rachel's mother had also been Pakistani, the similarities ended. Rachel had been wrapped in Pakistani culture despite being in England. Where Sally had continued from Primary School to the local comprehensive, Rachel had been educated with other Pakistani families so that from eleven years or so, her friendships and contacts would have been restricted to her own culture. Her father, Sally realised, who she'd believed to be a traditionalist, had modified his principles to embrace England and though a disciplinarian in all things, particularly education, he'd encouraged her and her brother equally. Shaping his face into the mirror next to hers, she silently thanked him.

Arif was waiting at his compound gates. "Asalaam Alaykum. You have walked. I thought you must be lost!" He led them through a neat garden to a shady veranda where a long table had been laid for tea and a girl of around twelve was manoeuvring a wheelchair into position. The child was tall, like her father who, she couldn't help noticing, had dark hair that curled neatly into the nape of his neck. He turned and Sally looked away quickly.

"Let me introduce my family." Arif raised an arm towards the wheelchair. "My wife, Faiza, and my daughter, Pazir." An elegant lady came through a door. "Ah, and my mother, Sultana Bibi." A boy of around ten was introduced as his son, Karim.

Sally was directed towards a seat to the left of Faiza who, she could see, was aged beyond her years. Colourful cushions in her wheelchair accentuated pale skin that hung loosely from her arms and through her thinning hair, the shape of her white scalp showed clearly. Though warned of Faiza's fragile state she was shocked and wondered what miracle was needed for her to recover. She took the proffered skeletal hand. "It's very nice to meet you. Thank you for inviting me to your home."

Faiza's watery eyes blinked as she nodded slightly and indicated the seat one past her own so that Pazir, having secured the wheelchair brake and offered her hand in an unexpectedly mature formal gesture, took the seat immediately to her mother's left, cleverly obscuring Sally's view as she cut food into mouth sized morsels and held the teacup to her mother's mouth.

Arif's mother excused the younger children to a separate tea indoors, complete with their own version of a French patisserie style chocolate cake like the one that Sally had seen sitting on a marble slab on the sideboard, and handed delicate china tea cups and plates of tiny sandwiches around the table. The twins, delighted to be free of formality, had taken Sammy and disappeared with Karim whose homemade peepshow theatre was providing fun for them all. The toy reminded Sally of something she'd once made with her father. They'd decorated it with painted sponge trees and matchbox buildings, and added cut-out characters on lollypop sticks. Arif passed a cup from his mother to Sally. "Forgive me; the name of your son?"

"He's Sammy. Well, Samuel really, after his grandfather." She thanked him for the tea. "Are you sure your son won't mind him being with them? He's still a baby."

"Karim will take care of him. Samuel is a good name; Christian." Sally glanced towards the house. "I am Muslim." he said, sensing her enquiry. "It is what I was brought up to be. I find many questions but it provides me with a moral compass. And you? I assume you are Christian?"

Sally hadn't felt a religious affinity since attending Sunday school as a child and found the cultural religiosity in Pakistan disconcerting. It intrigued her to hear Arif say he questioned the doctrine. "Like you, I was brought up with a strong religious code, but in my case it was Christian. My father was and my mother still is a believer." But she wouldn't claim to be a Christian. "In England it's different. Religion is personal. I think that here it's wider than that; more integrated."

Arif spread his hands wide. "That's a whole conversation. We could talk for many hours! You are right. Religion isn't only personal here in Pakistan. It governs all aspects of our lives. Personal, social, economic, political. Everything. We are Muslim; my wife, my children. And me too. It is evidence of my respectability." Arif smiled. "This is too serious for teatime. Please, tell me something about you. What do you think of our country?"

She hardly knew where to start. "There are so many faces of Pakistan and I've seen so few. But of course, meeting my father's family has been very special, and now that I've decided to stay longer I'm hoping to learn much more."

"Five months! There is time to learn a lot." He expounded the delights of Pakistan. "You have seen the landscapes here in the Hazara region but you should see more; Peshawar, The Khyber, Chitral, Shandur. It is different. Though Lahore is also interesting. I expect you have visited the Badshahi Mosque, the Red Fort, and the old city in Lahore. Are they not exceptional?" Sally nodded. "Shalimar Gardens? Jahangir's tomb?" She shook her head. "Ah, you must go and see the inlaid marble that is as beautiful as the Taj Mahal. Few visitors see it; you must make sure you visit." Brushing crumbs from the table he continued. "And I'm sure you have wondered about our politics, our government, our corruption." He rolled his eyes and his tone belied the gravity of his words. "Oh yes, there can be no denying. What you in the West call corruption is a way of life here, for the Government, the Army, Business. Everywhere. Even in sport where perhaps you might expect to find good 'sportsmanship' eh?" Arif's mother coughed her disapproval of the conversation and he acknowledged her with a slight nod. "Of course, not everyone is corrupt; some of us find it most distasteful. But even where it is not necessary it does exist. For example, when it happens in the sports where we are world leaders, it is an insult to our magnificent sportsmen. You watch our national pastime; cricket? And we are famous for our hockey. And polo too. Have you seen polo?" His eyes sparkled. "You must before you leave. It is a majestic sight!"

"I've seen the horses being trained in Race Course Park." She'd taken Sammy to the Lahore park several times. "But no, I've never seen polo played. Have you played?"

He grinned. "Oh yes, I like it too much. You know, we have

to change the ball many times because when we hit it so hard it is no longer a ball; it becomes... I don't know the word in English, but it has many sides!"

"Your English is impressive," Sally assured him, and told him about a film she'd once seen. "The film starred Steve McQueen. He played polo when he wasn't pulling off bank robberies."

"Yes, I saw this film too; I remember McQueen and also I think Faye Dunaway. What was the film called?"

Sally thought for a moment. "It was 'The Thomas Crown Affair'. I saw it maybe ten years ago. Do you remember the song *Windmills of your Mind?*"

"Ah yes! *The autumn leaves turning to the colour of her hair.*" A cough halted his bad singing and he ignored his daughter's giggle. "Have you visited a Sufi shrine and seen them whirl, crazed with drugs? Or watched hijras dance at a festival? Or drunk gin and tonic or beer that is brewed here in a country where the drinking of alcohol is prohibited? Yes, we are a crazy nation. Do you know how many languages are spoken here?" She shook her head. "No, I don't know either, I don't think anyone does. Some are only spoken in the mountains. Some are not recorded. But my dear, there are more than twenty in this province alone."

She realised why she'd failed to understand voices around her in Abbottabad. "Urdu isn't spoken here?"

"You speak Urdu?"

"I'm learning."

He nodded his head. "People do speak Urdu here and English is spoken in schools and businesses. But people speak Hindko and some speak Pashto. My wife is from this region; she speaks Hindko and of course our lingua franca, Urdu. But she doesn't speak English."

Sally saw Faiza glance at her husband and speak to Pazir, who translated her mother's words. "My mother apologise she not speak English but say she welcome you in our home."

Sally thanked her, "Shukria," then answered a few more translated questions about English weather and Birmingham, where Faiza's brother was studying to become an accountant.

When Faiza spoke again Sally looked at Pazir, waiting for her to translate what she assumed to be another question, but Pazir left her tea and manoeuvred the wheelchair from the room.

Arif's mother apologised. "Faiza is unwell."

Arif's eyes followed his wife from the room then he spoke quietly to Daoud. "The inflammation is not responding to medication and she has little strength to fight it herself." The two doctors switched to Urdu but their expressions and tone conveyed the gravity of Faiza's illness and it wasn't long before Rachel thanked Arif and his mother for the tea and said they should be leaving.

As she packed their bags the following day, Sally thought of Faiza's skeletal frame. Wasted bodies were found in famine or war zones, places where death was inevitable. They were not found in family homes. She recalled a line from *Macbeth*, learned for an English literature exam many years previously; *the way to dusty death. Out, out, brief candle! Life's but a walking shadow.* She breathed in Sammy's fresh air-dried shirts to dispel the musty humidity of the room, a smell she associated with the police officers, a man and a woman, who'd brought news of her father's fatal accident. She'd backed away from their sympathy into the living room curtains and gulped the dust of them into her lungs, hating the officers as much as the faceless driver who'd killed her father. Tucking the last of Sammy's clean clothes into her bag she saw Pazir's serious eyes and feared for her.

Daniel tapped on the bedroom door. "Arif talked to me today. He has something to ask you."

The lightness of his tone was intriguing. "Oh? Well, I've finished here." She followed Daniel into the family room where the rest of the family looked amused and curious at the same time.

Daniel spoke. "You like Abbottabad?" he asked.

"Yes, very much. I like the hills, and the climate. And I've enjoyed being here with you." Her curiosity was growing. "Why do you ask?"

"You said that you would like to do some work?" She nodded. She was intrigued. "We are wondering if you might like to spend a little time here in Abbottabad. Arif is asking if you might teach English to his children. He wants them to speak without an accent and says you speak it like an Englishwoman." She chuckled; did he think of her as Pakistani? "He would like to come and talk before you leave for Lahore, but does not wish to impose or offend. If you do not wish to discuss it he will understand."

Teaching children wasn't the kind of work she'd envisaged. But it couldn't be too difficult, she thought, after all, she'd been an "A" student at school. "I…. Well, I don't know." A focus, and of course, some income were attractive but there were practical difficulties. "How can I? It would need more than a few weeks to be effective; I'd need to live in Abbottabad. Daniel, you and Yalda have invited me to live with you in Lahore; we've made plans. And what about Sammy? I have him to think of him, too."

Daoud hit the core of the situation. "Yes, there are a number of things that need addressing. Living with Daniel and Yalda or living with us, it is the same thing." Rachel nodded her agreement gleefully. "But first you must decide if you would like to do this teaching of English."

Pazir's serious face came to mind, and then Karim with his theatre box. She'd liked the children and her immediate instinct had been positive. Already her mind was itching to create games and dramas to teach them. And much as she enjoyed being with Yalda, Saima and Aamina, there was a strong and mutual bond with Rachel. "Yes," she admitted, "I would like to do it. If it's possible."

Once the family machine moved into action any practical problems she'd foreseen dissolved. She'd stay with Rachel and Daoud and they'd care for Sammy whilst she worked. In return Sally would help the twins and the older boys improve their English too. In less than a week her and Sammy's belongings had been brought to her in Abbottabad and a time-table of teaching had been agreed. During the day she planned lessons, seizing on ideas from things the children said they liked to do, and as school closed she went to Arif's house to teach Pazir and Karim. Sammy, who liked nothing more than to be in the middle of everything to do with the twins, stayed happily behind.

At the end of the second week Arif arrived home earlier than usual, and listened to Pazir reading a story she'd written. "So the elephant painted his toenails pink to match the marble stairs in the palace, and everyone thought his feet were much smaller than they really were. No one ever again said he had big feet." She flushed with pride as her father applauded and asked if it was her own story. "Yes," she admitted in English, "I wrote it for Sammy and the twins. Sally is going to read it to them at bedtime."

"Well, they're lucky boys!" Arif turned to his son. "And you Karim, have you written a story for the twins too?"

Karim was less pleased. "No. I'm writing instructions to make a box theatre," he said in Urdu, "but it is too difficult."

Sally read what he'd written. "This is good Karim, but I think you need some new English words to finish it. You're very lucky because I know what some of them are. On Monday we'll finish this together."

Dismissing the children, Arif complimented Sally on her teaching and then enquired if she was still enjoying Abbottabad. "Have you been up to Thandiani yet?" he asked and hearing that she hadn't, recommended a visit. "It is very close, twenty five miles only, but the road is steep and winding so it takes more than one hour." She wondered if – hoped – he might be inviting her to join him and the family. "Thandiani means 'cold', and because it is high, it provides a very nice escape from the summer heat. It is very beautiful, with pine trees and grass so soft you have to keep touching it. We would take you but it is too far for Faiza at the moment. Perhaps Daoud will take you. I will talk to him."

She promised that she would talk to Daoud too, and then asked after Faiza. "How is your wife? I haven't seen her this week?"

"I think she is not any worse which is perhaps an improvement, Alhamdulillah."

That night Faiza's heart stopped beating. It simply hadn't the strength to carry on and in sleep her life came to an end. As was the custom, she was buried before nightfall and after the funeral prayers Rachel and Sally returned home leaving Daoud to accompany the men to the burial. Taking tea to the veranda they sat silently, each immersed in her own thoughts.

As a tear slipped down Rachel's cheek Sally put a hand on her arm. "I'm sorry. It's hard to lose a friend, especially one so young."

Rachel didn't respond immediately, and then she spoke quietly. "You know Sally, I never really knew Faiza well, but I liked her and yes, she was a friend. She was too young to die. The children are so young. I know that Arif's mother lives with them, but it will be hard for them all. Children need their mother." Her voice faltered. "Something like this makes you think of your own life, doesn't it? I wonder how my son feels not to have a mother."

"Oh Rachel. Maybe one day you'll be with him again."

"No. It cannot happen. He was told I have died too." Rachel shuddered. "I can't bear to think what would happen to the twins if I died." Sally opened her mouth to protest but Rachel silenced her. "It is possible, Sally. Daoud's first wife died and his boys miss her you know. She's still their mother."

Sally nodded. "But Daoud's boys have you."

"They do. But I'm not their mother. They call me auntie." Rachel shared a confidence. "I'm glad they call me auntie – I don't want them to call me Ammi. I never tire of hearing Tariq and Sohail call 'Ammi' but I'm selfish, Sally, I don't want to be mother to Daoud's boys. I cannot be their mother and they cannot be my sons." A small sob escaped. "He is fifteen years old now. My son. I saw him last year when we visited Peshawar; he's a man and I haven't seen him grow. I watched the house, Sally. It is very wrong that he believes his mother is dead."

Sally agreed. "Maybe when he is older? You could tell him the truth, when he's older."

But Rachel shook her head. "To him I am dead. He will never look for me, and how can I go to him? He won't know me and his grandparents will tell him I'm just a crazy woman."

Sally's mind went to Sammy, growing up without John, who she was almost sure was his father.

As if her hearing her thoughts, Rachel asked, "Will you tell Sammy about his father when he wants to know?"

What would she tell her son when he asked that important question? "It's difficult Rachel. I…." It may have been the emotion of the day or perhaps the impossibility of the question that caused the sob to break free.

"Oh Sally! I'm sorry." Rachel put an arm round her shoulders and the two women held each other, wrapped in sorrows that had little to do with the funeral they'd attended.

After a few moments Sally spoke. "No, no. It's all right. The truth is…" Shame had restrained her since arriving in Pakistan but shared vulnerability encouraged her. "The truth is, I'm not absolutely sure that Sammy's father is John." Seeing surprise though not repulsion on Rachel's face, she continued. "I think he is, because Sammy's so much like him, but I, well… I made a dreadful mistake." She told Rachel of her humiliation and remorse that kept her fears a secret, and how John's confusion over blood groupings had exposed the truth. "I can't imagine how I will ever tell Sammy what I did," she finished.

Rachel nodded. "Oh my goodness, it's difficult." She thought for a moment. "Perhaps you could just tell him about the blood group mistake? Why should you tell him about the other man?"

"That wouldn't be the truth. And if he ever found John…. well, what then?"

"You loved John, didn't you? I can tell by the way you talk about him. I think you still love him."

She shook her head. "No, I don't anymore. It's hard to be sure because I did love him, very much, and I still love what was, if you understand what I mean. And I'm sorry for what I did. If things had been different we would probably have married eventually and we'd have been a family and would probably have been very happy. But coming here, to Pakistan, has freed me. It's easy to stay with the past, but things do change. John was special, but I've changed. Actually, I think I was already changing before we split up."

"Maybe I should ask Daniel or Daoud to arrange a marriage for you?"

In the seriousness of their conversation she didn't see that Rachel was teasing her. "No! You mustn't even think of it."

"Arranged marriages work very well. And a Pakistani

marriage would keep you here in Pakistan!" Rachel grinned.

"No!" Shocked, Sally demanded, "How can you say that after your own experience? Your first marriage was terrible!"

"Well, yes. But that was a deceitful arrangement. My husband married me out of duty." Rachel glanced at the door and her eyes became serious again. "My husband…. he was having an affair." It was an afternoon for shared secrets. "With a man."

Sally thought she'd misheard. "A man! Are you sure?"

"I saw them. I'd been to the market with my mother-in-law and returned early. I found them in our room. The man left quickly and my husband was very angry with me; he told me that I would be killed if I told anyone what I'd seen or if I said anything to anyone. He wasn't lying. I continued to be his wife and told no-one. Even Daoud doesn't know. Please Sally, don't tell anyone." Rachel's hand clutched hers. "Promise me, you'll keep it to yourself? Please."

"But he's dead, Rachel. He can't threaten you now."

"I know, but my son must never know that his father was… like that. It would be too bad. Please, Sally, you must promise not to tell anyone."

"But he can't have been, well… you had a son."

"I became pregnant very quickly, in the first month. He was so pleased when I told him and I thought he loved me. But after that he didn't want… you know…. with me. At first I thought it was because he didn't want to harm the baby and I was touched by his thoughtfulness. I thanked God for his goodness. But as time passed, and after my son was born, he avoided sleeping with me. We didn't sleep together like that ever again. Sally, he only married me to please his parents and to protect himself. I was probably chosen because I was an outsider, from England." She pulled loose threads in her sleeve. "I know you see men holding hands. Even policemen. But that is friendship.

Women hold hands too. And we kiss each other. It is the Pakistani way; men for men and women for women. We don't mix until we marry. But for a man to be with a man? It's against the law; the law of nature, the law of our land and the law of religion. If people had known about Jabil it would have been very bad. I think his father suspected and was frightened, so he pushed for a marriage to protect him and of course, their reputation. If it had become known, his family would have lost face, and if the police knew it would have been very bad for him. He could have been lashed or even stoned. So you see, having a wife and especially a child made him safe."

Rachel's story belonged in history. It was, after all, nineteen eighty three. "Couldn't you have refused the marriage? Didn't you want to stay in England?"

Rachel's eyes widened. "How would I know who to marry? It's a big decision. My parents were wise and experienced. They didn't force me to marry Jabil, but I trusted their decision." Sally wanted to ask how her parents had known Jabil but Rachel held up a hand. "I know what you are going to say. You are going to say it was a loveless marriage. You are very wrong. A marriage is based on respect, on compatibility, on mutual expectation. These things start the flame of love that grows steadily to sustain the man and his wife throughout their lives. It is not like the fierce flame that flares up and then burns out quickly." Rachel threw her hands into the air and clapped her hands. "Poof! Gone."

"But your marriage didn't grow."

"Of course not. It wasn't based on respect, compatibility or mutual expectation was it? But my parents didn't know that. Jabil was the nephew of a man my father had known as a boy; our grandparents had been in business together. "

"When did you first meet your husband?"

"He came to England with his family, to visit me. I met him at the same time as my parents did."

"And you liked him?" She couldn't grasp the idea of marrying a man she didn't know.

"I thought he was handsome. He was educated, and well mannered. I thought, yes, this man will give me a good life. It will be happy." She gave a wry smile. "And it was the right decision at the time. To reject him would have saddened my parents very much, and anyway, there was no reason to do so. Sally, life is about compromise and understanding. Good family life comes from balancing the needs of everyone; it leads to happiness. When I was a girl my parents wanted me to be happy, which meant marrying and having children. My mother wasn't educated. She had no idea about study and university. I didn't question it. It wasn't an imposition; it was just growing up. And getting married wasn't an imposition either, it was what I expected and accepted."

Sally baulked at Rachel's reasoning but she was beginning to understand it. "Your marriage to Daoud is a good marriage. It wasn't arranged. He was your own choice."

Rachel's eyes twinkled. "We were wise and experienced enough to consider a second marriage for ourselves. But we sought our parents' approval."

Over the coming days Sally mulled over Rachel's words and speculated how love, articulated like this, was meaningful. She and John had expressed love, but had only discussed it in an abstract way, seeing it as some ethereal quality that enriched their lives rather than providing worldly guidelines with which to shape their future. She'd never taken love far beyond the starry eyed, idyllic beliefs established in childhood and adolescence defined by romantic songs, literature and films. Boy meets girl, flaming passion, the rosy glow, the violins. And whilst rationally she knew this to be illusory, subconsciously she'd searched for the flame and finding it with John made it reality. But she'd been enticed by a false flame. If – was it only two and a half years ago – she'd had respect, compatibility, and mutual expectation in mind, and if…

'If', her father had used to say, was a big word.

With Pazir and Karim's grandmother away, Sally had agreed to stay with the children until Arif returned from work, but with Sammy there, and his baby-talk Urdu already better than his English and easily understood by the other children, the English lesson deviated into Urdu again. "English please. I will only reply if you ask me in English!"

"My father will like too much my biriyani." Pazir had laboriously translated the recipe in her neat handwriting. "But he is old fashioned," she told Sally, "He cannot cook anything. I am going to write a cookery book for him."

"Your father will like …" Sally prompted, and waited for Pazir to correct herself, then agreed to supervise the cooking. "You can teach me too, because I need to be taught the secrets of biryani, and Karim and Sammy can help."

Sammy tried to climb on his mother's knee, insisting he too, could cook biriyani, but Pazir shook her head vigorously. "I can make the most delicious biriyani, but Karim and Sammy can't cook. Karim is a boy and Sammy, you're too small!"

"Nahin choti, larka barra!"

"In English, Sammy!" Karim laughed.

Consoling her son that he was indeed, not a baby but a big boy, Sally nodded her head at Pazir in mock agreement. "Yes, it is a problem. Boys cannot cook. And what happens? They grow into men who cannot cook either. You would think that someone should teach them before they become men, wouldn't you?"

Seeing the wisdom of Sally's words, Pazir agreed. "But they have to keep the secret of the biriyani," she insisted.

"Sammy, it's the black bits we don't want. We eat the white bits." Pazir scolded as Sammy's plump fingers scattered rice whilst Karim saw only amusement as peppercorns cascaded to the floor.

By the time Arif arrived home the kitchen had been cleaned and Sammy had been necessarily bathed. But the meal was ready and Arif's praise brought a rarely seen flush to Pazir's face. As Sally cleared the remains of the meal and the children settled in front of the TV she practiced Urdu on Arif, regaling him with tales of the cooking process. "You should have seen Karim grinding the spices," she laughed, "they were flying everywhere and he sneezed so strongly that you'll be relieved to know we started again!"

Arif's laugh triggered his mild, nervous sounding cough and then he thanked her for staying late. "Please, stay, and take tea," he invited and settling into a chair with her cup she prepared to enjoy his company. She'd noticed his hair was slightly longer and thought it suited him. Then she saw his solemn face and realised he had something to say, that this wasn't the sort of friendly chat they'd often had. She tensed. Were the children not making enough progress? Or were the lessons not sufficiently disciplined?

His voice, too, was serious. "I think you will be planning to leave us soon?"

"Yes." She knew he was aware that she would soon be returning to England. "I'd like to have some time with Daniel and Yalda in Lahore before I go; perhaps my last two weeks."

"You have been here now for almost four months." She waited to hear what was on his mind. "The work has gone well; Pazir, especially, has improved her English, for which I thank you. You are good with my children and they like you too..er, very much." He smoothed his hands along his trouser legs and coughed again. Sally waited. "You and I, Sally, we are similar in age." The disparity went unchallenged as Sally pondered the personal comparison. "I admit that I am… a little older, but not so much. As you know, I am a widower. I am able to offer a good home, and I would be father to Sammy. And of course, as a doctor, am fortunate to have a stable and secure livelihood." He stopped for a moment as if unsure of himself then took a deep breath. "Sally, I propose that we marry."

Sally blinked. Had she heard correctly?

"This is not good form and I apologise. It would have been better if I had first spoken with your mother but that is not possible. I have spoken with your uncle, Daoud. He has not objected and says I must speak to you directly." He paused, and then spoke less assuredly. "I am not sure of my words. Please forgive me."

As a proposal, it both astounded and thrilled Sally. Irrationally, and shockingly, she thought he must somehow have known of her nocturnal fantasies. But he couldn't possibly have, and she focused on what he'd said. Yes, he was a widower. But so recently, only three months had passed. Her voice returned. "I'm flattered. But Faiza… It's too soon."

He repeated himself. "It's because you plan to leave that I speak now." Apologising if he had offended her, he assured her that marriage needn't take place until a more appropriate time, and reaffirmed it was her imminent departure that forced his untimely proposal.

But what of love? He hadn't mentioned love. During the months she'd been teaching the children there'd been no indication of regard, romantic or otherwise, and the proposal was coolly rational. Had he too, she wondered, been indulging in a hidden interest that might be deemed inappropriate? The thought brought a blush to her cheeks.

Arif spoke. "I do not expect an answer yet. Please take some time. You will have questions. My religion perhaps? Though many who marry into the faith convert, I would not ask it of you. It is not necessary. Though it is the tradition, The Quran asks only that a Muslim marries 'people of the book" which includes Christians – and Jews too. My faith is important to me, but I would not ask that of you; it is too important." A white handkerchief appeared in his hand. "I know that your culture expects marriage to be a union of….," he coughed, "hmm, of love. I believe this too. My marriage with Faiza was a good marriage. I learned to love her as she did me. I have a regard for you. And you are a beautiful woman. I will come to love you too." He mopped his face with the handkerchief. "I would feel better if you could say something."

Her hand trembled on the chair arm. "I….I'm…I don't know what to say. I'm flattered by your proposal, but my plans don't – didn't – include a future in Pakistan." Her words sounded negative; she needed to think, to consider the impact of his suggestion on her and Sammy, on her family and friends, in England as well as in Pakistan. Her mother's voice told her, 'It's a crazy idea! Are you mad?' yet she almost accepted because of its recklessness.

"I hope I have not offended you?"

"No. No, of course not. I'm just…a little surprised. I need to think."

"Of course. I would prefer a considered response."

The smile that crinkled his eyes and reflected his uncertainty was, Sally thought, incredibly attractive.

A hint of autumn chilled the night air but Sally refused a taxi, choosing instead to walk and rationalise her thoughts before she joined the others. It was an outrageous proposal, and she wondered how different it might have been if he'd known of her fantasies. An image of Arif, dropping passionately to one knee was a joke that Sally might have once shared with Diane, yet would shock Rachel.

Rachel's words came to her; respect, compatibility, mutual expectation; the foundations of marriage. And Arif's proposal suddenly made sense. It was carefully considered, as she might have prepared a proposal for the board, those many moons ago. But there were no violins and she wondered how much she needed them.

Over the coming week she tried to visualise life with Arif. He was calm and reliable; a rock to her uncertainties. But he was sombre. Humour was important; would they laugh together? He'd laughed at Karim's efforts with the spices, and their conversations had often been animated. His recent widowhood was good reason for solemnity, but a proposal, though serious, lent itself to hope and cheer. Didn't it? She wished her friend Diane was closer; she'd be calm, dispassionate, and honest. Rachel, she knew, could not be unbiased. And Daoud, as Arif's friend of many years, would find impartiality difficult. She had at times, imagined herself and Sammy living in Pakistan, but not seriously. Sammy had adapted to life in Pakistan very quickly, but what of his roots in England? And vague dreams of a man, even a husband, and perhaps another child had always been firmly set in England, with an interesting job and her mother. England was home, and Sammy's too. He might speak Urdu, but like her, he was English.

Would Arif accept her as a working wife? She couldn't be a housewife.

And what about the violins? Where were they?

And what of her mother? Sally swallowed. It would be painful for her mother, upsetting her deeply to have her daughter and grandson living so far away. She didn't travel much further than Hastings, and flying half-way across the world to visit her daughter would, Sally thought, never happen. If Pakistan was to become her home, she would have to travel to London at least once, if not twice every year.

But was her mother a reason to refuse a new life for herself and Sammy? Sammy was thriving in the company of aunts and uncles, and he loved Karim, and Rachel's twins too. And Pazir was already a big sister to him. He adored her. Earlier that day, when Sammy had slipped and fallen, it was Pazir who had tickled away his tears.

Sally tested new imaginings; Arif. Pazir and Karim. And Sammy. Here in Abbottabad. And she found it wasn't a bad picture. She'd discovered a family life here in Pakistan that she couldn't give Sammy in England. It was, she thought, time to look to the future.

CHAPTER 11

Pie and a Pint

The ceremony had already started when John crept into the back row of the Registery Office. Mouthing his thanks to a couple who let him pass along the row to an empty seat, he squinted into low autumn sunlight that painted enormous Georgian window patterns on the wooden floor and saw the sun-hazed backs of Diane and Malik who faced a narrow faced, bespectacled man. Malik was speaking, repeating words the man had said. "....why I, Malik Farmara Njai, may not be joined in matrimony..." He looked across rows of heads; there were more people than he'd expected. He scanned the rows; seven in front of him, six seats at each side, calculating that must be almost a hundred people present. He'd expected less with it being a Registery Office wedding. Two rows of hat-topped heads and suited shoulders lined the front right rows; Diane's family, he assumed, recognising her mother, half veiled in navy gauze. And a few rows behind, a row of women would be Diane's friends. He wondered if any of them were alone. The registrar was asking everyone to stand. He rose, then froze. The long dark hair. The red hat. The tilt of the head. Diane had told him that Sally and Sammy were in Pakistan! He gripped the back of the seat in front of him and released his breath. Leaning forward unobtrusively he tried to see, but she was partly obscured by others. Where, he wondered, was Sammy? Had she not brought him to the church? He swayed gently to the left then the right. He couldn't see a child. Was there a man? Women were at each side of her. He puzzled why Diane or

Malik hadn't told him. What were they thinking of? He looked back along the row he'd pushed into, wanting to leave. He'd slip away; miss the reception. The ceremony finished and Diane and Malik were walking along the carpet, coming towards the back rows, with their guests following out from the front. He couldn't escape. She'd pass whilst he was still in his row; she'd see him when she passed. He rubbed his damp palms against his jacket; saw the red dress, the hat. She'd lost weight, was thinner. He saw her face. It wasn't Sally. It was someone else. The eyes, the nose. The mouth. Not hers. John swallowed, shuddered, and breathed. How he could have mistaken this woman for Sally, he told himself, was unthinkable. She was different, so different.

Her name was Lisa and she was Diane's cousin. She taught music at a school in Bristol and played cello in a string quartet. He bought her a Bacardi and coke, then another. They danced a bit, and talked. Later, at the end of the evening, he took her home. And stayed.

The bar was quiet. A mournful looking middle aged man studied a pint of beer whilst an older couple warmed themselves next to the log fire. His father was already there, waiting for him and looking small, John thought, at the end of a carpet that had been designed to hide dirt. Seeing him stoop as he stood, he realised age was beginning to disguise the man he called his father. "Pie and a pint?" he asked.

Wiping foam from his upper lip, John murmured his appreciation. "Mmm. That's a good pint. Any messages from Mum?"

"Just her love. She said you'll be round on Monday to go over the accounts." He drank from a half-pint. "You're ok, then?"

"Sure. Yes, I'm fine."

"Busy weekend?"

"Mmm. Yes. Always is, these days."

Reaching over an adjoining table for an ash tray, he repeated. "So you're ok then?"

"Yes. I said so, didn't I?" If this was feeling all right, John thought sardonically, he wouldn't want to feel any worse. Life wore like a heavy overcoat that he wished he could take off occasionally.

"You did. Yes, you did. Could do with a holiday, eh?"

"Yeah. But no chance of that before January."

"You need a good number two, that's what you need." Michael smeared bright yellow mustard over a chunk of pork pie and popped it into his mouth. Within seconds his eyes were watering and he cleared mustard from the remaining morsel. "Oh dear me," he coughed, "that mustard bites back!" And knowing that, in only the second year of business, a good number two was a dream he changed the subject. "You went to Diane's wedding?"

"Mmm. Mum's flowers looked nice."

"Yes. She does a good job with flowers. Good time?"

John stubbed his cigarette into the ash tray. The bar was depressing; he wished they'd met somewhere else. "Ok."

"Sally there?"

"What's this? Twenty questions?"

"I just wondered – I thought she'd have been there, and... well, Sammy too, and well, your Mum and I, we wondered..."

"Dad, they're in Pakistan. So they couldn't come, but if they had, I wouldn't have gone." He watched another drinker join the man at the bar. "So, what was your day like? Golf?" He'd grown accustomed to the occasional seemingly nonchalant enquiries about Sally or Sammy and just as nonchalantly, he evaded their interest.

"I think he's yours, you know. I think he looked like you."

His father's voice had been low, almost inaudible. "It doesn't change anything, Dad. He's Sally's. And Sally has him. So I can't." The truth was that Sammy was a part of him in a way that he didn't understand. "I don't know if I'm Sammy's father but I think I might be. I couldn't have loved him like I did if he wasn't my child, could I? There must be something biological that makes that happen, isn't there? Surely, you can't love a child completely if he's not yours." Realising his gaff, John stopped. "Oh! Dad, I'm sorry. I'm really sorry. I didn't mean that you and Mum….. Look, I'm sorry."

Michael drained his glass. "I don't know if you can love a child of your own more than a child who isn't. That's the honest truth John. But we loved you as much as we could. We still do. But we didn't have a child of our own, so we can't know, can we?" Regret sat heavily on his face.

"I know, Dad. I haven't always made it easy for you, and I know you had to work hard with me. Maybe it would have been different if I'd been a newborn when you adopted me. I don't remember anything from before but there's a door, a locked door, and there's a child behind it who's me, knocking and asking to be let in. In the story of who I am, the first chapter is missing. I've looked at men and women in the street and wondered, 'are you my father, are you my mother?' You've no idea how many new beginnings I've given myself." His laugh was flat. "My great uncle? Rothko! My mother? A artist's muse, and a brilliant cook. My father, a dastardly bastard but irresistible. There's more, many more. They're just the good ones." He chewed pork pie, willing the jelly to melt in the warmth of his mouth, but which was, like the pastry, solid. He'd made pork pies, hand raising warm pastry round moulds, and reducing liquor from simmered pig's trotters to pour over the succulent chunks of meat. They tasted nothing like these lumps of hardened putty that needed mustard to make them edible. "This pie's rough, isn't it."

Not ready to be diverted, Michael continued. "Your mother and I, we don't know much about your real parents, but you have the adoption certificate and your birth certificate too. Their names are on them. You can find them if you want to."

"No. I don't want to." He couldn't explain that behind the locked door were fears of what he might find. "Hey, we're having a pint, not a psychotherapy session." He stood up. "My round. Another half, or a pint?"

His father caught his hand as he picked up the glass. "I'll listen if you want to talk to me. Or if not, you could talk to the man you saw when you were ill. He was helpful ..."

"Thanks. I'll think about it. But let's just have a drink now, eh? Half?"

Talk to a psychotherapist? Sure, he could talk about the voices he heard in his head and a psychotherapist would listen. But everyone had voices like that, and one of his told him he didn't need a psychotherapist. Given the last year, there'd be something wrong if he hadn't pondered the connections and parallels of his own and Sammy's childhoods. If he hadn't been saddened, disturbed, upset, he wouldn't have been human. A therapist might use scientific sounding words to describe thoughts but it didn't change anything; it didn't fill the gaps. Michael and Frances had reshaped his whats and ifs and buts and he knew he'd been lucky. He should be grateful for that luck, and at a higher level, he was. But deep inside the demanding voices that searched for truth gnawed at the voices of rationality and reason, and refused to let sleeping dogs lie. Or deceive.

CHAPTER 12

Almond Sherbet

Peeping through her veil into the wedding marquee as she passed, Sally looked in wonderment at marigolds and jasmine entwined with sparkling fairy lights and shimmering, flickering oil lamps. It was like a scene from the story she had, as a child, begged her father to read, over and again; *Scheherazade and the Arabian Nights*. Each time Scheherazade's life was saved, she'd sigh with relief, yet listen fearfully again the next time. A moment of sadness tinged the day as she wished her father could be there to see her, resplendent in a sari the colour of fresh pomegranate seeds and draped with gold wedding jewellery, marrying in the country of his birth. She blinked, grateful that, at least, her mother had made the journey.

Rachel and Aamina escorted Sally into a small anteroom where a kaleidoscope of silks, chiffons and jewels dazzled beyond the mesh of her veil and she saw her mother and grandmother sitting together, repairing more than thirty years of separation whilst between them, Sammy tugged at his great-grandmother's hand and pointed. She raised her veil a little and waved to her son then let herself be guided into the garlanded chair, ready for the marriage ceremony to begin.

They'd kept her from Arif all week, and now the pre-nuptial activities and traditions were about to culminate in the signing of the Nikah. In two more days, they'd host a Walima reception together, but today, with just their families present, she'd become Arif's wife. On her arm the glass wedding bangles shone against the intricate henna patterns her aunts and cousins had covered her skin with. She preferred the simplicity of pale skin and hadn't wanted henna, but Yalda and Rachel had insisted a bride couldn't marry without such beautification. Likewise the hours of painful hair removal, the rubbing of golden turmeric paste into her skin, and the painting of shimmering red lacquer on her finger and toe nails. With her hair threaded with fake gems and face glistening with pearly powders she hardly recognised herself. Arif might well wonder who his bride was! However the dress had been her choice alone. The gold threaded bodice accentuated her still slim waist and cascaded down to gold-slippered feet, and she loved the lavish, dazzling brilliant excess of it, so excitingly unlike anything she could have worn at even the grandest occasion and so different from something she might have worn had she married in England.

Someone announced the arrival of the Imam and she felt a thrill of anticipation. In the year since Arif's proposal she'd learned to trust her feelings and, to her joy, find them reflected in him. Not only was he the handsome, gentle man she'd first met, he was intelligent, interesting, kind, and highly moralistic – something that had worried her for a while. She'd once contrived an evening alone when, in new salwar kameez and with hair freshly washed, her intentions had been clear. When he'd ordered a taxi to send her home she'd demanded to know what was wrong; did he not love her as he said he did? He'd held her hands and told her that he longed for their wedding night when then, and only then, their union would be complete. But, he'd said, he would neither tarnish their relationship nor offend her by taking her to his bed before their marriage. The waiting, he'd assured her, tested him as much as it did her but it would enrich their marriage. Though slighted at the time, she'd come to see his reasoning as part of her growing trust and love for him, as alongside her adoption of the Muslim faith, it evidenced a stability that she welcomed.

As a Christian by default if not practice, her conversion to Islam surprised no one more than it did herself. Having picked up a book with the captivating title of 'King of the Castle' at Arif's house she'd discovered, as far she could see, a balanced look at issues in the secular world. The gulf of misunderstanding between the reality of Islam and what she came to see as Western beliefs invoked vigorous debate with her Christian uncles, but the more Sally read the more her interest grew. Wanting to improve her Urdu as much as to broaden her understanding, she joined a group of young women to study and discuss Islamic issues, and enjoyed the debates that were enhanced by tales of hard fought battles that were not unlike those she'd encountered at Black and Emery. Through her learning she'd come to accept that gender roles could be complementary rather than competitive and that diversity within the faith was something to celebrate rather than regularise. Not only did it make perfect sense according to the laws of nature, it taught her about a lifestyle that she wanted to be a part of. When finally, surrounded by Arif, her family, and her new friends, she'd pronounced her formal declaration of faith it was a moment she would remember forever. With the words of the Shadaadah enunciated, she'd known, in her heart, that life was going where she wanted it.

As the sound of drums, voices and laughter drew closer women thronged to the door hoping to see the Barat; Arif with his family and friends, arriving and entering a second anteroom. Then they returned, and the Imam was in front of her. It was time. She followed the Imam's words, though she knew the contents of The Nikah well. A slight shake of her head was almost indiscernible as the Meher was read, and which they'd disagreed on. Arif had assured her this 'dowry' established her independence. 'I,' he'd told her, 'am responsible for providing.

It is my duty.' Protestations that it was inappropriate because she intended to earn her own money fell by the wayside and the clause had stayed.

As the reading drew to its close she responded "Gabool kiya," and registered her agreement with a decisive hand. Daniel and the Imam registered their witness and as they left to conduct the ceremony with Arif she felt sun shine in her soul. She was about to become Sally – Sarah – Lancing Arif.

She turned as Rachel tugged her hand. "Come on!" Passing the curtained doorway where Arif's deep voice could be heard agreeing that he, too, accepted the terms of the Nikah they continued to a mirrored alcove where he would come to claim her. Within minutes Quranic verses heralded his presence and then by her side, his fingers gently but deliberately brushed hers. She'd been instructed to keep her eyes cast downward and from beneath her veil she saw Arif's legs clad in cream silk trousers and on his feet, embroidered leather slippers. Then it was time for her face to be revealed and she wished again that she'd refused some of the make-up. What if he didn't recognise her? The thought started a giggle and as Rachel lifted the veil clear it almost burst from her lips as she saw, in the mirror, Arif wearing a majestic cream and red turban. A plate of fresh dates was offered and taking one, she bit half and placed the other half in Arif's mouth, her finger brushing his lip. Amusement dissolved. Their eyes met and she knew that the abstinence they'd endured would soon end.

A gentle tug at her skirts broke the moment and she saw Karim had brought Sammy to her, clutching a small red silk cushion on which nestled two rings. It had been her idea to exchange rings, and taking the smaller, white gold ring Arif recited some Urdu poetry as he slid it slowly on to her finger. In response she took the second ring, this time silver, but otherwise a larger replica of the first, and placing it on Arif's finger, spoke the simple words her father had said to her mother on their wedding day more than thirty years previously, "Humans have never understood the power of Love, for if they had they would surely have built noble temples and altars and offered solemn sacrifices. But this is not done." Her voice wavered, but only for a moment. "And most certainly it ought to be done, since Love is our best friend, our helper, and the healer of ills. With this ring I pledge you my love." Arif placed his hand against her cheek and she felt his ring, strong and cool against the warmth of her face.

Applause surrounded them and she ran a finger carefully under her eyes to draw the tears away from the kohl and mascara. Daoud was signalling they should lead the way to the wedding marquee and for the first time they publicly held hands as they crossed the room. Aamina passed a garland of flowers over Arif's head at the doorway, but once outside he stopped abruptly and roared in mock fury. "I knew it!"

She bumped into him and discovered yet another tradition that was new to her.

He roared again. "Bring me my shoes. I demand they are returned."

The shoe racks had been emptied and she watched as he pulled several rupee notes from his pockets to exchange for the red and gold embroidered shoe bags that giggling Rachel and Pazir held behind their backs.

It was evening when Arif attempted to extract his new wife from the restraining arms and mock keening of her family and escort her to her new home. Sammy's cries of protest at her departure added authenticity to the Rukhsati ceremony until his grandmother and Rachel bribed him with ice-cream and promises of stories, and they climbed into one of a row of taxis that waited.

Arif's mother, who had left early, was waiting to welcome the returning barata revellers home with glasses of cool, sweet almond sherbet, so aromatic and deliciously refreshing that as she inhaled the spicy floral aroma Sally asked that her new mother-in-law teach her how to make it. Sotto voce, Arif's mother whispered it was a special wedding night drink to give energy, then laughed delightedly as she saw Sally's involuntary glance at Arif, who she saw was looking carefully at something on the table. She joined him and saw a flat tray, half-full of what appeared to be watery milk.

"What is this?"

Arif explained it was yet another wedding tradition, though more amusing, he added, than serious. "Whoever finds the hidden ring will command our marriage," he said. Seeing a glint of gold in the corner, Sally's hand dived forward to find nothing more than the tray's motif, whilst Arif's swishing fingers fished out a small gold ring. "Ah ha, I am master!" he proclaimed, "I have the ring." Sally laughed and, as he handed it to Pazir, telling her it was a gift from her new stepmother, she squeezed his hand in thanks.

"Thank you." Pazir slipped it on to her finger and admired it then pulled at Sally's arm. "Come, you must come with me."

She looked at Arif, wondering what new trick or game was to be played, but he nodded, and she let Pazir lead her along the corridor towards the guest-room suite she'd stayed in when looking after the children when Arif and his mother had both been away. It was a cavernous space, though airy, and although soulless she'd enjoyed the luxury of the private bathroom and tiny dressing room. Opening the door Pazir pulled her inside and threw open her arms. "Da-daa."

Sally looked around her; the room had been transformed. A large bed, scattered with red rose petals dominated the room, and Pazir patted the crisp white linen. "It's a new bed!" She moved to the wall. "And there's air conditioning *and* a fan. Look!" She pressed a switch and soft white curtains fluttered in the stirred air.

"It's so beautiful! I can hardly believe it's the same room! It looks smaller."

Pazir ran to the wall. "It *is* smaller." She pressed her hand and slid a panel aside, revealing wardrobes that extended the length and height of the wall. "You have the other end," she said, sliding a panel at the opposite end and displaying the clothes she'd packed into a suitcase a few days previously.

Pazir kissed her and left her staring at a dressing table reflection that stared back like a stranger in a dream. Here she was, married to Arif, and surrounded by this fine room. She'd suggested they might change rooms when they married but had assumed a simple swap, perhaps with his mother.

Arif appeared at the door. "Welcome to our room." He carried a small bowl carefully towards her, his advancing image blanking the room. "Do you like it?"

"It's a palace." She was overcome that he'd done this for her.

"Fit for my queen." He took two glass bangles from his pocket, each decorated with white flowers, and added them to those already on Sally's wrist. "It's a tradition. White for new beginnings. You have to smash these if I die before you." He knelt. "This is a tradition too." He removed Sally's slippers and shyness washed over her as his gentle hands washed her feet in the perfumed water he'd brought with him. "I must now sprinkle this water in each corner of the house to ensure luck and prosperity." In the wardrobe behind him she could see the shell-pink, lace nightdress she'd bought in London; an extravagance that now seemed immodest. "I'll be back soon; in about half an hour. When I've said goodbye to our remaining guests."

She set about removing the multitude of hair pins and brushing the stiffness from her hair. She cleaned off layers of make-up then showered away the powders and potions that had embellished her skin. She rubbed a piece of fresh sandalwood on to her damp skin then, ignoring the London nightdress, dressed in a new shalwar kameeze and sat anxiously on the chaise-longue, wondering why, at the age of thirty-four and hardly a virgin, she felt so absurdly nervous.

The remains of her glass of sherbet sat on the dressing table and she rose – as the door opened. Arif took her hands and kissed her forehead, her nose, and finally her lips. She closed her eyes and absorbed the gentleness of his lips, of his hands and heard him speak, "Bismillaah, ir-Rahman-ir-Rahim." Laying down two new silk mats they prayed together.

Then Arif guided her towards the bed where, in a whirlwind of cravings and desires they matched each other in the love they took and gave as, like dancers, they moved with elegance then fervour until passion was spent.

Lying quietly against her husband, beloved Arif, she knew they'd been right to wait.

Slipping a few photographs into a letter, she wrote Diane's once familiar address on the envelope and took it to where her mother was packing the last of her belongings. "Room for a tiny letter?" she asked.

Sammy knelt on top of the suitcase hindering his grandmother's attempts to edge the zips toward joining and seeing his mother, jumped up and held out his hand. "I take it. I going to London with Grandma!"

Sorrow darkened his grandmother's face. "I wish you could Sammy but I'm afraid your Mummy would cry for ever if you came with me." She hugged her grandson. "But promise to come soon? With Mummy and your new Daddy."

Sally bit at her lip. Her mother mistrusted most of the world outside London; it would have been a huge effort to come to

Pakistan and she was intensely grateful for it. And now she faced
not only the journey home, but the pain of leaving them in a
new, distant life. Running fingers absently through Sammy's
tangled hair she reassured her mother. "We'll come, Mum. Very
soon. I promise." A car horn sounded and she handed over the
letter. "Here, can you find a bit of room for this? Here's Arif;
it's time to go to the airport." She picked up the case. "Come on
Sammy, say goodbye to Grandma. And give me a cuddle too;
we'll be back in a few days." Knowing Sammy's tears wouldn't
last long she kissed him and called for Karim and Pazir. His new
step-grandma had treats planned too, and she kissed him again,
and tickled him. "We'll bring a nice present back if you promise
to be a good boy." Indignant objections became smiles as Pazir
whispered something into his ear and Sally smiled gratefully as
they left. "I'll ring," she promised.

The excitement of an undisclosed honeymoon destination
mitigated the sadness of her mother's departure and Sally's
spirits lifted as Arif drove quickly along the Great Trunk Road,
eagerly indicating road signs that might or might not signify
their destination. "It's very beautiful," he told her many times,
"You will like it too much."

"Peshawar!" She guessed as they sped northward. "We're
going to Peshawar. Or maybe The Khyber?" Arif groaned in
defeat, so when they left the road towards Mardan, Sally was
surprised and the game started again. She studied possibilities
on the map. "I need a clue; I don't know this area." Corn and
maize fields lined the valley roads and ice blue water tumbled
over boulder-strewn river beds. In the distance trails of slow
moving trucks crawled on what appeared to be a ledge cleaved
into a mountainside. "We're going there?" she asked, aghast.

"That's the Malakand Pass" Arif grinned, as though it
explained everything.

She didn't know whether to close her eyes to the nightmare or open them to the dangers as Arif eased the car between elephantine trucks and rocks that marked sheer drops, or tucked behind a lumbering truck as yet another hairpin bend appeared. Eventually, the road widened and she relaxed. "Please tell me we don't come back this way," she said and shuddered when Arif told her the alternative route made the Malakand Pass look like a motorway.

Within a few miles it seemed they'd passed into an enchanted world. Sally looked, enthralled as craggy rocks became a lush green valley with tree clad hillsides and mountains that could have been Switzerland. "Arif! It's beautiful!"

He patted her hand. "This is the Swat Valley and it's the most beautiful place on earth! I knew you'd like it."

The sun had dipped below the mountain tops when they arrived at the hotel and Sally was already pleased to have the shawl they'd bought at a weaving cooperative on the way. With its softness round her shoulders, and sitting on the veranda of the white marble hotel that had once been the summer palace of the Wali of Swat, she decided that even royalty could not have been happier. A bird sang in a hibiscus tree, and to the east of the hotel, water could be heard, cascading. Behind and some way up the mountainside someone, probably a shepherd, trilled a flute. Was he playing to his animals, she wondered, or amusing himself. The hotel manager crossed the manicured lawns and she speculated the truth of his story that 'numerous royal personages, including Queen Elizabeth of The Great Britain' had stayed in the hotel. Even if it were true, she thought, no-one could have felt more like a queen than she did at that moment.

The baby must have been conceived during the honeymoon,

perhaps even in the bed that Queen Elizabeth had supposedly slept in, but at only eight weeks it was hardly considered a miscarriage. There'd been no test and although she knew without doubt that she'd been pregnant she linked the loss to either the skin rash that had erupted or the nasty flu bug that had started just after their return to Abbottabad. To her relief her afflictions didn't affect the family, not even Arif, whose minor but recurring skin irritations and chesty coughs appeared to be the hazard of his work. The miscarriage tarnished the happiness of the first few months of her marriage but she concealed sadness amongst the general melancholy of recovery from 'flu, consoling herself that it seemed unlikely she would have a long wait for another pregnancy.

The second pregnancy, three months later was indisputable. The test at nine weeks was positive and she basked blissfully in dreams of a child that would unite and reinforce this family that they had brought together. She saw Pazir 'mothering' the child; another boy she was sure. Sammy would be four; no longer the baby, and he and Karim would teach their brother to play cricket. And Arif, now almost fifty, would be kept young and lively by his new son's antics. Sally prostrated herself, even at her dawn prayers, and joyfully extended her prayers with duas so that when she agreed to buy Sammy a soldier hat in the market one day and he uttered 'Al-hamdulillah', she realised he'd got it from her.

The second miscarriage smashed her illusions. Writing a second letter to her mother only days after the first joyful missive was almost impossible and she postponed the writing. Although pregnant for only twelve weeks, she grieved the reality of the dreams.

When her next pregnancy extended to six, then seven months, her joy knew no bounds, and despite the burden she carried in such heat, she floated through her days until, waking in the night with cramps in her stomach she'd known something was amiss. A stronger cramp clamped her swollen belly and her frightened cry woke Arif. By the following day the body of her baby had been removed from her womb and she lay sedated in a hospital bed, curled into an ache that constricted her chest, asking herself, "Why? Why?"

Daoud promised a medication regime of drugs and supplements designed to help her become and stay pregnant but she recoiled from such interventions; a baby, she believed should be created by nature or not at all. Perhaps nature was telling her that, in her mid-thirties, she was too old to have a child; a price she must pay for refusing to allow her body to conceive when she was at the right age. The prospect of another miscarriage, another dead baby, was more than she could face and she found a doctor, a woman who had trained in America, who listened sympathetically then agreed it was acceptable to avoid a pregnancy in the circumstances and prescribed birth control pills for her.

With time on her hand and facing the reality that she and Arif were not to be blessed with a child, she considered her future. She looked about her as she went around the town, seeing where women were working and what they were doing. It was clear that opportunities, even for educated women, were limited. Most who did work did so only before marriage. But, she thought, there must be something worthwhile she could do. Recalling an exercise she'd done as a graduate many years previously, she took a sheet of paper and divided it into columns headed 'Skills' on the left and 'Enjoy' on the right. Starting on the left she wrote 'organising', 'motivating people', and 'communicating'. She added 'following instructions' then struck out 'following' and replaced it with 'giving'. It was a harder than she remembered. Had she changed so much, she wondered. Hadn't fifteen years of age and experience refined her skills?

Moving to the right hand column she wrote 'giving instructions' again then wrote 'teaching'. She'd enjoyed teaching Pazir and Karim well enough but not enough to extend it to teach Daoud and the boys – which she'd hardly done. But planning and creating activities had been satisfying. She added 'planning' and 'creativity' to her list, then pondered how could she say she liked giving instructions if she didn't want to teach? "Oh! It's too hot to think," she muttered, "and this is ridiculous." She pushed the paper away and rang Rachel.

"Come and have iced tea with me," she demanded, "It's too hot to do anything else."

But Rachel was busy. "I'll come at two o' clock," she said, "Before I meet the twins from school."

She wandered to the bathroom, picked up a damp towel from the floor, then into the bedroom and lay under the fan. Within minutes, its whirring lulled her into a dream filled sleep in which Sammy, a grown man, walked along a London street. She knew he was searching for his father and as happens in dreams he was suddenly John, not Sammy, and was searching for her, enraged because she'd not miscarried his baby. His anger was uncontainable as he strode up the street banging doors and shouting her name and she cowered behind her mother's door until suddenly he was there. She tried to run but the bulk of pregnancy hindered her and his hand grabbed on her arm and she screamed.

"Wake up." Arif was holding her arm. "Sally, wake up. You are dreaming."

She focused on his face. Her heart pounded with relief. Dear, kind, easy to love Arif. "I must have fallen asleep. It was dreaming about ...... about England. It's all right. It was nothing." The clock radio showed it was almost one o'clock. She'd slept for over an hour and here was Arif, home for lunch. Jumping from the bed, she washed her face and made for the kitchen. "There's dhal in the fridge," she called, "and I'll get chapati from the man at the corner."

She was clearing away dishes when Rachel arrived.

"Sallyji! I'm here for my tea and I've brought us some galub jamun."

Licking the sticky syrup from her fingers Sally picked up the paper on which she'd started her lists. "You are my good friend," she told Rachel, "so you must help me. What am I good at?"

"You are excellent at eating galub jamun," Rachel giggled.

"No, be serious. I'm going mouldy here on my own all day. I want to do something. But what can I do? You have to help me."

Rachel pondered Sally's list. "You are a good teacher."

"Not anymore! Pazir says she's too old to have lessons with me and Karim will be off to school in Chitral in September. He doesn't need me to improve his English; the school's run by an English Army Major; they all speak perfect English."

"Arif's sending him to Langlands? Will Sammy go too?"

Sally shook her head. "He's too young; he's only just finished kindergarten. And I don't want him to go away to boarding school. Ever. Otherwise I really will go mouldy!" She drank tea and reflected that Rachel was right; she was a good teacher, and good with people. Especially adults. "Rachel. I could teach adults. What if I taught English?" The idea warmed, expanded. "What if I opened a language school for adults? Just a small one, maybe even only a few days each week." She had another idea. "And you could work with me; your English is perfect. We could do it together!"

Two years later five staff taught classes in what had once been a house in the appropriately named College Road. Sally's advanced group were reading English language newspapers and discussing Benazir Bhutto's return to Pakistan. It was almost dark; the class was about to end. "How long was Pakistan without a Prime Minister?" Sally asked.

Ayesha, an assistant at the Habib Bank, answered. "For thirteen years, after Mirza dismissed Khan. Benazir will try but he may not be allowed. New parties do not mean fair election. That we have to wait to see."

"He?" Sally asked

"Ah, yes. *She* may not ...."

Hassan, an accountant, interrupted. "She cannot be prime minister. She is corrupt..."

Sally stopped him. "I'm sorry Hassan, it's seven o'clock. We must finish for this week." She handed out papers and told the class, "For next week I would like you to write an interesting article about something you have read in a newspaper during the week. You may agree, disagree or merely comment. At least three hundred words, but no more than four hundred. I look forward to reading your views." A newcomer to the class, Jalil looked at her blankly and she repeated the instruction in Urdu. "And don't forget," she added, "Practise, practise, practise. Read everything you can. Good night, Allah Haafiz."

At home Pazir had put the meal that Shamila had prepared on to the table and thanking her, Sally quickly greeted each of the family as she prepared to serve Arif from the array of dishes. His 'Bismillah' was almost lost in the first mouthful and she buried irritation at his poor manners as she apologised for delaying the meal. "The evening classes are very popular, but I think I must get someone else to teach some of them next term, maybe a new evening teacher. The day is too long for me to do it."

"Yes, you are right, and eating late is not good for the digestion. It would be better if you could do that." Arif had been supportive of the school and although he hadn't objected to her being late, his usual point that he preferred to eat earlier indicated his displeasure.

She began to eat the food though hardly aware of it as her mind sought to resolve the problem of late classes. There was a student, the daughter of a lawyer, who had an excellent grasp of grammar as well as good pronunciation and vocabulary. She also had a confident way with her. But the family might forbid her to work, particularly in the evenings, and Sally wished uselessly, that the girl was a man.

Karim's voice interrupted her thoughts. "Auntie?"

"I'm sorry Karim. I didn't hear what you said."

Karim's sighed, visibly cross. "My cricket whites. I said I need them for tomorrow."

No longer a child but not yet an adult, Karim had begun to assert himself. "Well I expect Shamila will have got them ready. Have you looked in your drawer?" Karim admitted he hadn't and she quietly suggested that it would be a good idea to check things before he spoke crossly to anyone.

Later, with her book open on her lap, Sally fought the heaviness of her eyes.

"Ah, I fogot!" She jumped as Arif suddenly got up from his chair and crossed the room to his briefcase. "Daoud gave me this for you this afternoon; we were at the same meeting." He handed Sally an envelope. "I hope all is well? I didn't know you had seen him recently – as a doctor, that is."

Sally's tiredness evaporated. She hadn't yet told Arif about her visit to the maternity clinic a few days earlier; she hardly dare admit to herself that she might be pregnant again. "Oh I expect it's my usual check-up," she told him, "it won't be important. I'll read it later."

Arif returned to his newspaper and she lifted her book as if the letter had interrupted some exciting passage.

215

"We haven't been to Lahore for too long." Arif's was reading the back page, the sports news. "Perhaps we should visit Daniel and Yalda next week." He peered over the top of the paper. "What do you think?"

"Yes. Of course. We should go." She continued to stare at her book.

His paper covered his face again. "Oh! What a coincidence."

"Arif. Tell me. Why do you want to visit Lahore next week?"

He peered round the side of the paper and grinned. "You know me too well my dear. The West Indies are playing Pakistan at the weekend. Imran Khan will be playing; he is very special. Why don't you call Yalda and if they are free I will book flights from Islamabad. It will be quicker than driving." He folded the paper. "I know you well too. You are not a good actress; for a start, your book is upside down."

She glanced at the book, which wasn't the wrong way at all. But he'd caught her out.

"Why are you pretending that a letter from Daoud is too dull to read?"

"I'm..." She stopped. "I'll open it." Sliding her finger under the seal she pulled out the paper and scanned the brief paragraph. The words *congratulations*, and *fourteen weeks* jumped from the page and even though the letter merely told her what she knew, confirmation made it real. She passed the letter to Arif.

"Pregnant?"

She nodded.

"But....."

She looked at him. Was he disappointed? "You are displeased?"

"But...No. It is a surprise. Did you miss your pills?"

"No. But I was sick. Do you remember? It spoiled our weekend before Sammy and I went to London in August."

"That was..." He counted months on his fingers, "three,

nearly four months! Sally. Oh my goodness. You are well?"

She nodded and bit her lip. Tears had sprung into her eyes. She wanted a baby; it was good news. But there'd been so many disappointments.

Arif almost fell over his paper as he moved to embrace her. "My beautiful wife, don't be unhappy. It is wonderful news. It is perfect. So long as you are….. are well." He kissed the top of her head then took her hands. "But you must be careful. Sit down. What about your school? You cannot do it … your must…."

"I'm well. I'm very well. You'll be saying I must put my feet up soon!" His attentiveness was as amusing as welcome. "I promise I'll be careful, and I'll organise the school so I don't have to do so much. Rachel can manage; we'll get another teacher or reduce the numbers of classes until I can work properly again." The news brought as much anxiety as joy. "Arif, we neither planned nor expected this. It's not in our hands and we must try to neither fear nor hope too much. Inshallah, we will have a child of our own. Daoud will take good care of me… us!" She rested a hand on her stomach and barely whispered, "I hardly dare believe it."

Every twinge or nauseous moment was a torment of worry that once again shadowed her pregnancy, though this time it was apprehension rather than misgivings that clouded the months. When, one bright and fresh February morning Daoud suggested a Caesarean section, Sally agreed readily and a week later the sight of a healthy and perfectly formed daughter was an intense relief – as well as a thrilling surprise.

"Arif!" Both she and the baby were cleanly presentable by the time Arif was permitted entry to her room. "It's a girl!" Experience had taught her that boys and men were something of a mystery whereas girls were intuitively understood, and she tingled with excitment at this prize she held in her arms.

"But you convinced me we were going to have a son. We do not have a name to give to a girl!"

They agreed on the name Hiba, meaning gift.

Nine days passed before Hiba snuffled peacefully in the small room that had once been their dressing room and where Sally, unable to take her eyes from the tiny face that slept peacefully in the lace trimmed crib, marvelled at the perfection of the tiny fingernails, the miniature rosebud lips and the dark hair that already curled. The discomfort of healing wounds mattered nothing; after months of anxiety she could hardly believe the tiny, fragrant mite that lay in the cot was theirs. She recalled how she and John had taken Sammy home six years previously. John had carried Sammy in his carrycot into the kitchen and looking around uncertainly had deposited him on the kitchen table as if he were a bag of shopping. Hiba's homecoming had been orderly by comparison; Arif had carried her in his arms as if a new baby arrived every day and laid her gently in the waiting crib. Hiba was, of course, Arif's fourth newborn and with Sammy, the fifth child to live in this house. It was a family home and he was father to both her children, including Sammy. One day, when old enough to understand, she'd tell Sammy about John. She'd find the words to explain what had happened but in the meantime Arif was his father and now he had a new sister as well as an older sister and brother.

In the distance she heard Sammy's voice calling, "Ammi. Ammi. Aap kahaan hay?" sounding like any other Pakistani child.

"Mien yahaan. I'm here. Just settling your new sister into her crib. Come and hug me. I've missed you so much!" Tucking the cover round Hiba, she turned as Sammy ran into the room. "Hey big brother!" At six years, her son was no longer a baby. His dark hair was as unruly as the day he was born but now it topped a tall, athletic frame that – except for the face which was still an urchin-like version of John's – could have been Arif's. "Come and tell me what you've been doing whilst I've been away."

Arif brushed his almost black hair carefully in the mirror as he prepared to join her in bed. She'd missed his presence whilst in the hospital, and watching his vanity, it amused her that he succumbed to – as so many middle-aged Pakistani men did – dying his hair. But it couldn't be denied that the dark hair contributed to his youthful appearance. He was still an attractive man. If someone had told her, six years previously that she would find herself in Pakistan, married to a good man, with two children and two stepchildren, a comfortable home, and running her own successful language school, she would have deemed it impossible. Remembering the old adage of her mother's, she counted her blessings.

"You're looking very pleased with yourself." Arif met her eyes in the mirror.

"I was thinking how fortunate I am."

"*We* are!" Arif corrected her. "We are fortunate indeed." He climbed into bed and pulled the wool blanket over them both. "Yes, fortunate we are. You are home again and we have our daughter." He sank into the pillow. "Does Hiba cry loudly?" he asked, "I hope she won't disturb the night."

He was a good husband but a traditional Pakistani man and Sally knew that it would be her duty to look after Hiba's needs, day and night. Arif's contribution, to provide for whatever was needed, was something he would do without question. "She's too tiny to make a big noise," she reassured him, and teased him with an afterthought, "for now…"

Just before dawn a whimper broke Sally's sleep and she slipped silently from the bed. "Shhh." She touched Hiba's cheek then gently shifted her tiny daughter on to her lap, wincing at the pull of the Caesarean wound. Hiba soon suckled greedily and she relaxed into the rhythmic tug at her breast, remembering the quiet, almost meditative experience of feeding Sammy and looking forward to the same intimacy with her beautiful new daughter.

At the photographer's request, Arif's mother pushed Sally's dupatta away from Hiba's face, and tried too, to push Sammy's mop of hair into more orderly behaviour. The picture captured, Arif called Pazir and Karim into the group. For almost an hour they gathered, rearranged, re-grouped and smiled until at last, the photographer said it was enough. Proofs would be ready in a few days, and copies a few days later; ready to send to her mother in England. And to Diane, who would like to see Hiba too. Sally would put a picture in with her reply to a letter that had arrived a few weeks ago, telling of, amongst other things, a contract Diane had secured to test ready-made meals for a supermarket chain. She had, amusingly, sub-contracted a curry recipe to John. Sally never asked how John was, but seeing his image in Sammy every day couldn't help but wonder occasionally where life's passage was taking him. Marriage and Hiba, and of course, her acceptance of Islam, had shaped her own life, but to her mother-in-law's occasional chagrin, she was still the English Sally she'd always been. Arif's mother had worried what 'people' would say when a new car had arrived for her shortly after the marriage and had asked why Arif didn't employ a driver if taxis weren't 'good enough' for his wife. Fortunately, more enlightened than many of his compatriots, Arif had made it clear that he thought her car sensible, both in practical and progressive terms. A similar argument had brewed over the intention to work, and failing again to win her son's support over his wife's 'behaviour', her mother-in-law had declared she would pack her belongings and live elsewhere. But a few days of treats and gentle kindnesses had placated the bruised sense of decorum and eventually she'd accepted, albeit coolly, that progress didn't always please. Sally knew that progress began to please when she accepted a lift to the market and then again, when eventually she'd allowed herself to be driven to the language school where she'd basked in the reflected respect her daughter-in-law received from those around her. The final approval had been Hiba. The new baby pleased her mother-in-law greatly and Sally's place as a most agreeable daughter-in-law was secured.

The only cloud on her horizon was the distance between her much blessed life and her mother's home. Kissing Hiba's tiny fingers, she told her of London and the grandfather she would never meet and the grandmother who lived in London, and promised to take her to meet her. Very soon.

CHAPTER 13

Salmon Tikka

They (whoever 'they' were) said that if you hadn't made it by the time you were forty, you might as well forget it and John couldn't help feeling that registering Seagrams as a limited company and signing a lease for the third restaurant just before his fortieth birthday were auspicious. Outwardly he insisted it was merely another birthday but privately he acknowledged the marker as being of some significance and the change of business status made little difference other than it had been the catalyst behind his new VW Golf. And Seagrams Cider Barn would be the third – lucky three – restaurant. As Managing Director, he stood a little taller.

If this fortieth year was a marker, it certainly wasn't the finishing post. Even with six years of hard work and tenacity behind him, John knew he couldn't relax. Seagrams had been the only restaurant in the village when he'd opened, but growing confidence in the economy and the lowest inflation in six years meant that new restaurants were popping up like mushrooms. Locally, two pubs were now producing food that was good enough to distract the less discerning of his diners, an Indian restaurant had opened – influencing him to introduce a tikka dish to his own menu – and Bath's proximity kept complacency at bay.

Lisa's alarm buzzed and he let her slip quietly from the bed. Their liaison – not a relationship, he insisted – had lasted for almost four years and as he saw it, had little to commend it except, like one of Alice's kittens, it had an inconvenient habit of purring along. When they spent weekday nights together, mornings started at Lisa's house for the convenience of her school days, which she began always with cello practice. In minutes a deep, sonorous tone forced him below the covers until, once tuned, something her more advanced pupils might practice later in the day drifted more melodiously up the stairs.

Lisa seemed to find the impending fortieth milestone amusing, and from the vantage point of some eight junior years suggested minor lapses in his memory indicated he was on his way over the hill. Or paradoxically, at forty, life was about to begin. Clearly it couldn't be both.

Heavy eyed and weary, he recalled the celebrations that had gone on late into the night before. Too late, for a week night. But it wasn't every day he signed the lease, the architect's drawings, and the Venture Capital contract. Until yesterday, the funding had been simply numbers with a lot of noughts, but now it was in the bank with personal guarantees that negated any protection the limited company status might have given. Daunting and exciting in equal measure, the project could either make him a rich man, or break him. But the cider barn project excited him. His third Seagrams. As a listed building, the visual character of the building had to be retained but the architect promised a contemporary light filled interior; a theatre in which his food would play the leading role. In the torpor of sleep drugged imagination the medieval barn became a huge conservatory, as luminous as if the sun was rising from its very foundations.

Stretching an arm from below the covers he pushed the door shut on the cello. His first stop of the day was to be Bristol's Asian market for spices, then on to Bristol Seagrams for the catch-up with his chef, Frick. Dividing time between two restaurants had worked well but that wouldn't stretch to three restaurants and though Alain advised him to hire chefs and focus on management, he didn't want to. He thrived in the kitchens. It was where his creative energy came alive. Only from the kitchen would the integrity and personality that was the heart of Seagrams continue to grow. But Alain did have a point; someone had to oversee the business and he'd been thinking of Julia. She'd been with him since the start of Seagrams, he trusted her, and he knew she could do it. But would she?

It was still early for him, but with Lisa now making kitchen noises, he got up. Condensation blanked the bathroom mirror, and helping himself to a clean towel he wiped it clean. His face, he thought, had a acquired a certain, distinguished maturity, and seeing a long eyebrow hair he scowled as he tugged it out, wondering if this sign of premature aging was inherited.

Fresh coffee teased John's nose. "For me?" He pointed at the coffee maker.

"Sure. Help yourself." Lisa went to 'do her face' leaving John to contemplate the hint of Sally that still lingered in her wake. Dropping two slices of bread into the toaster, he picked up the previous day's newspaper and read the sports pages until a click of heels sounded on the tiles behind him. "I'm off. See you on Friday. Don't forget to ring the barn dance musicians and the disco man." She offered a cheek and John kissed it dutifully.

"Mmm. I'll do it later. Pick you up at seven on Friday."

Holding his birthday party in the cider barn had been touch and go, but with the lease now signed all was possible. Having forgotten to make the calls the previous evening, he changed his watch to the other wrist. As a prompt, it never failed.

Sweet Potatoes. He'd go to St. Paul's to get sweet potatoes, and he could get garlic there too. Negotiating the morning traffic he compiled a shopping list in his head. Tomatoes, onions, fresh herbs, lemons, cucumbers. And yogurt; thick yogurt for the raita. And spices for the tikka; cardamom, cumin, turmeric, good hot Indian chilli powder. If he grouped the four spices there were eight things to remember. Lisa might suggest he was over the hill, but there was nothing wrong with his memory.

Laden with shopping bags as well as paperwork, John pushed through the double porch doors. "Morning."

Julia waved and continued her phone call. "Not on a Saturday for three weeks. I'm sorry. No, no tables at all. Yes. Your name and number? Thank you, I'll certainly call if we have a cancellation." She scribbled in the diary then came to help with the bags. "You've been busy."

"I have. Frick here?" The Irish chef had acquired his nickname when, on joining Seagrams, he'd introduced himself in rapid Irish that had reduced Frederick to Frick. He passed a bag to Julia. "This is for the run through; the rest is being delivered later." He flexed his numbed fingers. "I thought you were at Bathampton today?"

"I was. But I swapped to see your Salmon Tikka. Curry spices are difficult for wine but once I've seen and tasted it I'll know what to recommend. Frick's in the kitchen doing something to the fish."

Over the years, Julia's personality as much as her commitment and ability had made her a key member of staff, and his thank you – rewarded with one of her broad smiles and oft repeated 'no worries' – applied to more than simply being relieved of a few heavy bags. "Well, it's good you're here; I wanted to talk to you." He shook his head at her questioning eyebrow. "In a 'mo. I need to sort this out." He grinned to deflect any doubtful significance and went in search of Frick, who was, as Julia intimated, cleaning the salmon fillets.

"Morning Frick. Good, you've started." He stacked the

vegetables in the racks and put the spices and a sheet of typed paper on the counter. "The recipe's here. Once you've skinned the salmon it needs cutting into inch slices and marinading. The spices are here too."

Frick said something at speed that John assumed from the tone to be assent and he returned to the dining room where Julia had two cups already filled with coffee.

"I suppose you would know of noteworthy English wines, wouldn't you?"

"Sure. There are some." It might have seemed an offbeat question, but Julia tuned in quickly. "There're more vineyards now, and buyers are starting to show interest. It's still fairly tentative, and the wines are more expensive. Generally drinkers don't trust them. But there are some nice sparkling wines and some of the whites and rosés are pretty good. Not many reds though. I can get some to try if you want; Peter's got a few."

"Good idea. Local is the way forward now." With a flourish, he pulled papers from his file. "That's the deal! The new restaurant is going ahead." It would, he told her, work with local food producers as much as possible, which of course, included wine. Then he told her that he hoped she would manage the three restaurants. "So, what I want to know, Julia, is how you might do it – and if, of course, you want to?"

"That's two questions."

"True, but it's as good as one. Think about it and let me know?"

"I know now. The answer's yes." Like John, Julia trusted instinct. "Of course I'd like to think about how it might work though. Give me a few days?"

"Sure. Same time next week?" John had his thoughts already, which included a rise in her salary and a car, but he knew those weren't the things that would motivate her. She thrived on challenges. "You'll want someone at each restaurant you can work with, and you'll need to liaise with me too. And you'll need to factor in travelling time."

"Time's the easy bit. Peter's so often away buying his wines and now Adam's at boarding school, time is what I have." The word 'time' sounded like a commodity. "I'll have something for you this time next week."

She'd responded as he'd hoped, and happily he added the sweetener. "We need to look at your role too, Julia. Perhaps a new title for the new job? Something with Director in it? I'd like you to be involved at a higher level. Can you think round that too?" Her eyes widened, just slightly, but enough to know he'd read her well. He raised a hand in a high five. "Exciting, eh?"

Frick had started to prepare the vegetables, and John prompted him to wash the spinach three times. "It was picked this morning and came with the field; I paid the earth for it!" he joked. "Anyway, it was so good I bought it all." The dry ochre skin had already been pared from the sweet potatoes and setting the mandolin, John sliced the hard orange flesh into spaghetti-thin strands whilst Frick briefed him on the weekend. A waiter had called in sick on Friday and put pressure on the others, but, said Frick, the others 'did' busy in their sleep so it had been another good weekend. John wilted spinach leaves whilst Frick threaded strips of salmon and slices of sweet red pepper on to damp wooden skewers and placed them under the hot grill.

"Watch this Frick – it happens quickly." John dropped clumps of sweet potato into hot oil as Frick leaned over to look. "Keep an eye on that salmon too," he instructed as he extracted a crisp golden cluster of sweet potato and placed it carefully on absorbent paper. "The raita's ready?" Frick nodded. "Great. You do the second sweet potato and I'll do the fish – there's nothing

special about grilling fish." A pungent aroma of charred spices
filled the air as he turned the skewers. "Ok. We're done. Now,
this dish is visual; I want it plated like this." He shaped a round
of spinach in the centre of a large white plate then topped it with
crossed skewers of tikka. "You must – pass the lemon – work
quickly or the salmon will be cold." The fish shimmered under
a drizzle of lemon juice and he lightly balanced a sweet potato
tangle on top. "Easy! Your turn; you do one." He dropped a
small pot of raita on the plate and took it into the dining room
"Hey Julia. You want to try this?"

"I do." She exchanged a glass cloth for a fork and picked off
small pieces of potato and fish. Then she tried it with raita, and
finally, fish and spinach together. "Got it. A medium Sauvignon
Blanc, not too dry. Or if it has to be red, then Pinot Noir. It
needs something to stand up to the flavour of the salmon
without overpowering it but that doesn't clash with the spices."
She took another forkful. "That's a real nice dish. Looks great
too. I love the colours."

John picked off a piece for himself and hoped her new role
would keep her from the temptation of a fine restaurant, though
he doubted she would endure the formality and pomp many of
them nurtured.

Free evenings, so few and far between, were to be taken
advantage of, and John was showing off his new home to Diane
and Malik as much as celebrating the new venture. Diane had
fallen in love with the gleaming kitchen. "It's from a new
warehouse place," he told her, "in Warrington. It's Swedish;
you'd love it." Meanwhile, Malik coveted the leather Habitat
sofa and made himself comfortable next to Diane who was, with
Lisa, browsing the mail order catalogue looking for outfits for
Lisa's sister's (also Diane's cousin's) imminent wedding.

"Red. You look great in red." Diane held her finger on a red dress as she reached for pen from her handbag and in doing so dislodged an envelope that fell, unnoticed by her, to the floor. As John stooped to retrieve it a photograph slipped from the envelope and in an instant he saw Sally, some children, and a man. In the slow motion seconds of the moment he nudged the picture under the sofa and pushed the letter back into Diane's handbag.

When everyone, including Lisa, had gone home, John retrieved the photograph. Sally looked composed and elegant in her Pakistani clothes, and still very beautiful. A tall, severe looking man rested a possessive hand on her shoulder. He'd be the husband, and probably father of the two older children and, he thought, the baby. But it was the younger child who took his attention. The boy leaning nonchalantly against his mother's side was Sammy. Aged around six. John knew he'd be seven now; his birthday fell two weeks before his own. Sally had written a note on the back; *June 1987. With love from Sally, Arif, Pazir, Karim, Sammy and Hiba.* Diane had told him that Sally had married in Pakistan, and at the time he'd persuaded himself he had no feelings about it. But now, bile-like jealousy rose in his throat. This new family; the solemn man, the other children, excluded him forever. The man looked old, certainly older than Sally, and almost a grandfather to Sammy, a thought that gave him sour satisfaction. Sammy's little-boy face was perfect, as beautiful as...a memory stirred. He found and rummaged through a box of old photos until he saw the folded card, edged with embossed holly and reindeers. Inside was a picture of himself at eight, pleased as punch as he sat on Santa's knee. Putting the picture alongside the family group he saw Sammy's dark, unmanageable hair, the pointed chin with a hint of a cleft, the cheeks made round by a smarty pants grin, and saw himself. In that moment he knew with absolute clarity that Sammy was his son. Retrieving the old Doc Martin's shoe box from the bottom of his wardrobe he found the blue baby record card identifying Sammy's blood group from amongst his jumble of passport, electoral role registration, qualification certificates and other personal documents. Tearing it in half, then half again, he tossed the pieces into the bin.

Just below where he'd found the card lay his flimsy pink birth certificate, its creases beginning to disintegrate with age, and below that and less shabby, was his adoption certificate. The certificates revealed his birth name as Jonathan William. Frances and Michael had changed it to John when they'd 'made him their own'. But this wasn't what interested him. He read the birth certificate even though he knew the entry by heart. He'd been born at Bowthorpe Maternity Hospital, in Wisbech, on 28th October, 1948, in the County of the Isle of Ely. He'd looked it up; it was in Cambridgeshire now. Blue-black schoolroom handwriting recorded his father as Jack William Crowson, a policeman, and his mother as Gillian Crowson, both of 28 Church Road, Leverington. There could be very few reasons why a woman, married to the father, would give her child away. He'd often wondered if his father had agreed to the adoption, and if so, what he had believed to be the reason. The Wisbech telephone directory had shown a number of Crowsons; six of them with the initial 'J'. It wasn't too many to ring, but starting a conversation with, "Hello, I'm your long lost son" was inconceivable. Refolding the certificate carefully he replaced it in its dark box and, as he had many times before, promised himself that one day he'd find his father who he was sure was innocent or who must have been deceived into agreeing to the adoption.

"Reel ..., and turn ..., and cast ..., all lead down..." On a platform that looked like the best efforts of a village hall stage, two red cheeked musicians fiddled energetically whilst a third squeezed an accordion and a fourth man called the dance steps. Neither the caller nor the music could be much heard above the rowdy hilarity of dancers who skipped and stumbled through a Cornish reel. Barn dancing had been Lisa's idea, but from the centre of the chaos he was heartened that it was to be only a minor part of the birthday celebration. A disco would follow, and though perhaps less memorable, familiar flailing would be less challenging.

John 'led down', then noticed Lisa signalling wildly from the head of his row, and realised he'd missed the 'cast'. Next to Lisa, Diane was holding her sides as she laughed helplessly at a bemused Malik who faced the wrong way. Someone shoved him back towards Lisa and as he scurried back the caller shouted, "and lead down." He gave up. It was time for a drink.

From the bar he watched his guests cavort through something called a Devon jig. He enjoyed parties but he avoided dancing whenever possible. It felt unnatural to shuffle and sway clumsily, especially whilst around him, other people seemed to move rhythmically.

As the jig progressed he looked around at the barn. It was sound and in reasonable repair for its age, but turning it into a restaurant was a bigger project than the others had been. They'd already been restaurants and alterations had been minor compared with this project. He was under no illusions; there was a lot to do. A central, open plan kitchen was an unusual concept and had Alain not found a group of investors who specialised in restaurant refurbishments and who'd been impressed by his successes, it might never have got off the ground. Now, after months of preparation, planning, and finding ways through the plethora of regulations about everything from kitchen extraction to vehicle access, it was moving toward reality. The virgin space was a new canvas waiting for its first brush stroke; the digger, that would start work on Monday morning.

Lisa was walking towards the bar, her Sally-like curls bouncing round grey eyes and an elongated face that belonged to no-one but Lisa. "Drink?" he asked.

"A very long Bacardi and coke please. With lots of ice. That was hot work."

Her piano player's fingers caught his wrist as he turned to order the drink. "Hey! You haven't put your ring on."

The gold signet ring had been her birthday gift and it was a nice ring, but it symbolised Lisa's dreams of an engagement. And rather than attracting the proposal she'd hoped for, it repelled him. "Sorry. I forgot it. I'm not used to wearing a ring. Don't worry; it's safe. It's in the box."

"John!"

"What?"

"It's to wear! I thought you would have worn it, especially tonight." Lisa's mouth, turned down at the corners, gave her face an El Greco quality. "I thought you'd be pleased with it."

"I forgot," he lied, "come on, cheer up; it's a party." She pouted and said something that he failed to hear as the disco started. "Can't hear you," he mouthed, and pointed to where Diane and Malik sat with a group of friends. "Let's go over there."

Diane moved her chair to allow another into the circle, and John sat next to her. She'd recently relocated her business to a small industrial unit outside Frome where she employed five staff and now also, her husband Malik. He asked her how it was going.

"Good. Yes, good, thanks. We're working on a supermarket project – can't tell you which one – but it's a biggy. English food

for English freezers. Things like shepherd's pie, faggots, and…
get this; chicken curry!"

"Chicken curry?"

"Sure! We Brits love our curries; have done for centuries.
Did you know that the English have been eating it since the
middle of the eighteenth century? It's practically a national
dish!"

"Pull the other one!" But his scepticism wavered as he
considered the salmon tikka currently selling well in Bristol.

"Actually…" John could almost see the cogs clicking an idea
into place. "Do you fancy creating a tikka recipe? Something
along the lines of that salmon thing you cooked last week, but
that could be frozen?" His creative 'genius', as she put it, could
be marketed.

"Flatterer!" He joked, but as an idea it had something.

Lisa leaned across the table. "Come on you two! Stop talking
about work." Her piano fingers held forth an empty glass. "Let's
have another drink. This is supposed to be a party."

The interruption irritated him. "When work is so dull that it
can't be talked about, I'll be looking for something else to do." He
turned back to Diane and carried on with the conversation.
"You're doing some interesting stuff; I'll give it some thought. I'll
call you. Soon." Lisa was sulking. "It seems it's my round…."

He ordered himself a whisky and watched the dancers
shaking and shimmying as coloured lights synchronised with
Lionel Richie's voice. It was hard not to watch Sandy, who'd
arrived unexpectedly with Alex. She was dancing with Frick,
who like John, was finding it difficult not to ogle the svelte body
that moulded itself to the music. Her sequined black dress
flashed and sparkled in the lights, and the once red, spiky hair
was now a jet black, glossy crop that complemented the dress.
The music changed seamlessly and Sandy revolved, arms aloft
and hips swaying. Half way round her kohl rimmed eyes caught

his and he saw the words she was singing along to; *'I'm working my way back to you, babe.'* It had been almost a year since they'd last, to mutual satisfaction, renewed their friendship and he'd been surprised when he'd seen Alex arrive with her. When Alex had explained his wife was looking after their sick daughter John had assured him he didn't mind in the least that he'd brought Sandy and had returned a conspiratory flick of tongue against her cheek with true pleasure. Glancing at Lisa first he raised his glass to Sandy. It hadn't been difficult keeping her a secret as their occasional brief dalliances merged into his conveniently flexible work. But, inviting though the words of her song were, meeting Sandy over the next few days would be difficult. He inclined his head slightly and watched Sandy tell a disappointed Frick that their dance was over and walk to the bar.

"Hi." She turned to the bartender. "Small Harp, please."

"Hi yourself. You're looking as desirable as ever."

"You too." Sandy rolled her eyes suggestively. "Not bad for forty."

At thirty eight, Sandy wasn't much younger, but, he told himself wryly, there weren't many women like Sandy. "How long are you here for?" Her answer of four more days was pleasing. "You fancy doing something tomorrow evening?"

"I do."

Her directness was refreshing. "I'll cook; at my new flat." Somehow, he'd make sure he was free. He scrawled *'Flat 2, 4, Cavendish Crescent, Bath'* on a scrap of paper. "It's on the right, past the golf course. Eight o'clock?"

Lisa came to the bar, her eyes expressing distaste and disapproval as Sandy moved away. "Friend of yours?"

"She's Alex's sister-in-law. I haven't seen her in ages."

Sandy had pulled Alex to his feet and was leading him towards the dance floor where, to his dismay, she turned and winked at him. Lisa's voice was carefully casual but her eyes had narrowed. "Well, she looks very pleased to have reacquainted herself. You wrote something down for her?"

"I gave her the address for the Bristol restaurant. Is there something wrong with that?" Indignation at the cross examination almost justified his lie.

Lisa examined her nails. "If I misread the look she just gave you, why are you angry?"

"I'm not angry!" He'd raised his voice. Taking a deep breath, he forced calmness. "Lisa, this is my birthday party, it's not the place for an argument. She's an old friend, that's all. Let's chill. Do you want another drink?"

The moment passed, but it cemented his decision. He would end the… liaison. It had suited his lifestyle, and having separate homes had preserved his freedom, but it was never going to be the kind of relationship that Lisa – or he – was looking for. She'd reminded him of Sally, but, he admitted ruefully, only when she walked away. Sally's beauty had been deeper. Sally had taught him to love; to accept and be able to give love, and with her, he'd learned to believe in himself. She'd truly been his 'other half'. He could never have shared the John who'd cried over his son or the John whose confidence hovered behind a façade with Lisa. Lisa said she loved him, but it didn't inspire him. After Sally he'd resolved to never get involved again which, he thought, was why he'd been with Lisa for so long.

That night he feigned sleep as Lisa curled into his back and hooked a leg over his. The clock marked the hours as he contemplated tears and recriminations over breakfast, and noted that it might be provident to use the old coffee pot and juice glasses. Perhaps, he thought, he should write her a letter? Dear Lisa. Dear? Eventually sleep obliged and when he awoke, a letter wasn't even a memory.

With bleary hangover eyes the subdued breakfast mood didn't seem out of place. Tested and tasting words, he looked for the right moment until, with a surge of adrenalin, he let go. "Lisa, I need to talk to you." His hands clasped below the table and he took a deep breath "I've been thinking."

Lisa waited. "You've been thinking?"

"We've been together for quite a long time, and…." Lisa's eyes began to shine and he realised with horror that she thought he was about to propose. Words fell over themselves in the hurry to be out. "It's not working anymore. I think we should stop seeing each other." He grabbed his coffee mug. "We're not right for each other. We want different things from life." It was true; what he wanted was what he had with Sandy; no ties or lies. Lisa had paled. "It's not fair on you… us… continuing as we are." He took the signet ring box from his pocket. "You'd better have this back. It's not for me. You deserve someone who wants a life with you. I'm sorry, Lisa, but that's not me." There. He'd said it. It was out.

"You're dumping me?" Lisa blinked, her eyes full of disbelief. "I don't understand. Why? What's wrong?"

"Oh Lisa." He spoke calmly, even sympathetically. She'd done nothing wrong. "It's not working anymore. I'm not what you want me to be."

"But I love you." She reached a hand towards him. "We've been together for four years. We've had good times; it can't just finish. Talk to me, John. What's the matter?"

"Lisa, I'm sorry. I can't make the promises you want from me. Your sister is getting married and it's clear that you want the same thing. There's nothing wrong with that. In fact you deserve it. But that's not for me, Lisa. It's better you find someone who wants those things too."

"What do you know about what I want if you won't talk with me? I don't understand. Talk to me, John. Please." An empty silence seemed to reverberate. Then a thought replaced confusion. "Last night! It's that woman. You're seeing her." John started to deny the accusation but Lisa had jumped up. "This isn't about me, about what I want. It's about what you want. You're lying." His protest went unheard. "You're a loser, John Sommers, a bloody loser. You're forty, and you're still Jack the Bloody Lad. You need to grow up!" It gave him a little satisfaction that he'd been right to use the old pots for breakfast as Lisa slammed her coffee mug on the table and the handle snapped off. "You know what? You're right. I do deserve better than you. And it won't be hard to find!"

Her chair crashed on to its back and he righted it before following her to the bedroom. Electric rollers slammed into a bag. "Lisa. It doesn't have to be like this. I'm sorry it's not working. You haven't done anything wrong. Neither have I. It's just not going where either of us want it to." Shoes from the previous evening were screwed into the dress and hurled into the bag. He started to say they could still be friends but the words stuck as he realised he'd never felt they had been. With nothing more to say he left her to finish packing her things until, minutes later, he heard the door slam. Weak with relief he sat with closed eyes, counting slowly to calm his breathing, and then rang Diane to suggest she might comfort her cousin. Lisa's cigarettes were still on the table, and next to them, the signet ring. He picked up the cigarettes. It had been a week since he'd had a cigarette. He took one from the pack and lit it. The ring could be posted.

As he left, he glanced round the flat. He'd bring flowers back, lilies probably. He'd changed the sheets and put fresh towels in the bathroom. A new chapter was beginning.

Winding the car window down he let air blow its freshness into the car to dispel the trace of the White Linen perfume he'd bought Lisa the previous Christmas. Along the verges dandelions and daisies smiled their good morning and from the speakers of his car, Katrina and the Waves sang; *I'm walking on sunshine…*

It might have been his new found freedom, or the aftermath of Sandy's company, but when he woke to a work-free Monday-morning-sun rising in a cloudless sky, he had a crazy idea. The day ahead of him was as free as he chose to make it, and he wanted to drive to Cambridgeshire to see what kind of a place he'd been born in. Before sense challenged, he gathered jacket, wallet, keys, and sunglasses, and let the front door clunk decisively behind him. It would be a day out. He wasn't knocking on any doors. It was just a day out, in the sunshine, in his nice new car.

He'd been driving for more than four hours when he saw a Little Chef. A road sign had told him he was somewhere called Guyhirn, which he assumed to be a village though with little more than an indeterminately long road dotted with indifferent industrial buildings, squat dwellings and cultivated fields, he couldn't be sure. Somerset villages had churches, cottages and meandering lanes. Even main road villages had some charm. This one, though, did have a Little Chef! He ordered bacon and beans from a big bellied man who gave him directions to Leverington in an accent that, with its 'err's and 'oi's, sounded oddly like home.

A few trees and buildings interrupted the flat, black, freshly tilled fields that stretched to the horizon. Even the sky was endless. Poplar trees and distant church spires seemed to spike the heavens and he wondered if it was the vast prostration of the Fens that produced such clarity of distance. Driving slowly down the middle of the narrow road he avoided the fractured edges and pot holes and passed symmetrical redbrick semis squatting in symmetrical plots. In the village, newer houses, bungalows mostly, and more of the cube-like semis squatted together. This was Leverington. Place of his birth. He saw he was already on Church Road and slowed, looking at house numbers. Thirty-two, thirty. He stopped. Twenty-eight. The house sat sideways to the road so that a pebble dashed façade with plastic framed windows offered a blank face to the road. He pulled forwards a few more yards and saw the front of the house. A UPVC door was half obscured by a re-sprayed Ford Cortina. Behind the car, an open, wooden garage, more a large shed, sheltered planks of wood and a residue of building materials. John wondered if the rusty swing in the garden had ever been his, or if his birth father had ever put a police car in that very garage. He opened his car window, lit a cigarette and mused. This was where he'd lived for his first year and some of his second, and its proximity confirmed that, for most of his life, he'd been lying to himself. It did matter. Blood was thicker than water. And history was repeating itself; Sammy was growing up without his real father too.

He finished his cigarette and threw the butt to the ground. He'd seen the house, and that was enough. He wasn't ready for whatever might be behind the door. He started the engine just as a tall stocky man of about his own age stepped from the front door and looked at him suspiciously.

"You looking for something?"

"No. No, not really thanks." John hurried to reassure him. "I used to live here. A long time ago. I was in the neighbourhood and thought I'd take a look. For old time's sake."

"Yeah? When was that?"

"Oh, long time ago. I was a baby. Your place now?"

"Yeah mate. Been here six years. Been doing it up."

"Looks good." In the circumstances, the lie was acceptable. "You local?" The man nodded. "Don't suppose you ever heard of a Jack Crowson? He used to live here." The words had formed and sounded without thought, and with a bolt of fear it occurred to him that this man might be his brother.

"Crowson? No, mate. Hang on though, my Dad's inside.

Knows everyone, he does." John did a quick calculation; the father would be around the same age as Jack Crowson. In this community it was feasible they would know each other. He wasn't ready to face a father. Not yet. He needed time to think, to prepare. He considered driving away, there and then, but the Seagrams logo on the side of his car was as good as a calling card.

The man reappeared. "Dad says he knew a policeman once, called Jack Crowson, but he's been dead more than twenty years. Cancer, he thinks. His wife's living in Wisbech, with the son. They've got the greengrocer's on the High Street." The man was pleased with himself. "They relatives of yours?"

Never for one moment had John thought that his father might not be alive. He'd been something of an apparition, but he'd always been alive. His legs weakened. A dead father. A living mother. And a brother. He was stunned.

"You all right mate?"

"Yes. I'm fine. Sorry – Jack was – a good friend of my father's. Thanks though. It's good to know his wife is still alive though. I might look her up. Thanks." The man was inviting John into his home for a 'cuppa" but he wanted to go. "Thanks, but I've a long way to go, and I was just passing. Thanks for the information though. It's good to know...."

It was almost dark when he arrived home. The engine had drummed 'Jack Crowson is dead, Jack Crowson is dead' and he was pleased to shut it off. There was no grief. Just frustration and futile anger. From within a cocoon of indifference he'd never questioned his father's mortality. Now he felt cheated, let down. Again, Jack Crowson hadn't been there for him. He vowed to find a way to make sure that history didn't continue to repeat itself; somehow he'd find a way to communicate with Sammy. And he'd quit smoking.

That evening, for the first time since moving into his new flat, he was lonely. Even his thoughts seemed to echo. He put the kettle on, then switched it off and reached for the whisky. The familiarity of whisky called for a cigarette but he refused himself the pleasure and thought instead, about Leverington.

He hadn't much liked the Fens; though finding the house of his birth had been gratifying. Jack Crowson – he couldn't think of him in any other terms – had taken his secrets to the grave, but the woman he'd despised since childhood was still alive. Jack and Gill. He sniggered. They were certainly over the hill! One dead and the other... Gillian Crowson had no right to the honour of 'mother'. She'd rejected him, tossed him away. Frances had been all a mother should be, and more, at times, than he'd deserved. He recalled when at fourteen, she'd found him smoking in the garden and in the ensuing row he'd chosen words to wound. "You're not my mother," he'd shouted, "You've no right to tell me what to do." Michael had told him he was lucky to have her for a mother and he'd been right. But it hadn't stopped him hurling the same hurtful accusations again. Later, in therapy, the psychiatrist had plucked all sorts of truths from him, like the year he'd refused to give her a Mother's Day card and had told her why. He cringed now, at the cruelty. The psychiatrist had said that all children got angry and rejected their parents sometimes, but he'd known, with such accusations based on truth, that he'd hurt deliberately. The child in him could be excused childish behaviour but the man wondered if it wasn't too late to say he was sorry.

He wanted another whisky but the bottle was in the kitchen. Closing his eyes, he found Sammy, bright and without him in Sally's family photograph. There'd been a painting in which Branwell Bronte, unhappy with his own image in the family group, had tried to paint himself out. But the ghostly image remained. In the family picture behind his eyes, it was he, John, who was a ghost.

He turned on the TV just as a Government health warning advert he'd seen before started; it was compulsive viewing. Volcanic rocks crashed and demonic bells tolled as an ominous looking shadow chiselled the word AIDS into a tombstone. John Hurt's sinister voiceover warned of the deadly disease that had no cure. It was grim stuff, but quickly forgotten as he returned to Wendy Craig's TV family complaining as she dished up something inedible in 'Butterflies' on BBC 2.

In the days that followed, thoughts of Sammy increasingly wormed their way into work activities. In quieter moments he wrote imaginary passages that might form a diary, a sort of episodic letter he might give Sammy one day, and in pre-dawn half-light he visualised meetings where he and Sammy would fill in the gaps of their lives and the bond between father and son would be strong. He wondered if Sammy had any artistic talent and imagined him finding fame that had eluded his father. In imaginary letters to Sally, he sometimes asked to be acknowledged, in others, demanded a meeting with his son. But as days followed nights, John faced reality. Sammy lived with his Pakistani family, too far away for a relationship, and too complicated for the boy to understand. John wasn't a part of that family. All he could hope for was that Sally would, one day, tell Sammy about him, and that he would want to find his father too.

Frances pushed the ledgers towards him. "Well, that's that all present and correct. All's going well." She handed over her pen.

"Thanks Mum." He signed the sheets. "I'm seeing Alain on Monday, he'll be happy with this." He dropped the pen into his shirt pocket where it nudged the photographs of Sammy and the print of himself. "Dad playing golf?"

"He is. He'll be back around teatime." Frances held out her hand for the pen and receiving it, added her signature to John's, then turned the page and began to head up new columns. "Did you want him?"

"No, no, it's ok. I just wondered." He could feel the photographs against his chest. "Mum. Can I ask you something?"

She didn't need a crystal ball to know a significant question. "Go ahead."

"I, I well. Er…" It was ridiculous; he felt like a small boy. "I don't quite know what to do." He told himself to get on with it. "You see, I've been thinking. About Sammy." He could see cautious expectation on his mother's face. "And … about his father." It wasn't easy; he didn't want to hurt her, but this was important to him. "And that he might think about his real father. One day. You know; he'll want to know. I expect." His mother's eyes seemed to bore into him.

"You want to know about your birth parents."

It was disconcerting how she managed to get into his thoughts. He saw her chew the inside of her bottom lip; a habit that always manifested itself when she was upset or worried. He swallowed. He couldn't tell her about Leverington. And he didn't want to talk to her about the woman who'd abandoned him at the most innocent and vulnerable time of his life. He just wanted to talk to her about Sammy. "No. Well, not directly. I sometimes wonder about them; of course I do. It makes me realise that Sammy will wonder. About his father. One day."

Frances continued as if John had agreed. "We expected you to want to know years ago, but you always said you didn't want to know. The truth is, John, we don't know much. We gave you what we had, your birth certificate and the adoption certificate a long time ago." She chewed her bottom lip again. "We have some papers but I'd rather talk about this when your father's here."

"Mum, it doesn't matter." He didn't need the papers. He already knew more than papers would tell him. "It really doesn't matter." He pulled the two photos from his pocket. "Look. Look at Sammy and look at me."

To his surprise, she hardly glanced at the pictures. "I know, John. We saw a picture that Diane had, a few years ago, when Sally married her Pakistani man. We knew then. But after what had happened, and after Janine and Amanda, well…. we didn't think you wanted to know."

Amanda? Janine? He looked at his mother in surprise. "What's Amanda got to do with it?"

"Well, she's your child too."

He'd never seen Amanda, and the end of maintenance payments a few years earlier had, he felt, closed the link. Amanda had been Janine's child. The idea that she might one day contact him came as a surprise. She was as unreal as Sammy was real.

"No she…, well she's Janine's. Always has been. It's not like Sammy."

"Well, what next? Do you think that Sally will tell Sammy about you?"

Again Frances read his thoughts as if he'd spelled them out to her. Picking up a biscuit he studied it. "No. I'm not sure," he admitted, "though I hope she does." It was enough truth. The biscuit disappeared into his mouth and he kept Leverington to himself.

Conversion of the Cider Barn ran over by two weeks – due mostly to an underground river that flooded the newly excavated cellar. But now drained and dried and with the river re-routed, Julia's English wines sat alongside more traditional

French and New World wines, and above it, at floor level, a state of the art bar was ready to be stocked. Artwork had transformed the white, barren walls and embraced the previously vacuous space. The architect had been right to intensify the space with white and light, though before the pictures were in place John feared it had been overdone. With the art in place, the room had style. Seagrams style. The newly arrived Rothkoesque commission was waiting to be hung where, separated from the gallery by structural oak supports, it would be solitary but dominant.

Alain didn't understand art. He'd suggested that John could save the money by painting a panel himself, and the memory brought forth a hollow laugh. He wished he had the talent to express emotions in the way that Rothko had or Roly could. The portraits he sketched were good; they could be read, but abstracts were different. And Rothko's murals, a singular, interdependent work, repelled, whilst Roly's panels, individual and self determining, buzzed with energy. They had expression. He, John, couldn't do what they'd done.

Was it a coincidence that the panels were evolving towards four seasons? In the first, red and blue hues radiated like a summer sunset, whereas the second, a smaller monochromatic panel, brought bright winter light into the dark, narrow Bristol premises it had been created for. Now this panel, considerably larger than the other two, with three fresh green rectangular planes on an ochre base, suggested spring. Did it augur a fourth; an autumn?

The new panel shimmered as John circled it at a distance and became a stroll through spring woods at sunrise. Moving forward, he stood in front of it with arms raised as if to embrace it and with his face almost touching the surface, he inhaled slowly. In some crazy way he trusted these paintings. He'd often sat, silent and alone with the first commission, freeing his mind

CHAPTER 14

Dhal

"Hiba's sick and you are her mother. It is your duty to stay here."

Arif's tone was authoritative but Sally continued to gather her papers. She knew he didn't have a clinic that morning. He could stay with Hiba for a few hours if he chose to. But, though he adored his daughter, it wasn't his place to look after her and she knew it would be futile to suggest such a thing. She forced herself to speak calmly. "Hiba has a cold. That's all it is. Another cold. She's not a baby. She's six years old! She'll be fine. She's crying now because she wants her way, not because she's sick. Shamila's here this morning, and so is your mother. Arif, I have to go to work this morning; Mr Kahil and Rachel cannot teach three exam classes at the same time."

"My mother is old and still sleeping and it is not Shamila's job to look after Hiba. Shamila is here to relieve you of the household chores. She's not here to relieve you of your child!"

Our child, thought Sally. "Arif, I want to stay with Hiba. But how can I? Until Shazia comes back I have to teach her class. They have exams; it's their last class!" When Shazia had failed to turn up for work a few weeks previously she'd called at her home and found it empty. Her students had spoken of a charge of blasphemy, saying that the family had fled. "I'll call at Shazia's house again; the neighbours may know more. I'm sure she'll be back. I can't believe the family have gone, just like that."

"No, Sally. You must not go to Shazia's house!" Arif gripped her arm. "Listen to me Sally, you must not get involved. If there's any truth in the blasphemy rumours and you are seen to support her, anything can happen. Even though you are Muslim, some people don't like that you drive and work and such things. You must not draw attention to yourself in this way."

There was enough truth in Arif's warning for Sally to know she shouldn't intervene. But Shazia had become a friend as well as an employee, and she couldn't simply turn away. "There must be something I can do for her."

"Sally, there is nothing. The family have gone. Even if she were to come back you cannot employ her again. You must not go to the house or ask about her." Arif was adamant. "Sally. You must promise."

She knew that though the blasphemy laws outlawed criticism of all religions, in practice, accusations of anti-Islamic behaviours had become a cruel weapon, often based on no more than hearsay, and sometimes, lies. Most of those arrested were eventually released, but often faced retribution of some kind. Arif's warnings were justified, and she had to concede. Nodding her assent and with a heavy heart she reconciled herself to finding a teacher to replace Shazia.

The practical side of the dilemma resolved itself within a few days when the son of a student, a young man planning to go to university in England, asked if there were any opportunities to teach English before he went. His timely request, adequate English skills, and immediate availability relieved her from the inflexibility of classroom teaching and life resumed the normality of relative peace, broken only by the children's squabbles.

Having resolutely ignored bickering for some time Sally eventually interrupted. "Enough! Sammy, stop teasing your sister."

"He's stolen Bandy!" Sally could see Hiba's favourite toy, a bendy monkey, behind Sammy's back.

"Why is it always me who has to stop? She's never told to

stop." Sammy flicked the monkey back at Hiba. "You're such a baby!" At twelve, he was as robust as Hiba was not.

"Samuel, stop it. First of all Hiba's not well, and secondly, she's a lot younger than you. Can you tell me why you behave so childishly?"

Sammy turned away but not before she saw him pull a face at Hiba, whose similar response resulted in giggles. "I give in!" Picking up her handbag she told Sammy he was in charge. "I have to go to the market."

"I don't want him in charge of me," Hiba protested, "he's too bossy."

"You won't be, will you, Sammy?" She looked threateningly at her son. "Are you old enough to be responsible?"

Sammy pulled himself to his full height. "Of course." His voice cracked and Sally frowned a warning at Hiba, who seemed to find this recent change in her brother amusing.

"Well Daadi is upstairs if you *really* need her, but she's resting so try to not disturb her. Hiba, I'll get some yogurt to get rid of your nasty mouth thrush and it won't hurt to swallow. I'll be back in no time." Picking up car keys and umbrella, she instructed the children to behave, pulled the door closed and ran through the last of the rain to open the gates. Puddles soaked her feet as she unlocked and relocked the padlock, but at least the monsoons were warm.

The ground was steaming in sunshine when she returned and lying on the driveway an ink smudged pale blue airmail envelope, tossed over the gate by the postman, had become almost indecipherable. She tried to read the sender inkblot as she carried her shopping indoors and seeing Sammy watching a noisy TV programme, his leg swinging lazily over the chair arm, demanded he help her. Most of it's to feed you anyway," she told him. Unlike Hiba, who hardly even picked at food, Sammy's incessant hunger was a constant challenge. The contrast between them was remarkable; strong, healthy Sammy, and tiny, fragile Hiba who was susceptible to all the ills and ailments that blew her way. But she was a happy, sweet child and Sally thanked Allah for her family.

She dabbed the airmail letter dry with a tissue and slit the sealed edges carefully with a sharp knife – a method she'd discovered was particularly important if the letter came from her Mother, who got full value by covering the entire surface, precisely and economically, in tiny script. But this letter was an unfamiliar script and Sally looked curiously as she unfolded the page. She recognised the address immediately, and her eyes shot to the bottom of the page where the name, Michael Sommers, caused her to sit down sharply. John's father!

Dear Sally,

I know this letter will be a surprise to you, it being more than twelve years since we last spoke. Perhaps we should have written but we didn't have an address, and anyway, it wasn't easy. Now, I write because circumstances have forced me to contact you. I got your address from Diane.

Something terrible had happened to John?

I started to write many times. There is no easy or right way to tell you what I have to say, and so I will just set the words on the page. Earlier this year I lost Frances after a short illness. I know you were fond of her and I would also have written if that was all I had to tell you. But I need to inform you of her wishes too.

When your son was born, we were overjoyed. This you know. Within days of his birth we started an endowment with the intention of providing something for him, perhaps to help him go to university. We had great hopes for our grandson's future. The blow we felt when John told us what had happened couldn't have hurt more.

'*What had happened.*' Her very words! Guilt and remorse that she thought buried forever kicked her ribs as her eyes raced down the page.

Some years ago…… John work …… party at your friend, Diane's …
… photograph of your wedding …… Sammy….

The words described a world that Sally had once known intimately and which now excluded her.

……Frances's illness…. trust fund …. without our grandchildren….
As memories churned Michael's voice echoed love, shame, and heartache and she read that a trust fund, to be managed by their solicitor, would come into effect when Sammy reached thirteen. Michael hoped the money would provide for Sammy's education as his wife had wished, but it would need Sally's involvement to be administered and he asked her to contact the solicitor at an address in Bath.

The letter was succinct. It left Sally feeling weak.

"Maa!"

Sammy's voice intruded. "Sorry?" Looking at her son she saw John's features.

"I'm starving. Can I have some of these?" He'd discovered a packet of biscuits in the bags he'd carried to the kitchen.

Nodding, she returned to the letter. '*….without our grandchildren…*' She tried to read the tone. It was concise. But was it curt, or merely factual? She imagined Michael writing the letter with old sorrows overlaying fresh mourning as he carried out wishes that had been made in joy. Trying to set aside her own sorrows she wondered how she would shape her response. Condolences and sadness she truly felt would be the easy part. She'd liked and respected Frances and had occasionally considered writing as Sammy grew up. Each time, fearing rejection or worse, she'd veered away. But now she must write, and finding words to bridge the empty years would be difficult.

"Maa! Wake up! I've spoken to you three times!"

Sally looked at Sammy. "Sorry?"

"Ha! You're just like Hiba, you have a world of your own!"

"Sorry Sammy. What were you saying?"

"I was telling you that whilst you were out Pazir rang. She needs some money for books for her course. She said she'll try to ring again this evening."

She folded the letter and tucked it into her pocket. "Right. Thanks Sammy." Despite her heavy heart she couldn't help but be amused as he yawned dramatically and flopped back into the chair, actions designed to reinforce her awareness of his boredom. In another week the long summer break would end and he'd start his second year at the Abbottabad School, but this time as a boarder. Though only ten miles out of town, he'd garnered Arif's support to join his boarding friends, claiming he was missing too many activities and eventually, she'd agreed, reluctantly. With Karim now at college in Peshawar and Pazir in The States, the house appeared to be closing down around her.

"Sammy, would you mind making some tea?"

Sammy wound catlike, round the side of the chair. "Where's Shamila?"

"Come on Sammy. It would be very helpful if you'd clear up your breakfast things too whilst you're making tea. Shamila has plenty to do and she's not here to clear up after you, particularly when you don't get up until late."

Rolling from the chair, he lumbered his frame across the room. "I'm going. I don't need a lecture."

He wouldn't have spoken in such a way in Arif's presence, but distracted by the letter, she let it pass. 'Without our grandchildren'. Was Michael apportioning guilt or expressing sorrow? She didn't know what John had told his parents or what their reactions had been, and now, so distant in time as well as miles, it felt unreal. Perhaps it was she, Sally, who had changed. In embracing Islam she'd searched her soul, challenged her guilt, and found truths to live with. Sammy's birth had been a decisive step for her and John; one that might have strengthened their unity, possibly for the rest of their lives, had it not been for 'what had happened'. Though Sammy was clearly and thankfully John's child, their break-up was undeniably due to alcohol and adulterous sex, unemotional and meaningless and which bore no relationship to the passionate union that had once bound her to John. The part she'd played in the sequence of events and eventual outcome was deeply regrettable, but forgivable – as Diane had once insisted it should be. Before she'd accepted Arif's proposal she'd told him about John, and Sammy. And about James. For almost a week she'd waited to hear him say he no longer wanted to marry her but instead he'd told her that the past couldn't be changed. His only request, he'd said, was that they didn't speak of it again. But Michael's letter triggered once dormant emotions. Actions had consequences and there was no escaping the ripples of life.

That evening she showed the letter to Arif.

"We don't need this money," he said brusquely.

"Yes, but Michael wouldn't know that. They set up the fund when Sammy's future was insecure."

"It is secure now." Arif coughed the persistent cough that worsened when he was agitated. "So what will you do?"

"Your cough isn't getting better. Hiba was coughing today, too."

He took a small bottle from his pocket and rattled it. "Antibiotics."

"Good. Could you get some for Hiba?" He nodded.

She looked again at the letter. "I'll write, but it won't be easy. I don't know what to say. I don't know how Michael is financially. If he needs to use the money he should keep it, but I don't want to offend or hurt him."

Arif turned away. "I don't know what you should do but I pay Sammy's school fees. I am his father now; he knows no other. That's the way it is. You should see this Michael when you go to England during the December holidays and tell him so."

"You'll come to England, too?"

"No, I don't want to use my vacation time like that. You go. It's end of term so Sammy and Hiba can go; your mother will be happy to see her grandchildren."

The conversation was at an end but the letter dominated her thoughts throughout the week. As she sewed name tags on to Sammy's uniform, packed his trunks, encouraged Hiba to eat food, and taught English lessons at her school she composed and recomposed a reply to Michael. Eventually she wrote first to her mother, telling her that she, Sammy and Hiba would come for the Christmas holiday. Then she wrote a second letter, to Michael, asking if she might visit.

The night was eerily quiet and infused with white light when Sally woke. Somewhere in the house a sound had disturbed her sleep and she held her breath as her ears strained beyond Arif's chesty breathing. When she heard the sound again she recognised it. Used to nursing Hiba's feverish colds or bouts of sickness she was already running up the stairs by the time Hiba called, "Maa, Maa. I'm sick!" She found her daughter pale and shivering and smeared with vomit. "Oh you poor little thing!" Stripping the sheets from the bed, she wiped Hiba's face and carried her, swiftly, to the bathroom. It was very cold and she worked quickly, aware that she too, was beginning to shiver. Through the window the amber glow of the street lamp was alive with a flurry of white specks. "Oh! No wonder it's so cold. Look Hiba, it's snowing!" Within minutes, clean and wrapped in a blanket, Hiba curled into a chair whilst Sally changed the covers on her bed.

"Maa, will it be snowing when we're in London?"

"It might. But probably not. We have a lot more snow here than they do in London." Looking at Hiba's feverish eyes Sally wondered if they'd be able to leave for London in a few days time. "Come on little one; back into your bed." Climbing in beside her, she hugged Hiba's thin body and waited for her breathing to settle. But Hiba's body was hot; too hot, and when the shallow, rasping breathing didn't settle, Sally slipped from the bed. "I'll be back in a minute – I'm going to get some aspirin," she told her.

Shaking Arif's shoulder, she woke him. "Arif. Hiba's very hot. Come and see her."

Arif's voice, arriving ahead of his presence, startled the sleepy emergency room to life. "Pneumonia. I'm sure. Temperature's 39. There's sternal recession, her respiratory rate's 40 and there's no breath sound on the left side. I want oxygen and IV fluids. Get blood tests and a chest X-ray organised." His manner both reassured and alarmed Sally. A distant Call to Prayer sounded and she covered her head automatically as ward staff moved robotically to Arif's commands. Incongruously, a cleaning woman squatting in a corner paused her incessant crablike sweeping to gawp at the unfolding drama. Hiba's nose and mouth disappeared behind an oxygen mask and the white brightness of the room pulsed as Sally felt her legs weaken. Steadying herself against a stainless steel shelf a metal kidney dish skittered then crashed to the floor, and, as if suddenly aware of her presence, Arif handed a cannula to the duty registrar. He led Sally to another, empty room. "Get a taxi and go home. Hiba will be all right; the oxygen and antibiotics will take effect very quickly. Lots of children get pneumonia. She'll be home again in a day or two. You can come back in the morning, but go home now." Her teeth chattered and he rubbed her arms vigorously. "Go home. Keep warm. Sammy will be worried; go and tell him his sister will be home soon. I'll phone in a few hours. Come." He led her to the corridor. "Go that way, and tell the nurse at the desk to get a taxi; tell her I said so." She nodded reluctantly, trusting her doctor husband to perform whatever miracle was needed. "Hiba will be fine," he repeated, "don't worry." Her feet obeyed his instructions, taking her along the corridor but her eyes saw nothing except Hiba's face enveloped in the oxygen mask.

When Arif arrived home Sally was in the kitchen, stirring a saucepan of erupting dhal. Her eyes sought beyond his unshaven chin and grey pallor and he answered her silent question. "She'll be fine." He filled a glass from the water cooler. "It's pneumonia and there's empyema too. But she's having antibiotics and within twenty four hours we'll see a big difference." He rubbed a hand over his eyes and turned towards the family room. "Come. Sit with me."

"What's empyema?" She followed him.

"It's a sometimes side effect of pneumonia. It's infected fluid, or pus, in the pleural cavity. That's the space between the lung and chest wall." Her hand flew to her mouth. "Don't worry, the antibiotics will deal with it. It could take a couple of weeks for her to fully recover, and we might need to use a chest tube to drain the pus, but she'll get better."

"A couple of weeks! But we're going to London on …." The impossibility of the planned journey sank in. "It doesn't matter. We can go in the Spring holiday." An acrid smell drifted from the kitchen. "Oh no!" Running into the kitchen she found a layer of blackened lentils stuck to the bottom of the saucepan. "Oh chootar! That's all I need!" Carefully ladling the top layer to a clean saucepan she dropped the burnt saucepan into the sink and filled it with water.

"It's only dhal, dhaling." Arif's old joke, started on their honeymoon almost nine years previously, brought a half smile and she returned to his side. "It is only dhal," he repeated, pulling her close.

"I know. You're right. I was making it for Hiba; it's easy for her to eat. I can make some more."

Arif nodded. "It's a good idea. Even if she was well she wouldn't eat hospital food." He rubbed his red rimmed eyes and told Sally he would shower, eat some of her dhal, and return to the hospital. "I want to check she gets the right medication and on time."

When Hiba didn't improve the next day Sally stayed at the hospital. Snow continued to fall gently beyond the window, echoing the slow drift of Hiba's tiny chest under the stiff white sheet. Late in the evening Hiba's eyes opened and Sally moved quickly into her view. "Hello little one," she whispered. A wave of coughing wracked Hiba's body and Sally hugged her daughter tightly until the paroxysm subsided.

"It hurts, Maa." Hiba's voice, distorted behind the oxygen mask, was barely audible.

Sally wiped a tear that ran out of the oxygen mask. "Hush, don't try to talk. We'll ask Baba for something to stop it hurting."

Summoned by the coughing, Arif came into the room. "She shouldn't be coughing like that." He put his stethoscope to Hiba's chest and listened. "I've changed her medication; she's on a combination dosage now." He checked her pulse and muttered to himself. "Why isn't she responding?" Lifting Hiba's other hand, he looked at the cannula. "What the…. " Snatching her chart from the end of the bed he demanded, "Which nurse did her last checks?"

"I think she's called Ansari; the tall, thin woman. Why?"

Arif was out of the door before Sally had finished speaking, returning a moment later gripping the forearm of the startled staff nurse. "Look!" He held Hiba's hand for the nurse to see. "This is infected! Why has it not been checked?" Sally leaned over to see where Arif pointed and noticed a redness and slight swelling around the white tape that held the cannula in place.

257

"This is a hospital. Nurses are trained to look for things like this! My daughter is here because she has pneumonia. Do you want her to have septicaemia too? I want a cannula – a sterile cannula – in her *other* hand, and I want this cleaned. Properly and now!" His voice was compelling; the nurse moved quickly.

Once the procedure had been completed Arif adjusted the sheet and tucked Bandy under Hiba's arm. "It's no wonder so many of our doctors leave Pakistan. It's impossible to work here. This is the best hospital in Abbottabad and still we cannot rely on good practice. How doctors cope in the Government hospitals I do not know." Frowning, he looked down then bent and picked something up. "Look at this! I should be surprised but I'm not. It's broken glass! A phial has been dropped and no-one has cleaned up! Patients walk around beds without their shoes on – what are nurses thinking of!"

"Here, give it to me." Sally tugged several tissues from a box and wrapped the glass carefully. "Arif. You said Hiba should be responding. What do you mean?"

Arif sighed. "Hiba's pneumonia is caused by a 'flu bacteria. The kind of antibiotics I've given her should deal with it, but there are other bacteria involved; she has empyema. It may be that Hiba's resisting the antibiotics because she's had so many over the years." He looked at Hiba's hand again then lifted it to his cheek. "There's another antibiotic; a new one. We don't have it here. But they have some at the new Shifa hospital in Islamabad. I'm going to drive there and get some."

"Arif! Why don't you send a courier? You can't drive all that way and back tonight!" His face was grey and slack.

But Arif was adamant. The newly opened hospital, he insisted, was equipped with modern machines and apparatus, and whilst there, he would test Hiba's blood more specifically. "I'll test yours too," he said, explaining that Sally might have acquired Hiba's bacteria and be in need of precautionary medication. He drew the blood himself, first hers, then gently tapping at Hiba's limp, thin arm until he found a vein, he filled a second phial. Kissing the round plaster on Hiba's arm after he was done, and knowing it was never a breakfast treat, he promised to bring her some ice-cream for breakfast the next morning.

"Mmmm, Ice-cream sounds good." Sally tried to tempt Hiba to eat after Arif had left. Ice-cream alone might not be an ideal meal but it would, at least, provide some nourishment. "Shall I go and get us both some now?" When Hiba nodded, she went to the street where, within minutes, a youth cycled slowly past the hospital. "Hey!" She called, "do you like ice-cream?" Apprehension turned to amusement as she offered to buy him whatever ice-cream he wanted if he would go to the parlour and buy three tubs, including one for himself. It was a risk – he might go off with the money – but it wasn't much. Ten minutes later he brought back the ice-creams and some change, which she insisted he keep.

"Here we are Shehzadi." Lifting Hiba so that she was sitting, she arranged her pillows and moved the oxygen mask. "Ice-cream." Hiba opened her mouth to accept the proffered spoonful and let it melt in her mouth. "Well done little princess. Only princesses have only ice-cream for tea, don't they?" A tiny smile tugged Hiba's mouth and she accepted another few spoonfuls before turning her head away. "What? A princess saying no to ice-cream? Whatever will the king say?" But the effort of eating even ice-cream was too much and Sally willed Arif's speedy return from Islamabad.

Hiba slept fitfully into the evening, her rasping breath muffled inside the mask. Exhausted, Sally tried to doze in a chair though each bout of coughing brought a fresh prayer to her lips. Soft soled shoes came and went, methodically recording Hiba's temperature, pulse, and medications. As day faded, the blue light of snow half lit the room, and rubbing her eyes Sally got up and switched on a light. Once more, Hiba's tiny chest heaved and choked into another round of hacking and in the new light Sally saw her daughter's skin. It was grey, her lips blue. "Nurse!" she shouted, then screamed, "Nurse!" Hiba struggled to sit upright, arms reaching for her mother, terrified eyes pleading for her to stop what was happening. A nurse ran in then out of the room again, shouting for the doctor. Hiba sucked fiercely at the mask's ration of air and clamped her lips as if reluctant to release it. The nurse returned with a doctor. The room filled with people. A cardiogram came to life. Bleep, bleep. Another line was inserted into another vein. A doctor listened through a stethoscope, first to the right, then the left, then the right of her chest. The bleeping slowed and someone pummelled her chest, picking up the rhythm of the cardiogram, but the bleeps still slowed. Then stopped. They hoisted Hiba so that her head hung backwards like a ragdoll, and Sally watched a tube pushed in and in, further and further, until it could go no more. A bag pumped air into Hiba's chest and she watched it rise and fall again and saw the doctor listen right and left then extract the tube and push it in again. The bleeping didn't start again. Nor did the breathing. The only thing the doctor could usefully do was to catch Sally as her legs folded and she dropped to the floor. But he was too late for that, too.

Over the coming weeks she asked Allah over and again why he'd taken back the child he'd so reluctantly given. What had they done wrong? What more could she have done? She'd prayed, she'd lived in faith; what had Allah seen, in his wisdom, to take her beloved daughter? They, her and Arif, should have been taken first. Taking Hiba was too cruel for reason.

Sammy was brought home from his school, and Karim and Pazir came home too. It seemed almost normal, having the family around, except for the solemnity. It would never be normal again. Laughter, like Hiba, had died. In a house thick with grief they spoke only to say what had to be said. Arif went about his day, his so recently youthful appearance lined and grey as an old man. There was no chatter. No teasing. No banter. She watched Sammy stare blankly at the TV. He'd always been an easy child to be with; easygoing and easily read. He'd said nothing. Perhaps he imagined himself too grown up at twelve years; a man who shouldn't cry. He'd changed during the past year. Limbs had stretched. His voice was a man's. A soft balloon bulged the front of his throat. He'd sat motionless for almost an hour, and Sally had filled with irrational panic then relief as she saw his youthful head move a fraction. Then she grew angry. How could he watch TV? His sister had been dead for only one week. She started to demand he turn it off, then stopped and instead, went to the kitchen to make a meal. Dhal. She'd make dhal. She could do it without thinking. Food. Hateful, life supporting food. Taking plates from the shelf she counted out six, then remembering, put one back.

Hours, days, weeks, and then a month shuffled into the past. Sammy returned to school. That morning Arif had left with Karim and Pazir; taking Karim to his Peshawar college and Pazir to the airport. Arif's mother had taken her grief to Dubai and in its emptiness the house had a new silence that Sally embraced. Arif would be away for two nights, staying with an old friend in Nowshera, giving her freedom to submerge herself in the heartache that had replaced her daughter. She hadn't the strength to deal with Arif's sorrow as well as her own.

She went to Hiba's room. On the bed was Bandy, the toy she'd refused to sleep without. An elastic hair-tie lay on the shelf next to the owl alarm clock that still ticked as if time mattered.

Twisted into a hair-tie were wisps of Hiba's dark hair and Sally picked it up and stroked it against her cheek. The room might have been ready for Hiba to come home to, except Shamila's presence overlaid the tidy dolls, books, clothes and the clean, fresh bed. Still holding the hair-tie Sally lay on the smooth sheet and let her face sink into the uncreased pillow that had once been indented with Hiba's face.

It was dark when the phone woke her, and quite cold. Pulling Hiba's blanket round her shoulders she turned to the wall and put her hands over her ears until the ringing stopped. It was probably Arif, or possibly Rachel. Rachel, who still called almost every day. A worm of guilt wriggled into consciousness. She'd have to go back to work soon; Rachel couldn't carry it all for ever. But not yet, not yet. She looked over her shoulder at the owl clock; it was almost nine thirty. Having eaten nothing since the meagre breakfast before Arif had departed that morning- she hadn't wanted it, but everyone ate – she had a hunger. With them all gone she didn't have to prepare food, or eat if she didn't want to. But this hunger was new. After a few more minutes she rose from the bed and went to the kitchen. With a handful of biscuits she returned to Hiba's bed and slept until the Imam called the dawn prayers.

Perhaps because she'd slept in Hiba's bed, or perhaps just because she'd slept, she woke feeling unusually refreshed. Somewhere in her head a voice protested; 'mourn'. It insisted, 'mourn and mourn again'. But the new energy was irresistible. She had another whole, free day before Arif would be back and discarding her creased shalwar kameeze she stepped into the shower. Scalding water stung her scalp and cascaded down her body, filling her mouth, her nose and her lungs with steam. She lathered her hair and body and rubbed until her skin tingled and suds circled her feet. Then she scrubbed her skin with a sun stiffened towel until she'd punished herself enough for enjoying this undeserved solitude.

She wanted tea. And eggs. She'd have to go to the market and buy food. But people would see her, criticize the light in her eyes, the bounce in her step. Taking her as yet unworn burka – destined for the visit to Mecca they'd planned to make – she covered and hid behind anonymity. She'd buy chicken, fresh coriander and chillies. She'd prepare the meal for Arif's return the following day. Chicken, sizzling with spices and lemon. And she'd ask Rachel to come for tea, to talk about work. She tidied Hiba's room, smoothing the sheet and turning the pillow to hide the creases her head had made. Shamila would wonder if she saw a used bed and Sally had no intention of sharing the secret of her sanctuary with anyone.

After another night in Hiba's room she woke again with energy. With fresh tea in hand she picked up the papers that Rachel had brought and saw the first folder contained a batch of applications for the new term that Rachel had already registered. Eight already; a whole new class. Another folder was full of letters that Rachel had answered and needed no more than a glance and her initials to indicate she'd read them. The third folder held a letter clipped to a batch of papers which she quickly saw, was the lease for her school premises. Unlike the other letters, this one didn't have Rachel's reply attached. Sally read more slowly as the words became meaning. The family who owned the building were giving three month's notice of their intention to repossess the property. No! She read the lines again. Why? Rachel had told her she must look at the lease, but not why. The letter was dated the previous day; she had just three months to find new premises. And turn it into a school. And inform everyone – who might not … it wasn't fair! "I don't want to move." She protested to no-one but the page. Her eyes glazed with tears and the letter, then the lease and its folder, slid from her fingers to the floor, taking with them the energy she'd started the day with.

The sounds of the gates opening and Arif's car roused Sally from Hiba's room. She closed her eyes tightly, resenting his – or anyone's – intrusion on her solitude, then realised she'd done nothing to prepare the meal she'd shopped for other than rub spices into the chicken the previous evening. Hastily tidying her daughter's bed she ran through the house and into the kitchen before the front door opened.

"Sally? Ap kahan hai?"

"Arif! I'm here, in the kitchen." She went to greet him, wiping her hands on a cloth as if she'd been busily preparing food. "Let me help." Taking his hat she saw that the pallor of his face had, if anything, deepened. "The journey was difficult?"

Arif shook his head. "No, not difficult. Just tiring."

Where was the warmth of their reunion; a kiss on her cheek, an enquiry of wellbeing? The despondent silence lay heavy and she let her feet turn her away. "I'll make tea. Sit down; I'll bring it to you."

The room, with its curtains drawn against the sun was dark but heavy with heat. Placing tea and a plate of biscuits by the side of Arif, she touched his hand. "Arif? Are you sleeping?"

His eyes remained closed but his hand moved and covered hers. "Sallyji." After a moment his eyes opened. "Sit with me. Please."

She switched on the ceiling fan and sat below it, opposite Arif, and waited. There was so much to be said and yet so little they could say. Arif roused himself. "Sammy?"

"In school." Dust swirled in a sliver of sunlight. "Karim and Pazir?"

"Yes, they have returned. Pazir's flight left on time."

Her eyes followed the dust and her mind cried out to her husband, 'Talk to me about Hiba. She's here! Can't you feel her?' The tea cooled, the biscuits went untouched and the distance between her and the stranger she was married to lengthened.

"Nowshera? Your friend was well?"

Arif nodded. He stood, moved to the window and pushed aside the curtain, stirring more dust mites into a frenzy. "I've been to Rawalpindi. Not to Nowshera."

He'd lied to her? Why? Arif didn't lie.

He stood with his back to her. "Before I tell you what I have to say I want first of all to tell you that I love you. It's important that you know this is the truth. I hope you will one day be able to forgive me for what has happened and also for what..." Blood suffused his neck and Sally tasted foreboding. "When I took blood, yours and Hiba's, to Islamabad, it was to test not for pneumonia antibodies, but for this fear they call AIDS. You've heard of it, though no-one speaks of it. I couldn't do the tests in Abbottabad; people know us here."

Why didn't he turn and look at her? Why couldn't she move?

"I can hardly say this but you have to know. We have the virus. It is confirmed."

The table at her side fell sideways, her cup smashing into splinters and tea. She'd heard about AIDS; it had been on the news and in the newspapers when she'd been in London. It killed people, slowly. Dreadfully. The actor, Rock Hudson had died of it. And also Freddie Mercury, about two years ago. They'd said Freddie Mercury died of pneumonia but everybody knew he was gay. Photos had shown him like an old man, his skin stretched across bones like Faiza's had been. Faiza! She made the connection; pneumonia and Hiba, and Arif's words ricocheted off the gilt mirror frame, the wooden chair backs, the brass topped table.

"I am a doctor. But I've failed."

His voice, an echo. Hers too. Unreal.

"But it's a gay disease. AIDS is a disease of gay men!"

"My dearest wife, I have this dreadful virus, and I, may Allah forgive me, have given it to you. And our daughter. Because I failed to see. It is unforgivable. Faiza died because of me, and our little daughter, Naimah too. I believed we didn't have this virus in our society. I believed it to be not only a disease of homosexuality – the word sat uncomfortably – but a Western disease. I was blind. I allowed complacency to lead to this. Allah granted me a good life and I have not acted wisely. Many years ago Rachel's first husband died in my care and I now acknowledge his illness for what it must have been. A needle stick injury is careless; I remember he flailed about as I injected him. This is when I must have contracted this dreadful, hateful, and," he paused momentarily, "incurable virus."

Sally saw him turn, felt his hands take hers and saw his face before her. This man, this doctor who was her husband, was responsible for her treasured daughter's death.

"Our beloved Hiba is gone, and in all probability, Sammy will be alone before he is a man. If Hiba isn't enough, you'll bear this too."

Sammy? Here was another horror!

"Rachel will also worry, but it is a long time ago for her, and she and her family are healthy so I think she must be safe though I do not know how. I do not know how I have lived for so long without being ill. I suppose my cough and skin….."

Of course, Rachel's first husband!

"Sally, my heart is broken. I am sorry. I ask forgiveness without a right to expect it from you, but in hope. There is money; I will make arrangements for my Mother, and for Pazir and Karim, and for you and Sammy. I've made a new will…"

He'd known for a month! He'd not told her. Hiba's grey, frightened face appeared before her, her lips blue as she sucked for air, her terrified eyes pleading. Her head falling back as the tube was pushed down her throat. The pumping of her chest and the silent heart monitor. "Nooooo...." Sally's wail obliterated her husband's words, inflating and expanding into a howl that enveloped her, filled the room, became everything...

The first thing Sally became aware of as she woke was pain. Black, coarse pain that grated her skull, her eyes, her neck. It immobilised her. There was light beyond her eyelids and she slowly opened her eyes against the pain that stalked the careful movement and threatened worse. Then Arif, Hiba, and the pain exploded. Gasping, she jolted her eyes shut again. There'd been an injection in her arm. Arif, yes, it would have been Arif. She'd thought she was dying and had submitted and welcomed the unstoppable black wave. But it hadn't worked. With eyes still closed she wished death could be so easy. The throbbing in her head settled to steady pain and slowly she became aware of a hand holding hers and quiet words being whispered.

"Sallyji. Wake up."

She didn't want to. She couldn't. She wouldn't. Another scratch on her arm; this one brought white lightness. And quiet, gentle peace.

When she woke again Arif was still there, still holding her hand. She dared to think, remember, then to open her eyes again and saw him, grey and drawn. The doctor, who should have known.

Over the days that followed Arif told her about the visit to Rawalpindi. He'd been to meet a man, a victim of HIV, he said. Human Immunodeficiency Virus. In some cases, and as it seemed with him and possibly Rachel too, the virus didn't develop into AIDS, which surprised her as she thought that HIV and AIDS were the same thing and people died of it. But it gave hope. Hope that she too, might be one of the lucky ones.

Arif didn't look at her when he told her that babies could be born with it and also, could get it from their mother's milk. Ice chilled her bones. He was a doctor, he should have known. Because of him, those intimate, much cherished times had blighted her child's life. Her milk; the best she could give her own child had killed her. She'd turned from him then, and thanked Allah for the irony that Sammy, born from outside the marriage bed, was safe.

A few more long, silent days passed before Arif told her of his plans. "I cannot continue to work here in the hospital; they'll not have me." He was going to work with the man in Rawalpindi. "He's a brave man. As a Christian with HIV he has to face much discrimination. He has started an organisation to help other victims – Christians, Muslims, wives, children, anyone – with HIV. A doctor would be useful. His name is Nabeel Kumar."

Despite her anguish Sally felt some regard for the man's bravery.

Arif elaborated. "He couldn't find work so became a migrant worker in Quatar."

Sally turned her face away, hating this new enthusiasm that was creeping into Arif's voice.

"They make them take a blood test when they enter the country now, and Nabeel, well, that was how he found out."

"He works here now?"

"He runs a sewing machine repair shop, and has a clinic – of sorts – there. The UN and some international donors fund his work."

Arif planned to live in Rawalpindi during the week, though, he said, they might move there in time. And next month he was to travel into India with Nabeel where, although there wasn't a cure, they hoped to get drugs that might help – if they could smuggle them into Pakistan.

Rawalpindi? She knew no one in Rawalpindi or even nearby Islamabad. She looked at her husband sitting cross-legged on the floor, his eyes bright, his high forehead frowning with intensity as he explained this new world of hope and life and future, a world that included and yet excluded her and Sammy, and felt cold. Sammy, at only twelve years old, was going to have his future abruptly changed, and... she worked out with shocking clarity – she might live for only two or three more years. Then what? Arif would be alive? And what about Rachel? The drugs from India might (might!) help, but what future for Sammy?

In England, Sammy had a father. And a grandmother. And blood is, after all, thicker than water.

CHAPTER 15

Banana Cake

Michael was still sitting at the table when John came back to the kitchen. He looked small, deflated inside his skin. "Dad. Your tea." He pushed the mug forwards.

"Yes. Thank you." Michael's hands wrapped round the mug. "Neil and Linda gone?" John nodded. "I asked them to put her clothes into bags. For Oxfam."

"That's good."

"And I've told Linda she can take the flower arranging stuff. To give to Lucy. Lucy does flowers."

"That's good too. They're good people, Linda and Neil."

John took a knife from the block. "For you?"

For a moment Michael looked blank, then comprehended the change of topic. "Go on then. Your Mum reckoned Linda used to make those cakes to use up the bananas that Neil couldn't sell, and when he retired, she couldn't stop making them." He accepted a slice and broke away a corner. "She said Linda's cakes weren't as good as hers, but they all tasted good to me. I never told her so, though." He chewed the corner piece absently. "It must be eight years since they sold that business. Do you still get your vegetables from the new people?"

The banana cake story was as stale as the banana cake, and the new people weren't new people any more. "I do. Their stuff's fresh and they have a variety. Herbs too. They're good."

He started to clear away the tea things but his father resisted. "Leave it, John. Leave it for now." His eyes were pink rimmed and watery. "Sit down. Talk to me. It's been three weeks since

Frances died, and no-one even says her name. They think I'll get upset if they mention her. Even Linda. I'm grateful for what she and Neil are doing, but I wish she'd stop being so busy when she's here, and would just sit down and talk about her." Michael pushed his empty tea mug aside. "Tell me how you are, John. Tell me how *you* are coping."

Being busy, particularly around his father, was how he was coping. It was how they were all coping. "I don't know, Dad. Sometimes I forget she's gone and then I remember and it hurts that I could have forgotten. It's a surprise that she's not here, now, with us." He reached for an ashtray from the dresser and saw a card with a Picasso dove. "You've got some more cards. Shall we go through them?" It felt like a useful thing to do. "There's quite a lot; and letters too. We should answer the letters, and some of the cards too."

Taking silence as agreement, he put them on the table and opened the first one. "Brian and Jane." He thought for a minute. "Weren't they the people who lived across the road, who went to Bournemouth?"

Michael took the card. "They did. We went and stayed with them once. Beautiful gardens down there. And a theatre. The Winter Gardens. Your Mum pinched a cutting off their white begonias. She was always getting cuttings from somewhere or other." He picked out a second card and looked at the flowery water-colour before opening it. "Oliver and Susan. I play golf with Oliver sometimes." He read aloud. *We wanted you to know how sorry we were to hear about Frances. We didn't know her as well as we did you, but we remember the beautiful flowers she did for our daughter's wedding.* He looked at a potted hyacinth, flowering on the windowsill. "Everyone talks about her flowers."

As they read, Michael's eyes regained some animation. He read kind words from Diane and Malik and then picked up another one. "Anthony." He paused. "Anthony knows what it's

271

like. It's been four years since Moira died. Same thing. Ovarian adenocarcinoma." He pronounced the word as though he'd been using it all his life. "They caught Moira's earlier. You'd expect that, wouldn't you, with Anthony being a doctor. It was another five years before she died. Your mum was already in stage four when hers was diagnosed. Perhaps it was better that way. Not knowing, I mean. But it was too late for the surgery and chemo they gave her. It made her last months hell, going through all that."

John took Anthony's card and put it back with the others. "Dad, the surgery and chemo might have helped. It might have worked. But it happened so quickly. Last summer Mum was well. She was pleased because she'd lost some weight. She had no pain. Nothing until just four months ago." Four short months. He recalled how she'd stay in bed for a day or so every month when he'd been a boy. He hadn't understood it at the time, he'd just accepted that she wasn't well. When he came back from college, she was miraculously better; it didn't happen anymore. The oncologist had said there might be a link between endometriosis and ovarian cancer. "No one knew, Dad. There was no warning about the cancer until it was too late." Privately he agreed with his father and wished they'd spared her the traumas of chemotherapy and surgery. "We don't know what might have been, Dad, and we can't change anything."

Michael cut another slice of Linda's cake, his movements slow and heavy. "Have another piece." He offered the slice. "Do you want to read your Mum's will?"

He'd expected that, at some time, his father would mention the will and was curious, but felt ashamed that his thoughts had wandered into such matters so readily. There'd been money, inherited from her father some years previously, and through her generosity he'd started the Bristol restaurant. And she'd paid for his holiday in Greece. He assumed that any monies left would go to Michael. "Should I? Can't you just tell me what it says?"

"I've got a copy if you want to see it, but the solicitor will be writing to you. Soon. It's straight forward; a few bequests and everything else coming to me. The surviving spouse. Except for her shares. Her 'portfolio'." He mimicked Frances's voice, trying to make it sound amusing. 'Portfolio'. It echoed in John's head. "And a sapphire tie pin that belonged to her father. They're yours. I'll get you the pin later; it's in her jewellery box. And the solicitor will send you the shares stuff. "

John swallowed. He hadn't expected that. The stocks and shares were valuable; enough to pay off his mortgage if he chose to. Or think about another restaurant. It was hard not to be pleased, despite the circumstances.

"And it's not in the will, but she always told me she was going to give you her engagement ring. She didn't wear it anymore; it didn't fit her. But she hoped that, well, one day...
..." Michael's words trailed off. "Anyway. You'd better have it."

One day. Tomorrow? Any day? Words took you forwards in time but didn't stand still long enough to be caught. Frances had yearned for family and it had saddened her to be denied children of her own. To also be estranged from the grandchildren she'd have loved, nurtured, and spoiled, had been an added heartache. "I'm sorry I couldn't make her happy, Dad." An image of the old photograph of Sally and her family skittered through John's mind. "I'll keep the ring, and when the 'one day' comes, it'll be used." An empty promise?

"Ay, John. Do that." He gathered cake crumbs on the table. "There's another bequest." He pressed the crumbs on to his finger and ate them. "For Sammy."

"Sammy?"

"Yes." Michael's voice was carefully casual. "We thought about him a lot, you know. Frances worried about his future.

She wanted to help him have a good education and so she bought some bonds after she sold her father's house. They're tied into a trust fund."

Bonds? Trust funds? Astonishment overcame his initial outrage. Frances had secured a future for Sammy without discussing it with him. "She had it all worked out, didn't she?"

Michael shook his head. "No. She left that to the trustees; me and the solicitor. I've written to Sally."

This second revelation was undeniably an intrusion, and only with an effort, did he remain calm. "You have her address?"

"Yes. I got it from Diane. I wrote a few days ago."

He was astounded. The news that Michael had undertaken such things without telling him astonished him. He looked at the man in front of him, and saw beyond the seventy-eight year old frame to the man who had always known he was right – even when he wasn't. "You wrote to her. Without telling me?"

"You never wanted children. We wanted to do something for him."

"Never wanted?" John struggled to control his voice. "Dad, you have no idea. Why didn't you talk to me before you wrote to Sally. Why did neither of you talk to me about a trust fund?"

Michael looked away. "We thought you'd say no."

It was then that he realised what Frances had done and his anger dissipated. She'd been clever, very clever. She'd crafted a key for John.

Michael plucked a letter from one of the sympathy cards. "Do you remember Alice, your Mum's old friend?" It was a rhetorical question. "She says she'd like me to go and stay for a few days. That's kind, isn't it? Maybe I'll go." He folded the letter and laid it back on the pile. "One day."

With Frick away, and less than half of the tables occupied in the Bristol restaurant, admiration for what his mother had done was tempered by Frick having given his notice. He'd tried to dissuade Frick from the current trip to Belfast, sure that 'the troubles' as Frick called them, were no more than a local vendetta, but 'the troubles' had unnerved Frick's wife, and she was set on leaving England. The tin of paint thrown over the family car had been infuriating but had been passed off as malicious nonsense until the letters started to arrive. *The car was first* and *Get out or look out* had been followed by newspaper cuttings about the Warrington bombings. Frick's wife had become frightened and though he tried to talk Frick into a less distant move, Frick said they were fed up with looking over their shoulders and were going home. The final straw had been when his son had returned from school with a blackened eye, which might have been the result of a clash on the football field. But there'd been cruel words about Irish Catholics, and Frick had said they couldn't live like that. But he wouldn't go until he had a job, and that's where he was; at an interview near Belfast.

John was tired. As he called the final order he felt like he'd worked a long, hard shift rather than the quiet evening that had passed. "Normandy Pork, to go," and "Beef rump". Despite working all evening with food, he hadn't eaten since Linda's banana cake and taking a fresh steak, he slapped it on the hotplate. A handful of pre-fried chips went into the fryer, and he poured a large glass from the remains of someone's '87 Bordeaux. Months of watching his mother die and the emotional decline of his father had taken its toll. He was exhausted. Not just fatigued, but bone weary, and he longed for space and distance and energy. He wanted... a holiday! The idea rolled around a few times and he liked it. A few weeks somewhere, alone, was extremely tempting. France? It had been almost a year since Sandy's last visit and he imagined her face light with joy as he turned up, unannounced, at her home town, then he chuckled as he visualised the more likely dismissal. She barely spoke about her life in France, and he assumed she had a good reason not to share it with him. Perhaps she was married; he didn't want to meet a husband. The charade of a clandestine affair – if that's what it was – brought its own excitements. No, Sandy wasn't the answer. He thought of somewhere unfamiliar, exotic. Pakistan? The name rolled around his mouth a few times. Sammy would be eleven; an age where his education might be considered. Sally's husband – he tripped over the term 'husband' – had looked tall and severe, and military. An officer probably, perhaps one of the Generals he'd read about in the newspapers. Articles about Pakistan caught his eye. It seemed an unruly place, dominated by the military and religion, with politicians and ministers being shot and bombed. He'd read recently that Benazir Bhutto had become prime minister for the second time and that Western politicians were talking tentatively of economic and social stability. It might be a time to visit, though he'd never heard of anyone going to Pakistan for a holiday. He played with the idea for a while until sense told him of its futility.

But the seeds, once planted, germinated. He considered The States. Barrie Bates, his old college friend, rebranded (wasn't that the term?) as Billy Apple, working impressively alongside greats like Jasper Johns and Andy Warhol. Was he still in 'The Big Apple'? Probably not. Or he might take his mother's legacy and double it on the gaming tables of Las Vegas. Or go to the Grand Canyon. He hadn't had a break, a proper break, for years. Julia and his chefs would manage for a few weeks without him, and Alain could handle any crises. The idea warmed. New people, new foods, new ideas. It would refresh him, and Seagrams would benefit from that. As a student he'd tried to paint giant abstracts of the Grand Canyon, fusing dramatic landscape shapes with rock and river and sunset colours. With youthful delusions of brilliance he'd tried oils, then pastels, and finally collage, but they'd lacked conviction and he'd blamed the lack of realism in abstraction rather than his lack of skill. And because it sounded impressive. But the Grand Canyon was inspirational and he felt an urge to visit. Then reality asserted itself. All he'd been through was still happening; Michael, at the kitchen table, was bent by a loneliness he didn't know how to live with. John couldn't leave him. Not yet. Reluctantly, he put the dreams into his 'one day' box.

Fresh rain drops splattered the already shiny streets as he claimed space behind two chatting cyclists on a right turn. His father inhaled audibly, and he couldn't resist teasing him. "Don't worry. There're plenty more students. I'll bag a couple later." He drove on, newly accustomed to this quiet man his father had become. "Fifteen minutes, and we'll be there." Rows of bicycles, strong and determined, rested along the side of the Bodleian Library, some standing proudly upright, some battered and disintegrating, tangled into each other as if they'd given up hope. Like his father, thought John. In need of an overhaul, a refit. It had been a blessing when he'd agreed to stay with his gregarious bachelor brother in Oxford where music, books, eating and drinking, and of course, debate with Geoffrey's interesting friends, was not for the downhearted.

"You're here!" Geoffrey's rounded girth emerged from the front door. "Good-oh! I was watching out for you. Filthy weather. Come on in. Fire's lit. Tea's almost ready. I got some scones from the WI stall. Ate one already!" he guffawed. Two fat cats sat on piles of papers and books in the warm and dusty, cluttered sitting room. "So good you can stay a night too, John. Don't know how you can get away these days. How's business?" Before John could reply, he continued. "Booked a table at The Boathouse for tonight. Good traditional pub grub; beef casserole, treacle sponge. That sort of thing. Nice place, though a bit quiet." He passed the scones to Michael. "Not John's posh nosh, eh?"

Michael was already beginning to brighten. "Suits me, Geoffrey. I'm glad you're not going to ask John to cook for us."

John wasn't offended; it was small talk, and meant nothing. He retorted, "Sounds good to me, too. I'm glad you're not asking my Dad to cook, either."

As it can in spring, Friday's winter weather preceded the kind of day that promises the start of summer, when city dwellers covet houses on green hillsides and non-gardeners don their Wellington boots. John savoured the warmth as he drove home, and imagined customers flocking to a new, pretty, canal fronted restaurant. The previous evening's visit to The Boathouse had been disappointing. Until, that is, John saw the opportunity. Few customers wanted the flat beer, dull wine, or 'homemade' food from the freezer, and the nicotine décor and stained false oak bar wasted the pub's privileged location. As worn as the pub, the owner revealed a recent 65th birthday and a desire to retire, and John asked not if it was the right time or place for his fourth restaurant, but how he would make it his. In terms of timing, it was foolproof. The government had officially declared Britain out of this latest recession, and optimism and spending were increasing. There'd never been a better time to launch a new restaurant. With ownership of the Bathampton and Bristol properties and a long lease on the Cider Barn, funding wasn't going to be difficult. With his mother's legacy, he was now a rich man and wondered if he should keep his mother's portfolio and raise funds from investors or sell shares and invest the proceeds in Seagrams Ltd? The former would spread the risk but the latter would give him controlling share of the company. He laughed out loud; it had never occurred to him that he would wonder, one day, what to do with money! The risk on The Boathouse lay not in its location but in its distance from Somerset. Oxford appeared vibrant, and had a sizeable middleclass and student population, so it was promising. But its distance from the Seagrams hub presented challenges. He did a mental pros and cons exercise. Ticks; ripe for development, perfect position, keep Frick and move him to Oxford. Crosses; distance, unknown market. When the ideas dried up he began a new list, this time of questions. 1. How to fund. 2. Management – will existing structures expand. 3. Julia – Need her views. 4. Alain. He wants to retire soon. The list grew so that he couldn't remember what all the questions were, but the now familiar and addictive buzz of a new project was humming along with the car engine. He'd need to do some groundwork to present the project to the group who formed Seagrams' official sounding but casually informal Board of Directors; Alain, Julia and Trevor, the Bathampton chef. The other director had been his mother.

Taking advantage of the light spring morning John emerged from his flat in shorts and new running shoes and loped self-consciously along the pavement, nodding complicitly at a fellow jogger and hoping that he didn't look like the (slightly) tubby novice that he was. Within minutes his breath rasped and he slowed, regulating his pace to his breathing as it became clear that even on this fourth outing, he was still a beginner. The running regime had started after losing several squash matches. Forty-five wasn't young, but it wasn't old, either, and with new determination, he'd resolved to be a non-smoker. He looked intently at Bath's glorious Royal Crescent as if his slowed pace had been determined by an urge to study the grandeur, then moved on, round The Circle and retraced his steps towards the park. This, he knew, was where he'd find the real runners, and where, on his first few outings, he'd felt himself to be an impostor amongst the knotty calved men and pony tailed women who'd overtaken him with ease. But already there was a glow of companionship as he joined in, looking he believed, like a jock. In just two weeks as a non-smoker he felt fitter, and had even begun to appreciate subtle flavours and aromas. Just this morning there'd been a new richness in his coffee, and the fragrance of newly cut grass in the park was as sweet as when, as a boy, he'd thrown grass trimmings at his father. Remembering that reminded him that his father's lawn would need cutting whilst he was away. He checked his watch. He still had time before his session at Bristol to call at the house, cut the lawn, and check all was well.

Cheap, glossy junk mail protruded from the letterbox, and as he unlocked his father's front door, he tugged the post through. He'd let himself in many times before but this time felt different. Alone with the old curtain smell and a silence he could hear he gathered mail from the floor. Dust motes danced in yellow light cast by the door's stained glass panel and his eyes, distorted to an alien roundness by the gilt framed convex mirror, took in the regency-stripe wallpaper and faded Constable prints. Like the curtain, they belonged to a bygone time. The door to the kitchen door stood open and he could see the red Formica table, naked except for a cake tin. He hadn't been prepared for the lifelessness. This, he thought, was what death felt like; memory created expectations that reality failed to deliver. The kitchen had been a family room, a warm retreat and gathering point. He saw himself at the table, aged eleven, with his childhood friend Rick. Rick, who hated peas. Frances had cooked peas and they'd giggled helplessly as Rick flicked them, one by one, on to his plate and the room echoed momentarily with ghostly laughter. Dropping the post on the table, he opened the cake tin and found the remains of one of Linda's banana cakes robed in green fur. In a pot on the windowsill, dead daffodils sulked and hung their shrivelled heads, and outside, fallen forsythia blossom patterned the paving slabs and drifted against the wall. He made to go outside to cut the grass. But he stopped. If he cut the grass what would Michael have to do when he returned? Instead, he wrapped the remains of the banana cake in an unread paper, washed the tin, and replaced it in the larder. Tablecloths were kept in the drawer. Moving the letters aside he spread a bright cloth over the table and put the letters on top. Then he saw the blue airmail envelope, stamped in Pakistan.

He resisted opening it several times before doing so. Smoothing the tissue-thin paper flat on the table he looked at Sally's handwriting, very little changed despite the passage of almost twelve years. 'Dear Michael'. Sally expressed her sorrow at the news of Frances, and hoped that Michael and the family were finding solace. John spluttered. "The family!" He, John, was 'the family'. Why couldn't she have written *and John*? He skimmed the letter, seeking news of Sammy. *It comes as a surprise to learn of a trust fund for Sammy, and I'm deeply touched that you considered such a thing.* He raced on; Sally planned to travel to London at Christmas with Sammy and Hiba, and she would write to the solicitor as Michael had asked. He read more slowly, *Though it is important we discuss Sammy's future together before we can accept such generosity.* She went on to say she hoped to be able to see Michael in December and would telephone when she arrived in London. John swallowed. December! Almost nine months away. Sammy would be twelve. He'd been a baby when he left England. There was an address was at the top of the letter; Abbottabad. He had no idea where Abbottabad was, this place where his son was growing up. He considered writing soon, then decided it would be better later, nearer the time. Noting the address in his diary, he slipped the letter back into its envelope and scribbled a note on the envelope, *Sorry, Dad, hope you don't mind me opening Sally's letter.* Then he left the house to its ghosts.

But ghosts stayed with him and thoughts of the visit tempted him to write sooner. Letters formed in his head. *Dear Sally. Many years have passed since....*, or, *I was pleased to read your letter....* A thought, so basic, stopped him short. Did Sally want him as Sammy's father? She must – it was a fundamental truth. Over the years, her affair had faded into relative obscurity against the certainty of fatherhood, and though it had hurt deeply, time had softened memories and diminished the consequences. Whatever had happened between Sally and another man wasn't a part of Sammy and all he wanted was to be acknowledged and have some kind of reconciliation with his son. *Dear Sally*, he started again, and getting no further, shelved the problem for another day.

When Frick arrived back at work, John was keen to hear the result of the Belfast interview. "Hey, how did it go?"

"Ah, it was a good job, so it was," Frick fastened his apron and began to work alongside him. "But there were better than me for it."

"Well, they missed their chance with you." John commiserated, suppressing his relief that Frick wouldn't be leaving just yet. Planning approval for the Oxford pub was by no means secured and he didn't want to raise Frick's hopes with the prospect of something that might not happen. "Things ok at home though?"

"Oh, ay. Jenny's upset. She wants away, but I'll not go on the Nat King."

"Nat King?"

"Dole. Nat King Cole. You no heard o' that?"

He shook his head. "Anything from the police?"

"We'll be waiting for it." Frick never used a definitive yes or no, and in this instance John took his answer to be no. "The trouble is there're so many of 'em blowing in and we never see the same gard twice. But they're all the same, so they are. They say it'll be some chancer trying his arm, so unless they catch him rotten we've no chance."

All this had been said at a pace so rapid that John stopped preparing his lamb crowns to keep up. "Well it's good nothing else has happened. Given time, it might settle down. Are you sure that moving to Ireland is the right thing to do?"

Frick leaned on the back of his knife to crush garlic cloves. "I know what you're saying John, but Jenny's got it into her head, and it needs some neck to argue with that one. Right now, she's jumpy as a fiddler's bow. She won't let the kids out of her sight. They're truly fed up, so they are, and they're kicking off most of the time. I tell you, John, I'm glad to be here, so I am! If you're ever after having kids yourself, be warned. Your life'll never be the same again."

John pushed away the racks of lamb, now chined, and left the kitchen. It was difficult to comprehend how Sammy, in his life for so short a time, had had such impact. Blood thicker than water? That, and the parallel ripples of his own childhood, which had prompted a great deal of soul searching over the years. He recalled something someone had once said. Andy Warhol he thought it was. Time, he'd said, didn't change anything. You had to do the change yourself. He was both right and wrong, John thought. Time did change things. Time had sent his father to the grave before he got round to finding him and it made him determined to find a way to establish a relationship with his own son before it was too late. He declared too, that he would find Gillian Crowson, before time changed that too.

It was the worst kind of winter's day. A late dawn had hidden itself behind grey drizzle so that vehicles on the road loomed like phantoms and headlights wavered, ghoul-like. In front of John's car a lorry load of gravel dribbled water. It smeared greyness across his windscreen and John worried about having sufficient washer water for the journey. It was a slow drive. He'd left home shortly after five, and at almost ten he was still thirty miles from Wisbech. Time he'd allowed for a break to garner himself and gather his thoughts before meeting Gillian Crowson was diminishing. Her letter lay on the passenger seat but he didn't need it. *You have always been in my thoughts, and the prospect of meeting you again is beyond my dreams.* His heart had thumped and his eyes had brimmed with tears when he'd first read it, until the old voices had intervened. *Always?* If that were true, how could she have handed him over to a stranger? She'd mothered him for a year and a half before she'd given him away, and for more than thirty years he'd sought and never found reason other than, like Sally, she'd deceived her husband. In which case, Jack Crowson would not have been his father. A tangled web, indeed. But, unlike fatherhood, motherhood couldn't be compromised. A photograph, taken on holiday somewhere warm, had been in the envelope and he'd stared and stared at it, seeking a likeness in the low resolution picture and wondering if she'd stared the same, at the photograph he'd sent her.

There'd been two telephone conversations since the letter. The first had been stilted, and she'd cried. John hadn't; he'd forced himself to think of her giving him away, and later feared she'd thought him unfeeling. The second call had been longer. She'd asked about his work and he'd told her about Seagrams. She'd said she liked cooking too, especially baking. And she'd told him she didn't share her son's home as he'd thought she did. The son lived near, but she lived alone. Then they'd made the arrangements for the day that was unfolding.

The gravel lorry in front slowed to let a van turn right and John saw the Little Chef café he'd stopped at five years earlier.

He'd had bacon and beans then; overcooked and cold. But the coffee had been hot and strong, and that's what he wanted now. His watch said ten-forty. If he stopped he'd be late. But the temptation of coffee was great and he reasoned that if it had been forty-three and a half years since Gillian Crowson had last seen her him, another ten minutes wasn't going to make much difference.

Number 10, Victoria Road. The house suited the street name; a bay fronted, red brick Victorian villa, it had been a slightly later addition to the side of the neighbouring two-up two-down terrace. He hadn't smoked for more than six months, but he craved a cigarette. If Gillian Crowson smoked he'd have one for sure. Behind a net curtain a shape moved; she'd been watching, waiting for his arrival. Nevertheless he rang the bell and within seconds she was there. Gillian Crowson. Shorter than he'd imagined, with the Queen's grey hair and pearls, though he doubted the Queen would wear powder-blue fur-lined slippers. He fidgeted with his car key and his hands were sweating. He dropped the key into a pocket. Should he shake her by the hand? Kiss her on the cheek? Throw his arms round this long lost mother? Neither spoke then they spoke in unison; "Hello", and both apologised. "Sorry." "Sorry." He stepped forwards, shuffling sideways in the narrow hallway to allow her to close the door. Her face was flushed but a shaky smile lightened her eyes.

"Go through," she said. "First door."

"Thank you." The scent of lavender wax explained the gleaming oak sideboard and side tables.

"The weather's awful. You've had a long drive; sit by the fire. Here, have the easy chair." A large armchair stood next to a grate of glowing ceramic coals. "I'll make some tea. Make yourself at home."

The room sparkled with cleanliness. Even the leaves on the plants shone. He glanced at his shoes, wondering if he should remove them, but decided that as an afterthought it was no better than keeping them on. He desperately wanted a cigarette but couldn't imagine anyone had ever smoked in this pristine room. A group of photographs stood on the sideboard; family pictures in shining frames. He picked up one, then another. When she returned with a tray of cake and cups he'd replaced the first and was rubbing fingerprints from the other.

"Oh, that's Katherine's family." A small shiny table was pulled forwards and the tray of floral china crockery placed on it. "Katherine's my eldest." She pointed to two girls. "That's Fiona, she's at university in Leeds, and that's her sister Lizzie who's still at school, doing 'A' levels. And that's Bob, Katherine's husband." A kettle whistled from somewhere. "And that's Lorraine, my next one, with Mike and their daughter, Alice. And that's Matthew and Vicky, with their brood; Dominic, Lawrence, Richard and Rebecca." He felt weak, afraid he was going to cry, and was relieved when she disappeared again. These were his brother and sisters, in-laws, nephews and nieces. One minute he was an only child, the next, he was surrounded by kith and kin. There was another photo, black and white, with a man and woman on their wedding day, which could only be Jack and Gillian Crowson. His father had been a tall, heavy set man. And handsome. Gillian was much smaller, though taller than now, and very young.

A teapot was brought into the room and placed on the table with the china. He pointed at the wedding picture. "This is you, isn't it? How old were you when you got married?"

"Twenty one."

"So young."

"We did, then."

He'd already told her he wasn't married and she hadn't asked about children, probably assuming he didn't have any. "And this was my father?"

"Yes. He was your father." A gentleness softened her voice. "He's been gone for twenty eight years."

"Cancer?"

"No. His heart gave out in the end. It was a blessing; he'd been ill for a long time."

The man in Leverington had been wrong; it wasn't cancer. "He was ill for a long time? What was it?"

She waved him to the chair. "We've a lot to tell each other. A lot. But first, have some tea and get yourself warm." Two cups were filled. "Milk, sugar?" A smaller table was moved next to him and a cup placed on it. "Do you like banana cake?"

John laughed; he couldn't help it. "Banana cake? You've made banana cake?"

"I have. What's funny about that?"

"Oh, nothing really." He wiped his eyes; there was little difference, sometimes, between tears of laughter and tears of sorrow. "My mother's…" he faltered, "I mean…"

"Your other mother…"

He took up the term. "My other mother's friend used to make it all the time, to my other mother's chagrin."

"She didn't like banana cake?"

"She did, very much. We all did. Do. It's a long story."

"Ah. Another day then. We've a lot of those to tell each other."

He was warming to this woman, though owning her as a mother was a difficult step. He tried to visualise her as Frances, doing his accounts, and then with him as a child, perhaps on the beaches of Norfolk. But her face didn't sit in the images. As she talked he explored her face, searching for hints of likenesses but finding little more than the small cleft in the chin that he'd seen in the photograph of Sammy. He'd have to tell her about

Sammy. If they met again. After Sally's December visit. If someone had accused him of being superstitious John would have laughed, but with Christmas only a month away he was reluctant to tempt providence by saying aloud that they were coming.

"It was like a dream come true when I got your letter." Gillian's voice was quiet and John leaned forward. "It's such a long time Jonath… Sorry. You've been Jonathan in my head for forty five years. It's hard to change."

It was a small revelation, but it gave John courage that she'd cared enough to think about him for forty five years. "I think 'John' fits me now."

"Yes. I'm sure it does. I wrote a little card to you, every birthday. To Jonathan. With a few words about the family. I've still got them; you can have them if you want. Silly of me, I suppose. But I always hoped you'd come looking for us, one day."

This was a huge revelation, and tears hovered at the edge of control. "I'd like to have them." He spoke quietly. "I'd like to have them very much."

"I'll get them. Before you go." She inclined her head. "I was saying. It's a very long story, and I hardly know where to start." Her teacup began to rattle in its saucer and she put it down. "Your father, Jack, was ill for a long time. He had Pick's disease. I don't expect you know what that is?" She continued as he shook his head. "It's a kind of dementia. It started early, in his early forties and got worse as he got older."

John quaked. "Dementia in his forties! It's hereditary?" The question was brutally selfish but the prospect horrified him.

"It…. Well, yes. But not everyone will develop it. He was younger than you when it started. Jack's grandmother had probably had the same thing, but they didn't know what it was in those days. Neither his father nor his sisters had it. We didn't know what it was for almost six years; and even then, they couldn't be sure that's what it was because there was no way of checking. Not then. They can diagnose it now, with scans and things."

He did the sums. "He had it for more than twenty years? It wasn't what he died from."

"No. It might have been kinder if he had." A handkerchief in her hands was being kneaded into a ball. "Jack was a particular man. Shoes always shining, hair always trimmed. Then things changed." She picked up the teapot and topped his cup up. "He'd always insisted on a clean collar every day, so when he told me one day that he didn't need a collar I was a bit surprised, but to tell the truth, quite pleased. But then he got angry because he said his collar was too dirty to wear and shouted at me that I was a slovenly woman. He'd been such a gentle man and I didn't understand that he was ill. Other things changed too. He refused to eat apple crumble. Said he hated it." She laughed mirthlessly. "It had been his favourite. He started going to the pub and staying 'til it closed. I thought it was the drinking that affected him. I still didn't know he was ill. Not then. By the time you were born it was clear that something was wrong, very wrong."

John waited. He'd not heard of Pick's disease, but he couldn't see a connection between that and his adoption.

"Pick's disease changes people's personalities. It makes them do things. Things they wouldn't have done normally. It was difficult for me, looking after him, with children all still so young and my sister here too. My sister, Janey, lived with us. She was a couple of years younger than me, and when she was born the cord got caught round her neck and she was starved of oxygen. Anyway, Janey never grew up, not really. She never got any older than ten or eleven, even though she lived for fifty nine years. But she was my sister and I loved her. Through it all, I loved her. Right to the day she died. Anyway, Jack… he……

Well, Janey was your mother. I'm sorry but there's no easy way to say it."

John gaped. "But you…" Suddenly he realised what had happened. "You pretended I was your baby. You registered me as your child."

Gillian nodded.

"That's probably illegal." He could hardly believe what he was hearing and hardly believe he'd made such an inane comment.

"I did it for good reasons. Janey couldn't have looked after you; she couldn't look after herself. And Jack was your father. It made sense, John. And I still believe it was the right thing to do."

He was in the middle of an illusion, a fascinatingly compulsive story with fictitious characters. "But you gave me away." It was a statement rather than a question.

"I didn't have a choice. Jack took against you. He was unkind to the other three too but they were older and learned to stay out of his way. But when he started physically hurting you I had to do something. I was at the end of my tether. It might help you to understand that we women rarely ever had choices. We were dependent on our husbands. Jack was sick and he wasn't going to get better. But he wasn't liable to die soon either. They locked his grandmother away and she lived to see her seventieth year. Life can be very cruel. I couldn't lock Jack away, and I had no-one to turn to. My parents had already passed away. I'd had to put Janey into a home. The other children needed me. So I looked for a way out. I can't say that adoption was a choice. Choice is what happens when you have more than one solution. A children's home would never have been a real home, so though it broke my heart, I did what I did and I'll not say I'm sorry. But I am sorry that I had to."

The sun had broken through the grey clouds and light floated through the net curtains as if a new dawn was appropriate. John tasted salt and realised he was crying. He hadn't known either of his parents and never would. But here, in front of him was his aunt. His own blood. She was his family and it was she who had given him away, not because she didn't love him, but because she did.

Part 3

CHAPTER 16

Lentil Soup

Flat 2,
4 Cavendish Crescent,
Bath.
18th May, 1994

Dear Sally,

Many years have passed since we spoke to each other, and I hope my letter does not intrude on your privacy. I hope also, that you don't mind me writing.

Diane tells me you and Sammy are back in London for a while, and I understand you are unwell. I hope that your treatment in London is successful.

Diane also told me about the loss of your daughter. I am truly so sorry. Nothing can compare with such tragedy and I cannot contemplate your suffering. Life must have changed beyond all comprehension for you and please accept my deepest condolences.

Yours,
John.

He dropped the letter in the post box and breathed a sigh of relief that was no relief at all. He'd written numerous letters before this one, two had even got into envelopes, but the journey between pen and post box had never been completed. Now it was done; the letter was on its way and other than waiting for the postman, he couldn't retrieve it.

Having posted it he fretted that it was too impersonal, then too personal. And too short. He'd wanted to tell her he knew that Sammy was his son and he wanted to see him, to be a father. But that would be too abrupt. So much had changed; things were different and he feared she might return to Pakistan before he saw Sammy. "Reply, Sally," he whispered to himself, "please reply".

33 Coventry Street
Bethnal Green
London
29ᵗʰ May, 1994

Dear John,
Thank you for your letter. Yes, life has been difficult and your words were kind. To lose my beautiful daughter just before Christmas was almost overwhelming. And yes, with all of this, I find myself ill too. Life can be unkind.

Without my husband (he is in Pakistan) Sammy is my lifeline. He keeps me going. He's a smart boy and full of life as boys are. He was doing well at school in Pakistan and as I expect to be in England for some time, he's now in school here and I'm pleased to say, doing well.

I'm sure you will know that your mother provided for Sammy's education in her will, which came as a great surprise to me. I was sorry to hear that she had gone – I expect that you and your father miss her very much. She was a kind and lovely woman, who I too have missed. Please accept my sympathy for your loss.

As you said in your letter, many years have passed. It's too late for recriminations, though I still feel a great sorrow over what happened between us. But the past is gone, we have moved on, and I hope that you have found happiness.

With kind regards,
Sally.

Sally re-read her letter. It had been kind of John to write but his letter appeared little more than dutiful. She wondered, should hers be less warm? Or more so? Had she said too much about Sammy? Should she have mentioned Arif?

The last of the white glass wedding bangles lay on the dressing table and she picked it up. The first had broken on their honeymoon and Arif had teased her that it was grounds for divorce. This one would have been saved for Hiba. Cupping it in her hand she cracked it hard against the table edge and dropped the pieces in the bin. HIV, she thought bitterly, killed in many ways.

Flat 2,
4 Cavendish Crescent,
3rd June.

Dear Sally,

Many thanks for your letter. It was good of you to reply and thank you for your sympathy about the death of my mother. Yes, we do miss her. My father does particularly. I will pass your words on to him.

It's good to hear that Sammy is doing well at school, though it's hard for me to imagine him as a twelve year old – and a teenager later this year! I'm glad he's been a comfort to you, as I'm sure he'll continue to be.

I am aware of my mother's wishes regarding Sammy. We'd expected to hear from you on the matter but I can see how your planned visit to London didn't materialise. I believe you are in contact with my father's solicitor but if I can help please let me know.

I agree that what took place between us was sad but as you also say, time has moved on. I never married or found a partner, but you could say that I recently found someone special. I managed to trace my parents. It's a long and complicated story, but yes, I can say that I am happy.

Yours,
John.

He pondered his last paragraph, wondering why he felt a need to tell her about his parents. He'd almost said more but decided it would be imposing and left it as it was.

What he didn't say was what was at the forefront of his mind; that he wanted to see his son. The offer of help with Frances's bequest would show he meant well.

Bethnal Green
16th June.

Dear John.

What good news! I wonder how you managed to find your parents. It sounds as though it turned out well and I'm pleased for you.

You write of Sammy too, and I have included a photograph of him with this letter. In including him in her will it looks as if Frances was sure of something that I hope the picture will help you consider. I know a photograph isn't proof, John, but I believe, unreservedly, that Sammy is your son. I will tell him about you if you wish it, and if you are willing, I would like him to meet you.

If you agree I suggest you come here to London. My mother will be away on a church study day on Sunday 1st July and Sammy is proud of a delicious lentil soup he makes. Come to lunch.

With best wishes,
Sally

There. She'd said it. The letter was blunt but there wasn't an easy way to say to a man, "You are the father of my twelve year old son and by the way I'm dying of HIV!" If John acknowledged Sammy and things went well, she'd tell him why it was important that Sammy met his father. So little was understood about HIV and even here in England it punched a full factor of ten on the scale of fear. She hadn't told anyone about her status yet, other than her mother. Not even Diane knew. Her viral count was still low and the drugs were helping. Looking at John's letter, she bit the skin at the side of her fingernail. Sammy would need his father one day. What choice did she have? She could arrange for John to see her doctor or one of the counsellors at the Trust, who'd help him understand she wasn't dangerous to anyone.

And, she was more frightened than he could ever be.

One step at a time.

Bath.
Thursday

Dear Sally

Thank you for the photograph of Sammy. He's a fine boy, and looks quite tall. And familiar. I admit that I saw another picture of him some years ago and know that there can be little doubt about who his father is.

In my last letter I told you that I'd traced my parents. In fact, I found my aunt. My parents have both passed on and so I can never know them. This is not how I would like it to be for my (our!) son.

You said in an earlier letter that you have been ill. How are you? Diane told me you are unclear as to the nature of the illness but are getting treatment in London, which I hope is helpful.

Sammy is a cook already? I look forward to coming to lunch on 1ˢᵗ July.
Yours truly,
John

His son was cooking! John recalled something that Sally had once given him; a quote by an American columnist who wrote under the unlikely name of 'Miss Manners'. It had amused him and he'd kept it the back of the cookery book where, like a pressed flower, it still lay.

"There are three possible parts to a date, of which at least two must be offered: entertainment, food, and affection. It is customary to begin a series of dates with a great deal of entertainment, a moderate amount of food, and the merest suggestion of affection. As the amount of affection increases, the entertainment can be reduced proportionately. When the affection is the entertainment, we no longer call it dating. Under no circumstances can the food be omitted."

John was going to see his son. It wasn't a date, but the ingredients were there.

ACKNOWLEDGEMENTS

For comments, help, and perseverance, I thank;

My husband, David Lankester, for unwavering support, encouragement, common sense, and staying for the whole journey.

Lorraine Trendall-Moore, for suggesting I write a book in the first place, and dreaming up ideas – some useable.

Katherine Wiit, for diligent feedback and constancy.

Ros Hudson, for suggesting I should re-write the first chapter.

Vivien Turner, for an enthusiastic response and speedy editing - twice.

Penelope Wacks, for great feedback, particularly around the first chapters.

Carol Dilks, for encouragement and suggestions about the first chapters.

Steven Henson, for reading and honesty.

Gemma Joyce, for support.

Angela Partridge, for a thorough proofread and enthusiasm.

Maria Amjad, for ensuring authenticity of all things Pakistani.

Susan Fletcher, for motivating me to keep going.

Jackie Spurrier, for great ideas about cover design.

Rebecca Smith, for a thorough polish.

Ralph Ticehurst, for the Soup.

Amy Cooke at Matador Publishing, for not complaining when I finally re-wrote the first chapters.

Paul and Jane Eastwood, for valuable feedback on book covers.

Friends in Pakistan who, in their different ways, contributed to the novel, including Fareed, Shafquat, Sultana, Hector, Kiran, Sam, Asher, Nazir, Arif, Khalida, Ghazala, Saima, and many more.

And to the authors of the many books I found interesting, useful and illuminating, particularly;
    Khushwant Singh, *Train to Pakistan*.
    Geraldine Brooks, *Nine Parts of Desire*.
    Louisa T Brown, *Dancing Girls of Lahor*.
    Abraham Verghese, *My Own Country. A Doctor's Story*.
    Oswald Wynd, *The Ginger Tree*.